THE UNREC(

THE
UNRECOVERED

RICHARD STRACHAN

RAVEN BOOKS

LONDON • OXFORD • NEW YORK • NEW DELHI • SYDNEY

RAVEN BOOKS
Bloomsbury Publishing Plc
50 Bedford Square, London, WC1B 3DP, UK
29 Earlsfort Terrace, Dublin 2, Ireland

BLOOMSBURY, RAVEN BOOKS and the Raven Books logo are
trademarks of Bloomsbury Publishing Plc

First published in Great Britain 2025

A catalogue record for this book is available from the British Library

ISBN: HB: 978-1-5266-7053-3; TPB: 978-1-5266-7054-0;
EBOOK: 978-1-5266-7052-6; EPDF: 978-1-5266-7049-6

2 4 6 8 10 9 7 5 3 1

Typeset by Integra Software Services Pvt. Ltd.
Printed and bound in Great Britain by CPI Group (UK) Ltd, Croydon CR0 4YY

To find out more about our authors and books visit www.bloomsbury.com
and sign up for our newsletters.

To Polly, Cora and Maeve

The desert with all its arsenal of phantasmagoria was a theatre of shadows, a spectacle for men and angels. Only the shadows did not reflect the reality outside the cave. They were the projection of the world inside us.

Paul Evdokimov, *Ages of the Spiritual Life*

Lance-Corporal Lewis sings where he walks, yet in a low voice, because of the Disciplines of the Wars. He sings of the hills about Jerusalem, and of David of the White Stone.

David Jones, *In Parenthesis*

Part I

Friday 22nd March 1918

She had been at Roddinglaw House for six months when they brought the soldier from Jerusalem. She had seen the casualties of Messines and Passchendaele pass through, of Cambrai and Arras – the burned, the fevered, the shot – and so it was no real change to her routine when the Nursing Sister told her to stop what she was doing and help with the new intake. There was, after all, no end to it.

'And the trays?' Esther said. She was setting the trays for supper and it took a moment to drag her mind from the absorption of it, the hypnotic routine.

'Tell Miss Stewart to take over,' Sister said. 'I'll not have *her* fluttering over the men, for all the good she will do.'

Sister's face, hard-pressed, harried, was stern beneath the white cap. The long blue dress clasped her tightly at bust and hip, and her neck bulged at the high line of the collar. She folded her hands on her stomach like a priest Esther had once seen on the graving docks in Gibraltar, blessing the ships before the water surged back into the basin. For a long moment, as the late sun slashed through the windows of Roddinglaw, she felt the shadow of the Rock against her, the warm kiss of the Spanish wind. Her father at the wedding, his soft hand in hers, Peter standing tall beside her in his uniform.

With a severe look Sister bustled back to the entrance hall. She was always keen to mark the difference between the qualified nurses and the VADs, who were, she implied, little more than a spare pair of hands when an orderly was unavailable. Esther did not feel the insult. She was always being assigned night shifts at short notice or made to empty the bed pans and clean the sluice room, to scrub bath-tubs and scour pans and wash the encrusted bandages, but it was no more than she had volunteered for. She had wanted to put her hands on the sinews of the war, to help, to heal, but as she looked now at the baskets of silver knives and forks, the long line of wooden tables stretching off down the hall, unease returned to set its weight against her shoulders. Putting out trays and folding sheets and pillow-cases and padding splints and washing bedclothes, and then taking the plants in their bronze pots to be watered so the visitors would have something nice to look at – this was not what she was meant to be doing. They needed nurses at the front. At the front, men were dying.

She found Alice Stewart on the ward upstairs, in what had once been a walnut-panelled drawing room. Ten beds now hugged the walls, each clad in a coloured eiderdown. There were labels on the headboards showing name, rank and injury. Officers were in the east wing, other ranks in the west.

Alice had wheeled in the tea trolley and was teasing the men as she plumped their pillows, a medicine they craved more than any other. Some lay in their dressing gowns, resting a plastered leg or a splinted arm. Others sat around the card tables in the blue flannel suit and red tie of the convalescent uniform. The room was an open spread of the morning papers. Raking the print for word of their battalions or place names they recognised, the men were unusually sombre as they read of the German offensive. For all the wire on the beaches and the grey destroyers slipping through the firth, the war could feel very far away here. Now, resuming with a new and unexpected life, it had reached out and touched them once again.

'Anything I can help with, Mrs Worrell?' Alice said brightly.

'Sister asks if you can set the rest of the trays for supper. She wants me on the intake.'

Alice visibly wilted. Captain Moore, in an armchair by the window, roused himself from his newspaper.

'Hop to it, lass!' he barked. His grin was ferocious. 'Can't keep Sister waiting, can we? And if you can – by God, you're a braver man than me.'

There was a ripple of laughter, the crisp flurry of turned pages. Captain Moore was missing an eye but he had flipped the black disc of the patch up onto his forehead as if to more easily read the news. The puckered flesh there was inflamed, a stiff raw density to it.

'Nurse?' a small voice said at Esther's side. Lieutenant Goodspeed was lying in the bed nearest the door, a gangling, adolescent creature who seemed as fearful as a child when he spoke to the nurses or the VADs. The blankets were drawn up to his chin. His face was white with pain and he clutched his arm. 'I wonder, awfully...'

'Is it terribly sore?' She stood by his side, drew her palm across the sheet as if tucking him in. 'The MO's rounds aren't till this evening, I'm afraid, can you hang on till then?'

It was a question they had to ask, even knowing that the men would always say yes. The performance of it, the insincerity, made her feel hollow inside.

'I'll try,' Goodspeed said. His lips twitched into a smile.

Esther walked with Alice Stewart back to the grand staircase. The red carpet underfoot was threadbare and showed the smoky yellow weave.

'The boys seem a touch low this afternoon,' Alice said. There was a flat Derbyshire note buried deep in the heart of her accent. A tuft of straw-coloured hair had escaped from her cap and she kept wiping it aside with the back of her hand. 'But that Captain Moore's a card though, isn't he? I honestly think he's sweet on me.' She dug her elbow into Esther's side.

'They're all sweet on you. You're such a bright thing, so cheerful.'

Alice glanced over her shoulder and whispered, 'He's only got *one eye* though.'

'It could be worse,' Esther said, leaning close. 'There's many would be satisfied with only losing an eye, I'm sure.'

'Well, if any of them are sweet on us it's only because we're the first women they've spoken to in months who aren't French. There's no more to it than that, I'd wager.'

They came to the head of the staircase. Carved overhangs framed the tall windows, and through the glass the spring sun, low in the sky, blazoned the grounds. On the other side of the lawn a bronze horseman with shield and spear glowed on a marble plinth, and the broad oaks, budding in the season, shook their branches. Esther could see clouds drifting off towards Edinburgh. Everything was jewelled by rain.

'Anyway,' Alice said as they descended, 'it makes no odds to me how many of them are sweet or otherwise, and whether they've got one eye or two. If God keeps Georgie safe then we'll be married when he's back, and that'll be the end of it.'

God was invoked the same way Alice would cast a pinch of spilled salt over her left shoulder at dinner, or as she tapped the banister rail now to make her hopes come true. Esther was tempted to ask why, out of all the seething millions abroad, God would lay His hand over Georgie in particular, but she restrained herself.

'I like it sometimes,' she admitted. She smoothed a crease in her tabard. 'I mean, that you can talk to a man and know that there's no more to it than that. No expectations, no... I was going to say danger, but that's not quite the word.'

'I don't know about that,' Alice laughed. 'Danger sounds about right to me.'

'They need us more. That changes it, I think. Often it's just that they want to talk.'

'Lord,' Alice said. Once again she tried to restrain the lock of hair. 'I don't know that I'd ever exactly want to *talk* to them.'

The younger girl touched Esther's arm. Her face was flushed.

'Oh, but I'm terribly sorry, Esther, really I am. Talking about Georgie and getting married when, well... You know.' She took Esther's hand in her cool fingers and ran her thumb over the wedding ring.

'It's nothing,' Esther said, trying to reassure her. 'Truly. And let God keep George safe, for both your sakes.'

She took back her hand and touched the ring with her own thumb. She didn't know why she still wore it. Perhaps it was easier to give the men a clear signal from the start. There was such vulnerability in being wounded, and the heart often mistook the target of its yearning. The ring was like the soldiers' rank insignia; it let them know where they all stood.

'Tis a figure or a symbol, say, she thought. *A thing's sign: now for the thing signified ...*

The orderlies had left the main doors open. Billowing into the entrance hall came the spring breeze, smelling of the grass and the sea, the cold rain. The intake had already been transferred to the long gallery in the eastern wing. Beds had been found for the new patients, the red screens drawn while they settled. Sister and the MO, Major Lawson, stood in the aisle between the two long rows as if waiting to be summoned. The wall on the southern side of the ward, high to the vaulted ceiling, showed landscapes and portraits of old Roddinglaw worthies. The gilded frames caught at the gas lamps' tarnished light.

Major Lawson smiled as he saw her; it warmed his lean, ascetic face. He was small and compact, and wore his authority as easily and as neatly as his uniform.

'Thank you, Mrs Worrell.' He stepped aside for her. 'Always a compliment to your example, Sister, the way our VADs show such enthusiasm.'

Esther pitched in for the next half an hour, helping with dressing gowns and jackets, checking if anyone needed tea or water; always smiling, always looking them in the eyes and treating them not as patients but as men. Some of the other nurses referred to them as 'the boys', but Esther felt it was important always to think and talk of them as men. It wasn't a question of respect, not exactly, but it was a way of acknowledging the seriousness and the force of what had happened to them. In this ward alone some had been burned by shell fire. Others had survived gas attacks that left blisters on their skin and lesions on their lungs, or bore ridged and angry scars from bullets and shrapnel. There was trench fever, septicaemia, the cratered, weeping sores of gangrene. There were wounds that would never heal.

Major Lawson moved from bed to bed, his brown brogues clipping at the black and white tiles. 'All done? We'll start the rounds upstairs then, Sister.'

'Very good, Major.'

One man lay in a drowse at the end of the row. Ida Lambert, another of the VADs, had drawn the blankets down to his waist. His chest was encased in a shroud of bandages. The label on the bedstead identified him as Captain Daniel McQuarrie, 7th Cheshires: bayonet wound.

His eyelids flickered as Ida drew away. 'Poor chap,' she whispered. She touched the back of Major Lawson's hand, as if by accident.

'Our first from the Palestine front,' Lawson said. 'Penetrating wound through the centre of the thorax. Happened just before Allenby took Jerusalem.' He glanced at Esther. She could smell the clean citrus scent of his cologne. 'Missed his heart by fractions, apparently. I wonder what it was? Seems very wide for a bayonet.'

Esther took the water jug and refilled the glass at the side of the bed. A Boston fern spilled from a copper pot beneath the window, the leaves framed by the green glass and glowing with an almost tropical light. They walked back up the aisle.

'I fear our beds will be in greater demand over the next few weeks, Mrs Worrell,' the major said. He smoothed his moustache. 'You've read the news, I take it? The Germans seem to have thrown everything at us. The storm has broken, and alas, there is only so much medical aid to go around.'

'But every room's in service here as it is, sir,' she said quickly. 'Every bed is full.'

'The army would have us put up tents in the grounds, I'm sure, but I can't imagine anything more miserable for a convalescing soldier than being at the mercy of a West Lothian wind.'

They came out into the reception hall. The front doors were closed now. There were over a hundred patients in Roddinglaw but it may as well have been empty for all the noise they were making. From deep in the house came the ghostly wail of a gramophone. Brindisi, Esther thought. *La Traviata*. Her father had been a great one for opera.

'I have a mind to visit Gallondean along the coast next week,' Lawson went on. 'I was hoping you would join me to make our case. A volunteer nurse might help blunt the edge of an army doctor making the request.'

'Gallondean Castle?'

'If you could call it that.' He paused, turned on his heel to stare out of the gabled window beside the vestibule, hands clasped behind his back. 'The heir apparent has returned, from what I understand. His father died in India just before the war. I don't know the state of the house, but there will be empty rooms at least.'

'Of course,' Esther said automatically. She had found it best to agree to any suggestion the senior staff made. 'I'd be happy to.'

Lawson turned from the window and looked very closely at her. The late-afternoon sun fell through the glass and burnished his khaki jacket, giving a hard gleam to his Sam Browne belt. His eyes, ironic now and amused, were shot through with little shards of green.

'We will appeal,' he said, 'to his sense of Christian charity.'

After that there were dressings to be prepared for the following day, and then the joyless task of scrubbing out the baths and distributing the bedpans. Later on she helped with the drug rounds, pushing the trolley behind Sister as she strode through the wards. Esther was pleased to see Lieutenant Goodspeed given something to help with his pain. It never seemed to leave him, morning or night, and its origins were mysterious.

'The shoulder's no bother at all, nurse,' he would say. 'But in the arm it's like...' He groped for the words. 'It's like *waves* moving through me. Top to bottom. *Waves*.'

Then, steeling herself, Esther followed Sister into the west wing to help the amputees get ready for bed. As they came in the door Clemons and Reid, who had lost a leg each at Broodseinde Ridge, looked up from their game of cards. Private Hopkins winked at them as he shuffled on his crutch to the side of his bed. Corporal Prevost, who had lost both hands at Cambrai and had been peppered groin to throat with shrapnel, stirred in his chair and showed them all a cheerful grin. To Esther it had the same depth as the smile on a wooden doll's painted face.

'Tomorrow's another day, nurse,' Prevost said happily, as if another day without his hands was a treat he could barely imagine.

Esther nodded and made herself seem equally happy. She could never see him without thinking of the English cemetery in Florence, the cool tomb beneath her forehead, the smell of the Arno. Lying that night in the hotel bed, waiting for her husband to return.

When she finally climbed up to the old servants' quarters at the end of the day she was leaden with fatigue. While Alice and Ida whispered to each other from their beds, Esther tried to read for a few minutes from her volume of Browning (*Dramatis Personae*), and then from Elizabeth Browning's *Aurora Leigh*. In these few spare minutes her eyes couldn't quite catch the words though, and in any case they appeared on the page like a living rebuke: she hadn't thought about her own poetry for weeks. What would Aurora Leigh think of that? Or Elizabeth Browning, for that matter? They had girded themselves against an entire age in order to write, but here was Esther lying like a pallid rag, wrung out, with barely the strength to roll on her side and turn off the lamp. There was no fighting it now. She had to sleep.

The last few grains of Thursday – or was it Friday? – slipped through her fingers, and soon there was nothing left in her hand. All that remained was to lie there listening to Alice's adenoidal breathing on the other side of the room, Ida's velvet sighs as she settled herself. The darkness would soon deepen. Before she knew it she would have passed through that darkness into the light of another day. At the end of it Mr and Mrs Browning would still be waiting for her on the bedside table, and their verses would once more fall with no purchase through her drained, depleted mind.

Before she fell asleep, she thought about Captain McQuarrie in the ward downstairs. Palestine and the light of the desert places, the saffron light, Jerusalem nestled in the hills. And then she thought of water, of the North Atlantic chill; the rolling silence of the deep, the utter darkness at the very end of it, where no light could ever go. Down there, where her ghosts lived now, and waited.

From Jacob Beresford's journals, March 1918

The sea is barred with silver, cuffed and flattened by the wind. The waves are torn into scraps of tattered foam. Rolls of barbed wire sag on the beaches. The islands in the firth lurk out there, low and unsteady. Earlier, I saw a lifeboat from the station at Port Edgar struggling in the tide, bucking, grinding, the sound of its motor snatched away by the wind into the wider sea. I dread to think of the souls they must have to save in that water. I thank God and my enervated lungs that I am not in the navy.

I think often of the voyage that brought me from India, the wind towing the stench of the Bombay docks as the liner trawled through the bay. I can still picture the liquid phosphorescence of the midnight oceans strung out behind us as we sailed to Suez, those long trails of emerald and pearl. I remember sitting on the lawns in the sanatorium at Bhowali, staring out over the green hills of Uttarakhand and smelling the forest birch on the fragrant breeze. I hold onto that picture. And then from somewhere vague and unsettled, a place I'm still reluctant to visit in my mind, comes the image of the garden in the Civil Lines; the sun striking the shade house, the scorched brown grass at the height of summer. I can hear the mad, insistent warble of the brainfever bird... India, and then the ocean bringing me home, to Gallondean.

Of course, it has never really been my home. It is a puzzle to me even now. I cannot make the pieces fit. There are locked rooms, hidden stairways, priest holes, annexes tacked on over the centuries, storerooms choked with crates and boxes. There are shelves stacked top to bottom with ancient papers and documents, corridors blocked with old furniture. The factor, Mr Rutherford, has not been seen in some time, and has certainly not been keeping the place up. No doubt he's still been drawing his salary on my father's account though – yet another matter that I lack the energy or the enthusiasm to resolve.

The house luxuriates in the name of *Gallondean Castle*, but it is no more than the accretions of time upon the Norman core. There are three flat storeys of grey stone, the crenellations silver and wet above a squat tower. The windows look out onto a blustered shore, where the waves creep up the beach and hiss against the shingle. Sometimes I'll stand and stare across the water for as long as I can bear it. Drear and grey, and all the grey sea loping and unsteady, wrinkled by the evening breeze. Fife sits there beyond the firth, no more than a thin grey line when the fog doesn't obscure it completely. Warships prowl, belching smoke. The sky is a grim grey blanket. Everything is grey.

It is a place of oil lamps and kerosene, of darkness at midday. 'A perfect misanthropist's Heaven…' But this is where it must end. There is nowhere else to go. It will find me here if it will find me anywhere.

Earlier the boy from the village arrived with the week's groceries. He is a sallow creature, barely strong enough to pedal his bicycle. His front two teeth are missing and there is a cast in his eye that makes it look as if he's trying to peer over your shoulder. Fifteen years old or so, and yet he's barely five feet tall. I wonder if the war will come for him in turn? Malnourished, half-blind, and yet he could still carry a rifle or use his body to stop a bullet. Even now I expect it to come for me. My rotten lungs are no excuse. If I'm not already dead, then before the year is out, I will be in khaki with the rest of them.

He was amazed that I lived here alone. 'Tell your cook the pork's good for two days,' he said, and goggled when I informed him that I have no cook. Where are the servants? he must think. Surely a valet, a maid to do the cleaning? No, I wanted to tell him. I am the only living soul in Gallondean now. I have had enough of servants and cringing *ayahs* and housemaids. In Lahore we were so provisioned;

ironic that the colonial class often lives in greater comfort than the equivalent in the Mother Country. But then they do not have the heat to contend with here, the Indian heat; when the plains can barely support a European life, and all of society takes to the hills. That was always the time, my father said, when he did his best business.

I have often thought of asking the boy if he knew my father. Would they know his name in the village? Did the lord and lady of Roddinglaw receive him in those far-off days before the war, whenever he made the journey home? Or was he beneath their notice; a man, after all, who had to make his own living, and who made it by handling the dead?

No, I cannot imagine him surrounded by his servants, certainly not in this isolated place. God alone knows what impulse made him buy it. A secret snobbery, the desire for a grandeur he felt he'd earned through long labours? Who knows. In any case, the doings of our parents are of little interest to the young. Was it not Twain who said that at fourteen his father's ignorance was unbearable, but when he reached twenty-one he was astonished at how much the old man had learned in seven years?

I remember Bobby laughing at that. I remember Sarah, emerging from her room, passing me a brandy and soda, the cool touch of her hand.

This morning, while the weather was clear, I walked along the path towards Hound Point. The beaches are strewn with loops of wire, and although I can't for a moment imagine German troops landing here unopposed, still the wire remains. A reminder of the war, if nothing else. Given the scale of the German offensive in France, perhaps we shall see the Kaiser's men on British soil yet?

When I passed the Fishery cottage, about half a mile from Gallondean, I saw the hermit crouched in the back garden, sitting amidst the long spring grass and the early dandelions. I have often seen him flitting through the trees on the path to South Queensferry or hunting the foreshore for flotsam, his shirt tucked into a pair of ragged trousers, his feet bare. His white face has often peered at me from the black windows of his cottage, eyes wide, hair in two grizzled curtains framing an unshaven face. He called out as he saw me. I reconstruct the meeting here.

'The Lord of Gallondean!' he cried. 'You will forgive me for not visiting yet, sir. My own circumstances, you see, have detained me a while.'

'Circumstances?' I said. I was walking along the raised path that led through the trees and looked down on him.

'The other night there. You might have seen it, the lifeboat caught so ragged in the waves? That was on my account, I confess. Rescued, you see, and then I was in the lock-up for my troubles, and that kept me for some time from your door, and from paying my respects. I saw the light in your window though, high on the wall of Gallondean, and I knew that the lord must be home.'

The cottage behind him looked dim and shabby, the windows dark, the whitewash peeling from the stone. The garden was a jungle. There was an outhouse in one corner, fringed with bramble, and I could smell it from where I stood.

'I live at Gallondean,' I told him, 'but I'm no lord. I don't know where you have that from.'

I couldn't tell if he was mocking me. There was no side to him that I could see, no sharp edges. I should have left it.

'You live in the old house and are the rightful owner now though, sir,' the hermit said. 'Are you not? That makes you the lord as far as the legend goes, title or no title. There is none other after the death of your father, for which you have my condolences. He was always very good to me, in his way.'

I stopped again and looked back at him. The cottage was very drear on the foreshore. In bad weather it would be hard-bitten by the wind. Beyond it were the strings of wire on the beaches, the sea feathered and drab.

'You knew him?' I said.

'Indeed so, sir.'

I came down from the path and waded through the grass to the back gate. The hermit stood as I approached, his hands plucking at each other.

'How so?' I asked. 'Forgive me, but I don't see how your paths would have crossed. This cottage is not on his land as far as I can tell.'

'Your land now, sir,' the hermit said. He ducked his head. 'And your cottage as it happens, also. The deeds were in your father's name.'

I looked at him. The greasy tangled hair, the patched tweed jacket, the drab collarless shirt. He smiled easily at me. I had the impression of brown, irregular teeth before he sealed them away behind his lips. I could smell the drink on him.

'Who are you?' I asked, although of course I was already beginning to guess. 'What is your name?'

'I am Mr Rutherford, sir,' he told me. 'The factor, although that's a grand title for the duties I held, to be perfectly honest. I confess those duties are somewhat beyond me now. I can't set my mind right to them, as it were. Things intrude, often, with me, and I suspect I have gone downhill in the last few years.'

There was a thread of madness in his eyes. It was as clear as day. I had found him on a settled morning, but who was to say what storms the afternoon might bring.

'Well, I have no need of a factor myself,' I said. 'Do not trouble yourself on that score.'

He rushed through the grass and gestured to the back door.

'Will you come in, sir? I can offer a cup of tea, though nothing stronger I'm afraid. In honour of your father, so that we may at least drink something to his name.'

Against my better judgement, I agreed. Mr Rutherford ushered me across the threshold. There was a sharp tang of unwashed clothes, blocked drains, the wet ashes in the empty grate. The cottage was no more than two bedraggled rooms. We stood in what passed for his kitchen and I saw that there were empty bottles cast into a corner. Rutherford, grinning at this coup, fiddled with matches and pot and laid out two cracked mugs. I couldn't imagine spending even a single night in this hovel.

'We were all so sorry to hear of Mr Beresford's passing,' he said. 'The good folk of these parts. Although,' Rutherford winked, 'truth to tell, I'm not sure there were many knew Mr Beresford that well. Like yourself, sir, he preferred his own company on those rare occasions when he was here.' His eyes twitched and the grin he showed me was so fierce that I almost took a step back. With an effort he reined in his emotions. 'Cheers,' he said. 'And to Mr Beresford.'

We raised our mugs and I forced myself to swallow.

I drank as much of the tea as I could stomach. I saw myself for a moment, as if from outside, standing with this wrecked old man in the midst of such squalor; the stink of mouldering food, the saline reek of the seaweed on the shore. I felt reckless suddenly, and aggrieved.

'You said the lifeboat had rescued you?' I said. 'You were out in that weather, at night? Fishing, was it?'

Rutherford looked abashed. He hid his face behind the upturned mug as he slurped the dregs of his tea.

'Not fishing, sir,' he said. 'If only. No, I believe I was trying to reach Inchmickery. The monasteries out there – ruins now of course. I am so drawn to such silent places...' He laughed. 'It seems I'd taken a boat from Port Edgar, which went against me in the storm.'

'You know the navy have that island now,' I told him. 'You would have been arrested if you'd reached it. Perhaps you would have been shot as a spy.'

He cradled his empty mug, eyes downcast. 'I am treated with some leniency in these parts, on account, I believe, of my previous standing and my loss. And I do get odd notions now and then, I've confessed as much.'

'You're not from here originally, are you?'

'No, sir. Belfast, by way of the Borders.'

'And this loss?'

'My boy, sir. He was killed at Boulogne, very early in the war. It has been a trial to me, I admit.'

'Boulogne?' I said. 'But that's on the coast, surely? It's nowhere near the front.'

'Aye, sir,' he said. His face became as hard and unyielding as a wooden mask. 'They said it was an accident, but I know better. A young lad, innocent, and the French whores just waiting to take advantage, if you see.'

Again I saw that shift in him, the fierceness unmoored by grief. I felt a great fatigue settle on me suddenly. I gave Rutherford my condolences and made to go, and it was only as I reached the door that I remembered what he had said earlier.

'Legend?' I said. 'What did you mean? You told me I was the lord as far as the legend went.'

Rutherford's face came alive. He wrung his hands with pleasure.

'Oh, yes, sir, yes!' he cried. 'Your father was a great one for it, a *great* one. I have often wondered if he heard it himself before he died, God rest him. I did, you know. That's how I knew. I heard it, loud as you please. It near froze the blood in my veins!'

'Heard what?'

'The howling, sir. The howling.'

And then Mr Rutherford was so good as to brew another pot of tea and tell me about the legend of Hound Point, and when exactly I was going to die.

Tuesday 26th March 1918

The sound of screaming woke her. She had fallen asleep at the nurses' station, deep into the night watch. Silence, and then came again that despairing cry, hoarse, more grief than horror.

Esther pushed her book aside and rose uncertainly from the desk. Bad dreams unsettled the men most nights. The risk was that the other patients, surprisingly intolerant, would wake up and complain.

She followed the cry to the eastern wing, where Captain McQuarrie, the officer from the Palestine front, had half-fallen from his bed. He was struggling to pull himself back up, one hand on the bedside table, the other groping on the floor, his legs still under the sheets. His brown hair was dark with sweat and the pyjama jacket had come undone to reveal the white tape of the bandages around his chest. Some of the other men had briefly woken, but most paid no attention.

'John,' McQuarrie said, groggily. 'John, for God's sake…'

Esther moved briskly over the parquet floor and stooped to put his arm around her shoulder. There was a wild, acrid smell about him.

'Captain McQuarrie,' she said. She kept her voice firm and low. 'It's Mrs Worrell, Captain. I'm one of the VADs. You've been having a bad dream.'

She thought of calling for an orderly but she managed to get his head back onto the pillow, feeling the strain in her legs as she braced and lifted. He was a small man for an officer. Most of them had a foot in height and forty pounds on the private soldiers, but Captain McQuarrie felt very slight in her arms as she settled him. Dawn was not far off now and the dressings looked clean in the light that bristled through the window. They weren't wet under her hand. The wound had not opened.

'No need to call Major Lawson,' she said. She tried to sound as decisive as Sister, as breezy as Alice Stewart, but she didn't have the knack. She had never been altogether easy with other people. Too sharp, too self-contained, Peter had always said. The inheritance of an only child. He had disliked that about her. He had discovered too late that as a wife she was a poor adornment for a naval officer.

McQuarrie pulled the caul of the dream aside. His face emerged, clear, and he seemed himself again. He lay back on the pillow and blinked. Esther poured him a glass of water from the carafe and he sipped it thoughtfully.

'How are you feeling?' she said. 'Are you in any pain?'

He shook his head. He looked very boyish lying there, brown hair tousled by sleep, his thin young face clean-shaven. He managed a smile. Esther had the sense it had been dredged up from the depths of him. There was something stunned about him, disbelieving. His hands kept idly drifting to the bandages around his chest, as if reminding himself that they were still there, that all this had actually happened to him.

'I'm fine,' he said. His voice was weak and Esther had to lean in to hear him. 'I hope I wasn't shouting anything I might regret? Men do, you know. The most awful rot, you'd be embarrassed by it in the cold light of day.'

'I know,' Esther said kindly. She had heard it often enough herself; patients crying for mothers and siblings, for God or their closest friends. 'But you didn't.'

'I'm glad.'

She paused, unsure if she should continue. Sometimes the reminder was more than they could take. McQuarrie seemed calm though, now that the dream had moved away from him.

'You did mention a name,' she said. 'John.'

'Ah.'

'But nothing more.'

'Good. I'm happy to remember John. He was nothing to be embarrassed by. He'd been there from the beginning.'

'Was he a friend?' Esther asked. She knew the man was dead. Nothing in McQuarrie's tone suggested otherwise.

'Yes. A good friend.'

'I'm sorry. I'm very sorry.'

Esther smoothed the sheets, took the empty water glass and placed it on the table.

'Shall I leave you to sleep?' she said. 'It's not quite dawn, you've an hour or two yet.'

He gave an almost imperceptible shake of his head.

'I think I'll leave sleep for the moment.' He looked at the window behind the Boston fern; the dimpled glass, the green light rising as the sun came threading through the trees. 'Would you have anything to read? Just something to keep my mind from wandering.'

'There are the newspapers from yesterday?'

'Perhaps not right now. War news doesn't quite appeal.'

Esther thought. 'There's the library on the first floor. I'm not sure if it's locked at night though. I could go and have a look for you?'

'Don't trouble yourself, please.' He smiled again. It was a very old smile, Esther decided. It reminded her, with a force that she wasn't quite prepared for, of her father's smile. Patient and knowing, and generous to all mistakes.

'Wait there a moment,' she said. She stood up.

'I'm not going anywhere, I can assure you.'

Esther went back to the nurses' station and returned with her book. She passed it to McQuarrie and he read the gilt lettering on the spine.

'Mr Browning,' he said. 'Poems.' His tone suggested that he was willing to reserve judgement.

'Poetry's a bit of a passion of mine,' Esther told him. She gave a tight, deprecating shake of her head. 'I adore Browning. And Mrs Browning for that matter. I don't think any other book's been as important to me as her *Aurora Leigh*, although it is something of an epic. I'm not sure if you'd be quite in the mood for that one. And it's more of a woman's book, perhaps.'

'"*Round the cape of a sudden came the sea,*" he murmured. '"*And the sun looked over the mountain's rim.*"' His voice trailed away. He looked abashed. 'I've forgotten the rest. I'm sure I knew it once too. One of the short ones.'

She tried to keep the lilt out of her voice. 'You like his work?'

'I'm not too familiar with it. Fragments from school, although I'm sure Kipling's an admirer. I might have come to him that way. I can't remember.'

'Well,' Esther said, reaching out and tapping the cloth cover of the book. She was flushed with the embarrassment of sharing something she cared about. 'Hopefully you'll find him diverting at least. He can seem such an old Victorian, I know, but there's much to discover in him even now. All those voices, those stories and scenes, and ... I've always thought he seems surprisingly modern.'

'I'm sure I'll enjoy it. Thank you. Mrs Worrell, wasn't it?'

'Yes. And just call me if you need anything else.'

She went back to the nurses' station feeling oddly bereft. There was the privilege of sharing an enthusiasm, but as with all things borrowed or lent, she couldn't help feeling the loss as well. You gave something out and before long it was shared between all the other patients and you never saw it again. Alice was forever losing her copies of the *Illustrated London News*. She hadn't learned to keep what was hers to herself; in more ways than one, if Ida Lambert was to be believed.

Esther sat behind the desk and gazed up into the shadows that were flung against the ceiling, thick amongst the hammer beams. On nights like these she felt an almost religious awe that her life had taken such strange turns. It was hard to believe that she had ever been in control of any of it. She remembered the cold shock of England after a life spent in Gibraltar, the foetid cramp of Portsmouth, the massive grey dockyards fuming with ship smoke and industry. She had immediately missed the limestone blade of the Rock, that long, painted slice of shadow ever-present in her childhood.

And then the war had begun, and Peter had died, and before long her father had died too – faltering and sick and soon carried away. Fading in a clement season, the warm winter days short and still, the windows of the old cream-rendered house in the Southern District spotted with rain – but these were details that she could only imagine, because by then it had been impossible to leave England. The ship lanes were the preserve of trade and military vessels, and U-boats prowled the seas. He had died alone. Her father's friends had taken care of the funeral, but there had been no one to hold his hand as he slipped away, no one to kiss the cooling brow. The death of an old Gibraltarian wine merchant was no great tragedy as the battles began in France and Belgium, and the fate of his widowed daughter even less so. But when the house was sold, all Esther had left were the memories of a childhood spent in the sun-baked courtyards of the District, playing around Europa Point or sitting with her father in the long and sultry evenings while he untangled for her the intricate embroidery of family lore. Her grandfather had come from La Mancha, he had said. Her great-grandmother was a Berkshire woman. There were Roman Catholics in there, Methodists, Quakers. Perhaps even further back, dim behind the veil of history, there were *conversos* or men and women who had fled the Alhambra Decree. Who was to say? He would smile and spread his hands wide, all-encompassing, as if to offer himself and his story to the world entire; or perhaps to gather the world towards him instead and claim it all as part of his own heritage. That was Gibraltar for you, he said. One of the Pillars of Hercules, at which the human journey reached its limit.

By the end of 1914 Esther had found herself utterly alone, sitting in an empty house in Portsmouth with a sick apprehension of the wider emptiness that would soon consume her. They needed volunteers for the medical services, but she had applied only because the sense of that stretching emptiness was unbearable to her. Day after day, with no force or motive, no occasions to prepare for. She needed structure, she knew, purpose. Something more robust than poetry at any rate.

Sitting at the nurses' desk now, she looked through the words she had written in her notebook earlier. On the night watch she often turned over the lines and phrases that had occurred to her during the day, trying to find a shape for them, a sense of movement. These words were inert though. There was no life here, no hint of that world entire. She drew a line through them without a second thought and watched the daylight advance slowly across the chequered tiles of the entrance hall.

And straight was a path of gold for him,/And the need of a world of men for me.

THURSDAY 28TH MARCH 1918

'Christ, it doesn't half give me the horrors,' Ida Lambert said.

She looked up at the face of Roddinglaw; the domed finials, the yawning, iron-studded double door. In the soft spring air, the lawns very fresh and the blue skies whipped by strings of cloud, the power of the building was somehow lessened. They walked away from it across the crushed gravel driveway, their footsteps fading into the grass. Here and there men dressed in convalescent uniforms strolled in twos and threes, taking the air. There were plans to set up the lawns for croquet when the weather turned.

'I can feel every stone of it pressing down on me when I'm in there,' Ida said. 'And then the boys, all that pain. It's like an extra tonne of weight. I'm being crushed, Esther. *Crushed.* How can something so new hold such dread?'

The house didn't feel like such a burden to Esther. She quite liked the dull northern presence of it, the neat and restrained Gothic Revival, a modern reimagining of an ancient place. The towers were grey, square-based minarets, vaguely Moorish. The wings were flatly proportioned, massive, like the walls of a Tudor keep. Inside was a folly of clean, fan-vaulted corridors and gaudy stained glass, passages where strips of burgundy carpet led to curling staircases and narrow little chambers, or to wide and well-appointed drawing rooms. Every door seemed to lead deeper into an orderly and well-lit maze. It was Morris or Scott's view of the medieval; romantic, precise. It was easy to forget that Edinburgh was so near or that the house itself was less than a hundred years old. When the wind was up and the sea was arguing with the shore, it felt like a bastion of a much earlier age.

They came to the bronze horseman on the far side of the lawn. In its shade Ida lit herself a cigarette. She waved a hand towards the west, at the castle of Gallondean, the slate-dark wing of its upper storey just visible through the trees.

'Major Lawson says that old tower's an option, should we need to expand. Have you been reading the newspapers? France seems an absolute disaster, I can hardly believe it.' She crossed her arms and gestured vaguely with the cigarette. The smoke ribboned away into the still air. 'Imagine convalescing over there in the Castle of Otranto though, it doesn't bear thinking about. Imagine *working* there. The corridors are no doubt stuffed to the brim with spectres and headless monks.'

She leaned against the plinth and rubbed her cheekbone with the heel of her hand. The salt air had blotched her skin. She was a tall young woman, well-spoken, willowy, the bones prominent at wrist and neck. Esther had always felt she should be on the stage, or looming from the cinema shows they put on for the men in the evenings. Certainly not clad in the relentlessly unflattering uniform of the VAD.

'It won't be so bad,' Esther said. She didn't really believe it. 'Either here or in France. We'll hang on, you'll see. We have to.'

Ida sighed richly. 'You must read between the lines, Esther. It's all going wrong. The Hun is moving in *entirely* the wrong direction, at the cost of God knows how many lives.' In a declarative voice she said, 'I feel enormous presentiments of doom, Mrs Worrell. It's almost more than I can take.'

'Thank God we have a navy,' Esther said. She took the cigarette Ida offered, although she didn't usually smoke. 'And at least we're not overseas.'

Ida pinched the bridge of her nose. 'Lord, can you imagine? Triage in a field hospital the day after a big push? The mind boggles.'

Esther tried to imagine. It was half of what she thought about these days; the uses to which she could be put. Better there than here, and all it took was the courage to seize the moment and ask. But it was courage she wasn't sure she had.

Like schoolgirls, they glanced through the legs of the bronze horse in case Sister was watching them from the house.

'We're lucky in many ways,' Ida said wearily. 'I regret the glimpse it's given me though.'

'The glimpse of what?'

'The bare little glimpse of an untrammelled life. I wonder what we'll do afterwards. I positively leaped at the chance to do this, and it'll be hard going back into our cages afterwards.'

'Maybe we won't have to,' Esther said. Gibraltar and the colony swam before her eyes then, the pink and blue and yellow houses, the fig trees in the Alameda Gardens. Her father's musty warehouse near the docks, the woodchip and straw, the crates of *garnacha* wine and that oilskin ledger in his office. He would tear off pages for her to scribble her poems and stories on when she was a girl, keeping him company through the long, sun-slackened afternoons. That cage had been paradise, if she'd only known it.

'We'll see,' Ida said. 'When the boys return, if any of them do. Sometimes I tell myself that even *they're* lucky, being here. At Roddinglaw, I mean. They're alive, aren't they? But then with some of them you wonder how much has really survived. I had escort duty to the Royal Infirmary last week, and my God.'

She blanched and took a last fierce inhalation of her cigarette.

'Let me tell you,' she said, looking at her arms as if she'd only now become aware of them, 'I have a morbid fear of amputation. And then Sister being such a bloody tyrant, and Alice Stewart always wittering on about her Georgie – or flirting with the officers, the little slut. You'd never think she does so well for herself on the stipend Georgie's parents give her, would you? Lucky bitch. Honestly, without you, Esther, and our little chats, I would have gone mad months ago. I would have torn this bloody cap off my head and gone screaming into the night. It's the countryside, I think. I can't bear it. Farmhands creeping through the trees, toothless gamekeepers cackling over their snares... I doubt I've been for a single stroll around here where I haven't found some poor little creature ripped apart and strewn across the grass. All guts and feathers and fur, it's awful. Red in tooth and claw... But you volunteer, don't you? You can't very well walk away. *They* can't.'

'No,' Esther said. 'They shoot them if they walk away.'

'Good God.' Ida groaned. 'I just wonder how much more is to come. I wake during the night sometimes and hear them crying out, and I wonder if anything can be worth those dreams.'

Esther smeared the last of her cigarette on the rim of the plinth and watched the yellow paper crisp away. 'Do you still dream? I don't. Since starting here, I don't think I've had a single one.'

'Oh, I don't know. I wake up feeling so utterly worn out, dreams are the last thing on my mind.'

Esther looked up at the statue. The knight's face, fringed by a coif of sculpted mail, stared from his half-helm towards the trees. There was a hunting dog by his side, a greyhound or a lurcher weaving between the horse's legs, loping, head down. The bronze had been bitten by the weather and the armour was tarnished green. There was no name or legend on the plinth. Esther often wondered who it was supposed to be.

Ida rapped her knuckles on the horseman's heel. 'I dreamed about this chap, as it happens, last week. Or not dreamed exactly.' She crossed her arms again. 'Have you ever found yourself getting up during the night, but actually you're still asleep? You get out of bed, you go through all the motions, but you don't really know what you're doing? Half your mind's still in the Land of Nod.'

'I can't say that I have.'

Esther stood beside her. They looked up at the bronze warrior as he brandished his spear.

'Well, it's familiar to me. It happened a lot when I was a child, all feverish with growing. I was standing at the window recently and it was dark. You were on the night shift, I think. Your bed was empty. I looked out – or at least, I think I did.' She put on a cold and distant voice, an affectation that made Esther smile. Ida always came most alive in these moments of artifice. 'The moon was up, and all the grounds were bathed in silver. And as I stood there, the knight seemed to melt into the darkness, as though the dark itself had just reached up and washed him away. It was as if a great black sheet had been thrown over him, and when it was drawn back he was gone. There was just the horse standing there, his noble steed.' She shuddered and reached up to pat the dog's head. 'Even the poor old hound had disappeared.'

She put her fingers beneath her collar and drew out a silver chain, Christ crucified at the end of it. She clutched the figure in her fist.

'It felt like the war. Does that make any sense? If you could take the very essence of the war and boil it down and let it flow where it may. It felt like the war had swallowed him. And the war was here, here most of all. It didn't want to be anywhere else in the world.'

She kissed the cross and slipped it back beneath the high collar of her blouse. There was an ironic twist to her lips.

'You're not a Catholic, are you, Esther?'

'I'm not really much of anything.'

'God knows, I'm not at the best of times. But it slips out sometimes, you can't help it. Moments of crisis and all that.' She held her palm to her heart. 'Good Friday tomorrow, I mustn't forget. A day of sacrifice for sweet suffering Jesus.'

Esther had the feeling that Ida read more into her mild agnosticism than it deserved. Once, the younger woman had said, in a swoon of false jealousy, 'Such *wonderful* Iberian colouring you have. Levantine, even. You hardly seem English at all, really!' The fact that Esther spent her Sunday mornings in the dormitory only seemed to underline her suspicion. If the Presbyterian church in the village, the Episcopal church in Queensferry or the Catholic cathedral in Edinburgh didn't draw her to their congregations, then what else was she likely to be?

Esther refused to confirm or deny it either way. Let Ida hint and pry and prod. Let her see the shadow of the synagogue in Esther's eyes, if that's what she wanted. She remembered her father's hands spread wide, encompassing the peoples of the world, accepting all who had made him in the long drift of history.

'Of course, Major Lawson's a Catholic,' Ida said now. They strolled towards an oak tree on the far side of the lawn. A thick, saddle-backed branch was lowered to the ground by the weight of the years. Ida settled herself on it and kicked her feet through the grass. 'And he's not married – I've asked.'

'Isn't he a little old?'

'He can't be more than forty.' Her face took on the hard and economical cast of all young women talking seriously amongst themselves about marriage. 'And a surgeon, as far as I know. Little chance of him being killed, even if he was sent to the front.' She thought for a moment, as if she was totting up the figures in a ledger. 'And he's very tidy. Very *sober*. That has to count for something.'

'It does,' Esther agreed. 'More than you know.'

'It makes no odds, he only has eyes for you,' said Ida, without heat. It was just another part of the calculation.

'But I'm a widow. And not Catholic.'

'No. Neither you are. Then I suppose it all depends on how much of a romantic he is, doesn't it?'

'Men are always romantics,' Esther told her. 'It's the worst thing about them. They fall in love with their own illusions and then blame you when the illusion fades.'

'Really? How tiresome.' Ida raised an eyebrow. 'I defer to your experience. Is that how it was with you?'

'Yes,' Esther said, automatically, although she didn't say that with her the illusion had been conjured mostly from the other side. It had been the Royal Navy uniform, the lieutenant's banded lace on his cuffs, the vast and smoky bulk of the destroyer in the harbour. It was his black hair and hard grey eyes and the romance of the sea. But then where was the romance of the sea when the ship's hull had split open and the cold ocean was surging through the gap? Where was the romance of drowning in the dark? Despite everything, he hadn't deserved that. 'Yes, it was.'

'Well,' Ida sighed, 'at least you got the pension afterwards.'

'Quite. There's always that.'

Ida sprang up from the bough. She dusted the hem of her coat and together they walked back to the halls of Roddinglaw. The lights glowed pale and watery through the grid of lancet windows. As they approached the double doors, a long and heartfelt cry rose up from deep within the house. It bled into the breeze and was carried away, a distant lament.

Esther felt her heart skip, her step falter. She had never in her life heard such anguish before she joined the VAD. She had never known there was such pain in all the world.

28

'Bright eyes and a warm smile, girl,' Ida whispered. 'We can't keep the warriors waiting.'

'No,' Esther said. She looked back across the lawn, half-fearful, to the knight on his marble plinth. Childe Roland trawled the wastelands in despair, alone. The knights had all been killed, wiped away by the shade in Ida's dream. 'No, we can't.'

Friday 29th March 1918

At dinner Sister told her to help Corporal Prevost, a task for which few would willingly volunteer. When the toil was burdensome and grim, Esther had found it most often made its way into her hands; especially when it concerned a man who no longer had the use of his own.

The dining hall filled slowly. The men strolled through with their trays, their skin waxy and pale beneath the electric glare. It had rained that afternoon, a brief spring flurry, and lurking beneath the smell of boiled mutton was the rich scent of wet wool and boot polish. Everything felt too loud; the steel snap of the cutlery, the low rumble of voices, the screech of a hundred shifted chairs. Corporal Prevost crept at Esther's side like an obsequious waiter as she carried his tray. His empty cuffs were pressed to his stomach. Esther's face was already burning. She would never get used to this. But then, and presumably with greater force, neither would Corporal Prevost.

'Ever so kind of you, as always Mrs Worrell,' he said. 'Honestly, the trouble you ladies go to on my behalf. Well, it's a wonder and no mistake, and you must have so much to do on top of it.'

He made a ducking motion, grinned widely, wiped the sweat from his upper lip with his forearm. There was always this antic stream of words with Prevost, as if speech alone could postpone the moment of truth. She had often thought it would be better to do this in his dormitory, but no doubt that was only for her own benefit. None of this was his fault.

'It's no trouble at all,' Esther told him.

Prevost chose a corner table. He flopped into the chair and with a jerk of his head ensured he wasn't being watched. He kept his wrists hidden in his lap.

'I think you're all angels,' he said, too quickly. 'Truly I do. And then Sister, God help me...' He gave a stage shudder. 'She must have it in for you, Mrs Worrell, if she's giving you this job!'

Sweat beaded on his upper lip again. The skin there was raw. Alice had shaved him that morning and she had no skill with the blade.

'It's alright, Corporal Prevost,' she said quietly. 'Honestly it is.'

She had no words, nothing she could say that wouldn't centre the moment too closely between them. Quickly she cut up his meat. A tremor passed through him. He looked away as she began to feed him, piece by piece.

He soon fell into the rhythm of it. He chewed rapidly, swallowed, said nothing. His jaw jerked and snapped. At first he would dart a look over his shoulder to see if he was being watched, but by the time he was halfway through he had settled down. You could mask all this with words and good humour, but sooner or later the humiliation just had to be endured.

'Who'd have thought you needed them so much, eh?' He forced himself to laugh. 'Never gave tuppence for them before, but now I find they've all sorts of useful applications, don't they? Hands! Don't take them for granted, miss, that's my advice.'

Esther smiled at him. She crushed a boiled potato between the tines of the fork. Prevost, trying to pierce the plate with his gaze, opened his mouth. When he had swallowed, he said, 'MO reckons it's the Infirmary in a couple of weeks for fittings. Then maybe Roehampton, there's a hospital there specialises. Queen Mary's.' He gave her a hopeful grin.

'That's something to look forward to, isn't it?'

'Maybe I'll come out the other side like Captain Hook, eh?' Prevost laughed again. 'Could find all sorts of use for two hooks, I'm quite sure. Although he's a gentleman in the play, right enough. And I never did fancy the navy!'

There were clots of food at the corners of his mouth. Without thinking, Esther reached up with a napkin.

Prevost recoiled, his eyes wide. It was as if she had slapped him.

She felt herself redden and folded the napkin away. There were lines you couldn't cross. Evidently this was one of them.

'Speaking of Captain Hook,' she said quickly, 'I'd heard that some of the officers are going to be doing *Peter Pan* for one of the Saturday shows. Surely not?'

Prevost drifted back from whatever abyss he had fallen into. 'So I'd heard,' he said. 'Captain Moore taking the lead, as ever. Although what we've done to deserve it, Mrs Worrell, I don't know! If it's a choice between the officers prancing about in tights or a new Charlie Chaplin, then give me Charlie Chaplin any day of the week.'

He'd finished his food, and the knife and fork shook in Esther's hands as she crossed them on the plate.

'I don't doubt their theatrical abilities,' she said, attempting a wink. 'It's something else to look forward to, isn't it?'

'That it is, Mrs Worrell.' Prevost beamed. 'Maybe I'll put my name down after all. One of the Lost Boys, perhaps. Still, you can't fault their enthusiasm, can you? Irrepressible, that's what they are. Irrepressible!'

She was clearing up his dishes when she saw Captain McQuarrie at the far end of the hall, dressed in the convalescent uniform and carrying his tray. The book she had given him was under his arm. He looked shrunken, wizened almost, no longer the boyish young man she had gone to at midnight. She was surprised he had been given permission to leave his bed, let alone that he had actually managed it.

McQuarrie shuffled carefully to his seat, as if carrying something infinitely more precious than his dinner tray. Esther tried to catch his eye as she bustled past, but he had already opened the book and started to read. Every mouthful of food made him wince. She wondered what poem he was on, but there was such a strange and detached air around him that she didn't have the courage to go up and ask.

It was only as she reached the kitchens that Esther realised she had abandoned Corporal Prevost. When she went back into the hall he was gone. She imagined him creeping up to his ward again, sitting there patiently while he waited for the world once more to emphasise his utter helplessness to him. Like those Charlie Chaplin films he loved, it was a play of light and shadow on a flat screen, a world he could not touch.

That evening, sitting on her bed, she communed with the blank page of her notebook. It was quiet in the dormitory. Alice and Ida were both still working, but the silence was oddly inhibiting and the words and phrases only lurked beneath the surface of her mind, as reticent as ever. She looked at the page. She looked at the nib of her pen. Nothing cohered, and all was a formless sea inside her. Now and then a fragment floated by, a stick of flotsam that she couldn't quite reach, but how could you ever write about mere fragments?

None of this was really poetry, if she was being honest with herself. The words, the notebook, that limpid impulse, they were all just gestures towards a life that still had poetry in it. And if she let that go, she knew, then there would be nothing of her left.

She closed the notebook and resisted the urge to fling it across the room. Lying back, letting her mind drift, Esther swam softly over the surface of her week, the parade of broken images. Walking with Ida in the grounds, her dream of the knight in darkness. Staffing the linen press, changing bedpans, helping Corporal Prevost feed himself. Major Lawson's Catholicism, the arrival of the new intake. Charlie Chaplin and Peter Pan, and then Captain McQuarrie gliding like a starved saint through the murmuring crowd, the book under his arm.

After a moment her thoughts skimmed back to those warm days before the war. Peter in his uniform the day they were married, Florence on their honeymoon, the Duomo sitting there as if painted on the air, its thick wooden beams like brushstrokes. And then, her heart quickening, she drew closer to that dark moment in the hotel bed, Peter's mumbled voice in her ear, the hot stench of wine on his breath.

She passed a hand across her eyes. She could hardly breathe. Getting up, she opened the window and looked down onto the lawn below, the marble plinth, the oak tree where Ida had sat. She thought of the knight in Ida's dream. They were so eager for war in those days. God had given them licence. But then all those men in the house below her had been desperate for war as well, at least until the war actually found them. Until the shadow fell and wiped them all away.

Peter whispering in her ear, the sullen, lustful hatred in his voice. Her silent prayer.

Something flickered in her mind, a memory. From the bedside table she took up her copy of *Aurora Leigh*. She found the lines deep in Book II, at the point where Aurora's aunt has died and has liberated her from all expectation.

God answers sharp and sudden on some prayers,/And thrusts the thing we have prayed for in our face,/A gauntlet with a gift in't. Every wish/Is like a prayer, with God.

That was it. That was it exactly. The stink of wine in his mouth, the bed shuddering as he collapsed onto it, his words freezing inside her, a cold stone she had carried in her stomach ever since. In the awful weight of the realisation that descended on her, that she had imprisoned herself with this man, she had clasped her hands and prayed.

Esther clutched the book to her chest. She would write about the dread she had felt when she understood the trap she was in, about the selfishness of that prayer. She would write about the war. It would be a poem about Roddinglaw House and all the men who had suffered in that war. It was all there. There were so many facets to it, so much scope, so much of the truth to capture.

She turned to the window again. The trees out there were black. The moonlight was a silver filigree against the water. The evening had gained a clearer shape.

There was even space for the knight, she thought, a symbol of a more romantic age. A warrior, a Crusader, someone lost in far-off places, like Captain McQuarrie struck down before the gates of Jerusalem. Now there were no more quests, no more adventures, no more heroes to undertake them.

She closed the window. The bronze knight was a green silhouette. She must discover his name.

From Jacob Beresford's journals, March 1918

It was the day after his funeral that I knew my father wanted to kill me.

At the Gora Cemetery I stood before his headstone and read the inscription. It was plain and simple, as he would have wanted; no more than his name and the salient dates, and a single line of scripture: *Blessed are the dead which die in the Lord*. How many times had I heard him say those words.

The grass on the graves was dry and yellow, the headstones as pale as polished bone. The trees hissed and the breeze brought with it the acrid tang of the nearby canal. For the briefest moment there seemed not another soul in the world. There was just the parched air, the whispered conversation of the trees. It felt like a glimpse of the far and distant future; the British gone, their cemetery abandoned and all the graves reclaimed. The Hindus burned their dead, I knew, something that always seemed a more sanitary prospect to me in such a climate. If the body truly relinquishes a living spirit when it dies, then the fires of cremation seem commensurate to the glory of that sundered soul. Better surely than tossing a corpse into the mud and leaving it to rot. But then, unlike my father, I don't believe in the bodily resurrection. I was, in every respect, a disappointment to him.

I closed my eyes. I could smell the flowers, already wilting in the heat.

Bobby had done all the necessary. He had arranged everything. I knew my father had expected to end his days in the mother country, but he would have appreciated the irony of being buried by the same funeral directors he had personally established. I knew also that before the month was out I would never see Bobby or Sarah again. I had already enquired about selling the business. I had no intention of staying in India and taking my father's place. I was sick of Lahore, sick of the imperishable stink of formaldehyde, sick of the high, thin scent of bodies turning in the heat. I told myself that I was even sick of Bobby and Sarah's flat just off the Mall; the tired Arts and Crafts decor, the Félicien Rops illustrations rotting in their frames, the punkah hanging lifeless from the ceiling; all that decadent, Yellow Nineties inheritance from their own father, which they couldn't afford to replace or repair.

Bobby would no doubt see it as the most unforgivable betrayal when he found out that I had left. He would curse my name. He had worked for my father most of his life, tending the dead under his instruction, and would have thought himself due an appropriate reward. After all, hadn't we been such terribly close friends? But it was Sarah I would miss most of all. I knew that she did in some way love me, as I loved her. The heart would suffer, the soul would be stained, but I could not stay.

The wide streets of the Civil Station were eerily quiet when I came home that evening. I dismissed the servants and sat with a gin and bitters and thought over my plans. I was someone who had buried his father, a boy who had come into man's estate. I was free to go wherever I wanted. When the business was sold and the money was in my hands, I would disappear into the netherworld of the sanitaria. Bobby and his conceited self-pity, Sarah and the brittle demands she made on me, the hooks they had sunk into my flesh – I would put all that behind me. I would tear myself away and be free, left to commune in silence only with the germs in my lungs as they slowly killed me. Free from my father and everything he had ever expected of me.

But no. As it turned out at Bhowali, at Hawkmoor in Devon, I would not be free of him. I soon came to realise that he would follow me everywhere I went, to sanatoria, even all the way to Gallondean.

He had died in June, near the fierce peak of summer. The sun beat down on the city and the heat lay like a judgement on my father's house. My room was so warm that night, I barely slept. I remember groping for that excuse for months, whenever I brought the moment back to mind. Heatstroke, I thought. The lack of sleep, that imperial sun ringing like a great brass bell, the villa prostrate beneath it. In such a punishing summer hour, is it any wonder that the mind conjures phantoms? That's what minds do after all, when they can no longer take the strain.

At noon, the day after I'd put my father in the ground, I stood in the shadows of the veranda and looked onto the scorched garden. It was a furnace. A haze danced on the hot stone walls. Broken glass still littered the flagstones beside the shade house. I didn't have the energy to clear it away. The flowers within had wilted and died. Larkspur and hollyhock, sweet peas and nasturtiums. The white chrysanthemums most of all. My father's carefully nurtured little corner of England, killed by the Indian heat.

As I stared at the garden, the long apron of the lawn seemed to wrinkle and contract, like a slug sprinkled with salt. There were spots of light wheeling in my eyes, an acrid, metallic taste in my mouth that I last remembered as a child, when I'd choked on a two-*anna* piece. I recall my father cuffing the back of my head so I would cough it up. (I've always wondered if that's where it came from, my illness. The germs can live on surfaces for many years and lie dormant in the lungs.) The sun was so sharp that the garden had all the depth of a sketch on plain paper. I could have poked my fingers through it, torn it apart with a flick of the wrist. The air hummed. I swayed, the sweat streaming down my face. And then, as swiftly as a rail switch being tripped, everything was silent. The tracks changed, and I found myself somewhere else entirely.

Nothing moved or breathed or suffered. Nothing stirred. The droning insect day just ceased.

A spectre moved across the garden. A shade uncoiling, a black light reaching all the way to the Gora Cemetery.

All I could see were the fragments of glass, the crusted blood. Then the broken glass dimmed, and the shards winked out one by one. I could not explain it, then or now, but I knew. I *knew*. It was him.

37

All the light curled at the edges. I felt a surge in my lungs, the bacilli stirring in a frenzy. It was as if my chest was being crushed in a monstrous hand, and when I coughed my chin was red with blood. A shroud was drawn across my eyes.

I remember lying there on the veranda, fading in, fading out, beaten by the heat. I remember thinking, as the shade slithered across the blazing afternoon, that all this was no more than I deserved. But then I heard the sound of footsteps scuffing quickly across the terrace, a throaty feminine cry. Sarah was there beside me, her hand on my brow. Quickly the shade withdrew, and the Gora Cemetery reclaimed its dead. It was in no hurry, after all. There was no corner of the world to which I could escape where it would not follow.

'Be a light in the darkness, Krishna,' Sarah said, quoting from the *Gita*. 'Those who come to me go beyond the shadows...'

The candle burns low at my bedside as I write. Sarah's statue sits patiently at the end of my bed, projecting its inscrutable power. Nothing can touch me while it is here. I owe her that strange faith more than anything, taught to me during those last long days we spent together. Before I abandoned her.

Jakey is Sattva. He is the peaceful light.

I try to be, truly I do. I want to be the Light, pure and unsullied. I want to be what you saw in me, Sarah. Perhaps, while the Lord remains, a little bit of you remains too.

It was the de Gaillons who founded Gallondean, so Rutherford told me. The cotton merchants and calico printers who built Roddinglaw House came many centuries later, but in the early 1100s it was a family of Norman nobles, still with the Viking blood in their veins, who set down these stones. Barons and earls, hard men keen on fighting, their fathers had been ambitious knights in the Conqueror's service. They had been given land by a Scottish king and had headed north to take up their new estates. The de Gaillons found themselves with this wind-lashed stretch of coast outside Edinburgh, the Queen's Ferry near at hand, a patchwork hinterland of farms and villages behind them and a sullen population transformed on a king's whim from peasants to serfs. Feudalism came to the coast and planted its banner.

Little is known of Roger de Gaillon, who built the first tower house. The blunt columns and the recessed arch above the southern gate are supposed to be original, but it was his son, Robert de Gaillon, who turned it into a fortress. Legend and the long years have painted Robert in darker colours; a stern and violent figure who was killed in strange circumstances by his own son, William. Seeking intercession or forgiveness, penance or atonement, William then left these shores in response to the call for Crusade. Loot or pilgrimage usually sent the knights of Europe to the Holy Land – but William de Gaillon saddled his charger and answered the Lionheart's call for more austere reasons of his own. It was said that all sins were forgiven those who took up arms in defence of the Lord and Jerusalem.

As we stood in the clotted air of his shoreside cottage, I asked Rutherford how he knew all this. He didn't strike me as a scholar. There were documents, he said. Old books and volumes, accounts from more recent ages. By the seventeenth century the de Gaillons had died away and new earls had stepped into their place. Some were antiquarians and archivists, or just men with a passing interest in the history of their bleak and impenetrable fortress. They had marshalled the evidence and assembled the conjecture, making oblique reference to much older documents long-since lost to time. Before the war, Rutherford had been charged by my father to unearth all these accounts, if he could.

'And did you?'

'To the best of my ability, sir. Gallondean is a house with many chambers, as you know, many secret places in which to delve. It's strange how much remains when few are interested in it.'

'And what of this legend you mentioned?'

He gazed out of the window, as if the threads of the tale were laid out there amongst the marram grass, waiting to be gathered in.

'So it's said, William de Gaillon took his leave of Gallondean and set off on the journey to the East.' He pronounced the Norman name as he did the name of the castle: 'Gallon'.

'To atone for his father's death. Why did he kill Robert though? What was the enmity between them?'

But Rutherford didn't answer. He skipped forward and tugged at his thatch of hair. His eyes danced.

'Have you seen the statue, sir, on the lawn of Roddinglaw House?'

I nodded. I had noticed it when out walking, although I'd gone no closer than the treeline.

'The old Lord of Roddinglaw, sir, he had it sculpted a good few years back. I believe he was quite taken by the legend too, put out perhaps that he didn't feature in it himself. You know what toffs are like, very proud… He had gone to some lengths to buy Gallondean, so I understand, but it was your father won that auction by the higher price. As I'm sure I don't need to say, the statue is William de Gaillon no less, heading to the Holy Land, with his hound at his side.' He grinned, showing me teeth like a mouthful of gravel. His voice dropped. 'And it's the hound that's at the heart of it, sir. The *hound*.'

Alas, the dog's name hasn't travelled to us down the years, but it was apparently devoted to its master. Not willing to risk its life in the East, William de Gaillon had left it behind when he departed Gallondean. As he sailed to the Holy Land, leaving from the Queen's Ferry and heading towards France, the dog was distraught. When the boat vanished into the mist, slipping past the islands of the firth, the beast howled from that spur of land known today as Hound Point. Many months later, gripped by some strange frenzy, it ran back to that same spot and howled once more; and then, its madness spent, it curled up and expired at the exact moment William de Gaillon met his end in battle, three thousand miles away.

'The hound knew, you see,' Rutherford said. 'Such was the bond between them, that when the Saracens killed William, the hound knew! It howled and died clear away of a broken heart, as it will for all its master's successors.'

'So de Gaillon's heirs, the so-called Lords of Gallondean, they're party to this same legend, this curse or whatever it is?'

'The same, sir, the very same.' He twisted his hands together. 'When the lord's death approaches, Hound Point rings with the dog's ghostly howling, and the lord will know that his time is near. It happened for your father, sir. I heard it, I swear. And it will happen for you.'

I looked at him, so keen to be of service, his mad mind jumping back to a subject that had clearly preoccupied him for some time. All of it on my father's prompting too. I didn't believe for a moment that some spectral hound had truly marked the old man's passing, but clearly the tale had fascinated him.

'He wrote to you?' I said. 'Giving you instructions to look into this story?'

'Indeed, sir.'

'And you still have his letters?'

'Yes, sir,' Rutherford said, ducking his head again. 'Not here, but in Gallondean. There are volumes also, sir, and documents... some the worse for wear but they may be useful to you, if you find yourself equally intrigued. If, of course, the moment of your death is something that would be of interest...'

I felt the grip on my lungs tighten, the pressure shift and contract.

'Show me,' I said. I indicated the door. 'I think I have need of a factor after all, Mr Rutherford.'

Later: I can feel the darkness creeping in now. It crawls across the floorboards and through the mumbled stone of the corridors. It slithers past the dust-drenched tapestries and stains the narrow windows. The darkness, and everything it brings.

The statue beside me is no more than ten inches high, carved from grey and violet porphyry. Without it I would be lost. From Lahore to Bhowali, from Bhowali to Bombay, to all points west it has come with me. I glance now at the four arms holding the conch, the lotus flower, the discus and the mace. The face has such a calm self-possession that just gazing on it can still the beating of my heart. The shadow lifts a fraction. I will be *Sattva*, Sarah, I promise. I am the Peaceful Light. The shadow will have no hold over me.

Puja, she called it. Hanging lemons from the lintel, or breaking a coconut and scattering its waters around your bed. But where on earth would I find a coconut on this cold coast? For that matter, where would I find a lemon? What is fit for India is not necessarily fit for here, and so I have been forced to improvise. I have dredged up old apotropaic ideas from my childhood reading, like berried holly

41

hung above the door or garlic smeared on the windowsills. I have drawn a circle of salt around the bed; an old protection. I have lit the candle and I have said the prayer you taught me, Sarah:

Lord Vishnu, look over me while I sleep. Protect me, lord, from he who wishes me harm.

The shade swimming over the sun-struck lawn – how much longer can I keep it away? Cringing, waiting, refusing to confront it. Perhaps there is no alternative to the cold-blooded decision to fight, no matter what. The war will have me yet.

The wind batters the flanks of the old house. From somewhere in the firth a ship's foghorn blows, a sound deeper than the ocean. I feel the cough building in me again, rising like a bubble from deep water. I will gave way to it this time, hacking with a kind of ecstasy, pressing the handkerchief to my mouth, my head shaking like a dog's, all the veins thickening in my throat. And then I will take the handkerchief away and look, and I will count my days in the measure of the blood.

Tuesday 2nd April 1918

'It's going to flower early this year,' Major Lawson said. 'The cow parsley. And we're only just into April.'

He pointed to the sharp serrated leaves of what Esther had always thought was hogweed. Stands of it fringed the path, waist-high, very green in the sun-dappled shadows.

'I thought that was Queen Anne's lace,' she said. 'Sir.'

Lawson waved a gloved hand. 'You're thinking of *Heracleum sphondylium*, they're very similar. *Anthriscus sylvestris* is what we have here. Although honestly,' he said, as if sharing a confidence, 'there's something terribly pedantic about digging down into the Linnaean, isn't there? And the folk names are so much more evocative. Mother-die or wild chervil, or whatever you will.'

They walked on in silence. There was a band of trees hard against the dunes on their right, the sea beyond washing to the shore with a sound like ripped paper. The path was hard-packed dirt beneath their feet. Ahead and to their left, Mons Hill rose in shallow slopes, thick with forest. Again she felt the strangeness of that name, the appalling coincidence. To put wounded men in the shadow of somewhere that bore the name of the first battle in this war.

After a while, tentatively, Lawson said, 'Of course, I'm no expert.'
'Sir?'

He swept a hand towards the trees. 'I'm an amateur naturalist, at best. I've often thought it's our hobbies that tell other people who we really are though. Wouldn't you say? They're glimpses of what we truly care about.'

A space opened between them where she could have mentioned her poetry, but she left it unfilled. As much as she admired Major Lawson, she wasn't quite prepared to reveal a glimpse of what she truly cared about to him. Poetry was a secret thing, not to be shared.

'And do your hobbies extend to amateur dramatics, sir?'

Lawson blinked. 'Mrs Worrell?'

Esther, aware that she was perhaps overstepping the mark, said, 'I wondered if you would be joining the other officers for *Peter Pan*. Sir.'

'No, no, goodness me, no. Alas, my position means it's probably not wise. The mask of command and all that,' he laughed. He touched his cap, the dull badge of Asclepius struck by a shaft of passing light. 'But I would make a damned good Gentleman Starkey, I have to say. A *damned good* Starkey.'

'The men wouldn't mind,' she told him. 'I think they'd welcome a senior officer joining in, especially one they respect so much.' She gave a sidelong glance and saw Lawson blush.

'What the men would welcome and what the men need are sometimes two separate things, Mrs Worrell.'

'Then their gain is the stage's loss, Major. I'm sure of it.'

The path widened and the twin rutted tracks of the road began to sweep towards the gates of Gallondean. Beyond an apron of gravel and grounds thick with feathered grass, the house glared down at them. The windows were dark, and the stone was streaked with the morning's rain.

'Lord Weary's Castle,' Lawson said under his breath. He scraped open the iron gate and ushered Esther through.

'He's not really a lord though, sir, is he?'

'Heavens, no,' Lawson grunted as he shoved the gate back into place. They crunched over the gravel. The doors ahead of them were shut, two flat planes of darkened oak studded with iron nails. 'No, he's inherited the pile, but it's not an ancestral one.' He looked up at the pitted stone, the crenellated tower. 'His father bought it perhaps ten, fifteen years ago, as I understand. Made his money in the funeral business, of all things, out in the Punjab. Lord Roddinglaw was by all accounts displeased.'

'Lord Roddinglaw still lives in the house? I've never seen him. Although it is such a meandering old place, I'm sure I haven't set foot in half its rooms yet.'

'No, he's dead now, many years since. His widow owns the house, but she keeps very much to herself in Edinburgh. It was her offer of the building to the RAMC at the start of the war that put us all where we currently are. Most generous. Of course, none of us thought we would still be here nearly four years later...'

He raised a hand to the jamb, trailed it slowly back and forth as he searched for the bell. There was none. He looked at Esther and brought the heel of his hand down onto the solid oak.

'Let us hope the new Lord of Gallondean is less keen than his father to profit from the dead.'

She had seen him from the dormitory window many times, walking along the coast. It was hard to see such a figure in a landscape and not clothe it in romance, and from a distance he had looked almost Byronic to her; the black coat buffeted by the wind, the black hair uncovered, indifferent to the lightly falling rain. He walked with his hands in his pockets, his head bowed, giving the impression of deep thought and deeper torment. A shadow drifting along the shore.

Alice Stewart had pointed him out to her the day before. They had been taking in great armfuls of sheets and pillowcases from the washing lines at the back of the house.

'There he is,' she whispered, as if he could have heard them from three hundred yards away. She cocked her head towards the trees. Esther turned and saw the young man walking slowly along the path, on the far side of Roddinglaw's gardens.

'Who is he?'

'He's the chap who lives in the old tower,' Alice said. 'Beresford or some such. "Heathcliff" some of the other ladies call him, but I've always thought of him as Dracula. Doesn't he have that look to you? Lord, that book frightened the life out of me when I read it.' Alice's face became dark and conspiratorial. 'Catriona Swift stumbled across him in the woods the other day, when she was out picking daffodils for the foyer.' She gave Esther a pointed look.

'What happened?'

'Well, nothing,' Alice said, disappointed. 'She said he was just sitting there at the edge of the woods, lounging on a tree stump. But he was wiping blood from his hands, she says. Blood! And the look he gave her. She nearly jumped out of her skin. As if he wanted to *devour* her, if you take my meaning. All the girls say it. Someone's always peering through the trees at them, following them along the paths to the village, and always some poor little creature nailed to a tree or torn up amongst the roots. It'll be him, I wager.'

They strolled across the drying green, back to the tradesmen's doors. There was a narrow hall past the kitchens and the laundry rooms, where a long wooden table was set up outside the linen press for the women to fold the sheets. Alice flung down her pile and began to sort through it.

'And what I want to know is what someone so young is doing out of uniform? Tell me that, if you can. It doesn't look like there's anything wrong with him to me. Always out walking, in all weathers, or peering from the windows of his mouldy old castle. If you can even call it a castle.'

'I believe they do,' Esther teased her.

But Alice entrenched herself further on the moral high ground. 'And I'm sure *that* suits him right down to the ground.'

The rest of the afternoon had rushed by – cleaning, washing, overseeing deliveries of bandages and medicines; the goods truck rattling on the gravel driveway, the delivery men older and less certain of themselves, parsing the receipts with much frowning and licking of pencil stubs. Esther, as exhausted as ever, had moved through it all in a fog. Sister was constantly chivvying her, lashing the whip. 'Always a surprise that *you* became a volunteer, Mrs Worrell,' she had said once, 'when there's no money to be made…'

Later, not long before the patients were called for dinner, Esther had glanced into one of the former bedrooms on her way to the dormitory. Half a dozen men were sitting at battered old school desks arranged in a haphazard circle. Some were painting on small,

46

eighteen-inch canvases. Others, their fingers stained with ochre, palped and moulded blocks of ruddy clay, eyes fierce with concentration. Captain McQuarrie was standing there, just inside the door. He was hunched over slightly, his forehead damp, watching the other patients with the air of a schoolboy hovering on the threshold of a common room, the other pupils unknown to him.

'Aren't you going to join in?' she asked. She touched him lightly on the sleeve. He still had her book under his arm. 'I know some of the men find it quite restorative.'

McQuarrie, almost anxiously, gestured at the canvases. 'I'm no artist.'

'Oh, I'm not sure the quality of the end product is the point, Captain.' She knew she was using that bright and artificial manner again, the one all the nurses and VADs adopted when talking to the patients. It fell as naturally as the high-pitched, sing-song tone she might have used when talking to someone's dog or child.

'Perhaps I will then,' he said lightly, distracted. 'The clay appeals, I have to say. Making something, making it with your own hands...'

She tapped the cloth corner of the book. 'And how have you been getting on with Mr Browning?'

McQuarrie held out the volume, as if this was the first time he'd seen it. 'Very well,' he said slowly. 'At least, as far as I can tell. It's all a bit obscure, isn't it? But – yes, very well.'

'He does have a reputation for being difficult,' Esther admitted. 'Perhaps only partially unearned.'

'Some of the material though, it's a bit medieval... Always some dark tower or a troubled priest in the background, isn't there? Strange men killing their lovers.'

'Yes?' Esther said. She nodded, as if inviting him to go on.

'Storms and tumults and so on,' he said, looking apologetic. 'It all seems a touch old hat, that's all. A bit overdone. If you know what I mean.'

Esther felt loyalty flame inside her. There was the embarrassment of talking about what you loved, but there was also the affront when what you loved was slighted. Thank God she hadn't given him *Aurora Leigh*, the greater work.

'Some might say that,' she said. Her voice was colder than she'd intended. 'It's not the most generous reading, perhaps. And I don't think he's *obscure*. It's just that he lets his information unfold more gradually. You're never quite sure of the voice you're meant to be listening to.'

'I only thought, with the war…' McQuarrie dropped his eyes. 'I meant no offence. As I said, I haven't really started to think deeply about it.'

'I'm not offended,' she said, far too quickly. It was the one emotion it cost too much to admit. 'They're not my poems, are they?'

'I'm sure your poems are just as powerful, Mrs Worrell. Assuming of course that you write them.' He looked at the cloth cover of the book again and confided, 'No one underlines so much unless they're trying to learn something.'

Esther found herself making an awful, tinkling little laugh, as if he had caught her out in some sly game. She felt the blush on her cheeks again and stared at the paintings in the room, the men hunched over the school desks. She realised then that Corporal Prevost was sitting over in the far corner, his empty cuffs resting in his lap. There was a block of clay on the table in front of him, mumbled and squashed, two fringes teased out as if suggesting wings. With a lurch of horror that had her turning away from the open door, she realised that he had been trying to sculpt it with his wrists.

'But there was one poem that drew me,' McQuarrie said. He rifled through the pages. '"A Death in the Desert".'

'A favourite? You'll have to refresh my memory on it,' she said, trying to warm her voice. 'I can't quite remember.'

'Very interesting, it's—It's presented as this document that's been found in a hidden chest and…'

McQuarrie held her eyes a moment. His lips parted, but then he turned his head as if he didn't quite trust the words he had to hand.

'It's supposed to be about St John. An account of his last days, dying in a cave, despairing. Truth, and reason, and – this idea that man has three souls, body, mind and spirit, but…'

McQuarrie stared into the room for a moment, taking in the canvases and clay, the table in the centre where the finished sculptures were waiting to be fired in the ovens. Bowls, cups, a simple bust of a Classical female figure that owed far more to enthusiasm than skill. He slumped against the jamb suddenly and all the colour drained from him, like poison from a wound.

'Captain McQuarrie, are you alright?'

He waved her away. 'I'm fine,' he said. 'Truly.' He straightened up and touched his chest very carefully, laying the palm flat against his breast. And then he whispered, '*This did not happen in the outer cave,*' and shuffled to the head of the stairs without a backward glance, still clutching her book.

The man who answered Lawson's knock was hunched and grey, his face seamed and salt-bitten, mottled with drink. He peered at them through dull, suspicious eyes.

Lawson was unperturbed. 'We're here to see Mr Beresford,' he said. 'We are expected.'

The old man regarded them a moment, his eyes lingering less on Esther than on her uniform: the white cap, the red cross emblazoned on her chest, the long grey skirts. Without a word, he drew the door open and ushered them through. Major Lawson extended an arm and stepped aside for her.

Esther passed into the hard gloom of a shabby, ill-lit hallway. There was an oil lamp wavering in a pool of uncertain light at the other end, the glass bulb blackened by the flame, and a sharp smell of paraffin in the air. The rugs and carpets were threadbare. In places the panelling on the walls had come away, revealing the bare stone beneath.

They came to the foot of a staircase, some of the balusters bashed away, the hand rail shaking under Esther's touch as they climbed to the first floor. She could only think of young David Balfour in *Kidnapped*, sent up the dangerous stairwell by his unscrupulous uncle in the House of Shaws.

The old man took them through long and narrow corridors, past half-open doors that revealed rooms filled with piles of boxes or stacked old furniture. Narrow windows admitted spears of sunlight through their dirty glass. Major Lawson gave Esther a very pointed stare. He already had the answer to his question. Likely the war would be over before they could make this place the least bit habitable for their patients.

They came to a dim landing framed by two French *guéridons*, the gilt peeling, the mahogany chipped. On the other side of the landing there was another staircase of brushed stone twisting up into the shadows. There was a door to their right.

'Rutherford!' a hoarse voice called. 'Who is it? Where are you, for God's sake?'

The old man swept the door open and with a nod of his head saw them into the room. Duty done, he lumbered off down the corridor.

They came into what must once have been a library. To either side were shelves of leatherbound books, many gaps between the volumes. There was a strong smell of damp, and the light trickled only weakly through the arrow-slit windows. An oil lamp blazed on a long desk that bisected the room. For a moment the glare masked the man who stood behind it, his hands spread on the surface of a table that was covered with stacks of manuscript and parchment, old codices, manor rolls, sheets of vellum. As he stepped from the light Esther took in his black hair, the grey eyes sunk in a grey face, very thin, the temples high, the bones visible. It was the man she had seen creeping along the foreshore; the man who had alarmed Catriona Swift when she was out picking daffodils. Heathcliff or Dracula – and yet despite his appearance he reminded her most, with quick and sudden force, of her dead husband. For a moment it was as if Peter stood there before her, dredged up from the haunted deeps.

'Yes?' he said. 'What is it?' He looked very intently at Esther.

Lawson stepped forward and removed his cap.

'Mr Beresford? I'm Major Lawson of the Royal Army Medical Corps. You are, I believe, expecting us?'

Beresford did not bother to hide his irritation. He came from behind the desk and folded his arms. His voice seemed to be lodged in his throat and he had to force his words out. He was younger than Esther had first realised.

'A major. I don't know whether I should shake your hand or salute.'

'No salute required.' Lawson laughed. His eyes were hard. 'After all, you are not in uniform.'

'No,' Beresford said. He smiled. 'I'm not.'

He offered them nothing, did not even ask them to sit down. He leaned back against the edge of the desk, the lamp fuming behind him. The corners of the room were thick with shadow. Outside, in the late afternoon, the sunlight was thinning out. Esther tried not to look at him directly. She stood there with her hands behind her back, but she was aware of his gaze as it flicked back to her. She stared at the grim shelves of books instead, the leather covers bulging with damp.

'I mentioned the purpose of our visit in my note,' Lawson went on. 'As you know, Lady Roddinglaw has been kind enough to lend her property to the Medical Corps for the duration, and we've made good use of it for convalescing patients.'

'The good Lady of Roddinglaw,' Beresford said. He didn't try to hide the edge of cynicism in his voice. 'So very kind.'

'Indeed.' Lawson paused. 'Alas, space being what it is, and with Gallondean Castle so close at hand—'

Beresford gripped the edge of the desk. 'No.'

'Sir?'

'I'm sure your time is worth even more than the price I put on mine, Major, and I don't want to waste it. I'm afraid it's out of the question. You cannot have Gallondean for your patients.'

Lawson stared down at the toes of his polished brogues. With another light and not at all amused laugh, he said, 'I realise the house would need some improvements to make it fit for purpose, but our need is great. We are at war, sir.'

'Are we?' Beresford said. He looked again at Esther. 'Then at last I have an explanation for why there's so much barbed wire littering the beaches. It quite spoils my walks.'

'This is no time for frivolity, Mr Beresford. You must realise I am not asking for it personally but on behalf of the RAMC. It's for the wounded. If necessary, if absolutely necessary, the state can commandeer what it needs.'

'Can it indeed? How strange, when I thought the army was fighting to preserve our way of life, Major Lawson.' Beresford returned to his position behind the desk, trailing his hands over the manuscripts, the piles of letters, none of which looked to be in any better repair than the books on the shelves. 'Shall I suffer the state just to take what it wants from me, without recourse? You shall not have Gallondean. I cannot be clearer than that. If the army wants it, then the army will have to prise it from me at bayonet-point.'

Esther could see Lawson wrestling with anger. A mild man, one she had seen treat his patients with the utmost care and tenderness, he stared now at Beresford as if he wanted to stride across the room and strike him. What was that phrase he had used?

'Where's your sense of Christian charity?' she said. 'Men are dying.'

Beresford grinned. 'Ah, but I would never call myself a Christian.'

His teeth were bared. There was a glimpse of Peter's drunken anger then, her husband's restless temper, but the resemblance quickly passed. Beresford stared at her again, and then, as if stabbed by a sudden pain, he clutched his chest and turned away. He looked out of the window, his back to them. When he spoke, his voice was choked and gritty.

'Now, please, I have work to do. I cannot help you.'

Lawson looked at him a moment longer. His jaw was tight and there were spots of colour high on his cheeks. He replaced his cap and left the room without another word. Esther had to hurry to keep up with him.

As they cut along the path to the gate, the overgrown grass lunging at them from either side, Lawson peeled the gloves from his hands and thrust them into his pockets.

'Impossible,' he said, sadly. 'The selfishness, it's extraordinary.'

'I don't know what to say, Major. He certainly seemed very disagreeable.'

Lawson sighed. 'A shame though, of course. Allowances must be made.'

'Sir?'

'It's tuberculosis, clearly. It explains why he's here. The sea air. Although that damp and draughty old house can't be doing him any good. I shouldn't wonder if he has very little time left to him. If it's sooner rather than later, then I expect the army will get Gallondean all the same.'

Esther tried to agree, but the confrontation had shaken her. Again she saw the black hair, the grey eyes. So like Peter, she told herself, and yet her husband had had none of Beresford's cynicism, that anxious, barely contained scorn. But then she had to admit that she could barely remember what he had looked like now. In the end she had never really known him.

Esther glanced back at Gallondean before the woodland swallowed them. There, staring from the blade of a window high on the first floor, a pale face watched them go.

From Jacob Beresford's journals, April 1918

I can't think how to describe it, any of it. I must get it down while it's still fresh in my mind. Closer, he is so much closer now. I am almost thrilled to think that death is so near.

There are moments when I am overwhelmed, paralysed by all my fears. Exhaustion, fatigue – the pitch of high anxieties. Often I find myself in parts of the house, lacking all memory of how I got there. I black out; I swoon like a Victorian maiden. I surface amongst the trees or on the lawns of Roddinglaw with a storm in my mind. Only this evening I woke in the library, my head against the desk. When I came to, the reek of those mouldering books hit me with redoubled force. (I should throw them out. My father will have bought them by the yard, all the expected titles – Shakespeare, Ruskin, Carlyle, half of Greece and Rome. I cannot imagine he cut the pages on a single volume.) At the very least, the smell reminded me that I should gather up all the letters and manuscripts Rutherford had disinterred from Gallondean's cellars, because they will not long survive the damp in this room. Ruefully, I thought: Neither will I …

Absently, unsystematically, I began to pile everything together. Leatherbound codices; packets of envelopes sent from Lahore, the paper still redolent of sandalwood. Outside, the sea beat regularly on the stone, a slack tide rising to brush the terrace. The moon was waning, two-thirds bone-white, one third black.

I listened to the waves a while. A storm was rising, readying itself to lash against the coast. The house creaked and groaned, a floorboard settling here, a rafter there. Loose stone trickled through the walls like shale slipping from a hillside. It was the first time since Lahore that I had fallen asleep without Sarah's statue beside me, or a circle of salt on the ground.

Suddenly, and without warning, a sharp and searing pain flamed up in my chest. All the air fled away. I tried to stand and felt my head go light. The wick of the lamp crackled and the flame drew back. The sharp and urgent smell of the paraffin slowly faded. The library was lit only by the threads of moonlight reflected off the sea.

He was here. God help me, he was inside the house.

The heat of the Civil Station swept over me then. The parched heat of Gora Cemetery, the stink of the canal. The smell of chrysanthemums, the rising shriek of the brainfever bird, that dreadful, eclipsing moment—

The shadows flowed in, louder than the sea. Something slouched along the corridor outside. I gripped the arms of the chair. The darkness buckled where the door hung ajar.

I couldn't move. The breath heaved inside me but would not come. And then the door cracked, loud as a gunshot.

A swoon was on me, a great rushing tide of darkness. I remember reeling from the desk, crying out, sweeping the letters to the floor as I fell.

Hacking the blood from my lungs, head shaking, hands cupped to catch it, strings of fibre and mucus between my fingers. It was too soon. I knew too little. I didn't have even a fraction of the strength necessary to face it.

'Rutherford,' I spat. 'Help me, damn you. Rutherford. It's here!'

A light kindled. The old man's lamp, flaring in the darkness. My eyes burned. Frail as he was (I hazard by this point I was frailer), Rutherford stooped to lift me back into the chair.

'I heard you calling, sir,' he said, agitated. A blast of stale whisky buffeted me. His mad eyes rolled like marbles in their sockets. 'Did you hear it, sir? Was it there! Did you hear the hound!'

My breath settled. The pounding of my heart began to ease. Despite myself, I laughed, a desperate sound.

'No,' I said. I looked to the open door, the night lying heavily in the corridor outside. There was nothing there. 'No, I only thought – but I'm not ready to die quite yet, Mr Rutherford.' He helped me to my feet. I wiped my mouth with the back of my hand and saw the streak of crimson. 'Not when there's so much more to learn.'

Later. I had barely recovered from a night rendered sleepless with alarm when Major Lawson from Roddinglaw House paid his visit, begging for beds. I had forgotten the appointment had even been made. Rousing myself, quashing my anger, I looked up and saw Lawson step into the room, and beside him stood Sarah.

The ring of dark hair beneath the white circlet of the cap; the red cross on her tunic, like a Crusader's tabard. All I could see though were those tawny eyes, aflame in lamplight. How many times had I lost myself in those eyes...

The woman who stood there in a nurse's uniform was not Sarah, of course. But my heart was struck by the sight of her, and for a moment it was as if she had returned to me once more. For the first time in four years, it wasn't my lungs that prevented me from breathing.

Here, she had said. The garden still burned, but it was cool inside the house. She believed me, that was the thing. *Lord Vishnu is the Protector. He will keep you safe. There is no ghost or unquiet grave that can touch you while he is here.* She took my hands, laid them on the body of the statue. She hissed between her teeth, half-laugh, half-sigh. *I will stay with you, Jakey, for as long as it takes. Let me show you what true faith can do.* Her palm came up to smooth my brow. I thought my heart would break, because I knew that I was leaving and she did not. Poor Sarah. I couldn't make myself stay, although not a day passes when I don't yearn to catch the sight of myself reflected in her eyes. That flame of longing, of love, if love it was... *That cruel and miserable old man is gone. Fear him no more.*

But I do fear him, Sarah. I always have and I always will. I fear him, I think, even more than I loved you. At the end, I do not believe he was truly himself.

The rest of the meeting passed in a daze. I was weak, unbalanced. The attack had left me feeling frantic, somehow, almost frenzied. I refused Lawson's request. There is no time and no space, and I will not be interrupted now. When they left, I stood at a high window on the southern flank and watched them go. Back to Roddinglaw, back to the world as it is now and not as it was then.

Disturbed, shaken, I returned to my documents, my weapons in the war – the Georgian accounts of Scotland's last trial by combat, held in these grounds in 1597; the seventeeth-century antiquarian records of the Roman finds in Cramond. I called on Rutherford to bring me more, coughing into the palms of my hands, massaging my chest. More documents, more parchment, more information. I would build myself a fortress of ink and paper. I would know only the truth, and nothing else. I would be armed against it.

I tried not to think of the nurse, or of Sarah. There was only de Gaillon, and Gallondean, and the howling.

I have gone through his letters first, the instructions he sent to Mr Rutherford from Lahore. To see his handwriting again was a strange and dislocating thing. I remember it so well from school, all those terse missives that arrived term after term, exhorting me to do better. I felt pushed to the very edge of tears. We are never entirely free, it seems, of our love for our fathers.

I wondered at his changing state of mind as I read through them. At first each letter is filled only with routine instruction; ordering Rutherford to employ a new groundsman, say, or to ensure that preparations are made to lag the pipes for winter. He answers questions, comments on information his factor has given him, makes financial decisions which Rutherford is not qualified to undertake. It is all business and I skim through the contents rapidly, half an eye attuned to any mention of my name.

The letters are from 1911, 1912, 1913. I think back – 1913 was the year I came out to India from school. It was when I met Bobby for the first time, as my father showed me around the offices and mortuaries of the business. It was when I met Sarah at that Christmas party, gliding through the press in scarlet and black, a glass in her hand, those bright and wonderful eyes gleaming. My father mentions none of that, of course, but there isn't even an off-hand reference to the arrival of his son, whom he will have seen only three or four times in the past eleven years.

The tone begins to change in late 1913. Rutherford must have made some reference to the statue of the horseman at Roddinglaw, because my father is keen to follow it up. *He has never forgiven me*, he writes, *for acquiring what he feels should be naturally his.* (He? Lord Roddinglaw?) Then, later, *You refer to the legend, but I confess I've only heard of it in passing. Local folklore has never been of great interest to me.*

He returns to the subject again and again though, intrigued, drawn back, hooked on the mystery. *After all, I suppose in a way I am the Lord of Gallondean now.* He asks Rutherford to describe the statue in more detail, to sketch it if he has the skill. (No such sketch appears to survive.) He has his factor disinter whatever material is buried in the core of the house, old volumes in forgotten storerooms that legally should be in the library of the Faculty of Advocates. Rutherford is to collate any information he can find on Hound Point and William de Gaillon, the tale of a young knight killing his father and seeking penance on Crusade. My father seems to labour under the delusion that there will be some ancient rustic deep in the countryside who retains a folk memory of the tale, as if we were all living in the pages of a novel by Scott.

The letters become more frequent, the handwriting less clear. He instructs Rutherford to acquire material from various booksellers in Edinburgh and Glasgow; histories of David I and the Norman aristocracy in Scotland; collections of local myths and legends compiled by enthusiastic Victorian parsons. He suggests that Rutherford delve into far-flung university libraries and church archives, something that would only have bewildered the man. There are oblique references to my father's attempted correspondence with distant cadet branches of the de Gaillons, people who only seem to exist in the footnotes of Debrett's. He tries to track down former residents, tenants and owners from decades past. Even from this distance you can taste the mania, the obsession quickening as the months go by.

I do not have as long as I would like, he confesses. *Age and infirmity are catching up with me and my heart feels the growing pressure of the Indian heat. I have spent too long in my profession to hold any illusions about the body. The great leveller is near. Or, later,* You must listen on my behalf, Mr Rutherford. You must listen *for the howling.*

The last letter is dated 14ᵗʰ June 1914, a bare two months before the war began. At last I find mention of myself.

I will be returning later this summer with my son. Ensure the materials are ready for me to peruse. I would impress upon him the nature of this tale and what he must expect from Hound Point. The de Gaillons knew, down through the ages, and his own health falters. He is polluted in the lungs, infected I have no doubt through the louche company he keeps; half-castes and Jews, loafers and lounge-abouts, some of whom I am ashamed to say have remained in my employ longer than was proper. Just to be acquainted with them is a sickness of a kind. But all this will change. The air, the fresh sea air, the halls of a new ancestral home, will do us both the world of good. Together we will listen for the howling, and when it comes we will know. 'Watch therefore, for ye know neither the day nor the hour', so the Scriptures tell us. But we shall know; and such knowledge is a price far above rubies. A man armed with true knowledge can never be defeated.

The 14ᵗʰ June 1914. A Sunday, not long after church. It was the day he told me that we were going home, permanently. Bobby would be cast out of the business without so much as his severance pay. I would never see him again, and I would certainly never again see Sarah either. 'A whore,' my father had called her.I remember it well. It was the day I killed him.

The sky is dark out there. The sea rises, the weather turns. Another storm is on the way, the last gasp of winter. I think of India and the Gora Cemetery and the garden in the Civil Station. I think of her.

I must know her name. It is inevitable. I must know her name. I need, more than anything, the light she conjures in me.

Thursday, 4ᵗʰ April 1918

The weather woke her; violent, unrelenting. Her first thought was of Ida's dream, the darkness spilling over knight and steed and spiriting them both away.

She turned on the pillow, felt the swiftness of her heart beneath her breast. Ida was asleep on the other side of the dorm, one arm flung back, her breathing slow and regular. Alice's bed was empty; she had taken the night watch. The pale moon of her bedside clock showed that it was just past three.

Quietly, Esther put on her dressing gown and slippers and crept out into the corridor. She stood and listened. The panels of the windows shuddered in their frames. The wind blew high and clear, and then collapsed into a deep, subterranean groan. There was a hard knot in her stomach. Her mouth was dry. Something fretted in her. She couldn't put a name to it, couldn't gather it up and keep it still.

Alice Stewart was wringing her hands by the nurses' station when Esther came downstairs. She was pacing back and forth from the desk to the foot of the staircase, her face creased with worry.

'Alice, what's the matter?'

'Did the storm wake you too?' she said. She smoothed her apron. 'Lord, I know I shouldn't fall asleep on the night shift, but it's so difficult sometimes. And then this damned weather – it's like a hundred kettle drums banging together, isn't it? It's a wonder none of the boys have woken up.'

60

'I imagine they've slept through worse.'

The door to the downstairs ward stood open. Esther padded over the tiled floor and closed it. Alice gave her a fraught look, her bottom lip plumped out as if she was going to cry.

'Alice, for goodness' sake. What's happened?'

'It's Captain McQuarrie,' she said. Her hands found each other. 'The officer with the terrible chest wound. I went in to check on them all. I can't even say why... just this awful weather putting butterflies in my stomach, I can't settle for a moment. And then I saw that his bed was empty! Captain McQuarrie's. There's not a sign of him, and you know what he's like... Well, you worry, don't you? I'd hate to think that he'd got out and was wandering around in all this fret.'

The house sighed around them. Rafters creaked, windows rattled. Esther pushed open the door again, very quietly, and glanced into the makeshift ward. The smell of the sleeping men met her, the chemical flavour of their dressings, the rank underlay of rot and weeping wounds. There, faint in the light from the far window, she could see McQuarrie's empty bed. The sheets were neatly folded back.

She closed the door. On the near side of the hall the main entrance was locked and bolted. The great house was cold around them, but there was no channel of crisp night air to suggest an open window. If he had gone outside, then it hadn't been from here.

'Should we call one of the doctors?' Alice hissed. The louder the storm, the lower her voice became. 'What if he's hurt somewhere? He seems only half-awake at the best of times. And what if he's having – you know?' She pressed her hands to her head and gurned. 'An *episode*.'

Esther nodded. She tried to think. She was sure that he wasn't having an episode, whatever Alice meant by that, and if it was the case then there was no need to bother the doctors. She could imagine Lawson standing next to her in the hall, pondering the issue, being calm and reasonable and reassuring, and Esther standing there dressed only in her nightgown. Let that be avoided if nothing else.

If it had been any other patient but McQuarrie she might have been concerned. He was like a ghost already, floating unobtrusively through hall and corridor, detached, a dream of a man. But what had he really done that was so wrong? As long as he didn't disturb the other patients, what was to stop him rising in the night and taking himself from a place where he couldn't sleep to a place where, presumably, he could? Sometimes the only thing these men needed was solitude, so they could brood in silence on their hurts.

'No,' she said, trying to sound decisive. 'I'm sure it'll be fine. Trust me. It'll be fine.' She let her fingers rest on the door handle a moment longer. 'We'll keep this between ourselves, but there's nothing to worry about, I promise. He'll be back by the morning.'

Alice looked unconvinced, relieved only that someone else had made the decision for her. She sat back down behind the desk and rubbed her eyes with the heels of her hands.

'If you say so,' she sighed. 'But Lord help us all if something's wrong and the Major finds out. Or, worse, Sister.'

'I'm sure Sister won't find out,' Esther said. 'And if she does, well, it's just something we'll have to deal with when it happens. There are always positions going in the munitions factories, aren't there? Especially if you don't mind your skin turning yellow from the TNT.'

She left the hall before Alice started to cry and headed back up the stairs. The night rippled around her. The moon made everything seem barely real, like she was strolling through an illustration. It was only as she came to the long landing on the first floor, its burgundy carpet stretching out ahead of her like a tide of spilled wine, that she realised the knot was still in her stomach. Her heart fluttered. She didn't know what had made her get out of bed. For a moment she wondered if she was dreaming, as Ida Lambert had been dreaming when she saw the shadow devour the knight on the lawns outside.

Esther stood at the head of the stairs and looked down the corridor. It was so dark she couldn't see the end of it. Then, as the wind blew harder, the rich red carpet began to lift and contract, very gently, like a lung drawing in a breath.

It was a gap in the floorboards, she knew, an open space admitting the air. It was the storm pushing its way into every nook and cranny of the big house.

The carpet rose and fell and sighed again. The darkness beyond was as thick as deep water; and cold, very cold.

Esther gripped the banister. The knot tightened in her gut. The cold air slithered under the carpet. For a moment she was lying there again, waiting for Peter to come back to their room. She was listening for the sound of his drunken footsteps on the square outside. Pinned down, trapped, trying to breathe.

The dark shifted. The red carpet rose and fell and rose again. Something pale moved there. She could hear the shuffle of its feet.

The breath thudded from her. Two white shapes floated in the dark, swaying, coming near.

Prevost swam from the shadows, blind, half-dreaming, his arms extended. He didn't see her. The carpet shivered. His chest was bare, the shrapnel wounds raw and angry, but it was the sight of his stumps that froze Esther where she stood. She was in the English Cemetery again. The smell of the Arno, the cold tomb. Creeping near... that awful, apologetic smile.

They pick at the scabs, you know, make themselves bleed, Peter had said. *Damned beggars. They'd do anything for money.*

'It's my hands,' Prevost wept before he fell. 'God help me, lads, it's my fucking hands!'

Esther rushed to him. His eyes were lucid now. He trembled. She held his face, smoothed back his hair.

'You're fine, Corporal Prevost. You're absolutely safe. You're right here in Roddinglaw, it's all over. It's over. Nothing can touch you.'

Prevost looked up at her. 'I can still *feel* them, miss. Out there. I can feel them, rotting in the mud.' His body shook. 'And they were *mine*.'

FROM JACOB BERESFORD'S JOURNALS, APRIL 1918

Earlier I watched the dusk roll in. The sky was curdled, the clouds a crust of spreading dark. The waves slammed and scoured at the coast, and all the islands were fringed with lace; Cramond, Inchmickery, Inchcolm, Inchkeith. The storm came in. The wind tore shreds of foam from the waves. The trees thrashed and shook in the long green girdle of Mons Hill.

From the east window in the bedroom, I could see the string of pebble beach below, black in the dusk, the line of white dunes stained grey with rain. Rutherford was pounding down the shore, capering, his arms flung to the heavens. The sea was brutal now, catastrophic, waves of ice water shattering on the rocks. The old factor watched it with delight, raising his face to the sky as if begging the storm to pass through him. He howled and the storm howled back. I wondered again what madness I had let into this house by permitting him to stay.

He seemed to turn then and salute, raising his hands to the menhir of Gallondean, scraping back the drenched straggle of his hair from his forehead. The sky shook with thunder. The wind rushed faster and faster, thrashing against the shore, peeling off layers of sand from the dunes, so fierce that Rutherford was thrown to the ground by it. The waves mounted the shore, bursting against the stone, glazing him in a frost of salt. For a moment I thought he had been sucked back into the body of the sea.

Alarmed, I rushed from the room and coughed my way down the stairs, snatching up a lamp from the kitchen table that I lit with shaking fingers. I threw an oilskin around my shoulders, remembering the night last month when I had watched the lifeboat braving the coast to pluck Rutherford from the water. I pressed through the maelstrom and staggered down onto the dunes, hobbled by the wind. Great sheets of turf had been ripped up and the walls of the dunes were collapsing.

I cried the old factor's name, to no answer. The sea was black, not a speck bobbing in its sway.

'Rutherford!' I shouted again. I was rewarded by an inarticulate cry further along the shore. I coughed again, felt the blood fleck my lips. I saw him on his hands and knees scrabbling at the wall of the dune, like a terrier digging out a fox.

The shale crunched underfoot as I pressed on towards him, the sand stinging my eyes, my lungs heaving. The storm blew in too great a volume, and to swallow a lungful of air was like trying to gulp down a gallon of water.

'Here, sir!' the old man screeched. 'See it! Here!'

He lunged from the dunes, where the fringe of the grass had been ripped back. The sand trickled around him, a cascade. I lifted my lamp, its coin of light, as he held something out towards me; a shard of driftwood, a weathered rock. He turned it over in his hands, and then I was staring down into the brown flaking sockets of a skull's empty eyes. I could see the globes of femur and pubis poking from the spoiled sand ahead of me. Bones, buried in the earth. A skeleton, unveiled.

All the violence of the storm seemed to fall away then. I was deaf to it. I looked at the skull, cradled in Rutherford's fist, the black fissures, the bone like ancient ivory. Pieces came away in his fingers.

I stared sharply to the shivering trees ahead, where all the darkness danced. Something was watching, I knew. Something saw.

The wind howled on; but it was not the howling of the hound. No, it was not the howling, not yet.

Florence

Monday 29th June 1914

It was pleasant to wake up in Florence. The city felt like a dream; hard and soft, coarse and sophisticated. A portrait of the low medieval and the high Renaissance, it was more beautiful than she could ever have imagined.

They had looked for the spot where Savonarola was burned and had stared at the font where Dante was baptised. They had strolled for hours through the cloistered light of the Uffizi, summoning all the appropriate awe as they stood before Botticelli and Da Vinci and, for Esther's particular benefit, the *Madonna and Child* of Fra Filippo Lippi. "'I am poor brother Lippo, by your leave!'" she had declaimed, to Peter's uncomprehending stare. She added, 'I can't quite remember the rest. It's one of the longer ones.' They had stood before the pale and gleaming panes of the Duomo, Peter looking on with a residual Protestant scepticism; Esther, far better equipped to confront the numinous, with both an aesthetic delight and a faint moral distaste. All those pleas for intercession, the adorations, the confessions – it was beyond her. If there was God, there was God, she thought. Why this need for subordinates, for the mother and the child? Why torture the poor man and nail him to a cross?

Now, in the long aftermath of lunch, as the Tuscan sun began its slow withdrawal over the sloped orange roofs of the city, Peter eased back in his terrace chair and concealed himself behind the sheet of an English newspaper that was, as far as Esther could tell, full of nothing but the poor murdered Archduke. Rather the Habsburg heir, Peter had said, than the bloody Home Rule crisis. For her part, Esther resisted opening the pages of her *Baedeker's Northern Italy*. It lay there beside her black-bound notebook and her pencil. She was determined not to touch it. They had relied on its guidance in Rome, but with the same degree of faith that moved the pilgrims before the Duomo, she was sure that all she needed to comprehend the streets and sights of Florence was the life and works of Robert Browning.

Esther now watched her husband's hand emerge from behind his newspaper and grope across the table. Gently, she guided the porcelain coffee cup towards his fingers. The grand span of the Piazza della Signoria stretched away from them, like the planes of a capacious drawing room. The Neptune fountain chuckled to itself, green and blue behind its upcast mineral haze. The square edifice of the Palazzo Vecchio and its flat, Tuscan tower looked like an illustration she had once seen in a children's abridgement of Boccaccio. She turned and stared at the close columns of print with which her husband confronted her. He was, after all, a military man. It was only natural that he took an interest in such things.

'And do *you* think there'll be a war?' she said, more from a desire to break the silence than from any real interest in the nation's affairs. 'Just because this chap's been shot? The Archduke. Poor man. It's so very sad, and his wife too.'

She was drinking a glass of white wine the tawny shade of a church candle. It tasted of salt and currants and was as cold as a crystal stream. She wondered what her father would make of it, in his professional opinion. No doubt he would think they had been ferociously overcharged. She sipped the wine and watched Peter's empty cup reappear around the edge of his newspaper.

'I don't see why there should,' she continued. 'Just think of all the people who would be killed, it would be awful. And in any case, I don't see what it has to do with us. Not in the slightest.'

'By "us", Peter said, 'I assume you mean the Empire, and the Royal Navy?'

'Quite,' Esther agreed. 'Does Austria-Hungary have a navy? Does Serbia?'

His voice was mild. 'No. Or certainly not worth bothering about. But Germany does. They've been trying to catch up with us for some time.'

'And what does Germany have to do with it?' she asked.

'Hopefully nothing at all.'

'Exactly,' Esther said, implying that here she had gained a small but notable triumph. 'So I don't see what everyone's so worried about. Germany, Great Britain… it would be terrible.'

Peter sighed heavily and folded his newspaper, then signalled to the waiter. Esther sipped again while he ordered a brandy. She felt light-headed. She didn't like wine as much as she should, she decided, silently asking her father's forgiveness, but you drank when and where you were expected. She much preferred the nutty, sharp taste of the Italian coffee, the gorgeous richness of it. She would have drunk that all day if it didn't keep her up at night. She loved the fiercely bitter liqueurs and *digestivi,* the glorious flavours that seemed to infuse every part of this country.

'If the Habsburgs attack Serbia,' Peter said, bracketing his words with his hands, 'there's a risk that Russia will step in on Serbia's side.'

'We're on to Russia now, are we?' She frowned. Esther often enjoyed pretending to be more confused about these issues than she really was, knowing that Peter would relish the opportunity to explain it all to her.

'Indeed we are,' he said with a smile. 'And if Russia becomes involved, then so might Germany, on the Austrians' side. And then France would become involved. And then, heaven help us, so might the Empire and no less a force than the Royal Navy, with Lieutenant Peter Mark Worrell at the very tip of Britannia's trident.'

Esther dismissed this with a wave. 'Well, it all sounds very complicated.'

'It is.'

While he waited for his brandy Peter emptied the carafe of wine into his glass and tossed it back. His face was slightly flushed from the sun, his hair damp.

My husband, Esther thought. She tried the sound of the words against her mind's ear once more, so odd and unaccustomed. Would she ever get used to them? Sitting there without his uniform Peter looked strangely diminished, but even a month after the wedding she couldn't quite believe that she belonged to him. There was no greater step in a woman's life, she had been told. She liked the cold spark of the wedding band on her finger. She liked walking the streets with him, her arm in his. She liked the weight of his body pressed against hers in the night, the feeling of being crushed by him, filled out, although in Rome more often than not he had fallen asleep, half-dressed and wholly drunk. But then she had married a sailor, she reminded herself. That's what her father had said, a wine merchant who never touched a drop. What were sailors without their rum?

She felt the pang of his absence. But she was a woman now, she told herself, and no longer a girl. When her mother had died, at a time when Esther was far too young to remember, she had become her father's friend and helpmeet as much as his daughter, but a woman's world had opened up to her now. With tears and joyful regret, she had put her father aside.

'It's a pity we couldn't have found somewhere nearer the Arno to stay,' she went on. 'With a view, and with characters like Miss Lavish and Mr Beebe – wouldn't that have been fun? And some dear cockney woman running the *pension*, and everyone jostling for position at the dinner table.'

She laughed lightly to herself. Peter gazed at the globe of brandy as it was placed before him, breaking off for a stilted '*Grazie mille*' to the waiter, before turning to Esther and saying, 'What on earth are you talking about?'

'In the novel, darling. The one I was reading in Rome. Never mind...'

Peter tossed back half the glassful and swirled it around his mouth in precisely the way he rinsed his teeth when he remembered to brush them before bed.

'What shall we do now?' he said. 'Back to the hotel, view or otherwise? I'm feeling that bottle of wine, I don't mind saying.'

'Oh, Peter, but really,' Esther said. 'There's still so much to see, and it's not even three o'clock.' She ticked them off. 'Michelangelo's tomb at Santa Croce. The Giardino dei Semplici. And the Piazza di San Lorenzo, I simply must see that.'

Peter finished his brandy and then sighed again, as if she had read off a list of onerous chores. His eyes strayed to the square of his folded newspaper. 'What was that last one again?' he said, off-hand.

'It's where Mr Browning found the Old Yellow Book, I told you. In the market there. He drew on it for *The Ring and the Book*. Oh, I *must* see it.'

'Whatever for?'

Esther groped for her reasons, which she had failed to articulate more than once on this honeymoon. She looked at her notebook, as if the answer might be sketched there in its pages.

'Your problem,' she said with mock severity, 'is that you don't like poetry. And yet you know how much it means to me. I have never made a secret of that.'

'I like poetry,' he said, aggrieved. 'Always have. Listen. *My bed is like a little boat,*' he declared, flattening his palm against his breast and staring up at the rooftops behind her. '*Nurse helps me in when I embark;/She girds me in my sailor's coat/And starts me in the dark.* There, you see? You see if I don't.'

'But surely that's verse, darling, not poetry?'

'How dare you! You won't find an officer or rating in the navy who wouldn't shed a tear at that. Or the old navy prayer: *O Eternal Lord God, who alone spreadest out the heavens and rulest the raging of the sea...* What's that if it's not poetry?'

'That seems quite grand for the navy,' she admitted.

'Thomas Cranmer. *The Book of Common Prayer*, which you'd know if you weren't such a godless heathen. Anyway, read me some of yours then,' he said. He lit a cigarette and sat back in his chair, peering at her through the rising smoke. He pointed at her notebook. 'Your *poetry.*'

'Oh, I don't think so,' Esther said. The very idea. 'Goodness, no, I couldn't. I couldn't, and it's not – oh, Peter, no.'

He stared at her for a long moment that she found difficult to bear, his eyes hooded, his smile to her mind unnecessarily provocative. The mood was on him. He had been like this in Rome, especially after lunch or dinner. On their last day, at sunset in the Forum, he had loudly doubted her accuracy when she described what the ruined buildings in their original state might have looked like, dismissing it as all out of Baedeker anyway; and besides, in the end, who particularly cared? 'It's just a load of bloody ruins.' Esther had turned from the pillars of the Tabularium and forced herself to agree, just to keep him happy. It was his mood, that was all.

Quick as a snake, his arm lashed out and took up the book. The stub of his cigarette fumed between his lips, his eyes squinting through the smoke as he flicked the pages back and forth.

'*Peter*,' Esther said. 'Give it back to me this instant.' She reached for it across the table but he drew away. She sighed with exasperation.

'Always scribbling in this damned thing,' he muttered. 'Always mooning and staring and pondering with your pencil on your lip.' He turned another page, scanned the words as if checking a bill of sale. Esther felt grateful for the spurs and tangles of her handwriting then. Her father had always despaired of it. 'Look,' he said, rousing himself. 'Here we are. What on earth are we to make of this?'

'Peter, I forbid you to read out any of that You are *utterly* forbidden.'

'"Less again the fires dance, amongst the acres of the stone,/and something once more…" Something, something… God, Esther, your handwriting's like a *child's*, it really is. "Then something the virgins' house, and in its absence something pray." I mean, honestly.'

Tears pricked her eyes.

'Give it back to me,' she said. 'Please. You've no right.'

'No right? I'm your husband, aren't I? I've every right. And what's it all about? *Virgins*? I mean, for God's sake. Is any of this about me? Us?'

'The Vestal Virgins,' she said, as if it had been wrenched from her. 'We saw their temple in Rome.'

'Darling,' Peter said, mollifying now, 'I don't know why you bother with it, that's all. It's hardly Shakespeare, is it? And you spend so much *time* on it.' He sat side on, his legs crossed in their cream flannel, and stared towards the statuary in the piazza. The fountain was gilded by sunlight. 'I suppose it's good to have an interest,' he conceded. 'It gives you something to do when I'm away, but all that time, all that energy… I'm only thinking of you, dear, you see that, don't you?'

'Of course I do.'

He showed her the smile, half-cynical and half-adoring, that had so beguiled her when they first met, strolling in their groups past the Post Office on Main Street. Officers and girls, and his ship just docked in the harbour.

'I'm ever so sorry,' he said. He was drenched with sincerity now. He placed the notebook back on the table and reached for her hands. After a moment she gave them to him. 'I'm a beast, aren't I? But you must forgive me, of course you must. Do you? Say you do, please.'

'I forgive you,' she said quietly. She kissed him lightly on the cheek.

'Excellent!' Releasing her, killing the stub of his cigarette in the ashtray, Peter called the waiter for the bill. 'Now, anywhere,' he said. 'Anywhere you wish to go in this gorgeous chocolate box of a city, that is where we shall go. Florence is your oyster, my dear. Michelangelo's tomb, old Mr Browning's second-hand book market. Anywhere.'

Esther thought. She unravelled and folded away the little thread of misery that had wound itself around her heart. She looked across the piazza at the dun brick and the ochre stone, the gleaming white marble, the crenellated battlements of the Palazzo like the empty clockwork gears of a broken pocket watch. She felt immensely tired of a sudden, and not even the sharp Italian coffee could wake her. On the other side of the piazza a Cook's group filed past, huddled together and driven without mercy by their guide towards the cloisters of the Uffizi. A buoyant flood of Italian voices reached her from the streets behind, and the sun, briefly veiled, came out anew and struck her across the eyes. She wanted to be on her own, she realised. For perhaps the first time she understood that being married meant never being on your own again.

Thank God we have a navy, she thought, and ships far out at sea…

She rallied herself, picked up her notebook from the table, watched Peter reach for money as the waiter drew near.

'The English Cemetery,' she said, firmly. She had already noted the address that morning. 'The Piazzale Donatello, north-east of here. Half a mile or so.'

Peter looked at her askance. 'And what could you possibly want to see there?'

'It's where Mrs Browning is buried,' she said. Despite herself, the old enthusiasm rose to the surface. 'It's important to me. I've never read her *Aurora Leigh*, but I shall buy a copy when we get home. I wouldn't enjoy it half as much if I hadn't paid my respects first. She was an extraordinary woman.'

He shook his head, affectionate in his disbelief. 'I'll never understand you, Mrs Worrell. I could have had my pick of empty-headed young women, but I'm glad to say I've ended up with a wife whose head is full of old poets and older ruins.'

'And new poets as well,' she said. 'Even poetry has to change with the times.'

'Let the times look after themselves.' He stood from the table. 'And let us swim along in their wake, hoping we don't drown.'

He looked very stern and tall and strong suddenly. A mariner from an ancient northern tale, grim beneath his levity. He held out his hand and she took it with a smile.

They headed deeper into the grid of streets. Tall yellow buildings with flat projecting roofs loomed above them, blocking out the light. Esther gripped Peter's arm. She knew the general direction they were going and was determined not to rely on her guidebook. They were, transparently, two examples of the English abroad, but Esther didn't want to pronounce herself a tourist quite so openly. With no recourse to Baedeker, she wanted to suggest that she had brought to Florence both a nobler and a more artistic frame of mind.

Peter's mood began to curdle the further they went and the longer it took to get there though. Before long he was hectoring and chivvying her, his hands in his jacket pockets. Esther suspected he was feeling the effects of his lunch. All that wine, and a mountain of *Pappardelle al Cinghiale*.

'Are you sure you know where this place is?' he complained. 'Christ, I feel we've been walking for hours.'

'It's not too far away now,' Esther said, as brightly as she could manage. They had been walking longer than she had expected and she was feeling a little fatigued herself. Dusk was near, but although the sun was slipping languidly behind the rooftops the streets were still warm and dusty. She was parched. There was a café on a corner ahead and Peter surged off to claim a seat on the terrace outside. He ordered a glass of beer, a tonic water for Esther, and then quietly vanished into the gloom beyond the open shutters. Esther could smell grilled meat and olive oil, that ever-present bitter tang of coffee. She sat quietly and clutched her notebook and waited for her husband to return, meeting nobody's eye.

When Peter came back he flopped into his seat and sighed grandly, refreshed, his face lighting up as the drinks arrived. He drank off half the glass of beer while Esther sipped her tonic water. When the waiter brushed past with a tired and lugubrious expression on his face, Peter called for a brandy.

'Another?' Esther said. 'It's not even five o'clock.'

'It isn't? By God… Where does the day go, Esther? Where, I ask you?'

He looked coldly at her.

When they had disposed of the drinks, they walked on in silence. Esther held on tightly to Peter's arm. She tried to imagine moments like this in the future, moments of strain where it was not immediately obvious where the strain was coming from. He would be at sea an awful lot, she knew. He had made that perfectly clear to her before they married, as if it were the sort of thing she might hold against him. Esther had always been too frightened to interrogate whether that had been part of his appeal for her in the first place. There was a tremendous romance in waiting for the sea to give you back your husband. A brave mariner patrolling the oceans, he would be gone for weeks and months to the old grey widow-maker. Each time he came back he would reappear like someone new or only half-remembered. No matter where they ended up living though (Peter was arranging for a house in Portsmouth, obviously), Esther knew she would be spending most of her time alone. No company but a maid and perhaps a cook if he could stretch to it. 'I suppose your scribbling will keep you occupied,' he had said, not long after the ceremony in the register office. 'At least until any children arrive.'

The streets became quieter. Tourists were now nowhere to be seen, and the Florentines were noticeable only by their absence. Anyone they passed on the other side of the road seemed to move furtively, cupping a cigarette in their palm and scurrying along the pavement in the shade of those white and yellow buildings. Now and then a beggar would appear, shabby and down at heel, unshaven, hand extended for a coin. Some had sores on their faces, or empty sleeves pinned up on one side. They fixed the English couple, the rich English couple, so generous, with sorrowful and almost pitying stares, as if they felt ashamed that these visitors were being exposed to such degrading sights. How Florence has fallen, they seemed to suggest. From the days of the Medici to this human wreckage before you…

The beggars clearly didn't move an inch of Peter's soul, not even a woman who came creeping from a side street with a baby bundled in her arms, drawing back a flap of the cloth to reveal a crown of infant hair and a crust of dried cradle cap. The child whimpered. The mother showed an open palm, her eyes liquid and very dark, mumbling the words '*Per favore, per favore*' over and over again, like a mendicant's prayer. She smelled stale and unwashed, a ripe oniony stench, but then Peter was stepping around to Esther's other side and drawing her away with his arm across her shoulders. He commanded the beggar woman to leave them with a sharp and peremptory, 'No, thank you.'

'Shouldn't we give her something?' Esther said in a whisper. She drew closer to her husband. 'For the child…'

'It's why they have children in the first place, the brutes,' he said. 'They pick at the scabs, you know, make themselves bleed. Damned beggars. They'd do anything for money.'

On her own, Esther knew she would have fallen prey to every beggar in the city. Peter saw them as mere obstacles to be batted aside, just another distasteful aspect of the European streets, like the ubiquitous spitting, the remorseless electric trams, the stray dogs and children, but she would have handed out money until she didn't have a coin left in her purse. She was honest enough to admit that it wasn't because she was especially virtuous or charitable; she simply would have had no other means of making them go away.

As they continued, Peter was inescapably drawn to every café and *trattoria* they passed, quickly checking the coins in his pocket and signalling for a waiter before they'd even taken a seat. He would disappear to empty his bladder, and then knock back brandy or beer or vermouth as if they were regrettable taxes he had to pay in order to use the facilities. Esther declined the tonic water he seemed to think she wanted, and eventually he stopped ordering it for her.

In a café close to the Piazzale Donatello, which had in fact been some distance off their route, he finished his drink, tossed down a handful of coins and threw back his chair. Esther stood up from the table and said, 'Perhaps we should head back to the hotel instead, Peter? Only it is rather self-defeating to keep drinking every time you need to relieve yourself. You're never going to catch up, as it were.'

He stared at her. His face was hard and bare of any expression. For the briefest moment she thought he was going to slap her. She hadn't realised how drunk he was.

'Don't,' he said quietly. 'Don't you *dare* patronise me. Do you understand?'

His eyes brimmed with anger. He turned away and walked on and Esther followed him, a few paces behind.

She tried to settle her thoughts, to untangle her nerves. It occurred to her that she couldn't even remember the moment she had agreed to marry him. From the instant Peter had kissed her in the Alameda Gardens, lost in the plangent dusk, the scent of fig trees heavy around them and the traffic whispering on Europa Road, he had driven them both in this direction. A wine merchant's daughter with the blood of Spain and Portugal lurking in her veins, given the chance to marry an officer in the Royal Navy – why would she ever have said no?

At length they reached the English Cemetery, an oval of parkland ringed by a fence of wrought black iron. The streets split and curved away on either side, and the buildings frowned down at the field of graves. The stones and monuments stood in white rows beyond the archway, shaded under branching limes. There was a smell in the air of dust and herbs, a blocked drain somewhere in the streets behind them, the scent of all the trees and flowers relinquishing what they had taken from the sun. The smell of the Arno, she thought, ripe and sluggish. Esther crossed the road towards the gates. Peter followed, as gloomy and resentful as a schoolboy dragged to chapel on a cold Sunday morning.

'Is this it then?' he said. 'God, it's enormous.'

'It isn't. It's barely anything at all. Honestly, it's so quaint.'

'And do you have the least idea where this grave is?'

'Not precisely,' she said. She cleared her throat. 'I thought looking for it would be half the adventure.'

'The adventure?'

'Something we could do together.'

He threw his arms up. He had followed her through the gates but now he stopped and jabbed his folded newspaper at her.

'Esther, listen to yourself,' he said. 'I am *not* going to spend the next three hours trawling through this bloody boneyard searching for – you know, I've even forgotten exactly who it *is*.'

'Elizabeth Barrett Browning,' she said. Her voice was high and shrill. 'She was a great poet, and she was married to Robert Browning. They eloped and moved to Italy, to Florence. She died when she was only fifty-five.' She couldn't stop herself. On she went. 'She was very famous. Very famous, and far more celebrated than him.'

'Well, there we are then.' Peter smirked. 'There we *are*.'

He gestured vaguely at the gravestones, the tall white obelisks of the monuments. His collar was slightly askew and a lock of his black hair had fallen over his eye. He looked very handsome, Esther thought, which surprised her. Here in the Florentine dusk, dishevelled and drunk, and at a moment when she didn't think she'd ever loved him less.

'Aren't you coming?' She held up her guidebook. The cover was dark with the sweat from her palms. 'Perhaps there are directions in here, I haven't—'

Peter grunted and swiped the book from her hand. He stooped and snatched it up from the gravel and flung it across the gravestones, where it spun and tumbled like a great red and white bird. A magpie cackled from a lime tree deep in the cemetery.

'Bloody Baedeker,' he said. His voice was thick. 'Bugger Baedeker! It's supposed to be a honeymoon, Esther, not a bloody tourist trip. Should have gone with bloody Cook's if that's your attitude, saved myself a bloody fortune! Eyes only for each other,' he muttered, 'and not for every scattering of ancient stones you stumble across or a load of corpses in bloody graveyards.'

'Peter, why are you being like this?'

She couldn't look at him. She drained her words of every note of pleading. The mood was on him, stronger this time. The only thing to do was lash herself to the mast and wait for the storm to pass.

But then, as if summoning the energy would be too much for him – he was too tired, too drunk – Peter seemed to deflate. The anger sped away. He looked regretfully to where he had thrown the book. She thought he was going to say something, but then he turned on his heel and left the cemetery.

'Where are you going?'

'To get a bloody drink.'

'*Peter.*'

'I'll see you back at the hotel,' he said over his shoulder. 'Pay homage to your dead poet. And find your own way back.'

Even now Esther wondered if it had all somehow been her fault. She had nagged at him, she had been too critical, too much the wheedling shrew. Why shouldn't he enjoy a drink or two on his honeymoon, without his wife badgering him about it? But it hadn't been her fault. She was sure of that, and she held onto the knowledge very tightly. She watched him disappear down the street. She didn't look for her Baedeker. Let it be lost. She had no more use for it. She was where she needed to be already.

Blindly she followed the paths between the stones. The cemetery itself was small, but wild and tangled, a place apart from the city. She passed monuments and statuary, carved marble urns and crosses, table tombs and towering commemorative pillars. Cypress trees reached up as tall as church spires, narrow and straight and serene, boldly framed against the sky. They smelled of cedar and pine, swaying gently in the breeze that reached around the brow of the graveyard. It refreshed her. She felt very hot, as if Peter's words still smouldered in her flesh, but she chose not to dwell on them now. Let them flow into the past, not to be repeated even in memory, and as the sweat dried on her skin so too did the force of those words fade from her. All that bluster and rage, all that drink in his blood. He would be contrite in the morning, she knew. Let him be contrite.

She found Mrs Browning's grave as the light began to turn. It was a white marble chest tomb raised above a ledger stone on six Corinthian pillars. The whole structure was perhaps a head taller than Esther, although it seemed larger. Mrs Browning's profile looked off to the left in sculpted bas-relief, the letters EBB and her dates carved at eye level on the base of the chest. The grass around the grave was thick but well-tended. Someone had placed a dozen white chrysanthemums on the ledger.

She stood for a while with her hand against the stone. She ran her fingers over the poet's recessed initials and tried to conjure some significance from the moment, a sense of guidance perhaps or understanding, a feeling of culminated knowledge. Elizabeth would have been Poet Laureate if they hadn't gone for Tennyson. What would Robert's *Men and Women* have been without her? What would Robert have been?

She would read *Aurora Leigh* when she got home, she decided. That would be it. She would become a poet. There was nothing else for her to do. All her will and energy would be poured into it, and as though to seal this promise to herself, Esther rested her forehead against the stone. A monument always seems to promise revelation, and in the end reveals only what you already know to be true.

All the storm of Peter's displeasure was blown away by the smell of the cypresses, the cool breeze, the chatter of the birds skimming the gravestones in the growing dusk. She remembered the time he had given her lemon macarons from the French patisserie on Main Street. She remembered the ruby brooch he had bought for her in Hong Kong. Once, as they strolled in the Alameda, he had taken her broad hands in his, had stooped and seemed to count her fingers, and then deeply kissed the pleats and creases of her palm. He had taken a lock of her dark hair and held it to his mouth, his arm a band around her waist. Gifts of incense from Macau, as if she were an idol to be worshipped. Silk from Beirut and wine from Marseilles. Greater gifts were given in the words he used to praise her beauty. She felt the world had come to her in his person, brought to Gibraltar on the ocean tides and girded by British power. He thought her half a Spaniard; she thought him carved from northern ice.

Esther raised her forehead from the edge of the tomb. Hold on to what you thought was the memory. Think as if all the words he spoke back then were true. There is only what you want him to be, rather than what he is.

The beggar emerged from the tree-lined lane ahead, pushing through the leaves. It was a woman with pale blue eyes, her dark hair half-hidden by a shawl. She looked cold, although the evening was warm and balmy. She smelled strongly of urine, and when she smiled, that tragic, apologetic smile half-disgusted by its own ingratiating falsity, her face looked as though carved from wood. There was no spare flesh to it, no surplus. There was no abundance to her.

'Please,' she said, in English. 'Please…'

Esther felt herself recoil. She couldn't help it. The woman advanced, creeping, hunched.

'Please…' she said again.

She reached out and the sleeves of her tattered dress drew back. Esther looked at the woman's hands but the hands were not there. A shadow moved over the cemetery; the passage of the clouds, streaming west.

Each wrist ended in a stump. Loose skin had been folded over the bone, weeping and red where the stitches had come away. Crystals of black blood made a crust against the flesh. The smell was appalling. What was in the woman's eyes was not even pleading, or a desire for money. 'Please,' she said.

Esther stumbled, fell back. She sprawled in the grass and cried out, and the woman, concerned, made as if to help her. How? With what?

'*Mi dispiace…*' Esther whispered.

Gravel crunched beneath her heels. She was running, the skirts of her dress drawn up. The path unravelled before her, the leaves whipping back on either side, and then she was through the gates and out into the streets. Before, they had felt quiet and drowsy in the peaceful afternoon; now, they felt utterly deserted. The cafés were shuttered and silent. The pavements were empty of people. The buildings, so tall and stately on their narrow roads, now loomed like ruins, hollow-eyed, abandoned. All life had been scoured from the streets, given over to the dust, and her footsteps rang out like the sound of the last survivor fleeing a doomed city. She was weeping, but she couldn't say for whom. For herself, for Peter. For the Archduke and his wife, their lives snatched away at the point of a pistol. For the girl she had been just a few months ago, or for the beggar woman whose eyes had asked for death or recognition, or for simple, honest revulsion at all the horrors she had endured.

It was getting late when she reached the hotel, past the Piazza della Signoria, pausing to draw a handful of water from the fountain to cool her face. She walked on more cautiously. The hour of the promenade was here and the streets were filling up once more. Families, tourists, young couples and their chaperones. *La Passeggiata*. For the Italians it was still early, but Esther craved only sleep. She felt every eye on her, every unembarrassed and openly curious stare. She passed on.

Peter was not there. She sat in their room and drank a glass of wine and shivered. She hid her notebook under her pillow, and then after a moment took it out and placed it in the depths of her bag. She would only look at it again when she was back home. She envied Elizabeth Barrett her illness then, the ailments that had kept her secluded in her father's house with nothing to do but read and write. What paradise. What luxury. Esther could have had that, instead of this.

She stood at the window and looked out on the noble little square, the palazzo, the green and dusty trees. She would write. She didn't know what yet, but it would come. Poems, bold and allusive, of many voices. Moments and events and the measure of things. She would speak in the words of people trapped by their circumstances, people groping for beauty and grasping only regret. She would make her own meaning in this world, this life. She would live in the words she wrote and be happy. That was all she wanted.

He came back later that night. She heard his footsteps in the hall, the heavy, blundering tread of someone half-heartedly aiming for silence. The door cracked open. He sighed. The door closed. The rustle of discarded clothes, the dip and then release of the mattress as he slumped down to remove his shoes.

The stench of wine preceded him. Esther pretended to be asleep. She lay on her side, her back to the room, her hands folded against her stomach.

The cold rise of the sheets, the weight of him falling into bed. A moment's pause, the drunken flare of propriety, and then his hand was on her shoulder and his breath was hot against her neck. He was naked. The smell of wine, fingers palping at her breasts, the hard pressure of his penis in the small of her back.

'Esther,' he slurred. 'Let's get this off then, shall we? Come on, off, get it off...'

His mouth at her ear, the whispered words as he shuffled and lifted and groaned.

'That's it, my girl, that's it, wider... Come on, come on, tell me what you are, yes. Tell me, you are, aren't you? *A dirty little Jew...*'

She thought then of the Archduke and his wife, the account in the morning paper. There before her was the motorcade slowing to a crawl, the assassin crouched on the running board as he aimed his pistol, death in his eyes, fanatical.

Let the war come, she prayed. *Please God, if you are there, let the war come soon and take him away from me.*

The woman reaching with hands that could no longer feel the world, no way to touch it, no way to mould it to her will. Esther cried then. From somewhere over the rooftops in the south of the city, near the banks of the Arno, a dog began to howl. It sounded so lonely, she couldn't bear it. She thought she would die.

PART II

PART II.

Saturday 13th April 1918

The trail skimmed the coast and curled through the overhanging trees, a flat dirt path under a latticework of branches. Esther walked it quickly, passing through the grid of shadows, arms folded across her chest and her head down. Alice Stewart's tale of young Catriona and Jacob Beresford was one thing, but Ida Lambert had also felt herself being watched or followed on this track. 'A gamekeeper checking his traps would be bad enough,' she had said with a shudder, 'but the shadows have eyes out there, Esther, I'm sure. The crack of a twig, a rustle in the undergrowth – haven't you heard anything? I tell you, I wasn't alone this afternoon…'

Dracula, Heathcliff… But even if this was no more than a case of Ida's zest for drama, Esther still took care. It was a solitary mile between Roddinglaw and South Queensferry. With the sea on one side and the trees on the other it was easy to feel yourself far deeper in the countryside than you actually were. There would be no one to hear your cry for help if you were compelled to make it, no matter by whom.

She came out into the town at last and strolled up onto the hard-packed span of the High Street, past the tea rooms and the bakery with its jostling line of sailors. Everywhere you turned there were sailors from Port Edgar, and they seemed so much younger than the boys who'd crewed the ships in the days when she had first met her husband, the Jack Tars staggering through the streets of Gibraltar.

Esther could smell the gasworks beyond the harbour and the grain from the distillery. The rail bridge soared across the firth, a vast spun confection of red steel roaring as the trains passed through. She paused a moment beside the steeple of the old tolbooth, where the clock tower showed ten-past eleven and the date of the Golden Jubilee.

Jacob Beresford was standing outside a public house on the other side of the road. He was wearing a black Crombie buttoned to his throat and looked painfully unsure whether or not he should enter. He stood aside to let a group of soldiers pass in. She thought he looked like a lost little boy, scanning the crowds for his mother and trying to build up the courage to ask a policeman for help. Her heart went out to him, a great flood of sympathy that she barely had time to acknowledge, because he turned then and saw her, and the breath was seized in her throat.

The resemblance to her husband struck her again, a stunning blow. It was like Peter was peering at her from the other side of the road, all his confidence turned to doubt. He was Peter; but then the veil lifted and he was just a tired young man, frail and lonely and ill.

He scrambled to compose himself as she crossed the road. Again, Esther felt a strange compassion for him. Tuberculosis, Lawson had said. She couldn't think what it must be like to live with that sentence in your lungs. She thought of the blood Catriona Swift had seen on his hands as he sat amongst the trees.

'Have you changed your mind yet, Mr Beresford?'

'Excuse me?'

He was a few inches taller than her and had gained height from the edge of the kerb, but even so Esther felt that she was the one looking down on him. He was bareheaded, his black hair pushed back. In the smoky light he looked very pale. Perhaps that was why he was waiting outside a public house. They did say a glass of porter put iron in your blood.

'The new beds we need at Roddinglaw,' she said. 'The news might have escaped you, but the casualties are fierce. Gallondean would be most useful to us. And to them.'

Beresford smiled thinly. 'You've seen inside Gallondean. Such a gloomy old place. It would certainly be no favour to them, or to you. It's barely habitable.'

'And yet you suffer these terrible conditions yourself,' she said. 'You're a martyr, Mr Beresford.'

'There's much we can put up with when we have no other choice.'

'I know. I'm a VAD.'

He laughed. 'I take your point.' He gestured to two men sitting on a bench further up the street, wounded soldiers from the hospital at Bridge House. 'But would you put men like that in the cold and the damp, when that's precisely what they've escaped from?'

'Well, as it happens, we have men from further afield. Palestine, for one. Perhaps the cold and the damp is precisely what he's looking for.'

'Then he must be enjoying West Lothian.'

'Oh, immensely. I'm sure he'll find it impossible to tear himself away when he has to go back to the front.'

Esther had only rarely played tennis in the Victoria Gardens at home, and then rather badly, but she imagined this was what it felt like to reach the end of a successful rally. Her blood was up. She had an electric sense that there was nothing she could do to fumble the ball. She could simply score her point and win the game, whenever she chose.

'Well,' she said, turning to go, 'I'm sure there's enough to occupy you in Gallondean with all those skeletons, Mr Beresford. It's no doubt replete with them.'

'One skeleton, merely.' He grinned and she could see his neat white teeth. 'And the university has its claws into it now. I'm not sure they'd give it up without a fight.'

The discovery of the burial last week was still a great topic of conversation in Roddinglaw. Esther had seen the men from the university on the shoreline, standing with pipes in their mouths while they directed the sullen, elderly labourers to dig apart the dunes. The police had arrived first, by all accounts questioning both Mr Beresford and his factor, but the age of the bones had put them firmly into the hands of the academy. Mediaeval, she had heard. Another body seeded in the earth, to go with the Roman remains at Cramond, the prehistoric finds by the River Almond. There was barely a square foot of Europe that wasn't a mortuary of one kind or another. All those bodies planted in the soil.

'I'd be happy to tell you what little I know of it,' Beresford said quickly. 'Perhaps you'd like to join me in some refreshment?'

'In a public house?' She read the sign above the door. 'The "Hole in the Wall".'

He showed her an acid smile. 'Do all the drunken sailors put you off?'

'My husband was in the navy,' she said. 'I'm well acquainted with drunken sailors.'

He glanced at her hand, where the gold ring still shone. 'He's overseas?'

'Under them, rather.' She heard herself utter a harsh and rather frightening laugh. The spirit of Ida Lambert moved through her, clearly; and she was a bad influence. 'He died very early in the war. His destroyer was sunk by a German mine.'

'My God,' Beresford said. 'I'm so sorry. Forgive me, I—'

'There's nothing to forgive. We all have our losses.'

'Indeed. And I thought the tea rooms on Hopetoun Road might be more appropriate than the Hole in the Wall.'

Esther, drawn by the sound of a train cutting smoothly over from Fife, glanced up the curve of the High Street towards the grand span of the bridge. The engine drew a long tongue of smoke behind it. She could hear the raw clatter of the rails, the hiss of the pistons.

'Have you been to the Hawes Inn?' she said.

'I can't say that I have.'

'I've been looking for an excuse to go. Allow me to offer you some refreshment there instead, Mr Beresford. And it's Mrs Worrell,' she said. 'Esther Worrell. It occurred to me that you don't even know my name.'

'Then you must call me Jacob. Please.'

The Hawes Inn seemed no more than a jumble of huts in the shadow of the bridge. Esther ordered them a pot of tea and they sat by the sea-facing windows in the common room. The tide was out and the wet black wood of the pier was raised up from the water. Children were scrambling for crabs in the shell beds beyond, hunting for the lucky pennies passengers often threw from the trains as they crossed over. The sunlight streaming through the glass put some colour into Jacob's cheeks. A waitress, morose and distracted, brought over the pot and two cups, a jug of tepid milk.

'I'll be mother,' Jacob said as he poured. The tea was the colour of rust.

'Have you ever read Robert Louis Stevenson?' Esther asked him. She sipped her tea and watched him over the rim of the cup.

'Of course. When I was a boy. *Treasure Island* obviously. *A Child's Garden of Verses*.'

'*Kidnapped*?'

'Oh, certainly. And *Catriona*.'

'Then you'll know that this is the very inn where David Balfour is brought before his uncle sells him into slavery. Stevenson stayed here himself when he came up with the story. Isn't that something.'

'My word,' Jacob said. He looked around the room as if expecting Stevenson's ghost to emerge with an impish smile from the shadows. It was, she thought, the first unfiltered expression she had so far seen on his face. 'All this time I've been living nearby and I had no idea. Of course,' he said, looking carefully at her, 'I always preferred *Dr Jekyll and Mr Hyde*. All that darkness. All those secrets.'

'Of course.'

'I think I was quite a morbid little boy. I rather liked the idea that you could have a double, a part of you that could get up to all sorts of terrors, and another part that would never know. You could be a monster with a clear conscience. All little boys are monsters, in their way.'

Esther sipped her tea again, giving herself time to reply. She looked from the window to the empty shore, the ships moving through the firth. They were bringing the Grand Fleet down from Scapa Flow and Port Edgar would soon be teeming with even more sailors. Not for the first time, she wondered where she would be now and what she would be doing if Peter had lived.

Reaching back into the conversation again, picking up the thread, she said, 'He has such range, doesn't he? All those old writers do. I loved the South Seas tales when I was a girl. So exotic. And Conrad as well, in a different way, and Kipling obviously.'

'Kipling goes without saying.'

'Major Lawson mentioned that you had been in India before …'

It was half a smile, half a grimace. There were dark circles under his eyes. Esther watched as Jacob refilled their cups. He turned from the table to cough lightly into his hand.

'Major Lawson…' he said. Then, 'India's not quite as exotic as you've been led to believe from the stories. Not the British part anyway. In the end, it really is all just *chota pegs* on the veranda and complaining about the natives.' The smile switched on suddenly, like an electric light. 'I'm exaggerating of course. You're a keen reader then?'

'You seem surprised.'

'Perhaps. It's unusual for a naval officer's wife.'

'And what about a naval officer's widow?'

Jacob blanched at that. He held his cup in both hands and laughed nervously. She could see the surface of the liquid tremble.

'I had friends in Lahore who took literature very seriously,' he said. 'Anything modern, although you tend to be out of the run of things over there. It's still very Arts and Crafts, if you know what I mean.'

'Modern? Like whom?'

He waved a hand. 'Oh, they were very keen on the new poetry. *You* know. That magazine by Harriet Monroe. The later Yeats. Ezra Pound… sundry other Americans whose names escape me. What was that movement, a few years ago? Very refined, very precise. A sort of oriental delicateness to it.'

Esther dredged her memory. She felt exposed suddenly, unmasked, as though forced to prove an interest she had only ever feigned. Any talk of movements or aesthetic programmes always left her feeling vaguely anxious. She hadn't read a poetry magazine since before the war.

'Imagism? I remember that made a bit of a splash. The brevity of it terrified me.'

'That was it. Anything new, they were all for it.' He laughed again, fondly. 'She hated the Georgians, I remember. All that rustic honesty. A landscape and a comprehending eye…'

'She?'

'My friend,' he said, too clearly, too quick.

Esther tilted her chin. 'I was quite fond of the Georgians. Before the war, but I don't know if any of them have written since. Lawrence keeps writing, certainly, but then he always seems to go his own way.'

'Lawrence, my God,' Jacob hissed. He glanced over his shoulder. 'Have you read *The Rainbow*?'

'No,' she said. 'But then who has?'

'Not me for one.' He sat back. 'You know, I was very nearly impressed there, Mrs Worrell.'

Esther let him see her smile. Their eyes met, briefly. She held his gaze and then looked away.

'Rupert Brooke was passable,' she said. 'But who could write that kind of thing now? Who could believe any of that? After this war.'

'No one.' Jacob looked down at the drift of leaves in his empty cup. 'The war. You couldn't write an *Iliad* about this, could you? That's all finished with.'

'But Homer's so violent. Take the gods away and what are you left with?' She gestured at the room around them, the lace on the tables, the wood panelling, as if all this illustrated her very point. 'Violent men killing each other. Maybe the *Iliad* is exactly the poem the war needs.'

She was talking too loudly, she knew, and shrank slightly in her chair as Jacob leaned towards her.

'And do you write yourself?' he asked. A beat, a bare moment of pride or defiance, and then she nodded. Why deny it? She felt she could tell this man and he would understand. He wouldn't laugh or think to scorn the effort. 'I thought as much,' he said. 'My friend… she often talked like you. About literature. She wrote poetry.' He looked again through the bare window at the withdrawing sea. 'Truth to tell, I never thought much of it. I think she put too much of the gods in it, perhaps.'

'Maybe you'll think better of mine. There are no gods in it at all.'

She vowed silently not to mention Robert Browning. But then, what would Pound's work be without Browning? Browning could be as modern, as *new*, as any of them.

Jacob made an ironic little flourish with his hand. 'In any case, I wish you every success. It takes courage to create something in an age like this, giving form to the formless. You're planting a flag for life.'

It was impossible not to make the comparison. She remembered Florence, sitting in the square as the sun beat down, Peter, like Romney in *Aurora Leigh*, scorning the very idea that a woman could be a poet. Now here was Jacob with his cup raised in salute, assuming success was merely something she could work towards. No, he was not like Peter, not at all.

'Courage? I'm not so sure. Real courage would be making braver decisions.'

'Such as?'

'Driving an ambulance. Working in a munitions factory. Volunteering for a hospital at the front. Or even just deciding what to do when the war's over,' she said. 'If it ever ends…'

'The war's swallowed everything, hasn't it? The future seems so thin now, it's barely worth considering.'

Of course it wasn't, she thought. For him, with his lungs the way they were, the future was far from guaranteed. As he surely knew, there could only be darkness ahead of him.

'London,' Esther told him. 'I always dreamed of London, or Paris. Poetry.' She smiled weakly, embarrassed. It all sounded so absurd.

'Ah,' he teased. 'The *demi monde*?'

'Why not? I think I've had quite enough of the *monde entier* to last me a lifetime.'

Jacob laughed at this, his hand rattling the cup in its saucer. There was colour in his cheeks now, real colour, not just the reflected light. Eyes turned towards them across the room, but Esther didn't care. The war had swallowed everything, after all.

'Very good, Mrs Worrell. Very good.'

'Mrs Worrell,' she said, with half a sigh. Spurred on by those mildly disapproving looks, by the conversation and the line it had taken, she added, 'I suppose if the *demi monde* is calling, we should use our forenames, shouldn't we? Esther, please.'

'And what was your maiden name, Esther? You should use it for your poetry. Stake your claim to posterity under the name you were given, not the name you took.'

'Benady,' she said.

'Unusual.'

'That's Gibraltar for you. There's half the peninsula in my background, I'm sure. Castilian knights, Portuguese merchants, Galician peasants. Not to mention the English traders and all the rest.'

'And which were your parents?'

She saw her father's brown and gentle eyes. 'A mix of all of them, I expect.'

'You do remind me of her, you know,' he murmured.

'Who?'

'My friend.'

He stared closely at her. Esther, mildly alarmed, pivoted away. 'But we've talked so much about me this morning,' she said. 'We haven't begun to touch on you. And you never did tell me about the skeleton in the grounds.'

'Something to be saved for another time,' he said. The tea was finished. The morning had bled into the afternoon. Jacob signalled to the waitress as he reached for his pocket book. 'And I do hope there is another time.'

They left the inn and walked past the soaring red pillars of the bridge, to the gate that led on into Roddinglaw's grounds. Jacob offered Esther his arm. After a moment's hesitation she took it. They walked on into the mottled light, the tide on their left beginning its long advance towards the shore. He coughed once, his mouth hidden behind a handkerchief. She felt it wrack him, its clenched fury. The illness, devouring him.

She heard the crying from the bottom of the stairs when she returned to Roddinglaw. It was Alice, wailing – and Esther's first thought was for the path she had just walked with Jacob, the figures Alice said were always peering from the trees, the animals rent and torn by forester or gamekeeper and strewn along the trail. She took the stairs two at a time.

Alice was sprawled in a chair over by the window, on the other side of the dorm. One hand was clawing rhythmically at her face, while the other clutched the rag of a telegram. Her eyes were wild.

Mousy Catriona Swift knelt, shaking, at Alice's side. Ida Lambert stood next to them, her hands at her mouth, her blue eyes as wet as melting ice. She looked up as Esther came into the room.

'My God, Alice,' Esther said. She went to her, touched her shoulder, felt the shudder of the sob as it moved through her.

'It's Georgie,' Ida hissed, as if in confidence. 'He was killed in France. His parents just sent a telegram.'

Esther closed her eyes. She said nothing. She cradled Alice's head to her breast. She could feel every breath, every flicker of the blood in her veins.

'I'm sorry,' she said. 'Oh, Alice, I'm so sorry.'

Ida was weeping too, very quietly and decorously, and on a cruel impulse Esther wondered how many of those tears were real. It was only then that she realised Ida wasn't in uniform. She was wearing what looked like a child's nightdress and a pair of open-heel slippers. Her hair was down, her face freshly scrubbed. Ida saw Esther looking at her and grinned. '*Peter Pan*,' she whispered. The excitement was fierce in her. 'I'm going to be Wendy Darling!'

'You must hold yourself together,' Catriona pleaded, hands clasped in Alice's lap as if praying to an idol. 'For Georgie's sake, for the memory of him!'

'Oh, my God,' Alice wept. The hand that gouged at her cheek sought the crumpled slip of the telegram. 'We weren't even married yet, we didn't have the chance, we didn't…'

'Alice,' Ida said, gripping her other shoulder. 'Please, my dear, you mustn't fret so. It'll be alright in the end, I know it will.'

'Ida's right,' Esther said. She neither meant nor believed it. The worst that could happen had happened. 'I know it feels like hell itself now, but in time…'

'But what am I going to *do*?' Alice wailed.

'You needn't worry,' Ida said with confidence. 'His parents are *bound* to keep on paying the stipend.'

'Ida!'

She looked at Esther, hands raised in surrender. 'I'm just trying to be *helpful*.'

A voice spoke from the open door. 'None of you are. Not one. You're neither use nor ornament to the poor girl.'

Sister stood there, the hard starch of her white cap and the thick blue dress, her stark expression, making her seem as stern as a graven image. Even Alice stopped crying, but then she looked at the telegram and grief swept over her again.

Catriona stood up and drew back. Ida cautiously stepped away. Esther squeezed Alice's shoulder as Sister advanced, and then the older woman gathered her in, drawing her over to Ida's bed where they both sat down. Sister rocked her gently, pressing Alice's face to the crook of her neck like a child in need of soothing.

'This will pass,' she murmured. The frown was still carved onto her face. Sharply, she kissed Alice's forehead. 'Lord knows, this too will pass, my girl.'

The other women moved silently away, as though furtive or ashamed. As quietly as she could, Esther changed into her uniform for the afternoon shift, while Ida flitted off back to her rehearsals. As she struggled into the pinafore and settled the cap upon her head, her hair gathered back into a tightly ravelled bun, Esther listened to the rise and fall of the young woman's weeping. Another death, another brush of grief's awful attention, reaching all the way from France. All this sorrow soaked into the beams and joists of Roddinglaw, leached into its foundations. What was it Jacob had said? *The war's swallowed everything, hasn't it?* The war, a great maw gorging on human lives, shovelling the corpses in day after day, hour after hour. The image lurched to the forefront of her mind and she couldn't push it away. She felt weak, diminished, and for a moment even crossing the dormitory felt like too much of a drain on her strength. But then she heard the rumble of Sister's harsh affection, the grain of comfort as she rocked Alice in her arms. The strength must be found all the same.

Esther straightened her cap and headed for the door, ready to bring whatever comfort she could to her patients. Ida, Catriona Swift… they might not understand Alice's grief, but the men would. The men knew what it was to lose someone, to have them taken by the war. Swallowed, she thought. Devoured.

Monday 15th April 1918

Cardiac output was clearly reduced, but there was no suggestion of a tamponade. His heart was free from strain.

The ring of the stethoscope left a faint red circle on McQuarrie's chest. Major Lawson moved around the chair and pressed it to his back, listening to the sigh and rush of the tide within.

'Very good,' he said.

Pulmonary volume was unaffected. The thorax had been fully drained and remained so. There was no sign of infection, which was a miracle in itself. Even the catheter incision was nicely sealed, like a pair of prim and disapproving lips. The main wound was as curious as ever, of course. Lawson pressed a finger lightly along its border and watched the scar tissue buckle and rise under the pressure.

'Excellent,' he murmured.

It was a radial penetration. Were the Turks using round blades on their bayonets? It reminded him of a patient he had seen before the war, a child who had fallen from a tree and impaled himself on the railings of a local park. McQuarrie's wound was oddly similar. Even the dark spiral of bruising, the mottled, subcutaneous trauma, was not at all what he would have expected. It seemed as though the skin and the flesh and the bone had all recoiled from the core of the wound. If he didn't know better, he would have speculated that the interior had been cauterised in some way. That no organ had been penetrated was extraordinary.

'Well, this is all looking absolutely splendid,' Lawson said. 'There aren't many men who would be back on their feet four months after a wound like this.'

All the words and phrases were automatic. So many of his colleagues assumed their honorary ranks entitled them to affect a military bearing, whatever that meant, but Major Lawson had taken his sensitivities into uniform with the rest of him. A wounded soldier wants only competence and sympathy, not orders.

He replaced the dressings. 'Our VADs are becoming quite expert with these, aren't they?' he said. 'Mrs Worrell, was it...?'

'No,' McQuarrie said. 'I'm afraid I don't know her name. One of the younger ones. The ones who blush when they touch you.'

Not Ida Lambert then, Lawson thought dryly to himself. *There's one who wouldn't hesitate to touch a wounded man, I'm quite sure.* 'Yes, some of them do seem rather overwhelmed, don't they? Still, where would we be without them?'

McQuarrie laboriously put on his shirt, wincing at the effort. Lawson helped him into his jacket and wrote up his notes while the other man fastened the buttons.

'You're sleeping well?' he asked, looking up. 'No issues there at all?'

'No, Major.'

Lawson smiled and tried to seem less formal. 'The storm didn't wake you up last week? I confess, I barely slept a wink. I know the weather in Scotland is proverbial, but the last month or so has perhaps taken it a little far.'

McQuarrie said nothing. Even the smile he gave in answer was distracted, as though with no reference to the words the doctor had said. Lawson was no psychologist, and Roddinglaw was certainly no Craiglockhart, but he did wonder at the state of the young man's nerves. There were no signs of distress or panic, and he had heard no reports that McQuarrie suffered from nightmares. He could eat, he could sleep, he could talk if he wanted to. Very little seemed to disturb him, and yet there was something amiss there all the same. Being in his company was, to a degree Lawson wasn't quite prepared to admit, very slightly disturbing.

'Even a spring storm can be reassuring though, can't it?' he said, as he looked over McQuarrie's file. 'No matter what happens in the world, the seasons stay the same. The flowers grow, the fields are verdant, and then everything slowly fades and is replaced once more.'

'Everything fades,' McQuarrie quietly agreed. He looked up at the cold glass of the window, the overcast sky. 'It reminds me of the hills.'

'Yes?' Lawson said, his pen paused over the notes.

'The storms there, I mean. The winter storms, in the hills before Jerusalem.'

Lawson watched McQuarrie's face, expecting emotion, the betrayal of memory perhaps, but it was as cool and serene as ever.

'That must have been an extraordinary sight,' he offered. 'To see the walls of the holy city, Jerusalem itself, well...' He was careful not to let his own feelings show. To see where Christ had been cruci-fied, to see the tomb that couldn't hold Him. He gave his notes an unnecessary shuffle.

'I didn't see them,' McQuarrie said. He sounded almost apologetic. 'The walls of Jerusalem. The rains were too heavy and I couldn't get close enough in the end. The landscape is so difficult there, and then there was this.' He touched his chest.

'I'm sorry. I mean, to give it all such a Romantic glaze. I doubt there's anything that could so obviously mark me out as a civilian, despite the uniform.'

'We're all civilians,' McQuarrie said, as though to reassure him. 'My company sergeant, John Allynson, was in the professional army. A real twenty-year man. The difference between us was almost comic.'

Lawson pressed no further. The 'was' stood out in the territory of the sentence like a red flag.

'Well, quite. But I can't think of another place in the war freighted with more significance. You must have felt like one of the Crusaders of old, I imagine. It was quite a Christmas present for the rest of us.'

'Major?'

'The taking of Jerusalem. I was genuinely moved when it was announced, I have to admit. To think of it in Christian hands again, for the first time since... When? The twelfth century?'

McQuarrie smoothed down the hem of his jacket. Lawson felt vaguely that he'd offended him.

'General Allenby was quite clear,' the young man said. 'No one religion has sole claim to the city. Or, perhaps, all of them do. All three parts of Abraham's soul. Body, mind and spirit…' He smiled then, embarrassed, his lips pale and his face oddly flushed. 'I expect the trick will be getting them all to agree to that, won't it?'

'A trick that I have no doubt only the most skilled magician will be able to pull off,' Lawson sighed. 'I firmly believe the religious impulse is one of mankind's finest, but only a fool wouldn't admit that it can so easily be twisted into something dark.'

'Evil is often wrought by hands that would do good, Major.'

'Quite so.' He looked again at the medical file, noting the address. Before the appointment he had checked it on the city map. 'You live near here, don't you? I see from your notes that the family home is along the coast in Newhaven. That's not too far. It's possible you could be transferred to your parents' care until the medical board. I could make that recommendation, if you like?'

'That should be changed,' McQuarrie said, his voice very soft. He rubbed the stubble on his cheek. 'We sold the house after my father died, near the start of the war. I'm surprised the address is still on the file.'

'You said "we". You have family nearby still? Siblings, your mother?'

'There's only me. My mother died many years ago. My brother Simon, he died…'

'The war?'

'Loos. In 'fifteen.'

Lawson, solemn-faced, bowed his head. 'I'm sorry. My own brother died on the Somme. Even now, I—'

He was surprised by how easily the words failed him, and how quick was the rush of emotion that thickened his throat. Unbidden rose the memory of Charles as a boy: the way he sleepily marched into the kitchen each morning, dishevelled, still in his pyjamas and dressing gown. The ragged thatch of his hair, the furious intensity of the games they had played in the nursery or on the floor of their father's practice when there were no patients around. My God, he thought, and it felt as if he was realising his loss anew. It was something he would register again and again with the same ruthless certainty for the rest of his life. His brother was dead. He would never see him again.

Lawson cleared his throat. If McQuarrie had noticed his distress, he gave no sign of it.

'Well, regardless,' he said, 'Roddinglaw is more than happy to have you here, Captain.'

'There's nowhere else I need to be, Major.'

McQuarrie stood up from the chair and looked around the office, taking in the slanted ceiling, the view to the forested ground at the rear of Roddinglaw, the long road towards the village.

'You don't get the view of the sea on this side,' he said. He finished buttoning his jacket.

'Alas, no. Perhaps it's a good thing,' Lawson said. 'I'm sure I would be too distracted otherwise.' He gave a perfunctory smile, aware of how much work he still had to get through this afternoon. And then there was Mr Beresford to think of too... 'All those big ships in the firth,' he explained. 'I've always taken a somewhat boyish delight in the navy, although I don't have the stomach or the sea legs to be a ship's surgeon.'

McQuarrie gripped the back of the chair. Lawson wasn't sure if he had heard.

'And the coast as well,' the younger man said. 'The way the waves come in, the sound of them against the rocks and the sand. Exposed there on the shore.' He darted in before Lawson could reply. 'I wonder, the skeleton the other week, after the storm...'

Lawson brightened. 'Oh, yes, most interesting, wasn't it? Something to do with Gallondean Castle, I expect. The building is far older than you would think.'

'I wonder though – did you manage to see it? The skeleton. Before they took it away? Did you see the bones?'

'Very briefly,' Lawson said.

He had chatted idly with the professor from the university, an anthropologist. There would be a proper chair after the war, he had claimed, a proper archaeological basis for all this, not just day labourers hacking at the earth. The skull had leered silently from his hands, still clotted with dirt. The bone was stained almost black. It had been a wonder to see it, quite chilling on that cold shore, with Gallondean rising so dark behind them. Lawson had seen any number of bodies in his career, but the bones of that skeleton – their position in the ground, the way the coffin had crumbled around them, the very manner of their discovery – had genuinely disturbed him. It was the age of it, he supposed. The superstition of the earth holding its secrets deep, of long-buried things coming back into the light.

McQuarrie moved to the door. His clutched the handle. 'And did you notice...' he said, faltering as he searched for the words. He was sweating, Lawson saw. 'Did you notice...'

'Yes?'

'The hands,' he said. He opened the door a crack. 'I wondered only... did it still have its *hands*?'

FROM JACOB BERESFORD'S JOURNALS, APRIL 1918

I woke early this morning, dog-tired, weary. I dreamed about those old bones, clawing their way from the ground, the empty skull dressed in my father's face.

The damp had spoiled the tea in its caddy and for breakfast I drank only wine. I ate the remains of some bacon that I fried to within an inch of its life. Gnawing it from the knife, staring out at the wrack of water, the greasy stones on the shore, I couldn't believe that any of my illustrious predecessors had lived like this. The cold goes through to the marrow. This place decays further by the day; only this morning, as I strained to open a window, I found the edge of the frame crumbling in my hands. The rugs and carpets are rotting. The boards underfoot are buckled and damp. Squalor, hunger, despair. Of course, they were fighting men back then, tougher than any now living. I am not, nor have I ever been, a fighting man. I run, I flee, I escape. I run until there is nowhere left to run to.

But no more. The sword of knowledge is in my hand now. Every day it grows sharper.

My sojourn to Queensferry went far better than I expected. I had seen her the week before, walking along the path on a Saturday morning. Presuming that this was something she did every week, I planned accordingly. It's no more than a mile through the trees, and when the weather is fine the walk can even be pleasant – the sea slurring at the shore, the branches whispering above, the momentary sense that you're strolling through an unspoiled wilderness.

I left early, hiking along the trail, the slopes of Mons Hill behind me and the great iron strands of the rail bridge stretching ahead. I waited in the streets for two hours, enduring the hostile stares of the sailors and soldiers who no doubt resented me for being out of uniform. (There should be some badge or token to mark our status, the sick who cannot fight. The bloody rag of a handkerchief, say, hanging from our breast pockets. A dab of gore on our chins, coughed up from our corroding lungs.)

I don't know what I'm playing at, or why. All I know is that I felt a great need to speak to her again. It was out of the question to present myself at the doors of Roddinglaw, and so I was forced into this absurd charade of patrolling the High Street, peering in the windows of the tea rooms like a suitor who'd misplaced the object of his affections, as if she were a hat or a book of poems. I felt as nervous as a schoolboy. The exercise had left me weak, and the length of my deception was a mystery to me. Why was I bothering? In some strange act of sympathetic magic, I thought I could atone for what I had done to Sarah by venerating this stranger who wore her face, the way Sarah prayed to Vishnu by kneeling to his image. Did I only now understand what I lost when I left her behind? Her faith in me, her strange and indefinable love? In her presence I was a flame that could burn every shadow to ashes.

The resemblance buckled the moment she called my name though. Esther Worrell was Sarah and she was not. She was the echo of the guilt I felt, and she was nothing but herself – a young woman, a widow, a volunteer in the medical service with vague ambitions to be a poet when the war was done. Esther Worrell, Esther Benady as was. For long moments as we spoke over tea in the inn where Stevenson conceived *Kidnapped*, all very civilised, all very calm and collected,

I consciously pretended that I was talking to Sarah. I overlaid her manner so vividly onto the ordinary woman before me that I began to feel almost deranged. I could smell her again: the scent of her body, that subtle aroma of saffron and sandalwood, the jasmine of the garlands in her black, black hair, and the rich, earthy smell of her henna tattoos. I thought I would choke, my mind reeling as I recalled them, one by one. I must have seemed insane.

My God, Sarah – all I have of you now are the tokens of your half-grasped faith, and my own delusion that Esther Benady displays some hidden facet of your soul. And yet no force on earth would recall me to Lahore and to your arms again. My father was right, I fear. It was a sickness, of a kind.

I felt his shade again. When the bones were revealed, that shard of malice roused itself. It was watching, waiting. As Rutherford grovelled on the storm-lashed beach, I felt my father's hatred, live and present, peering from the trees.

The skeleton has alarmed me more than I can say. I sent Rutherford off to the village to report it, and it was soon to vanish into the clutches of policemen and professors. My first thought was of the Gora Cemetery, where the flooded canal often washed away the graves and revealed the bodies of the dead. The rain-flecked wind, so cold, seemed to carry for a moment the ghost of high summer in Lahore, and as the grave was excavated, that awful skull screaming silently out of the past, Gallondean began to feel even more like a mausoleum. Drenched in the dark, its stone corridors and oak-panelled rooms loud with the whispers of the dead, the house responds. Something has been uncovered, I feel.

Something has come out at last into the light.

To my surprise Major Lawson has paid me another visit, independently this time, and without Esther Worrell in train.

Rutherford announced him and I showed him into a cluttered drawing room on the first floor, little more than a cell strewn with tattered rugs, a tall armoire in one corner and the windows frosted with decay. My erstwhile factor sullenly coaxed a fire in the grate.

'Wood, sir?' I sent him for coal. Grumbling, no doubt annoyed to have been dragged from his whisky, he soon returned. While we waited for Rutherford to finish, Lawson looked around the packing crates and stacked furniture, all the evidence of my father's doomed attempt to build a new life here. When the old factor finally left us alone, the flames writhing across the coals, I asked how I could help. This time he had not come to beg for beds, he said, but to bring his doctor's eye to bear on my lungs.

'You have a physician in Edinburgh?' he asked.

I poured us whisky and cautiously sipped from my glass, trying to seem off hand and cynical. 'I haven't had the time to make arrangements.'

'I can recommend someone, if you like? Your condition seems to be advanced, Mr Beresford, and I would strongly advise regular observation. You're on the doorstep of one of the greatest medical schools in the world here, you should have no difficulty finding a doctor.'

'I've had my fill of physicians,' I said. To underline the point, I coughed into my fist. Despite my words I was actually touched by the gesture, that he took his oath seriously enough to check on me after the scorn I had shown him before. 'They only ever recommend fresh air, and I have more than enough of that here.'

'In Gallondean Castle?' He swirled the whisky in his glass, motes and spokes of amber glittering in his hand. 'This place will be the death of you. I can barely breathe myself for all the damp in the air. I'm convinced half the smoke from your chimneys is backfilling into the rooms.'

I smiled. 'I have no complaints.'

'If you're amenable, I can check on your condition whenever I have the time? Unofficially, of course. My conscience won't allow me not to make the offer, at the very least.'

I demurred. He was sensitive enough not to pursue the matter. How rare a quality, not to insist on your own virtue. I have to admit that Lawson seems a more serious figure than I realised and is genuinely interested in those he tries to help. As we sat there drinking our whisky, warmed by the fire, I almost felt that I was talking to some idealised version of my father. The doctor and the undertaker, both dealing with the frailties of the human body, the mysteries of the encasing clay.

We talked for a while, touching on other, less contentious issues. The German offensive, the situation in Ireland, if and when the Americans, for all their boasting, might finally make a difference at the front. The great antiquity of Gallondean.

'It's from "Gaillon", I told him. 'It's a town or village in Normandy. The "Gallon" of Gallondean comes from the de Gaillon family who founded the place. A corruption, I assume.'

'Fascinating,' Lawson said. 'That it's still here, I mean. That it's still standing after all this time.'

'And what of our recently disinterred friend?' I said. I tried to seem frivolous about it, or at least no more than morbidly curious. 'He must be equally old, surely? I saw you in discussion with the university men when they were digging the poor fellow up.'

Lawson became more animated at this. 'Indeed, yes, and the gentlemen from the museum. They all seemed most exercised by it. Apparently the find is quite a rare one. Strange, don't you think, when so much of the Roman past is still visible in the ground here?'

'It is medieval then?' I asked him.

'They seem confident that's the case. From what I can gather, the skeleton is incomplete. The hands, you see, possibly severed before the body was buried, although I'm sure the archaeologists still have an awful lot of work to do on it. The coast has eroded over the centuries, quite significantly. I wouldn't be surprised if much of it had been taken by the waves.'

'I suppose so.'

'Just think, Mr Beresford,' he said eagerly. 'When it was first built, Gallondean wouldn't have been placed quite so precariously near the shore. No doubt many of its lords and knights have been lost to the waters, if they were buried in the grounds here.'

I wasn't so sure, but I let Lawson make his assumptions. Evidently he has more of a taste for the Gothic than I realised. For my part, I know there is a Norman church on the edge of the village nearby. I suspect most of Gallondean's scions are at rest in its crypt, their graves long forgotten. To be buried in the grounds, unmarked, speaks to me of something and someone quite different.

I could only wonder if it had something to do with the first de Gaillons, Gallondean's prodigal sons – and fathers. I thought of William sailing for the East, his dog howling from the mist-wreathed shore, the corpse of his father behind him and the stain of that murder on his soul.

One more thing to note – Lawson's reaction when I mentioned Esther Worrell. He made his sally about the beds and I spoke her name in passing, and the flush was on his face immediately. The mumbling speech, the darting eyes. I smiled to see it. Infatuation, as clear as day.

I said nothing about meeting her in Queensferry, or about my own interest. I was surprised at the stab of jealousy I felt. How strange to think of this kind, intelligent man as something of a rival. It spurs me on, I find, makes everything seem that much more urgent. If I were a decent man, I would step aside and encourage her in his direction. She could do no better, I'm sure. But then I am not, after all, a decent man.

Friday 19th April 1918

The men, as boisterous and excited as children at a pantomime, filed in and took their seats. At the side of the stage Lawson could see Captain Bressett, one of the commissioned RAMC doctors, sitting at a Console piano. His fingers called forth a quick flurry of notes, his face strained and nervous. The stage was just the bottom quarter of the hall marked off by a line of empty chairs. Plain muslin curtains were drawn across the frontage from a sagging rail, and partly visible behind them was a painted backdrop of a children's nursery at night. The dining hall had been used for cinema shows, singalongs and recitations; for music hall numbers, magic sets and amateur routines – anything to make the long convalescent days pass more quickly – but this afternoon it was going to witness a performance of *Peter Pan*, staged by the pressganged players of Captain Moore's amateur troupe.

Lawson sat near the back of the hall, by the main door. He could see Lieutenant Goodspeed with his traumatised arm and Corporal Prevost with his missing hands both peering around the curtain. There was Captain Magallanes with the gas gangrene still bubbling in his hip; even Lieutenant Gourlay limping into position, his legs weak from the shell burst that had wounded him at Ypres. Lawson thought they all seemed as anxious as if they were about to go out on a trench raid. Miss Lambert stared frantically from the door to the kitchens, looking as if she was going to vomit. Captain Moore was standing at the side of the stage, sipping from a flask, his patch flipped up. There was something maniacal in his remaining eye. Not for the first time Lawson recalled that the captain's men had affectionately dubbed him 'Murdering Moore', and that he had won the MC at Mametz Wood.

The lights dropped then and the hall fell into darkness. The rumble of voices was oddly soothing. It reminded him of the vast canteen tent at the base depot in Étaples, during his brief few months at the front. The same rolling tide of masculine voices, the tang of a similar excitement. The great adventure, yet to begin.

Sister passed down the aisle and nodded briskly at him. Lawson resisted the impulse to salute her. He saw Daniel McQuarrie float like a phantom through the shadows, flitting to an empty seat at the other end of the row. He craned his neck to look for Mrs Worrell but there was no sign of her amongst all the silhouetted heads. There were a handful of the other VADs and nurses, orderlies, kitchen staff, a number of patients who had been assigned to him, an even greater number of those who hadn't; but Esther Worrell remained for the moment out of sight. He chided himself for caring, and for keeping a chair conspicuously empty beside him.

Mrs Worrell, he would say in a stage whisper, half-rising. *Please, I've saved you a seat…*

Pathetic. He smiled to himself, generous to his failings. If given the chance, he would sit there beside her in perfect silence, scrupulously ensuring that his thigh remained a decorous distance from her own, and not once speaking in the safety of the darkness what was on his mind. *Her*, that she was on his mind, always. That almost Sephardic beauty, the droll cast of her amber eyes, even just the smell of her as she passed him in the corridors. She was like no one he had ever met. She was the light of Spain and Portugal, the warmth that enveloped the gates of the Mediterranean. Jewish, Miss Lambert had hinted once with heavy dread, her hand lightly resting on his sleeve and her teeth primping her bottom lip. Lawson had turned away in distaste; Ida Lambert was ever a one for rumour and gossip. Even a hospital was just a stage for her, a place to stretch her new-found wings. And as if that would matter to him anyway, even if true. As if, in fact, it would not deepen the attraction, the respect, he felt for Esther Worrell.

But no, there would be none of that between them. If he could impress some sense of himself on her, then it would only be through the things that he tried to uphold every day: duty, honour, responsibility, all that dry old stuff. If she was to trust him, then he had to show her that he could be trusted, and the best way to do that was to say nothing. Nothing at all. Let her be ignorant and unaware, while in his heart he was aflame.

Lawson rubbed his temple, pushed back with his palm a stray strand of hair. He looked around the hall, wondering when everything would begin. The play had never been published, but apparently Captain Moore and Miss Lambert had jointly adapted Barrie's novel for 'the stage'. The mind boggled. He wondered who would play Peter. Like a nod back to the gilded days of the Elizabethan theatre, it had become a role for a young woman; Cecilia Loftus the last time he had seen it, he recalled. Ida Lambert was clearly taking a major part but he didn't think she was a likely candidate – she was too tall for Peter Pan, too lithe, too much of a woman. A few days earlier he had overheard Captain Moore relishing the prospect of Alice Stewart in the part, so that he could wrestle her in the climactic battle. 'But then her chap got himself killed,' he complained, 'and now she's too bloody upset.'

It won't be Mrs Worrell, Lawson thought. His mind refused the very image. It would be beneath the dignity he assumed for her, and in any case he could see her now, sidling her way to a seat at the front with the other nurses. There were a dozen rows between them. Wouldn't that always be the way?

Lawson crossed his arms and tried to relax. He stifled a yawn. A brash melody crashed through the hall, Captain Bressett hammering the piano keys. The curtain was swept aside. Pandemonium... and then the roar of enthusiasm that greeted the players was unbridled.

The stage is in darkness. Three shapes are slumped in three camp beds. Light flickers on, revealing them as Wendy, John and Michael. Miss Lambert is Wendy, clad in ill-fitting lace. Her eyes shine like stars, enraptured. Then, grotesquely, Corporal Prevost scrambles on from the wings. He's been cast as Nana, the Newfoundland nurse. He clambers across the stage on his elbows and knees, a sheepskin strapped to his back and the stumps of his wrists held up. He looks in agony, but every time he gives a gruff and hearty bark the audience erupts.

The biggest cheer is for Captain Moore, who bounds into the nursery with a look on his face not far from naked bloodlust. The flask is visible in his pocket. He is Mr Darling, rendered here as a thrusting young company commander barely able to control himself. They do the routine about the children's medicine. 'I am not frightened,' Moore cries.

By the time Peter Pan arrives, the audience is in hysterics. Goodspeed is in the title role, creeping onto the stage with none of the bounce and dark vigour normally associated with the boy. Lusty jeers and whistles meet Miss Lambert as she crawls out of bed in her nightdress, her cheeks red, the sheen of sweat on her forehead insistently lit by the dazzling beam of light that represents Tinker Bell. Someone off-stage projects it from an Orilux trench torch, and Miss Lambert frequently has to raise a hand to stop it from blinding her. Everything feels like it's happening in a dream.

'Why are you crying?' she quavers as Goodspeed weeps, his head on his knees.

'I always want to be a little boy,' Goodspeed says. His voice trembles. 'And to have fun!'

There's a needle of pain in those words that threads every man in the room together. The charge is extraordinary. A sob, somewhere in the darkness.

The children accept Peter's offer and are seduced from the nursery. There's no stagecraft here, no wires and pulleys or smoke and mirrors, and so they feign flight by leaping and jumping across the floorboards. The hall shakes. The portraits rattle on the walls. Goodspeed clutches Miss Lambert by the waist and tries to fling her through the air. Her breath catches and she shrieks. Goodspeed's face melts with pain. He looks like he's going to faint. Prevost barks at the door, but it's a noise that sounds more like someone trying not to be sick. Moore laughs uproariously from the side of the stage, sucking on his flask. And then the act is over, the muslin is drawn, and in moments they're off to Neverland.

Angry muttering. Hoarse whispers from behind the screen. The door to the kitchen creaks and slams. Captain Bressett conjures a jaunty tune from the piano. When the curtain falls away again the painted backdrop is now harsh jungle and pools of still water, a pirate ship lurking in the bay.

Tinker Bell zooms and flashes. Wendy is shot. The Lost Boys hum and haver. Slightly, Nibs, Tootles and the rest, young patients who were waist-deep in the mud a few weeks back, hands on the stocks of their Enfields or fumbling for their Webleys. In ragged tunics and short trousers, hair tousled, they look like boys indeed.

As Captain Hook, Moore is a man possessed. He is in his element, sneering and shouting, deadly and seductive, capping a fearsome and self-loathing rage with a murderous delight. The role of Hook fits him like a glove. The other pirates, Smee, Starkey, Bill Jukes, are as nothing in his shadow. The fight with Peter Pan becomes so ludicrously one-sided that the audience ends up cheering on the pirates. Goodspeed shudders as Moore clubs his wooden sword away – and then Hook escapes and Peter is left alone on the rock, waiting to drown.

All the men in the audience hold their breath in anticipation. This is it. This is what they have been waiting for since the performance began.

'To die...' Goodspeed says in half a panic, his voice reedy, '... will be an awfully big adventure.'

Silence. The last four years have been smoothed away in an instant, levelled by a charitable hand. The storm has broken and passed on, and the clear skies will dry the rainfall from the earth. No one has really died. No one has been lost, and all the Lost Boys are back safe with their mothers. Death is once more just another adventure.

Someone further down the row staggers from his chair and slips past, knuckling his eyes. The main doors clatter and fall silent. The maudlin tune Bressett plucks from the keys begins to falter. Across the sea of heads, Mrs Worrell stares in half-profile at the stage, her eyes wet and gleaming. Everyone is thinking of their childhood games. Pirates and Indians at the bottom of the garden. Lost Boys hiding in the trees, clambering the wooden rigging of the bedroom stairs, staring from windows transformed into the prows of pirate brigs. All of them grasping again at the chance to come home when the game is over.

The rest of the play blurs past. The Indians fight the Pirates and the Pirates fight the boys. The audience watches respectfully, mollified now, somehow content. The ritual has been comprehensively enacted. The children want to go home. The Lost Boys caper. Even Captain Moore is somewhat more contained by the end. A strange doubling to see the same actor in both roles, as Captain Hook and Mr Darling, but this has become the tradition. The model of order turns into the agent of chaos, and then once more back to order. The father who protects you tries to kill you for a while, before finally gathering you close.

There's light and ribald laughter as Moore enthusiastically embraces Miss Lambert, the VAD beaming with delighted terror – and then at last the show is over.

Daniel McQuarrie slips away as the audience begins to clap. The men stamp their feet and hammer the backs of the chairs. The players bow, Moore taking a triumphant swig from his flask as the applause washes over them. Daniel nods to Major Lawson in the back row, finds the door, strolls through the entrance hall with its grid of tile, seeks the cool evening and the fresh grass outside, the April air. He remembers a chill spring day, following his father down George Street to the box office, his brother Simon holding his hand. The streets were very cold around them, almost like autumn with that granite-hard Edinburgh wind. The trees in Princes Street Gardens had been black and bare.

The old man paid three shillings for the family circle. Then it was back towards Broughton Street, a Saturday matinee, although in his memory it is already getting dark by the time they arrive. The Theatre Royal was ablaze in light, the posters proclaiming the first performance since the Duke of York's in London. The smell of old and weathered sweat as they came inside, and then the performance dissolving into its heady myth. The children fly from the nursery, Neverland before them. The Pirates on their ship and the Mermaids in the lagoon, and Tiger Lily and the Indians, and the underground house with its tree trunk chimneys. He is ten years old and he has never seen such magic.

He walks across the lawn. The soft velvet evening gathers him in. The wind stirs the greenery. The bronze horseman steadies his steed, spear struck out towards the east. Daniel moves through the trees and sits for a while in their shadow, watching the starlight and the moon glint in narrow lines of silver from the waves. There is nothing but the motion of the water.

Minutes pass, an hour. Movement catches his eye. A figure is walking along the shore, a young, dark-haired man, thin, with a high forehead. His hands are stuffed into the pockets of his coat. He pauses at the tideline, stares out at the rucks and corrugations of the evening sea. After a moment he crouches and picks up a stone and then throws it savagely into the water. The motion is so violent that it wrenches a cough from him. He's overwhelmed by it, bent double, hacking and retching, his hands splayed across his mouth. He groans and spits onto the pebbles and then seems to recover himself. Massaging his chest, sighing, he stares back out to sea. The lightless shapes of passing ships, the mass of the islands; Inchcolm, Inchmickery, Cramond near at hand.

Daniel watches him silently, the way he glares at the waves. It's the face of a man he's seen before, stalking the trees and the shoreline, furious at his own despair. It's a face he has seen staring down at him, devoid of mercy. He's sure of it.

The same dark hair, the same gleaming cynical certainty, the ironic dread. One face refines the other, and slowly, slowly, both faces swim more easily into view.

The young man turns and casts a last look towards the trees and to Roddinglaw beyond them. Daniel hears his sad, defeated sigh before he trudges back along the shore, his feet crunching on the pebbles. Gallondean Castle is a tooth of black stone in the distance, gnawing on the night.

Daniel releases the breath he has been holding. His hands shake. He watches the young man until he has disappeared. He stands up, gives a last glance towards the water surging and falling back, the bands of platinum and silver painted by the evening light. There is a clean sharp smell in the air. He must get back before the darkness comes. Back to the dormitory, and then to the space where he can hide until the morning, where nobody can find him.

It all feels much closer now, more certain. The skeleton has been uncovered, the shadow is loose. There is clay in the art room to make the jars, and then he will wait for the signs he cannot remember.

This did not happen in the outer cave.

One of Barrie's models for Peter Pan was a boy called George Llewelyn Davies, a nephew of the playwright Guy du Maurier. Daniel remembers reading it in *The Times*, Davies' name pulled out of the casualty lists for special notice: March 1915.

Even Peter Pan can be killed in this war, it seems. He is a boy who will never grow up.

Sunday 21st April 1918

With our backs to the wall and believing in the justice of our cause each one of us must fight on to the end …

Field Marshal Haig's order had been quoted in the newspaper the week before, but Esther hadn't seen it until yesterday. She had been too busy, all her time and energy claimed by the hospital's routines. Whatever scraps left to her were consumed by thoughts of Jacob Beresford, and by the words she tried to commit with bloody-minded compulsion to her notebook each night. Both things were matched in her mind; the high coins of colour on Jacob's cheeks, and the lines she always scored out on the page with a miserable curse.

She saw again those grey eyes, keen as her husband's, staring feverishly at her across the table. *You're planting a flag for life*, he had said, but she could have done with an aim less lofty and inhibiting. The war, Florence, Roddinglaw House, the knight on the lawn. She had made no headway with any of it. In the end, she lacked Browning's gift to clothe a tale in verse, in an unreliable voice that you couldn't quite bring yourself to trust.

Then, tidying up the dayroom, she had found a copy of *The Times* from last week and the piece caught her eye. The British lines were being hammered. The German offensive was rolling on, and all that could stop it were men's bodies. She had stood there staring at Haig's words, and then she had looked at what surrounded her; the wicker chairs, the overflowing ashtrays, the half-read books and the half-drunk cups of tea, men drowsing their way to recovery. Through the window she could see the lawns extending to the shore far over on the left, the patients out there playing croquet in their dressing gowns. After Peter had died she had placed her fate in the hands of the Voluntary machine, and the machine had delivered her to this place of absolute safety. It wasn't fair. She almost saw the words written down before her. *I don't deserve this.*

The story in the newspaper sent her now to the panelled door of Major Lawson's office, deep in the east wing. She knocked tentatively and after a moment heard Lawson's muffled voice calling her in. He was sitting behind his desk, an open file spread out in front of him. She brandished the newspaper.

'Have you seen it, sir? Have you read Haig's order? It's a *storm* over there.'

'All the more reason then,' Lawson said, as if guessing her intentions, 'to take shelter where you can.'

'But they're *dying*,' she said.

'They've been dying for almost four years, Mrs Worrell.'

She looked again at the close print, the bare words. '"Our backs to the wall"? How can it be worse, how can it be *even worse*, year after year?'

'Alas, it was never good.'

'But *now*, can't you see, it's—'

'It's that this time the Germans might win? And here you are, Mrs Worrell, risking nothing. Is that it?'

'I just want...' she began, but Lawson held up his hand.

'That's the point, surely? None of this is about what we *want*. It's what we must *do*.'

She felt herself deflate. She had confronted him as if it were his fault. The buckling defences, the withdrawals, the battalions cut off. Her own self-righteousness appalled her.

He tidied up the file and returned it to the side of his desk. 'You've said before that you feel the need to go to France, but that's not a decision I can make for you. It's up to the VAD to allocate their resources. I'm not sure what I can contribute unless it's to tell you in no uncertain terms that you must not go.'

Relenting, with an open palm he indicated the chair on the other side of his desk. Esther sat down and folded the newspaper in her lap. It only occurred to her then that the information was a week old. Anything could have happened since, although if the war had come to a sudden and unexpected conclusion, she presumed she would have heard.

'It's no hardship for you to say that, sir,' she told him. 'My husband, had he lived, would have had me sitting at home doing nothing, I'm quite sure.' She held up the newspaper again. 'But men are filling gaps in the line with their *lives*. Their very lives. I only want to help,' she said, as if pleading for intercession. 'The best way I can.'

The wind breathed amongst the trees outside. She could hear the calm spring music of the birds. Lawson steepled his fingers. 'And what makes you think you're not doing that already? Because you can sleep in a warm bed every night? Because you have no fear of being killed by a bombardment or a machine gun? You don't have to be risking your life to do your best, or for your efforts to be worthwhile.'

'You make me sound like a petulant child,' she said. 'Or, worse, a romantic.'

Lawson sighed and rubbed his eyes. 'I don't think you're ignorant of the facts, if that's what you mean. One cannot work in any capacity in the medical services and retain illusions about war. Tell me,' he said, 'do you think I'm wasting my time here, or that I'm not exerting my every capacity to help?'

'Of course not, Major.' She felt herself colour.

'Then don't assume you're not equally valuable. You are needed here, Esther. Your work *here* is vital, more than you realise. Don't be so eager for the adventure,' he said, 'or the sacrifice.' His jaw tightened and he forced a smile. 'I know whereof I speak. I would not exchange Roddinglaw House for Loos in 'fifteen, or anywhere else on the front for that matter. I am needed here. And I believe you are too.'

'"They also serve",' said Esther sadly, '"who only stand and wait."'

'Yes, well, quite.' Lawson fussed again with his papers. 'But then Milton was never one of my particular favourites.'

He looked more leniently on her.

'One way or the other, the war will be over soon. Either we will win, or we must withdraw from the continent. But it would be a fine thing to see it through to the end, wouldn't you say?'

Esther, chastened, left his office feeling strangely more upset than when she had gone in. He was right, of course. As she passed down the stairs she looked at the newspaper in her hands. The Portuguese divisions had been annihilated. Messines Ridge had fallen. The River Lys was under fierce attack. Why charge headlong into that, with no more skill to your name than the ability to tie a reasonable dressing?

A window on the staircase admitted a wash of golden light. Sunday light, late afternoon, very still and clear, while the ground beyond fell away into a tangle of elm and beech. The sea was hidden from her. The branches of the trees were still dark in places, bare as bones, but here and there the buds were quickening. Rain had passed over recently. There was a scattering of drops against the glass. The house felt very still. She thought of Major Lawson sitting behind his desk, late on a Sunday afternoon, perhaps the words of the Mass still chiming in his ears or resonant in his soul. The sky was darkening outside and she thought of Jacob Beresford on the shore, facing down the wind.

Why go indeed? But why not, when there were so many distractions, so much distress, to escape from?

She had seen him again on the foreshore that morning, standing there as if he had been waiting for her. Or, and it was a possibility she didn't examine too closely, perhaps she had only gone walking in the hope of meeting him. He had been looking out to sea, his coat unbuttoned and streaming back from him like great black wings. He heard her feet crunch on the shale and turned, scowling. Gallondean stood further down the coast, blurred in the sea haze, squat and square, something in its dark aspect like a severed head planted on the shore, peering at them through sightless eyes. Sunday lay heavily on the land. The church bells had stopped ringing in the village. All the faithful were at prayer.

'We meet again,' Jacob said. The breeze took his words and smoothed them away. 'Will you walk with me a while, Esther?'

'Of course. If only to be on hand when you catch your death with that coat unfastened.'

Amused, and as if under instruction, he buttoned it up. He liked her sharpness, she could see.

'There, nurse,' he said. 'Safe as houses.'

He hiked up the pebble beach and joined her on the path. He set his eyes on her and Esther allowed herself to meet them, and tried to ignore the beating of her heart.

'I want to show you something,' he said. 'Or somewhere, rather.'

'Oh? And is it somewhere I wouldn't have noticed before?'

They were heading in the direction of Queensferry again, taking the coastal path through the trees and alongside the low-sloping bulk of Mons Hill. They had passed back this way last weekend, heading from the Hawes Inn.

'Possibly. Although I'm not sure the significance would have been obvious to you. It wasn't to me, I have to admit. Not until very recently.'

'I'm intrigued.' She made the decision to slip her arm into his, an easy gesture that she told herself meant nothing. 'You must know this part of this coast very well, you always seem to be tramping along it.'

'It's either that or spend all my days in Gallondean with Mr Rutherford.'

'I was wondering where you'd found him. He seems...'

'He does, rather, doesn't he? Another inheritance from my father. He was the factor. I would say I've kept him on for sentimental reasons, but truthfully he knows more about the house than I do. More about the grounds, their secrets...'

'I was sorry to hear about your father. He passed away in India, I understand?'

'Passed away?' There was sudden scorn in his voice. 'Such a pleasant euphemism. As if we were just strolling from one state to the other. Better to say he crashed, or collapsed, or something more violent. I saw many a corpse when I was in India, when he dragged me through the back shop of his business. Believe me, none of them looked like they'd "passed".'

She felt his arm stiffen. He gave a derisive snort and looked out over the sea.

'Misanthropy doesn't suit you,' she said lightly. 'And you're far too young to be so jaded.'

'We grow up quickly in the East.'

'It's not grown up to be so sceptical,' she told him. 'Or so cynical.'

'The old have wisdom, you mean? Try telling that to the boys in France.'

Esther withdrew her arm.

'We had a performance of *Peter Pan* in the big house yesterday,' she said. 'The men put on these shows now and then, entertainments so they don't all go off their heads with boredom. The whole thing was a riot. But you could see them all reaching out, reaching back, trying to touch something of their childhoods again. Something innocent. They still believed that such an innocence was there, I think that's what I mean. It hadn't been corrupted or revealed as something false by their experience. There was still something good behind them, and hopefully in front of them too. There was no cynicism in any of it, and if anyone has the right to be cynical then surely it's a man who's been wounded at the front?'

'Meaning that I don't have that right?' he said. He seemed curious, nothing more. 'I suppose that's true. When I die, it won't be by bullet or bomb, I know that much. But do I have a long and happy life ahead of me?' He made a low *salaam*, feigning dignity and seriousness. 'Well, we shall see. After all, we're almost there.'

'I didn't mean to be so harsh with you,' Esther told him. She took his arm again. 'I have to confess, I find you quite provoking, Mr Beresford.'

'The use of my surname alone is a suitable chastisement, Mrs Worrell. Forgive my cynicism. I forgot I was talking to a poet. It is of course impossible to create great art without a fundamental optimism.'

Fine manners were always a suitable refuge, Esther thought, a reliable breeze to blow away the tension. 'I'm not so sure about my optimism,' she admitted. 'You know, I wanted to write in some way about the war, but here it feels so far away… I think my art exists only in the conception of it.'

'Then that's half the battle, surely? Nothing can grow that isn't first conceived.'

Esther didn't reply. She didn't want to admit that the conception was as hazy as the details, and the intention was growing fairly thin as well. She had no confidence in any of it, no faith other than in her own blind determination. After all, not a single word she had written had ever been published, and the only person who'd read her poetry was her late husband. His verdict had hardly been a ringing endorsement.

The path ahead now curved at a sharp angle to their left. To the right, beyond the trees, framing a spur of land that hooked out into the water, was a beach of pale yellow sand. Marram grass fringed the dunes, shivering in the breeze. The water was dark and heavily scored with foam. It burst against the rocks.

'Here we are,' Jacob said. 'Beyond this narrow bay...'

He let go of her arm and strode onto the shoreline, passing to a bluff that hung over the beach like a pediment on the far side. Rocks were heaped at its base, the hard-packed sand rising above them in mounds and barrows, bordered by the salt grass. A path twisted around the side of the bluff and Jacob clambered up it quickly. There was an eagerness in him now, a boyish excitement. Esther drew up her skirts and followed.

The tide was in, still shallow at this time of day. She could see the sandflats just beneath the water. Beyond them, rising from the sea perhaps a hundred feet out, was a slump of black rock greasy with seaweed. A cormorant squatted there, spreading its wings and showing them its profile. She could see the three blunt humps of the rail bridge at Queensferry. A glint of light, the smoky rush of a passing train, and then all was silent save the crashing of the waves.

'Here we are indeed,' she said. On the promontory, barely a dozen feet above the beach, the wind was fierce and insistent. Her hair streamed back and her eyes watered, and she had to raise her voice to be heard. 'But where exactly is here?'

'Here,' he said, spreading his arms. 'Hound Point. This is where it will happen, Esther. This is where I'll hear it. And then I'll know, and I'll be ready.'

He told her then about Hound Point.

Shouting into the wind, he told her about William de Gaillon and his father, Robert. About Robert's death at his son's hands and William's penance for his killing, his decision to bear arms in the Holy Land in the name of Christ. He described the boat passing through the water, the oars beating the tide as the knight was ferried to the waiting ship, the dusk coming on and the black shadow of Gallondean Castle flecked with torchlight. He spoke as though he had seen it all happen, thrusting out his arms to show from where de Gaillon had sailed, pointing back towards the castle further down the shore, or on towards the islands that broke the tides, and then to the wider waters where the Forth decanted into the cold North Sea; and then France ahead, and Italy, the long journey on to war and Jerusalem. He told her about de Gaillon's hunting hound, his beloved retainer, wailing from the spur as his master sailed to war.

'Where we stand now,' he said. 'Right here. They say that when William de Gaillon was killed in battle, the dog howled here one last time and then joined him in death. That statue on Roddinglaw's lawn? That's William and his hunting hound.'

'I had no idea,' Esther said. She looked dubiously at the dunes and the marram grass. It was like the grave they had found, she thought, the bones by the shore. Another secret hidden in the earth.

'It was my father's obsession. The old house is overflowing with the accounts he collected. Documents, papers. I've barely scratched the surface of it.'

'He was obsessed with de Gaillon? The knight?'

'With the hound.' Jacob grinned, and his teeth looked for a moment like a dog's, eager and sharp. 'The hound is supposed to howl from this spot when the lord of the castle is about to die, so the legend says. A lord who killed his father... And I am now the heir of Gallondean.'

He believed it, she saw. Or, at the very least, he wanted her to think he did.

'It sounds like *The Hound of the Baskervilles* to me,' she said doubtfully.

Jacob smiled at that. 'Conan Doyle is an Edinburgh man, isn't he? Who's to say one legend didn't inform the other. I will find out soon though. I know it.'

'But you don't believe in it yourself,' she said. She thought of Wendy Darling in the play, her benign indulgence of Peter Pan's fantasies. 'Not really. Do you? You can't.'

He opened his arms to the wind and breathed deep. The flush on his cheeks deepened to something healthier, more vital. His voice was high and thin.

'I thought it was just some sad eccentricity on my father's part, something encouraged by that mad old sod Rutherford. I don't know, I still can't… But then I saw the bones, when the storm stripped the earth from the land. I've come to think that those bones were part of it. It began to make more sense to me, had more force behind it.' He struck his chest. 'I *felt* it. History had reached out and touched the legend. I think they're the bones of Robert de Gaillon. I'm sure of it. It's the skeleton of William's father.'

'You can't possibly know that.'

'I *believe* it,' he said, fierce, almost joyous. 'The body exiled, buried beyond the grounds, no safe harbour in the village churchyard. He was cast out, Esther. Cast out.'

He turned and took her hands. She felt herself pulled towards him – and then he was kissing her, his mouth hot, the fever rising in his blood.

She clasped his fingers. His arm encircled her waist, drawing her in. Esther, blank with shock, uncomprehending, reached up as though to push him away. Flashes of memory, the flame of old senses rekindled; Peter enveloping her, the musty male scent stoking a fire in her belly. She opened her mouth wider, gripped him, still part of her reeling back, but then Jacob turned his face aside and broke away from her, his eyes brimming. She stumbled back, hand to her mouth, skin raw where it had met the bristles of his unshaven lip, and despite the wind that coursed and hammered at the point, she felt hot, fervent in this heady cloud of air.

'Jacob—'

'I'm already dying. I know that. My lungs are killing me. I stand here now most days and imagine him sailing away to war, with sword and shield and spear. I stand at the window of the library and I wait to hear the howling, and when I do I'll know that death is finally with me.' He laughed and turned back to embrace the wind. 'I've been running from it since Lahore, frightened and ashamed. But now I know. I can stop it, Esther, at last.'

'Death?'

'My fate! My father!'

He grasped her shoulders and brought his face near to hers.

'Come with me next week,' he said. 'When you're free. We'll spend the day together, we'll go into Edinburgh, take tea at the Caledonian. We'll walk in the Gardens. We can do whatever you want. Come to Gallondean, stay with me, I'll...'

She brushed the back of her wrist against her lips. The wind snatched at her hair and at the hem of her dress. 'Jacob, I'm sorry, I—'

'Esther.'

The sun was high above him. Weakly it caught the drops of water in his hair and made them glisten. She turned and scrambled down onto the path again, the grass sighing on the dunes. She looked back at him, standing there on the edge of the shore, all the myths and legends buried beneath his feet. Peter had walked away from the gates of the English Cemetery, but Jacob would have thrust his hands into the soil and gripped the bones. That was the difference between them.

'Please,' she said. 'I can't think. They're such feeble words, I know, but I mean them all the same. I didn't expect this, not any of it.'

'Esther, forgive me.'

It seemed to her then that there was nothing to think about, as he stood above her on the dune. All the misanthropy had fallen from him, torn away in scraps and tatters by the wind. The rocks were ringed with a belt of foam. The cormorant raised its glossy wings and lumbered through the water, dark as shellac.

'I'll see you again, Jacob,' she told him. She kept her voice as level as she could. 'I want to. I won't leave it like this, I promise.'

And then she was running off across the sand, her skirts held up, and the trees were swaying to meet her, Hound Point abandoned behind, a lonely spur of land thrown into the grasping sea.

The legend, once glimpsed, builds its own momentum. You cannot live in this place and not respond to such grim mythology. The haar unravelling off the sea forbids reason. The shadows that fall on the cold stone conjure madness. The wind whispers secrets in the dead of night as it mumbles through the gaps. My father threads his way through all the rooms and chambers, watching, waiting. He is in every drop of condensation on the windowpanes. He is in the creak of every floorboard, in every scurrying rat as this house slowly collapses around me. He is in each mote of dust that rises from the manuscripts I draw towards myself.

Volumes accrue to me, day by day. I fill in the details and the context – who these people were, why they were here, what they thought they were doing when they sailed off to war. Armed pilgrims travelling immense distances to the lands where Christ had once walked, to wrest Jerusalem from the Saracens. I remember Esther saying there was a patient in Roddinglaw from the Palestine front. I wonder now if that man's feet ever walked the same paths as William de Gaillon's, if he spilled blood on the same battlefields.

My days and nights are full to overflowing with this stuff. I read William of Tyre on the Kingdom of Jerusalem, his *History of deeds done beyond the sea*. I parse Ambroise's *Estoire de la guerre sainte*, and the *Itinerarium Peregrinorum et Gesta Regis Ricardi*. My schoolboy Latin, first sharpened on Seneca and Caesar, is stretched beyond its bounds. I read about King Richard and the Siege of Acre, the massacre of the prisoners there, the Battle of Arsuf and the charge of the Hospitallers. Philips, Hughs and Fredericks swim in my mind, getting mixed up with Guys and Conrads and Raymonds, page by page, battle by battle, march by march. I scour the local records sourced by Rutherford for my father: prosopography accounts compiled in the Georgian age; genealogies; folk tales; incomprehensible reports from the Court of the King's Bench. I sit on a goldmine of documentation here, an archive beyond price. Firm and reliable detail eludes me though, and in its place lurk only rumours, innuendos, overblown denunciations, pulpit-speeches limned with fire. Robert de Gaillon was no mere warlord, I'm beginning to find; not just a brutal man insisting, say, on his *droit de seigneur*. He flits through the records like a ghost. *Unholy, blasphemous, diabolical* are just some of the terms that colour his name. But why? What on earth did he do?

As I read through all these murky histrionics, this medieval melodrama, I find myself wondering where exactly Robert's son fell. What stretch of desert or cleft in the hills claimed William de Gaillon? In what thicket of thorns or scrub was his body laid, while here, thousands of miles away, a dog howled on a lonely shore at the moment of his passing? What crimes or transgressions made him, with a holy fury, judge his own father with his blade?

Earlier, Major Lawson paid his now-customary visit. Routine enquiries about my lungs, my fever. 'Any episodes?' he asked, and at once I thought of Esther fleeing across the sand. 'No,' I replied. I have no idea if my mania then was caused by the disease or by the piece of land where I stood. Either of them could have brewed a madness in me, although in truth my lungs feel far less constricted at the moment. Eased by the floods of sea air I inhale every day, no doubt, hiking back and forth from the castle to Hound Point. Waiting there on the cusp of evening, poised for that spectral hound to claim me. Esther will return, I know. I'm sorry I frightened her, but I know our paths will cross again. I feel her lips on mine still and I know this to be true. When I am with her I burn, and the flame is a wholesome thing.

Lawson stayed a while after the preliminaries. He was keen to deploy his stethoscope but I palmed him off with whisky. Why bother telling me what I already know? We sat in the library, in the midst of my documents. The desk is strewn with them. It must seem a grand imperial project to the outsider, a massing and collating of important evidence, rather than the rabbit holes and goose chases of an obsession, and a second-hand obsession at that. He made no mention of it. He has a doctor's discretion.

The wind slammed into the castle walls. There is no breaker out there to shield Gallondean from it and we get the full force of the elements here, unvarnished. Lawson looked to the window, where a square of the blue evening was fading into black.

'You're a doctor, aren't you?' I said. 'I mean, that's what you are, what you were, before the war.'

'It's my profession, yes.'

'You trained here? In Edinburgh?'

'Manchester.'

'But you've served at the front as well? Before coming to Roddinglaw House?'

'Yes,' he said. He sipped from his glass, warily.

'Then you've seen...' I tried to put it as delicately as I could. 'You've seen the human form in many states, so to say. Unpleasant states.'

'I have.'

'And would you say...' I smiled to give him advance warning of how ludicrous the question might sound. 'Would you say that any of those sights, horrible as they might have been, made you think that perhaps the soul...'

'The soul?' It was Lawson's turn to smile. 'What of the soul, Mr Beresford?'

'Are you a religious man, Major? A Christian?'

'I am.'

'Only, I think if you had asked me four years ago whether I believed we each house an eternal soul, I would have laughed at you. The wry cynicism of youth and all that. But now, I'm not so sure. I think something does survive the body after death. Something remains, something numinous, a shadow of what once was.'

'Not a shadow,' Lawson said. 'I don't think that. It is ourself, I believe, as we are and were and will be. The body isn't a prison, after all. The body and the soul together are who we are.'

'And the resurrection of that body? Plain low-church Anglicanism always seems to fudge that part rather, doesn't it?'

Lawson laughed. He emptied his glass and placed it on the table in front of us, his fingers lingering a moment on the rim.

'As a Roman Catholic I don't have the luxury of fudging the issue, alas,' he said. 'Paul tells us the dead shall be raised imperishable, as Jesus was.'

131

I leaned forward in my chair. My face felt hot as fire. The darkness twitched in the corners of the room. Coals smouldered in the grate.

'But what does that *mean*? That the corpses claw their way out of the grave? That the torn and the fragmented, blown to pieces in Belgium and France, somehow gather those scraps up again and become whole? How can you, a medical man, think that? You've been elbow deep in matter your whole career, surely?'

He turned a tolerant gaze on me. 'Keep in mind that nobody knows,' he said. 'It's only to God that such things are certain. But I believe that a risen body will be provided, the same as it was when it was whole, but made immortal. Not the body that was destroyed, but a new and spiritual body exact in all particulars.'

'And children?' I said. 'The old? They come back in this new body as they were when they died? Then in the life to come, a father who had died young, say, would appear still young in the eyes of his elderly son? Or do they age or grow young proportionately, and everyone finds some strange average, or...'

Lawson shrugged and showed me his open palms.

'These are all details,' he said. 'It's speculation. It's not for us to know, other than in the broader truth. It's only atheists who seem to need certainty, isn't it? As a Catholic I'm quite comfortable with doubt.'

'It makes you more steadfast in your faith, doesn't it? Not less. But where is God in all this slaughter?'

'God is in the fact that you think it slaughter.'

'So the war – all the dead in France and the Dardanelles and Palestine, and at the bottom of the sea – they will all come back?'

'They will,' Lawson said. 'Because they must.'

'Extraordinary,' I said, but not to mock him. He was utterly sincere. I wondered if it stiffened his rigour to believe such things when dealing with the wounds of modern war. All those torn-off limbs and ravaged faces will be remade anew, imperishable at the final judgement. 'And I wouldn't say I was an atheist.' I shrugged in my turn. 'I wouldn't say that I was anything. But I do believe in the soul, I think. The soul or something very like it.'

'Then there's hope for you yet, Mr Beresford,' he said.

Later: A breakthrough. I sketch it here, another note as I grope towards the truth. In the documents gathered by Rutherford on my father's instruction, I have found an account from the 1820s, an Edinburgh lawyer's itemisation or inventory in preparation for Gallondean's sale. The house was then in some disrepair and the new owners (illegible) had plans for renovation. Rooms and their condition are described. The structure is coolly appraised. The grounds are dismissed with a note of their bare acreage. And then there is this:

> *The old chamber has been sealed, where de Gaillon's hands are said to have wrought their evil; and of the severed hands themselves there remains of course no visible sign.*

The severed hands? And what is this evil? What exactly did Robert de Gaillon do?

The old chamber has been sealed... But what has once been sealed can always be reopened.

Friday 26th April 1918

Spring sunlight, glassy and cold, sparkles in the grass. Daniel fastens his coat and puts his hands in his pockets. He walks swiftly across the grounds, boots stained black from the dew. A chill breeze fingers the wound in his chest, frisking under the bandages and dressings. When he breathes he can hear his breastbone creak. On warmer days he can barely feel it. Only when he takes the stairs more swiftly does the pain pulse inside him, thinning his blood, making his limbs shake and his lungs contract. Slowly, very slowly, the body begins to heal.

The taut grey lines of Roddinglaw fall away behind him. He reaches the lane that skirts the rear of the house and ribbons on towards the village. A horse across the fields on his left, a brown thumbprint in the grass, snorts in the cool morning air. The husk of a dead tree, its trunk hollow, throws its branches against the sky. In the grass he finds the plucked and ravaged corpse of a tern, its head missing, its wings pinned out in the turf. He takes a feather for his buttonhole, stoops a moment to address the wide, still air, level and motionless, the breathing silence of the country.

He walks the mile to the village, taking his time, listening to his boots scuff on the cinder path. The sea feels distant now, screened by Mons Hill and the Roddinglaw estate. He can smell the grass and the spring flowers, the sweet farmyard scent of earth and open land.

In the village he hitches a lift from a cart taking urns of milk to Newhaven. The driver's face is creased with age, his hands like knuckles of wood on the leather reins. He clicks his tongue and the horse trots on, dragging its burden. The clatter of its iron shoes is oddly soothing. Daniel leans back on the side of the box and closes his eyes against the sun. The smell of the beast, its snort and whicker on the long road that leads past Dolphington Burn and the Craigie farms, takes him back to the Judean hills. He thinks of the sorrel mare clipping through the high pathways, her soft brown eyes, the saddle bags slung across her back. Enfields sheathed in their oilskins, clips of bullets, a sack of grenades.

'Wait, John,' he mumbles, surfacing from a doze, unsure for a moment if he has said the name aloud. The cart driver says nothing, close as only country folk can be close, inhibited maybe by the convalescent uniform. Perhaps there is a son out there and the thought of him coming home in such a uniform is only slightly better than the thought of him not coming home at all. So many people must stagger though their days, nerves shredded as they wait for news. It's always worse to wait than to do.

The need had come on him, deep in the night. As soon as the dawn began to pink the sky, he was gone, leaving the hospital behind. Roddinglaw is changing now. The old guard are passing on as more and more new patients make their way to the makeshift wards. Captain Moore has been discharged, rubbing his vacant eye socket and making his departure with a smuggled bottle of gin, wishing everyone a swift recovery so they could go back to killing Germans as soon as possible. His barely masked misery at being out of the fight lingered in the common rooms. Moore had gobbled up news from the front, almost hoping that the situation would get worse so that in its desperation the army would turn to one-eyed men to make up the ranks. That ruthless bark of a laugh, the one blazing eye, the black patch flipped up onto his forehead – all of that boisterous presence strangely missed now. *Peter Pan* was his last gift to the men. A sense of lassitude has fallen on the hospital with his absence.

Daniel's thoughts wander. Palestine and Roddinglaw, the storm-struck earth where the skeleton was found, the mustering camp at Étaples. He thinks of St John in the poem, musing in his cave on the white lies that illuminate a greater truth. Touched by the numinous, even as his spirit succumbed to the weakness of the clay. Three souls reside in man, St John teaches: what *Does*, what *Knows*, what *Is*. Did Daniel leave behind what Does in Palestine? Did he spew out what Is into the desert? Could he now be only what Knows, even though there is so much he can't recall?

He thinks of the Sunday gone when he was walking by the shore and saw Mrs Worrell fleeing through the glade, clearly distressed. Then later, as he sat a while in the green shadows, seeing the young master of Gallondean returning along the beach, kicking at pebbles, his mouth sullen. Daniel had crouched and watched, and in the lines of the young man's face he had again seen that other face, long and thin: a face that he knows.

It is hunkered in a cave, glaring and mad.

A wildness surges in him at the memory. He breathes deeply and settles himself. He is in no danger, not yet. Darkness prowls this blustered coast. It haunts the dunes and the woods, it creeps through the corridors of Roddinglaw. It has followed him all the way from Palestine, but it will not find him unprepared. He spends hours in the art room now, silent alongside the men who paint and draw, as he sculpts and moulds and makes. Clay jars, none of them bigger than a few inches tall, each fired in the ovens to a fierce durability, each filled with earth he has taken from the ancient grave by the edge of Gallondean.

The jars are almost ready. They are important in some way that still eludes him, but all he needs to do now is remember the right words and symbols. Then the dark will have no purchase on him.

He alights at Granton Square, here on the northern edge of Edinburgh, the old hotel puffing smoke from its chimneys, the tram-cars clacking around its perimeter, the air sharp with the lingering smell of herring and whale oil from Newhaven along the coast. He thanks the driver, who nods brusquely, eyes squinting against the light. Daniel watches the cart lurch onwards, its iron-rimmed wheels turning towards Newhaven High Street.

He cuts up the side of the square and heads towards Trinity. Granton falls behind him, its ringing harbour where the minesweepers are moored, the sulphurous smell of the crushed stone from the nearby quarry. Soon appear the high, wide houses on the hill; lodges and manors, terraces and villas, all the merchants' country homes inherited now by a prosperous middle class, solid and imposing and sealed behind high walls and hedges. He passes the United Free church at Wardie, its sandstone shining in the morning light, the Episcopal church on Trinity Road with its piercing spire. The streets are silent. The villas, some with their curtains drawn against bereavement, are quiet as tombs. Beech trees sway on the corners, bowing their heads and scattering an early fall of budding shells onto the pavements.

A darkness before his eyes. There's a taste of metal at the back of his throat. A turn and then another turn, crossing the bridge over the railway line at Newhaven Junction, the air grey with the smoke of a passing train. There's a gritty, mineral flavour to the breeze after the clean open skies by Roddinglaw. He turns at last onto York Road, faltering now, the pain swimming faster through him with every step. It's too far for him to have travelled, too soon.

He sits on the pavement for a moment, resting in the shadows cast by the looming trees, and gathers his breath. The street is empty. There are no lights in the bay windows of number ten. The door is closed. He doesn't know who lives here now. When his heart has settled, he steals across the grass, passing down the left-hand side of the house towards the back garden, glancing in at the window onto the sitting room and its unfamiliar furniture, the room airy and uncluttered.

The garden is a sheet of grass bordered on three sides by flower-beds. The hornbeam shivers. Green-painted chairs ring an iron table on the lawn. A paved path follows the line of the house to the back door. He tries the handle, feels the latch withdraw, and sweeps the door wide open into the kitchen.

The air smells of brewed tea and baked bread, vegetables, boiled meat. No one challenges him. No one appears to notice a sudden change in the air or rises to investigate the noise of his entry. He stands there for a moment and listens, breathing gently through his mouth as his heart clatters in his chest. The wound throbs beneath the dressing. It is the very core of him.

He wanders through the house. Everything is different. The rugs underfoot are new, there are pictures on the walls that he has never seen. It seems cooler and less cramped, as if the windows have long been thrown open to blow away every last trace of the Victorian age. His father's life, reducing year by year to the confines of the parlour and the kitchen, the bed made up on the settee, his Bible, is no longer part of the house's memory. His footsteps ring on the bare floorboards at the borders of each room before sinking into rug and carpet.

Upstairs he finds the room he shared with Simon, before his brother graduated to his own room at the top of the house. Their fretwork models are gone, the Empire drum and the pushalong toys, the soldiers, the cricket bat and stumps. In their place is a well-kept bookcase, an overflowing basket of sailor dolls and teddy bears, an old rocking horse, a boat with half the blue paint chipped from its hull. The wallpaper is brighter and plainer, the woodwork is painted white. The fireplace is protected by a stained-glass screen showing the animals marching onto the Ark, behind them the frothing jungle foliage of a world on the cusp of being drowned.

He lies down on the single bed, on top of the coverlet. The wound is aching now. With each pulse of his heart it sends a black tide washing over him. The house, the seat of all his memories, had called to him in his dreams, and all he could do was answer. The war has brought him back to where he started, only to say goodbye to who he once was before the war began. Before his faith was vomited away, before his brother had died, when they had sat that last night in the garden and listened to the bats flitting through the fading dusk.

Sprawled out in a room that doesn't remember him, Daniel sleeps for a while. The morning slips away. A square of light slides across the carpet. When he wakes, he wonders if they've missed him at Roddinglaw. They'll be looking for him now.

A voice says, 'Who are you?'

Daniel lifts his head from the pillow. A boy, not much more than eight or nine, stands by the open door. His arms hang at his sides. He isn't afraid.

'Are you lost?' he says. 'Are you a soldier?'

'Yes,' Daniel answers. 'To both. I'm a soldier, and I think I'm lost.'

'Well,' the boy says, 'this is where I live.'

'I once lived here too.'

The boy shrugs, as though unsurprised. He sits down on the floor and toys with a puzzle piece. Daniel raises himself on his elbows. The pain in his chest has slackened but he feels threadbare and weak, worn out. He doesn't know how he's going to get back. Perhaps he could stay here, sleep in his old room, slide back into a life he should never have left.

'Is your mother here? Your father?' he asks the boy.

'They're around.' He appraises the wounded man lying on his bed. 'Are you hurt?'

'I was.' Daniel taps his chest. 'But I'm getting better.'

'Was it the enemy?'

'To be honest, I'm not sure what it was.'

'How can you not be sure?'

Daniel considers this. 'War is a strange business. Not all of it makes sense in the moment it's happening.'

'But you've fought?'

'Yes,' Daniel tells him. 'In the East. In Palestine.'

'Were you in Jerusalem?' The boy tosses the puzzle piece aside. His collar is open and there's a grass stain on his bare knee. 'Father said that was the greatest prize of the war.'

'No. I was wounded before I could get there. I'd like to go, though. Just to see what all the fuss is about.'

'Perhaps you will, one day.'

He smirks and gives Daniel a sharp glance. Daniel meets his eyes and it's only then that he realises. Of course. The light has moved away from the window now. They are facing east, away from the sun.

'I didn't expect to see you,' Daniel says.

'I have to go soon,' the boy tells him. 'It's getting closer. But you know that, don't you?'

'I know. I can feel it.'

'You'll hear it before the end. But you shouldn't be afraid.'

There's a dragging, tearing pain in his chest. He feels light-headed, oddly free.

'I came when you called,' the boy says. 'But you did not see.'

'No. Perhaps I didn't.'

'I was there all the same.'

'By then it was too late.'

'It's never too late. Never.' The boy looks to the window, the sky as white as a sheet of paper. 'It's a cemetery, in its way,' he says. 'All of it, every inch. Every patch of ground. Things buried, things hidden. Other things dug up and brought out into the light.'

'I know.' Daniel nods, closing his eyes. He feels the darkness crash in waves over him. 'The jars. I remember the jars. I've filled them with earth already. Earth from where the bones were dug, on the shore by Gallondean. It's the same earth, isn't it?'

'It's all the same earth, Daniel. Every bit.'

He nods. With an effort that makes his neck tremble, he raises his head and looks onto the empty room. He can hear voices downstairs, the firm shutting of the front door. He croaks and cries out. He is sick, he tells them, he's ill. Help me, please.

There is a wounded man in this house, but they should not be afraid.

Saturday 27th April 1918

The rabbit's guts were drawn, the viscera strung around the base of the tree in many-coloured ribbons. Heart and lungs and liver had been trampled into the grass. The rest of the creature was nailed to the trunk at head-height, the black eyes dull as stone, grey fur matted with blood. The carcass yawned at the breast, a mouth of red secrets.

'Farmers,' Jacob said by way of explanation. He stared into the trees, as if expecting to see one of their distinctive breed leering from the scrub. 'You'll find none more superstitious, let me tell you. They're forever nailing up stoats and crows to scare the others off. And what's the result? Nothing but a nice meal conveniently laid out for their fellows.'

He frowned and gripped the collar of his coat. His face was pale. Gently he guided her away from the scene and back onto the path.

'It's just horrible,' Esther said. 'All of it, just horrible.'

'Bloody peasants. Pay no mind to them.'

They were heading back from Queensferry, where they had been to the tea room on the high street and had talked only of incidental things – the weather, the sea, how pleasant the farmland was around them, how cold Gallondean got at night. Drowning in all the proprieties, neither had felt comfortable confessing the truth of their feelings, their uncertainties, with each other. The clash of cup and saucer, the chatter of the conversation surrounding them, made the truth impossible. Esther, as if tormenting herself, kindled those wild feelings again: the tension in his body when he kissed her, the heat of his lips. She squashed them down, doused them in the cold water of her will, almost aggrieved at the power they had over her.

The air was cold this afternoon. The sea was oily and black, slopping up against the shore with a sound like a blocked drain. The night before Esther had asked Alice Stewart if she would like to come along, as chaperone or companion. The walk to South Queensferry would do her good, she had said. The sea air, a cup of tea, and really, Mr Beresford was far better company than you would expect. She had pointed vaguely in the direction of that old dark house, crumbling on the shore, but with a wan expression Alice had shaken her head.

'He looks a cruel man to me,' she whispered from her bed. The light of the full moon was stark and white as it glared through their window. Ida Lambert was on the night shift and her bed was empty. Esther knew she would have been drinking in every word otherwise. 'Be careful, Esther. He looks like a *German*. And that pathway, please – you must be careful. Ida says so too, what with those poor little beasts you always find down there.'

'Oh, Alice,' Esther had said. 'I'm sure it's nothing more than your imagination. The war, this place – all of us are on edge, I think. I'll be fine.'

'Yes,' Alice had said. Her face had grown cold. 'You would go, wouldn't you? You people always go your own way.'

Then she had turned on the pillow, showing Esther her back. There was nothing else to say.

There was sense in her fears though. Esther looked to the trees lurching on the slope, the blurred motion of their branches in the quickened breeze, the darkness that lurked beneath them. Jacob walked on the other side of the path, head down, brooding. Neither of them had exchanged a word since they had found the dead rabbit. Ida's loitering shadows, she thought, stalking their prey. *Farmers indeed…*

Poor Alice. Esther told Jacob about her as they walked, how Alice thought of little else now since she had received the telegram from

Georgie's parents. She couldn't change a dressing without seeing the same wound that might have carried her fiancé away.

'And what does "killed in action" really mean?' Esther said. 'Shot? Blown up? Left to die in a shell hole with his guts hanging out? It's horrific. The blandness of it, the things it did not say.'

'Poor girl,' Jacob said. 'All griefs seem to flow from France. All roads lead there.'

'We're lucky, I suppose,' Esther agreed, although luck seemed an odd way of putting it. 'Not to be near where the battles rage. The war never comes any closer than the sea.'

The subject hung there between them like a covered frame in a gallery, almost inviting the observer to whip aside the cloth. So far Jacob had said nothing about what had happened the other day, but as they passed on he took her arm and she was content to be drawn closer. Whatever fever had gripped him on the bluff seemed to have withered for the moment.

'I've been thinking of how to apologise to you,' he said. 'About my behaviour last week. Hound Point, I might have seemed a little exercised... It's the illness in me, that's all.'

'It's getting worse?' Esther asked.

'It's unlikely to get better.' He tore a stalk of grass from the verge. 'Your Major Lawson says a certain excitement or fever is common.'

'Major Lawson? I wasn't aware that – does he see you, does he come to Gallondean?'

She felt an odd pang; pity, or a jealous blow. Not on her behalf, but vicariously for Lawson, if what Ida Lambert had claimed was true and he genuinely carried a candle for her. Poor Major Lawson, she thought. But then there was no guarantee Jacob had told him anything. What, indeed, was there to tell? What exactly was happening here?

'I have the feeling that he's a very great man,' Jacob went on. 'A great doctor in any case. He recognised my symptoms and keeps trying to convince me to seek proper treatment, and—'

'And you're not?' Esther said.

Jacob sighed and tossed his stalk of grass into the bracken. 'No. No, I'm not.'

As though called out by the conversation, he began to cough. There was no force behind it. To those who didn't know it would have seemed no more than a clearing of the throat.

'All this,' Esther began. She mirrored him and plucked her own blade of grass, tearing it until her fingertips were stained green. 'What you said last week about Hound Point, this calling, this spectral howl...'

Jacob looked abashed. He laughed to himself, his lips pale. Esther felt her anger kindle.

'You're really going to wait here to die?' she said. She flicked the torn grass away. 'There's no further purpose to your life? Just sitting in that place, poring over the dregs of your father's obsession, trying to convince yourself it's true? Documents and papers and dust, an old legend no one remembers.'

They had reached the narrow bay now, Hound Point beyond it. The gap in the belt of trees, the slope down to the open sand, the gathered rocks foaming in the spray. Jacob stood and looked off towards it. Beyond, far beyond, great rolls of cloud were tumbling over the coast of Fife.

'You don't understand.'

'Then make me understand.'

'I have no intention of just allowing myself to die here,' he said. His voice was weak. 'None at all. When the thing that will kill me comes near, I will kill it in turn. It's that simple. I will destroy it, turn every last blazing ray of the light against it...'

'Jacob, you're not making the least sense.'

'And what's your purpose then?' he said, facing her. 'Patching up men who've passed through half a dozen hands already? Changing bed pans and washing linen? If you want to go to the front, Esther, then do it. Risk everything, seize everything. If you want to write poetry, then write it. Gather what you may, write what you can, only don't let yourself be held back by...'

'By what?' she demanded. 'What do you think is holding me back?'

He paced to the edge of the beach, his hands in his pockets, and kicked at the sand.

'The dark,' he said. 'The spectre, creeping ever nearer...' He turned to her again. 'What did you feel when your husband died?'

Formalities, decorum – he didn't seem to care about them at all. Esther felt them swell up and crash around her, the conventions of a world already shaken to pieces.

'What did I *feel*? What do you think I felt?'

'It was a relief to you, wasn't it? It was a freedom you'd never thought to have again.'

'How dare you?' She reached for fury but it wasn't there. She would have to conjure it from scratch, but then part of her thought: why shouldn't he dare? Why shouldn't she?

Jacob smiled widely. For a moment his face looked bare of flesh; cadaverous, a grinning skull. 'Whether he was a kind man or a brute, a loving man or a bastard, it doesn't matter a damn. You were released all the same. What was it like, I wonder, the moment the telegram came? Oh, I've seen them, Esther, going from door to door. The yellow slips in the hands of the postmen, the death notices marched up the streets of every village and town and city, the drawn curtains and the weeping mothers. But you didn't weep, did you? I can see it, I can almost see it as if it is right here in front of me... The keys to your prison, and a pension into the bargain, and the whole world open to you at last. Only you're too frightened to leave. You've been confined for so long you can't imagine anything else.'

It was the arrogance, the certainty, but it was the little hint of truth as well. She flew at him then, ferocious, and rang a gunshot slap across his face. Jacob lurched back with the red imprint of her palm on his cheek. He stumbled, laughing still, a grotesque guttural sound that quickly turned into a bone-deep, hacking cough. He dropped to one knee in the sand, fingers up to his mouth, tears springing from his eyes. There was blood in his hands.

'Jacob, my God.'

She knelt by him. She could feel the pulse of his heart, the tired labour of his lungs. She drew a handkerchief from her sleeve and dabbed the streaks of blood from his mouth, wiping his tears away with green fingertips.

'Esther, I'm so sorry...'

'When you kissed me,' she said, half in a whisper, 'was that the fever's fault too? Was that for me? Or was it for your friend?'

She fell against him and he rose to meet her.

'Come with me,' he breathed against her skin. 'Please, Esther. I love you. Come.'

Lahore

Saturday 13th June 1914

Jacob had always thought the shade house looked incongruously like an austere native temple, torn up and transported to this suburban garden deep in the Civil Lines. The laths were of Indian rosewood, and each end of the narrow, L-shaped building was capped by a wooden finial. Morning and evening his father could be found worshipping in its narrow aisles, breathing in the scent of his English flowers; geraniums and heliotropes, hollyhocks and lady's mantle, white chrysanthemums. Dawn and dusk were his favourite times of day. Of everything in his father's life – his work, his son, the investments and interests he maintained back home – Jacob always thought he loved the shade house most.

It was early, not much past six. He stood at his bedroom window and looked out onto the garden. The light was already punishing, all blare and fury. There was no hinterland to it, no softness to its edges. He closed the shutter and flopped down onto his drenched sheets, trying to push the darkness of his dreams away. The shadow lurking in the doorway, something about oil in his lungs – coughing, always coughing, spewing it up in thick black strings…

He groped for the carafe of soda water on the bedside table and drained it. There was brandy in the parlour, he knew. There was whisky in the cabinet and a bottle of gin. He stared up at the immobile punkah above him. Six was too early. Six was practically the middle of the night.

The quiet snip of his father's secateurs floated across the garden. The faint and resinous scent of his pipe tobacco reached him, the drift of a mumbled hymn.

… Shake off dull sloth, and joyful rise/ To pay thy morning sacrifice…

Then rising and rising, higher even than the roar of the motorcar passing on the road, came the shriek of the brainfever bird. Shrill, insistent, hysterical. He covered his head with his pillow.

A year of this. A year of formaldehyde and heatstroke, of snakes in the garden, of his father's stern and disapproving glare. A year of the brainfever bird.

A fire burned in his chest. A tightness squeezed his lungs.

Shake off dull sloth…

Jacob went back to sleep.

It was Mr Beresford's habit to spend Saturday afternoons visiting his suppliers in the city – manufacturers of embalming fluids, providers of ice, farriers for the horses – and so it was with mild surprise that Jacob, coming through from his bedroom in his unbelted paisley dressing gown, saw his father standing there in the doorway of his study. The old man's expression was his habitual one, hooded and bloodless, his mouth downturned beneath the broad black line of his moustache. His spectacles caught the light and made two gold coins of his eyes.

'Father,' Jacob said, wondering how many times he had said that word in his life. Precious few, he should think.

'Jacob,' Mr Beresford said, as if to say he expected as much. The moustache twitched. 'Your plans for this afternoon?'

'Very busy, I'm afraid, Father. I'm late as it is.'

'Doing?'

'I'm meeting Bobby Dunstan. And his sister. A stroll in the Gardens, perhaps afternoon tea at Faletti's. They have so few friends of their own…'

Mr Beresford looked at him gravely. 'I strongly suspect that Robert Dunstan has more friends than you realise. But then you are nineteen now, and it is for you to make your own mistakes and deal with the consequences of them. Or so, at least, I have always thought.'

'Indeed, Father,' Jacob agreed.

'Indeed,' the older man said, turning, and for the briefest moment allowing his face to show a sketch of pain.

Jacob could feel his pulse beating madly in his temples. The familiar fire was brewing in his lungs and he only wished this moment would end so he could indulge himself in a long and luxurious cough.

'Is that everything, Father?' he said, his voice rather choked. 'I expect I shan't be back for dinner.'

Mr Beresford turned again. His face was oddly waxen, the eyes sunken and black. He looked old, Jacob realised.

'My own father...' he began, but then seemed to think better of it. 'What do you know of this city, Jacob? Of India?'

'Father?'

'We are at a crossroads here, my son. A literal crossroads. The rail lines link Peshawar to the north, Delhi and Calcutta to the east, Bombay to the south. Millions of people passing along them day after day, night after night. Increasingly, the roads are given over to the motorcar. Ships pass in untold numbers over the oceans of the world, flying the British flag.'

Jacob shifted his weight from one foot to the other while he waited for his father to reach the point. His mouth was parched and his chest felt fit to burst. He could almost taste the brandy that was waiting for him in the parlour.

'What I did, Jacob,' Mr Beresford continued, reaching out and laying a hand on his son's shoulder, 'was to find a market for what people will always need. Always. You find out what people need, and you sell it to them. Do you understand? That way lies...'

He looked up to the corners of the ceiling, down to the interlocked polished rectangles of the parquet floor.

Jacob said, 'Lies what?'

'*Freedom*, of a kind. The freedom to know that you are doing honest and useful work, to the best of your abilities. There is nothing greater.'

'I understand,' Jacob said. 'Truly I do.'

The glint of passion faded. The mask, briefly raised, slipped once more into place.

'You are idle,' his father said, resigned. He shook his head. 'Bone idle, and self-indulgent, and with no more care than for your own pleasures. You have barely applied yourself to the work I set you, and you show no aptitude for it in any case, let alone any interest. One year,' he said, raising a finger. 'Do you remember what was said? One year.'

Jacob nodded attentively. He vaguely recalled arriving on the boat from school, wilting in the heat as the liner docked in Bombay, then withering for three days on the train, half-stunned, as it slowly cut up towards the Punjab. He remembered sweeping in great clouds of steam over the River Sutlej, but by the time he reached the bungalow in Donald Town he was sicker than he had ever felt in his life. Most of what was said to him over the next few weeks, or what he might have replied in turn, was a mystery.

'One year to find your vocation,' his father continued. His face was stern now. 'And let me tell you, Jacob, in no uncertain terms – that year is up.'

'I'm sorry, honestly I am. I will apply myself, Father. If not at the family work, then I'll find something I can commit myself to. Journalism, perhaps, and you know I've always been most interested in the wine business, or ...'

Swimming in from the wilder seas of his memory came Bobby's request. He had forgotten that. Now, however, was very much not the time to raise it.

'This discussion will be continued in the evening,' Mr Beresford said. 'I shall expect you here at a sensible hour. We will talk further then.'

He closed the study door behind him and locked it. Then, without another glance at his son, Mr Beresford strode to the front door where the gig was waiting, leaving Jacob to dismiss the servants and rustle up his morning brandy himself.

Faletti's sat low and broad on the other side of a wide concrete courtyard, Indo-classical, like a great Minoan temple where they worshipped the gods of Theseus and Ariadne. Jacob smoothed his hair as he passed through the foyer and entered the bar. There was a drizzle of perspiration on his upper lip. He scanned the corner booths, brushed away the waiter who stood with folded napkin at the entrance, then saw Bobby's raised hand as he half-stood from one of the round tables in the centre of the room. Jacob wiped the sweat away and swept over as Bobby signalled for another drink.

'Jakey boy!' Bobby crushed his cigarette in the ashtray. 'I thought a gin and lime to start with.'

'Sensible choice, sensible choice.'

'I thought so. You can always rely on me, Jake, you know that.'

Jacob sat down and in moments the drink was at his elbow. He sipped the gin and looked around the room. The bar was still half-empty at this time, and frequented mostly by commercial travellers or the more affluent tourist. Beyond, in the glimmering foyer, he saw a trio of porters arguing over a stack of trunks.

A fan turned lazily on the ceiling and spread a disc of cooler air around them. 'Always choose this table if you can,' Bobby said, pointing upwards. 'After the street outside, it's positively arctic.'

He leaned back in his chair and lit another cigarette. He was at least a head taller than Jacob, leaner and bonier, a rangy, restless presence who rarely sat still. While Jacob draped a half-interested gaze over the other patrons, Bobby pierced them with a less forgiving stare, as if searching out enemies or potential friends. He passed quite well in the hotel's subdued lamplight, certainly far more than he did in the streets outside. But now Jacob came to think of it, he wasn't sure that he'd ever seen his friend in the hours of day. Just in bars and in the back rooms of his father's business, fiddling with the gravity jar or drawing hot water from the Ascot with a corpse on the table before him. One of the many reasons they favoured Faletti's was the presence of all the Italians and Germans, the Indian elite. It was a more international clientele in which they could blend without question.

'No sign of your sister?' Jacob said, trying to sound uninterested. 'I thought she was joining us?'

'She'll be here. At the moment she's no doubt stewing in the company of all those actors and musicians and poets at the Bhati Gate.'

'Try dragging her away,' Jacob laughed. The Walled City was somewhere he had never been, in the long year that he had lived here. The Kipling story was enough for him. He felt no need to explore it for himself.

Bobby gave him a close and half-amused stare.

'Are you feeling alright, Jakey boy? To my trained and expert eye you seem not quite up to dick?'

'I'm fine, absolutely,' Jacob said. He coughed into his fist and felt his head go light. 'No, only it's… bad sleep, and dreams, and so on.'

'Dreams?'

'Odd dreams,' Jacob said. He wondered if he should go on. Bobby could be merciless when the mood took him. 'Always the same kind.' He laughed. 'I'm choking on great clouds of black smoke… hacking it up, you know, coughing it all out.'

'How awful. And then you wake up screaming?'

Jacob forced another laugh. 'Hardly. But honestly, I can't sleep more than one hour in three. I'm exhausted.'

They fell into a brief and companionable silence, while Jacob rubbed his chest and tried to push the image of the dreams away. Night after night, as if something was trying to burst out of him, black and oily and dark…

Bobby, sipping his drink and making a noise as if something had just occurred to him, turned back to Jacob and raised an eyebrow. He put down the glass and drew a palm carefully over his lacquered hair. When he spoke it was in a casual, self-effacing tone.

'Mmm, your father,' he started. 'Did you…?'

'Oh,' Jacob said. He quickly drank while he tried to summon an excuse.

'Only you did say that you would ask him,' Bobby said.

'No, ah… Yes, I did, but I haven't…'

Bobby, clearly crestfallen, masked it with a sharp and cynical smile. He wagged a finger at the younger man. 'You're too frightened of him, lad. Don't I always say? He's your father, he's not God.'

'Isn't he? You should tell him that.'

Fumbling for another cigarette, Bobby leaned in closer. 'But seriously, Jakey boy, we *need* it. You know that. And what's five hundred pounds to him, hmm? He must clear more than that a year from his investments alone.' He sighed. 'Sarah's going to be devastated. America, San Francisco... she's set her heart on it.'

'Don't tell her,' Jacob said quickly. 'I'll ask him, honestly I will. Tomorrow. This evening.'

'It's just an advance on your inheritance, remember to say it like that. For an investment. But we *need* it, you see? All three of us. Then we can get out of here at last. Start up somewhere new.' He spread his hands wide. 'What else has your father trained me for all these years, if not to take my skills further afield?'

Jacob, with a dubious expression, said, 'I'm not quite sure that's how he'd look at it.'

'However you look at it, people will always need their dead buried, won't they? And why not in San Francisco instead of Lahore? The United States, Jakey boy, that's the future.' He looked past Jacob's shoulder suddenly and ground out his cigarette. 'But here's Sarah now,' he whispered. 'No more about this, right? We'll speak later.'

'Of course,' Jacob said, feeling his heart lift. He turned, stood awkwardly, saw a young woman in a cream ruffled blouse and a long crimson skirt approaching their table, her black hair hanging to her shoulders in curled tresses. Eyes like tourmalines, he thought. Like yellow jade or jasper. My God...

'Sarah!' he said, struggling against another impulse to cough.

'Jakey!'

She smiled, all teeth, leaned in to kiss him on the cheek. He saw at once that she had the brass wedding band on her finger. Bobby did the same. In places like Faletti's it was sometimes easier to pretend they were a married couple rather than brother and sister.

'Now tell me, Jakey,' she said, sitting close as Bobby raised a finger to the waiter. 'How *are* you? How are you *really*?'

'I'm wonderful, Sarah,' he said, abashed, and then in a voice of mock-passion: 'Now that you're here that is.'

He kissed her hand. It was all he could do not to suggest they should leave for the Dunstans' flat at once. The waiter brought over three more gin and limes, and in a sudden rush of excitement Jacob called for champagne.

'Goodness.' Sarah clapped her hands. 'What on earth are we celebrating?'

'Decisions,' Bobby said, raising his glass. 'Decisions, actions, determination. Friendship.'

'Oh, I'll drink to that any day of the week,' Sarah said. The champagne arrived in its ice bucket, three flutes chiming in the waiter's other hand.

'Sarah,' Bobby said, 'you *do* drink any day of the week.'

The afternoon bled away, faster than the level of the champagne. Outside the sun hammered on the dusty streets, but in Faletti's it was all ice and crystal and polished marble countertops, the gleam of porcelain and mahogany. Jacob looked at his friends, and with the alcohol pounding in his blood didn't think he'd ever been happier.

'Light, Love and Life,' Sarah declaimed. She drained the flute. 'Is that not the core message of the *Gita*, hmm? The three Gunas of Nature, the three states of the soul, the three of us wonderful friends.'

'And which am I again?' Bobby said, wearily. 'Am I peaceful light, I forget?'

'Goodness no,' she said happily. 'You are *Tamas*, the lifeless dark, of course.'

'Of course.'

She tapped Jacob on the shoulder. 'Jakey is *Sattva*, being and harmony. *He* is the peaceful light.' She touched her breast. 'And I am *Rajas*, all passionate, restless life. Don't you see?'

'It seems so obvious when you put it like that,' Bobby said, his voice very dry. He refilled their glasses. 'You're pulled in so many odd directions, my sister, truly you are. Can't *you* see? All this mystical nonsense, honestly.'

'Ah,' Sarah said, bright-eyed. 'Is that what a four-thousand-year-old religious faith is? I hadn't realised. Mystical nonsense, of course.'

'Now, now,' Jacob cut in.

'They wouldn't even let you in the temples. And you look just like any other Englishwoman when you go through the Gates, despite the way you dress.'

'I'm *not* though, am I? An Englishwoman.'

'You could be if you tried. It's all in the eye of the beholder, my dear.'

'I've never been in the Walled City,' Jacob interrupted hastily. 'After reading "The City of Dreadful Night", I wouldn't dare. Or do I mean "The Gate of a Hundred Sorrows"?'

'Either,' Bobby said. 'Neither.'

'Oh, come now,' Sarah leaped in. 'At least Kipling is from here. Top to bottom, like it or not, he knows the city. He knows India.'

'He knows his own idea of it,' Bobby said. 'And he knows that very well. But he's old news now. He's no Lawrence.'

'Who is?' Sarah, stealing one of her brother's cigarettes, leaned close to Jacob and said in a stage-whisper, 'Pay no mind to him. He's still annoyed he couldn't meet the Webbs when they came last year. Or was it the year before? You're such a terrible socialist, Bobby. *Terrible.*'

'I'm a democrat, not a socialist.' Turning his eyes on Jacob with a very specific glare, he said, 'Hence San Francisco. Hence America.'

Sarah tossed back a lock of her black hair. Jacob wasn't sure if she had heard. Her eyes caught the light.

'Well, it's all just politics, isn't it?' she said, dismissing socialism, democracy and everything in between with a wave of her hand. 'It's all just temporary stuff, here on earth. The eternal, Jacob my dear. That's the only thing. That's *everything.*'

'I agree with you, Sarah,' Jacob said. He rested his head on her shoulder. 'Absolutely.' And through the wreath of cigarette smoke that crowned Bobby's head, he saw the other man looking at him with a wry amusement.

Later, and how much later Jacob couldn't have said – the third bottle, the fifth or sixth gin and lime? – he slumped in his seat and watched Sarah return gracefully and with seemingly no ill-effects from the champagne along the tiled corridor that led to the ladies' powder room.

A tall young man detached himself from the marble curve of the bar then. He was dressed in a cream flannel suit, his neat dark hair combed back and his face sallow and thin. There was an urgency in the way he crossed the gleaming floor. Before Sarah could reach their table, he had taken her firmly by the crook of the arm and turned her towards him.

Jacob saw the flash of alarm in her eyes, the way she composed it quickly into a sneer of amusement. The man muttered darkly at her but they were too far away for Jacob to hear what he had said. Sarah detached herself, her face very slightly flushed, and returned to her seat with a laugh. The dark-haired man stared at her for a moment, before heading back to the bar and dashing off what remained of his drink.

'Who on earth was that?' Jacob said.

'Oh, pay him no mind.'

Bobby looked at her carefully. 'Another one of your admirers, Sarah?'

'Just some German fellow, you know how they gravitate to Faletti's. An engineer or one of those Forestry types. Very serious, very *Sturm und Drang*. Very German.'

'Did he hurt you?' Jacob said. 'Did he…?'

'Are you going to defend my honour?' she said, cupping the side of his face with a palm. 'You're *too* sweet, Jacob. *Too* sweet. Isn't he sweet, Bobby?'

'He's awfully sweet,' Bobby agreed. 'He's a very sweet young man.'

'My knight in shining armour,' Sarah said, and she rewarded him with a kiss on the cheek. 'See? Don't I always say you're the one among us who truly *shines*?'

Jacob blushed and looked with undisguised malice at the German, hunched over the bar. He half-hoped the man would turn around and see, and then half-worried what on earth he would do if the fellow actually did. Fistfights were unheard of in Faletti's – it wasn't that kind of place – and in any case, Jacob hadn't been in a fight since he was eleven years old. The German stayed where he was though, staring into his glass and brooding with what Jacob thought was typical Teutonic gloom. Honour satisfied, Jacob turned back to Sarah and Bobby.

'Well, I think it's an absolute bloody disgrace,' he said.

They continued drinking, Bobby and Sarah talking in that bright and off-hand way that Jacob had always found so charming, as if their lives weren't so circumscribed that this whole afternoon was only possible on the unspoken assumption Jacob would pay the bill when they were finished. As he looked out of the windows that gave onto the courtyard, he saw that the sky was getting dark. Evening was coming on, another day drowned in gin and champagne. He thought of his father tending the English flowers in the shade house. Monday to Saturday was work, and Sunday was church and the mandated day of rest. The old man wasn't even a member of the Punjab Club. He had no friends, as far as Jacob could tell. He had work and his investments back home, and that seemed to compass all his life. And what compassed his own? He didn't even pretend to an interest in his father's business, no matter how many times he was reminded that one day it would all be his. Gin and champagne, and the bars of Lahore's more upmarket hotels. Was that enough for him? But then what else was there in this world?

He rubbed his chest cautiously and took a sip of air. What indeed?

The German had been standing at the bar all this while, drinking, sometimes looking meanly over his shoulder at them. Jacob was ever aware of his dark looks, his strained and saturnine expression, the clench of his jaw. Somewhere in the pit of his stomach he felt alarmed, but with all the champagne in his blood the nerves couldn't shoot their message any higher. He laughed, he touched Sarah's arm. At one point he even had the boldness to lean over and kiss the corner of her mouth, but always he kept half an eye on the man at the bar, the gleam of fury in his eyes, the knuckles white on his glass.

Finally, when they had finished another bottle, Jacob shaking out the last few crystal drops, the German stalked over to stand beside their table. Conversation died away, but all three of them looked at him with the same expression of ironic amusement. Jacob hid his laughter behind the rim of his glass.

'Miss Dunstan,' the German said quietly. His English was clear and precise, with little trace of an accent. 'Please, I must insist. If you would only come and speak with me for a short moment, I'm sure...'

Sarah looked through him, as if at a mirage. She sipped from her glass and then sighed lightly, turning to stare at the windows and the dun stone of the hotel courtyard beyond, stroked now by the fading sun.

'You're sure what, exactly?' Bobby said. 'Hmm?' He held up his hand. 'Sir, don't you know this is my wife?'

Jacob nearly choked. He watched the German twitch a glance towards Sarah's ring finger. He went crimson.

'Your *wife*? But I...'

'I would advise you to choose your next words very carefully,' Bobby said. His eyes were dead, his voice cold as stone. Jacob felt his heart beat wildly in his chest. When he wanted to, Bobby could be terribly convincing. He really should have been the actor. Not Sarah.

She turned in her seat and, with an excess of warmth, took the German's hand.

'Herr Löwe,' she said, as though patiently explaining a difficult concept to a child, 'I'm sorry if there's been any misunderstanding. I'm sure the fault is *all* mine, truly I am. But as you can see, I'm enjoying a drink now with my *husband* and my dear friend, so really, you *mustn't* make a scene. Be a good gentleman, please.'

'Gentleman?' he said. 'Gentleman... You dare, and I have never been so, I...'

He stood there above them, his fists clenched. Jacob could feel Bobby stir on the other side of the table. The German cast a red glare into Sarah's face, turning it like a lighthouse beam on each of them in turn. When it came to rest on him, Jacob had the strangest feeling that he was looking into a mirror, his reflection twisted and distorted somehow. But then the moment passed and the feeling withdrew, leaving him taut and frightened, and with his lungs burning, burning in his chest.

'You people...' the German hissed. 'You *scum*. You make me sick. Sick!'

He dashed the champagne bucket onto its side and stormed off, feet ringing on the tiles. A tide of half-melted ice cascaded across the table. Sarah barked with laughter. Waiters were approaching. Jacob swept up a rock of ice and sent it sailing across the room at the German's retreating back, already taking out his pocketbook to pay.

Only Bobby still sat there, motionless, a cigarette fuming from his lips, his eyes narrowed against the smoke.

He looked at Jacob, and then Sarah was taking his arm, laughing, and dragging him from the chair.

SUNDAY 14TH JUNE 1914

Someone cried out on the Mall Road, deep into the night. Jacob woke, turned in the bed, flung an arm across Sarah's legs. His mind was reeling. The air was very still. A lamp flickered in the corner of the room and there was a smell in the air of stale cigarette smoke and whisky, the sweet tang of their bodies.

Sarah groaned in her sleep, shifted, drew Jacob's head in close against her breasts. Her skin was damp. The sheets were tangled around his legs. Above the bed, the punkah hung motionless. A candle burned across the room, in the niche where Vishnu sat in garlands of star jasmine and lotus, amongst all the English flowers he had picked from his father's shade house.

I will give him to you, Sarah had said the night before, as she slipped into the bed beside him. *You are the peaceful light, Jacob, and that can be a fragile thing. But the Lord will keep you safe. He will look over you and preserve you, against all the powers of the dark. If you go to him, you know you'll go far beyond the world of shadows...*

Jacob hauled himself up on to the pillow and lay on his back, trying to stop his head from swimming. The cry came again from the Mall Road, almost like a dog howling, but then it slowly faded away towards the Walled City in the north. He coughed once, tried to contain it, felt it raging mightily inside him. God, it was too much. It was far, far too much, this *pressure...* He felt glazed in sweat, feverish.

There was a scratch of light across the room. Bobby had struck a match, revealing himself sitting naked in the chair by the shuttered window. He lit his cigarette and the tip cast its glow against his face.

'What time is it?' Jacob said.

'Late. Or early, depending on your perspective.'

'I should get home soon. My father...'

'Can you feel it, Jakey boy?' Bobby said. He peered through the slats of the shutter.

'What?'

'The heat. I sometimes think it's thicker in the night than it is during the day. There's no motion to disturb it, you see. It just lies there on the city like a sheet of lead, impenetrable.' He looked at the bed, his eyes skimming over his sister's slumped form beneath the sheets, the curve of her hip, an arm outflung. 'Do you remember when you saw your first dead body?'

'Yes.' Jacob sat up and fought against the rolling nausea that sat up with him. 'When my father first brought me round the mortuary. I couldn't believe…' He cleared his throat. 'I couldn't believe that was what he expected me to do with my life.'

'And yet it's what he did, isn't it? It's what I do. It's how he paid your way through school. It's how he brought you out here; it's how he can afford to return to England once or twice a year. There's money in the dead, don't forget that.' He drew on his cigarette, expelled the smoke in one long blue plume. 'The first body I ever saw was my own father's,' he said. 'You know, in many ways I think it was the happiest day of my life. To look down on a dead parent is quite the thing. You feel suddenly free in a way you never have before.'

From the bed, Jacob searched the shadows for his clothes. Self-conscious in a way he would never have been during the night, he wanted only to get dressed and go. Every time was like this, in the blear aftermath as the sun began to rise. And every time he said to himself, *What am I doing here? Who are these people?* He felt sick.

'Jacob,' Bobby said, his voice very low, 'I'm serious. You know I am. It's life or death for us, truly it is. We can't go on like this. That bloody German in the bar. He's not the only one, you've no idea… She's going to get herself killed one of these days.'

'I know,' Jacob said. He was almost pleading, as if he were the one begging for a favour. 'I know, and I'll ask him the moment I get back. My father. The very instant.'

'Five hundred pounds. That's all we need.'

'And you'll get it, Bobby, I swear. You and Sarah.'

'We're counting on you, my friend. My brother. We're counting on you.'

'San Francisco,' Jacob said. 'America. Just think of it, Bobby.'

'It's all I ever do.' He crushed his cigarette in the ashtray and sat back in the chair, his legs crossed. In the dim light Jacob could see the sheen of sweat against his skin. 'Now get some more sleep. Get some rest. You know what Sarah's like first thing in the morning...'

He stopped for a moment at the corner of the path that led up to the front door, half-blind, as though the sun had scorched his eyes away. The bungalow was a low block of shadow ahead of him, the windows diamond-bright. Threads of darkness swam across his sight. He tried to breathe but there was not enough air in the world to fill his lungs. At the peak of every breath there was only this tightening in his chest, a burning, and the dreadful sense that the next lungful of oxygen would be his last.

Jacob leaned against the gate post and gathered himself, spitting on the kerb, puffing, trying not to be sick. The heat was ferocious. He had no idea of the time. He only hoped his father was still at church.

Stepping into the shade was like having a glass of cold water dashed in his face. He listened to the silence of the bungalow, the faint murmur of the servants in the kitchen, the light and pulsing beat of the crickets in the garden. Quickly padding over the parquet floor, he slung his jacket over a chair and prised open the cabinet in the corner of the parlour. A brief struggle, a manly grip on his nausea, and then he tipped a hearty swig of brandy into his mouth and gulped it down.

'Saints alive!' he hissed. He tipped the bottle again. 'Lord preserve us!'

He closed the cabinet and listened to his heart thump and flutter. The pressure in his lungs slackened. The coolness of his bedroom beckoned, the closed shutters, a damp flannel across his eyes. Once again he cursed the stubbornness that kept his father from Simla or the hills when the summer fell. He had no social position, that was the problem. He was little better than a tradesman, someone who dealt only in the darkest material. There was no place for him in that world.

163

'Jacob.' His father's voice came from the garden. Jacob felt like weeping. The brandy was sour on his tongue. 'I would see you out here. Now, if you please.'

He was in the shade house, tending his plants. Jacob crossed the dazzling lawn, smoothing his hair down, already enraged but trying to compose himself. As if on cue, the brainfever bird began its maddening song, the high and frantic chirp ascending from the branches of the almond tree. It was like a nail being hammered into his skull. He rubbed his chest and opened the glass door to step into the shadows.

His father wore a green-stained apron. His sleeves were rolled up and he had on a pair of tough canvas gardening gloves. By his feet there was a stack of faded stems, a scattering of brown petals. Mr Beresford did not turn to face his son as he entered.

'Did you know that my greatest expense when I first started work in India was for flowers? Endless flowers, vases and vases of them, wreaths and bouquets. This was before I branched out into embalming, still not a widely practised technique. You needed flowers when the body was being viewed, to mask the smell.' Mr Beresford reached in amongst the roses and cut with his secateurs. 'I can't recall when I first wanted to grow the flowers I loved in my youth. English flowers, the ones you would find in an English garden. The heat is too much for them in the end though,' he said. 'They are not native to this place, alas, and yearn for more temperate climes. They fade and falter, and eventually pass away.'

'Then why do you bother?' Jacob said, bluntly. He leaned against the staging and ran his fingers through the moist earth. 'What's the point?'

'The point is to strive for what is beyond us,' his father said. His voice was mild; he had taken no offence. 'Always. To struggle, to achieve, to graft new life in the most inhospitable places.' He cut in again, snipped, dropped another dead flower to the floor. 'There are more sentimental reasons,' he admitted. 'A reminder of home. A little glimpse of where we came from, and where we will return.'

He put down the secateurs and faced his son. Jacob, still leaning against the bench top, palmed the sweat from his face and tried to stop his legs from trembling. He was desperate for water. The pain in his chest flared up and surged to the base of his throat. His head was light – and always, over everything, came the sharp, chiselling call of that fucking bird outside.

'I see now that this is a mistake though,' Mr Beresford went on. 'Some blooms are not fit for these conditions, and to keep them here is cruelty. It is a death sentence. They must be uprooted and returned whence they came, so they may grow properly.'

He pushed past Jacob and took off his gloves, which he laid on the shelf beside the door. Bars of light and shadow fell on him from the ceiling laths above.

'You mean me, I take it,' Jacob said. He coughed, as though underlining his point. 'You want to send me home. Back to England. I've failed your expectations, is that it? Whatever they were. It was always a mystery to me.'

'I want us both to go,' Mr Beresford said. 'Together. There is nothing here for us anymore.'

Jacob laughed, incredulous. He coughed again, spat slightly, rubbed his chin with the heel of his palm. The brainfever bird began another trill through its relentless motif.

'Nothing? Are you quite serious, Father? *Nothing*?' He waved his hand, taking in the garden, the bungalow, Lahore. The flowers in the shade house. 'What about... And your work, for God's sake? The business? How on earth would you run it from the other side of the world?'

Mr Beresford did not seem to hear him. He peered through the slats onto the baked sheet of the garden.

'I remember,' he said, 'for many years, I tried to secure the contract for the army cantonment at Mian Mir. That was in the golden age of cholera though, and if there was one thing you could rely on soldiers to do back then, it was to die regularly of disease. But, alas, it was not to be. The civilians who either through duty or circumstance couldn't escape from the plains in the hot season... *that* was where my fortune was eventually made. In Lahore, Bombay, Calcutta. But it's a thin fortune, my son, although I've invested it as wisely as I could. I have property now, outside Edinburgh, that interests me. It interests me very much. I would see it once more and introduce you to it. So, enough. It is time to go home, before it's too late.'

Jacob shook his head. Bobby and his five hundred pounds. San Francisco, America. A new start.

'I came here on your instruction,' Jacob said. 'I did what you asked, and I made no complaint. And now you expect me to leave behind everything I have here, everyone I know, my friends—'

'Your friends are idle bludgers, nothing more. Robert Dunstan is a leech and his sister is a whore, and despite Robert's undoubted skill at the work I set him, I regret more than I can say that I ever allowed you to come into contact with either of them. You disgrace yourself by associating with them, and you disgrace my name. But no matter. The business will soon be sold and you will have nothing to do with either of them again.'

Higher, screeching, hysterical – the bird called again and again from the almond tree, and in the ragged pause before the call resumed anew Jacob felt the pulse beat hotly in his throat. He turned and coughed into his fist, tears springing to his eyes.

'I won't do it,' he croaked, hunched over. 'I'm not bloody leaving. And if you speak of her like that, of Sarah, how dare you, I'll …'

'Sarah Dunstan is a whore,' his father said, with precision and without emotion. 'She is a half-caste whore rented out by her brother, who should be trading cloth and trinkets in the Anarkali Bazaar rather than pretending she has anything in common with decent people. And that's all there is to it.'

The fume of blood in his lungs. He coughed and retched, then looked up to see his father frowning down at him. Jacob, bent double, glanced into his splayed hands and saw the blood in his palms. Carried on the tide of that blood came a wave of fury. It crashed over him.

Teeth bared, feverish, the bird screaming from the tree – Jacob stared up at that face he loved and hated so much, its eyes black. Spluttering, hacking up a string of drool, he swung back his arm and dashed his fist into it.

Mr Beresford gave no cry. He spun around, hand reaching for the glazed door, his fist punching through it and the pane shattering around him. He fell to his knees and pitched forward, and Jacob saw a shard of the broken glass, like a jagged tooth, slide smoothly into his neck. The remaining glass fell to the ring of paving stones and smashed, a swatch of crystal. There was blood on the lawn, blood on the stone. His father, trying to roll off the broken frame, vomited a red sheet and then was still. Jacob stood above him, teeth still bared in some mad rictus, hissing for breath. Those slivers of glass, stained, seemed to catch all the light and contain it. Everything else was dark.

He looked to the almond tree but the brainfever bird had flown away. The garden was quiet.

To look down on a dead parent is quite the thing, Bobby had said. *You feel suddenly free in a way you never have before...*

PART THREE

PART THREE

From Jacob Beresford's journals, May 1918

She had bought the statue from a market trader in Calcutta. She said to anyone who would ask that she had a Spanish grandmother, and made no mention of the orphanage at Kidderpore where her father had dumped her when his dissipations overwhelmed him. That was often the fate of Anglo-Indian children, although she could pass better than most. It was Bobby who collected her when she came of age and who brought her back to Lahore. Their father improved for a while, made money from gambling or vice or from dealing native art, and then quietly passed away having cleared at least three-quarters of his debts.

Vishnu preserves, an oath frequently on Sarah's lips.

Her mixed blood ensured that the temple was forever closed to her though, and so she assembled her own version of the faith. She created rituals to form a scaffolding around her day, to give her life a kind of shape. For as long as the scaffolding stayed up, then so did she. Translations of the *Upanishads* or selections from the *Rig Veda* formed her prayers. With no teacher or temple to guide her, she took glimpses of religious spectacle on the streets of the city and reframed them in her own mind as acts of private devotion. She pondered nightly on the mysteries of a faith that was closed to her, and then her half-starved visions of the One would be brushed aside so she could ready herself for a Saturday evening in the smart bars and hotels along the Mall. It was a predominantly Muslim city, and without the gods of old India she could well have embraced the god of Abraham. It could have been Marcus Aurelius or Neoplatonism or Madame Blavatsky. It had to be something. When there is nothing, there must be something. The emptiness of the void is not a natural state. The dark must always be balanced with the light.

She stayed with me for days after my collapse, when the shadow in the garden seemed to lurk in all the hidden places, stalking the margins of the shade house, insinuating itself into the corners of my mind. There was no one else I could have talked to about it: only her. I sent everyone else away, the servants, the staff. I spent the stifling nights trying to sweat the fever from my blood, and Sarah was with me until I regained a kind of balance. She wiped cool flannels across my brow, held the bowls into which I spat the productions of my lungs. It was getting worse. I knew now that I would never really get better.

Sitting vigil, praying and burning incense, Sarah remained. When I was well enough to get up, she brought out the statue of Vishnu. Deep in the night we pushed the furniture back and rolled up the rugs, and surrounded by a ring of candles we sat cross-legged on the parquet floor as she taught me the prayers that would protect me. All my father's Arts and Crafts décor, the uninspired choices of a man whose taste was formed in the 1880s, seemed to vanish around us. We were two figures in a cave, huddled against the dark, hoping that the fire would keep us safe. Vishnu was that abiding flame, Sarah told me. There was no darkness that could quench him, no shadow he could not burn away. He is the one against whom no victory by the dark is possible.

In my ignorance I always substituted him for God, but Sarah told me no; he is only part of the eternal One. There is Brahma who creates, Shiva who destroys, and in between, bringing balance to both, there is Vishnu who preserves. All have their part to play in the cosmic order. All combine their aspects in the holy triple-crowned spirit of Brahman.

'Don't think there's only *bad* and *good*,' she said once, 'and that you can only be one or the other. *Tamas* must exist, or *Sattva* would have no power. There is bad and good and the state in between, that draws from and feeds both. You must not draw too much from one or too little from the other, that's all. Ask Bobby.' She winked at her brother. 'He's the expert at playing both sides against each other, after all.'

And then she laughed, and Bobby laughed, and I laughed to see them both, my friends. The three of us, the holy triple-crowned spirit, and only my father standing beyond us in the outer dark.

For Bobby all this was pure indulgence, although he was happy for her to please herself with whatever philosophy most appealed. I have often wondered if at the core of his friendship with me there was a very simple desire to find a safe harbour in which he could berth his sister. That's all. He could see the probable shape of her life, and it worried him. But he never looked far enough to see the probable shape of mine.

What would have happened to me in all the years that followed if I had never had the example of Sarah's faith to protect me? Vishnu and my circle of salt, the flame of the eternal light glinting behind my eyes. How long would I have survived with that shade dogging my steps if I'd had no means of keeping it at bay? Is it Vishnu that keeps me safe, or is it just my memory of Sarah? Her face, her eyes, her dark and oiled hair, the smell of her skin when I was in her arms; the love that at times was so strong it nearly broke my heart.

Perhaps as that love fades, that faith she had in me, then so too does my safety. That's why I reach for Esther now. When it is entirely gone, then my father's grim shadow will draw near at last.

Dracula, some of the nurses are pleased to call me. Esther admitted as much that night. A vampire, preying on virgins…

'But you are no virgin, are you?' I had murmured, as she lay there in my grasp. 'You're a married woman.' Brushing my lips across her stomach, inhaling the scent of her, pretending with every shred of my will and imagination that it was Sarah's body spread open beneath me. I wonder, when she looked back at me over her shoulder, deep in the heart of it, her face flushed and her hair damp against her temples, who did she see in turn? Who did she look on with those citrine eyes? What phantom rose to meet her from the deep?

I find my attention turning inward again. In the cold mornings, when the spray salts the window glass and the sea lashes the terrace, I fall into my father's delusions and fire off letters to whoever might have lived here before; temporary residents, the scions of a dead aristocracy.

I am the current owner of Gallondean Castle, I write. *I believe that you too once lived here, and might have been contacted by my father...*

I wonder at the reception these letters encounter. Do they go straight into the fire, or do they call up memories too fraught to be revisited? All I need is someone to write back, anyone, just to tell me that I'm wrong. There is no such thing as Hound Point. It is a name on the map, a scrap of land, a legend. Nothing more. Gallondean is just an old house, very old, long past the point where it should have been pulled down. There is no shade haunting my footsteps, because there is nothing beyond death. Nothing. Your father died, and he will not come back.

'Rutherford,' I call, and the old retainer comes cringing into the room as I thrust the letters at him. He posts them for me in the village and I wait restlessly for him to return. Sitting in the kitchen at the cracked wooden table, shivering in my coat, a mug of black tea in my hands, I listen to the tide. Mice creep and flicker across the flagstones. From places deep within the castle come dreadful moans, haggard screams that billow down the chimneys. Are they the work of tormented spirits, the ghosts of old denizens, or just the protesting joints of a place long battered by the sea? I would accept either explanation, the state that I am in. Hours pass, days, and I have no idea where they go.

When Rutherford returns, we take up our oil lamps and delve into Gallondean's secret places. The deeds of the house are our treasure map. Attics, shut for decades, are uneasily broached, revealing footprints in the inch-thick dust. Witch bottles crusted with iron nails and ancient urine are disinterred from bricked-up storerooms. Walls are tapped for hollow panels. Windows are daubed with whitewash and then ticked off from the grounds to see if one mysteriously unmarked pane might reveal itself. In the great hall, once a place of feasting, now just a wood-panelled cavern in which my footsteps fall dead, I listen to the sound of things rustling under the floorboards.

The first week of May has slipped by. All my days are like this now. In reel and rout I parse the old parchment, I stride and mutter and fret. I press a forceful hand to my burning breast and walk the pathways, the beaches, the lonely moonlit corridors. Every midnight I find myself standing in the cellars of Gallondean, the wick guttering in my oil lamp and the fever guttering in my lungs; listening, just listening for the spirit of the de Gaillons to guide me.

Thursday 9th May 1918

The spring days marched on, the grass greener than it had been in months. Through the window a veil of sunlight and fresh rain fell and made everything sparkle as if newly wrought. Esther eased herself from bed, placing her book on the stand beside yesterday's newspaper. Hazebrouck was still in Allied hands. The Germans were running out of steam, everyone said, their last great gamble down to a diminishing hand and the dice refusing to roll in their favour. And yet there had been a quarter of a million British casualties since March. A quarter of a million men in no more than six weeks. Men like this; like Prevost and Goodspeed, and Captain Moore with his one fierce eye. Men like Daniel McQuarrie, estranged from himself, in limbo.

And it was not just men who were prey to violence and disorder, not in the depths of these awful days. She looked at Alice Stewart's empty bed and a thread of ice ran through her.

Esther had just returned from a short walk the previous night when she heard the news. She had been thinking of Jacob Beresford. She could still feel his fingers inside her, opening her like the rabbit on the path, the whimper in her throat, his breath hot against her neck and his teeth on her breast. The moon was a flaring silver disc, and as she came back into the grounds of Roddinglaw there was uproar. Two policemen stood flanking the open door. There was a flash of torchlight amongst the trees. Patients milled on the grass, hands in their dressing-gown pockets, some smoking, others pacing back and forth. Esther hurried quickly over the grass. She thought at first all this was for her benefit, although she had surely not been out late enough for an alarm to have been raised. It must be a patient then, she thought. Someone has deserted.

Ida Lambert had met her in the hall. Major Lawson was standing by the nurses' station under the curve of the staircase, talking to an older man in a rumpled brown suit who was scribbling down notes in a pad.

'Esther, thank God,' Ida hissed. 'You could have been killed… they still haven't found him!'

'Who? Ida, what's been happening?'

'It's Alice,' she said, her voice barely above a whisper. Her lips were chapped and red, as if she had been biting them. She drew Esther away, towards the door of the eastern ward. All the pleasure of the performance was in her face. 'She's at the Infirmary now, in town. My God, Esther, I've never seen such a sight. It's a wonder she made it back, blood all over her!'

'But I just saw her this afternoon, I helped her with the dressings…'

'She was attacked,' Ida said, eyes wide. She rubbed at her cheek. 'Stabbed in the back on the path from Queensferry. I must have walked that path myself a hundred times – didn't I tell you I'd felt someone following me before? Everyone says it. And here's the bloody proof! And you know what else everyone's saying, of course?'

'What? Who?'

Her eyes shone. Esther couldn't decipher the look Ida gave her then. Clearly relishing the fact that she was the one to break the news, Ida leaned close, her red lips parting, and said, 'It was young Dracula. *You* know.' She gripped her arm until, suddenly furious, Esther pulled it away. 'Jacob Beresford. The Lord of Gallondean.'

She stood on the corner of the lawn now, clutching her notebook in the spring sunshine, her copy of *Aurora Leigh*. Wood pigeons waddled through the grass like old matrons in white bloomers. Robins flitted from the fir trees and perched on the bronze spear of the knight on his barded steed. Everywhere felt the sun and the clean wash of rain, the smell of the sea and the strong weight of all this comfortable silence. Some of the patients were watching the treeline on the other side of the lawn, scanning the belt of firs that screened Roddinglaw from the shore. There were others beating the bounds with cudgels and croquet mallets, convinced that the woods sloping up to Mons Hill concealed a predator. Esther had heard some of them muttering darkly about Gallondean and the young man who lived there; a sallow cast to him, they said, furtive, a deviant look. She would sweep past with her head down while they talked, as though they would see in her face some hint of Jacob's attention, a trace of loyalty or tenderness towards this sinister figure. Poor Alice Stewart, crashing through the brush, screaming, screaming...

Esther thought of the rabbit unravelled on the tree when she had passed that way with Jacob a fortnight ago All the women who worked here had similar tales to tell of the brutality of country ways: foxes hanged by the neck from fenceposts, moles nailed to vermin boards, the tattered aftermath of midnight predations... and the growing sense that there was someone out there in the woods, watching them, stalking them like prey, holding in check a murderous desire.

She could see Gallondean's crenellated tower half a mile away, an ashen crown risen in the woods. An old house waiting to become ruins, Jacob Beresford planted in the middle of it like a rotten seed, raging.

She felt crushed. She ran her fingers along the feathered edge of her book, the cut pages. Push all that away for now, she charged herself. Think of nothing. Think for the moment of anything but Alice Stewart, and Jacob, and the dead things smeared across the grass.

The morning, clear and warm, passed slowly away. Esther spent an hour in the shade of the horseman, sketching, noting, pulling words and phrases from one side of her mind to the other and hoping the passage of her pen alone would drag some sense or insight behind it. As the sun turned, curling towards midday, she put her notebook aside and read for a while from *Aurora Leigh*. She was into Book V, the poet recounting the failures of her later work, when she became aware of Daniel McQuarrie standing by the side of the plinth. His hair was neatly combed, his tunic buttoned, and yet for all that he still looked half-asleep. Gaunt and somehow absent, as if her mind had conjured up a memory of him, rather than her looking on the living man.

'Captain McQuarrie, how are you feeling? You had us worried the other week.'

'I'm sorry,' he said. He put his hands in his pockets. 'Major Lawson was very disappointed in me.'

'Like getting a telling-off from the headmaster, I expect.'

'Something like that. I think he has higher expectations for wounded men. He told me they had a Guards officer here once who smuggled in bottles of whisky and sold them at a profit.'

'The scandal of it.' Esther hesitated. 'He said you'd been home. Major Lawson, I mean. You'd been to the house where you used to live.'

'That's right.'

There was no urgency in him, no need to explain. He leaned against the plinth and looked down at the grass.

'I imagine that was quite difficult for you. It always is, going back to somewhere we once knew. I dream of Gibraltar sometimes, especially here.' She looked up at the sky, the washed-out blue. Streaks of cloud were now threading in from the east. 'It's nice today but the heat's nothing to the Rock in May.'

'It wasn't as hard as I thought it would be. In the end, I saw everything I needed to see. Sometimes just seeing it can be enough.'

'Well,' she began, and then thought, *Enough for what?*

'And please,' he said, as he sat down on the grass, 'you must call me Daniel.'

In a conspiratorial tone, Esther said, 'We're not really meant to use patients' Christian names. Bad for morale, or discipline, or what have you.'

'The army's always worried about morale or discipline or what have you,' he said, tolerantly amused. 'I think it spends more time fretting about that than anything else.'

'You make it sound like a sentient thing.'

'I wonder if it is. It's like a great slouching, jealous beast, sometimes. Confident one moment, and then gnawing itself with doubt the next.' He gazed up into the blue and closed his eyes. 'Sometimes it even pulls miracles out of the bag.'

'Miracles?'

McQuarrie crossed his legs and rested his elbows on his knees, his chin in his hands. He looked like a little boy hunkered down in the dirt. 'They're trying to break us in France,' he said quietly, 'but we're still hanging on, aren't we? Who would have thought? And then taking Jerusalem... Do you know, I was told that was the greatest prize of the war.'

He said this with an almost sad astonishment, that anyone could ever think such a thing. Esther cleared her throat. 'But you don't think so?'

He shook his head, shrugged. 'It's not for me to say. I've never seen it, after all.'

He was trembling, she saw, very slightly. With concern, she said, 'Are you sure you're alright? You do look terribly pale.'

'I'm fine.' He rubbed his chest. 'It's getting better. Slowly, but better. Rest, I think. Just rest...'

She set the book down on the grass. 'Well, rest or no rest, there's a curfew this evening, remember. We'll have you all locked up after seven.'

'Of course. I was sorry to hear about Miss Stewart, is she—'

Esther felt a coldness trickle through her stomach. Guilt? Or fear that he was going to mention Jacob, the Lord of Gallondean. *Dracula*.

'She's in the Royal Infirmary. I haven't been to visit her yet, but the Major says she's doing well. Physically. I think it's been more of a wound to her mind than anything, the sheer horror of it.'

McQuarrie said, 'Getting wounded is like that.'

'Of course, goodness, what – I'm sorry, Captain. Don't listen to me. I'm very distracted, I'm not myself.'

He nodded at the notebook. 'Too upset? Or too deep in your researches?'

Esther glanced down at the oilskin cover, the blunt nub of her pencil. The horseman loomed over it, casting his shadow.

'I was trying to…' She threw up her hands. She couldn't have said a word of this so easily to Jacob, never mind to Major Lawson, but it was somehow easier with McQuarrie. It was what she imagined talking to a priest must be like, unburdening yourself and expecting in return not just the judgement but the penance too. 'They're poems,' she said. 'I'm trying to write a poem. Something about the war.' She laid a palm against the marble plinth. 'And about this knight and—' She groaned and pressed her fingertips to her eyes. It was as well to speak what was on her mind as keep it silent, for all the good it would do. 'And about you, I suppose.'

'Me?'

He cupped his palms in his lap. For a moment, so pale and at peace, he was like a friar begging for alms.

'Not you specifically, you understand,' Esther told him in a rush. 'But Palestine, Jerusalem. A soldier in the desert, in the war.'

'I'm not sure I follow.'

She pressed the bronze again. 'I want to write a long poem. A great, dramatic monologue, a voice, a story… About a knight, this knight, going off to the Holy Land, a Crusader. And there would be another Crusader, a warrior striving in the same place but hundreds of years later, as if it was the same war, the same voice, the same mix of motives. Ideas of chivalry, and purpose, and…'

The words came tumbling out. She laughed and could feel the colour in her cheeks. It was so easy to be embarrassed by yourself. *Three Hail Marys, my child, and…* She didn't know what other penance a priest might set. Major Lawson would know, but she would never ask him.

'And about myself as well,' she admitted. 'My fears, my experience. It all sounds such a grand project, doesn't it?' she said. 'Ridiculous. I'm not in the least equipped to carry it out. What on earth do I know, apart from myself and who I am, and I barely know that. I can't find the right words, and now with everything that's happened here, it's…' She smoothed her palm against the horse's hoof. 'It's as if I doubt every mark I've ever put on paper.'

'*What he considers that he knows today/Come but tomorrow, he will find misknown.* You should think of your Browning,' McQuarrie said.

'"A Death in the Desert". Truth becomes a deadened thing and needs love to pierce the doubt. Isn't that it? Perhaps love will help you pierce the veil, Mrs Worrell.'

'Love, yes,' she said, but the very word made her feel morose. Jacob Beresford, Hound Point, the gunmetal sea. She flinched from love. What good had it ever brought her? 'There's always love, isn't there?'

'As for Palestine, I'm not sure I can help you. I was just one soldier and, truth to tell, my war ended strangely.'

'Strangely?'

'It's always a strange thing to be wounded. There's no other word.'

A cold breeze was coming in now. Esther looked off towards the shore, as though Jacob might be walking through the trees there, waiting for her.

'I'm glad Mr Browning could give you that at least,' she said. 'For all his obscurity.'

McQuarrie smiled shyly. She had the sense of a wave passing over a quiet sea, a ripple of wind in a still field of grass.

'I've lost count of the times I've read it now,' he told her; and then, quietly, 'Studied the lines to the point they've lost nearly all their sense...'

He ripped grass from the lawn and leaned back against the plinth, looking up at the knight as it towered above them.

'Do you think Christ really caused the blind to see?' he said. 'Did John truly bear witness to the Crucifixion? Or were all these miracles just the necessary tales? I wonder. The stories we need to lead us towards the truth, where the truth is a far stranger thing than could ever be imagined.'

Esther, taut and unsure, let the silence stretch a moment. 'I couldn't rightly guess. Who's to say?'

'The poem says a man must act in concert with his natural need for truth, and not expect truth always to strike him between the eyes. We can't all be as lucky as St Paul, can we? Illuminated on the road to Damascus, and suddenly just... *knowing*.' He reached up and touched the narrow, crooked paw of the knight's hunting hound. 'I've always liked this dog,' he said. 'I can't think why, being always more of a man for cats.'

'Where do you go at night, Daniel?' she asked him. Suddenly she had to know. It seemed important that he told her, although why and for what she couldn't say. Did he spend those lonely hours wandering through the trees, strolling the quiet bounds of Roddinglaw? Somehow she didn't think so. 'Do you go outside? Into the grounds?'

He looked embarrassed. 'I didn't think anyone had noticed.'

'Only me. And Alice, but she won't say. Not now.'

'There's a place in the house. One place where I feel safe,' he said, 'and where I can close my eyes. Sometimes I go there. It reminds me... When I was hurt, they took me to the monastery at Mar Saba. I remember Father Bakirtzis, one of the monks, the silver Christ on the chain around his neck. The monks would help the wounded drink, holding ladles of water to our mouths. I remember the pale ochre tiers of the monastery, the silence, the desert. The weight of the wound in my chest. I felt safe there. I wish I could have stayed, sometimes.'

'You don't think this is a safe place? Roddinglaw?' She was aware of how grave she sounded, as if they were both delving into things that were better left unsaid. But she had to know.

Daniel looked over at the house, so solid, so fine and well proportioned; the relic of a more confident age. 'No,' he said. There was a quiet and almost stern assurance in his voice. 'I don't think it is.'

Above them the knight sat with his spear aslant, the dog weaving nose down through the horse's legs. The mystery of that tale, Jacob's obsession with it, hung heavy in her mind for a moment, as though the breeze itself carried echoes of that ancient howl. A lost thing mourning its master, leashed by nothing but its love.

'Have you been along the coast?' she asked Daniel. 'Have you been by Hound Point?'

'Not for an age. Not since I was a boy. I rambled all this coast when I was young.'

'Someone,' she said, and then the same trusting courtesy that had let her talk about her poems made her name him. 'Mr Beresford, I mean, the young man who lives at Gallondean, he told me about it. A local legend, some old tale about this knight. A Crusader heading off to the Holy Land, leaving his hunting hound behind.'

Daniel stirred beside her. 'And the dog howling from the point when the knight was killed,' he said. 'I remember.'

Esther was jolted by relief. A tale only gained substance in the telling, after all. 'Then you've heard of it?'

'Dimly. Years ago. Perhaps my father told me of it.' He laughed, such a sudden sound that Esther nearly jumped. He unfolded himself from the grass in a great rush and took in the sight of the horseman anew. 'I'd completely forgotten. And here he's been in front of us all this time.'

'Hearing that story of the hound, the knight who killed his father...' She stood up beside him and laid her hand against the plinth. The cold bronze shone a rich mahogany above them. A fighting man, a warrior, looking for penance in the blood he could spill, even if it was his own. 'It is a dark place, isn't it? I think you're right. I don't know why I haven't seen it before.'

It wasn't the story, of course, so much as the man who had told it to her. She knew that, but there was a difference between what she felt she could tell Daniel McQuarrie and what it was sensible to do. Some things must be kept close after all.

'I keep thinking of that body buried on the shore by Gallondean. All those years underfoot, its bones huddled in the ground. Sometimes we forget that's where the dead are, don't we?' she said. 'France and Belgium, or Palestine and the Dardanelles, or Britain itself. Always beneath us, everywhere. Beneath us in the earth.'

'It's the same earth, Mrs Worrell,' McQuarrie said. 'Every bit.'

From Jacob Beresford's journals, May 1918

Another creature in the grounds, mangled, undone.

I found it where the path branches off towards the grounds of Roddinglaw, a stoat or some other mustelid, taut on a wire as it dangled from a branch. The eyes had been cut away and the guts slithered from the long and sinuous trunk. The hide was peeled back. Anyone could have walked into it as it hung over the path; the nurses, say, or one of the recovering patients. This is no farmer's vermin board, despite what I said to Esther on our walk. These are signs, portents. These dead creatures are whetstones to keep the shadow sharp.

The longer I spend in Gallondean, the more it feels as if the house itself is watching me, collaborating with my father's shade. Vishnu has not yielded yet. But then the night is so much larger than him, and the darkness is infinite.

Today Esther slipped away from Roddinglaw and spent the afternoon in my bed. We met at the gate, half-hidden by the ferns, all the cow parsley in the grounds surging up around us, coils of bramble against the walls like the barbed wire rolled up on the beach. She took my hands and we kissed, each kissing our memories.

'I haven't spoken to Alice yet,' she said. 'Miss Stewart. I'll visit her, I've duties at the Infirmary next week, and… Oh, Jacob, it's terrible. They can't possibly believe it's you.' She hesitated; not by much, but certainly by enough. 'Can they?'

Rumours abound. It was a deserter from the barracks at Craigiehall. It was a desperate German sailor, washed up on the coast from a stricken U-boat. It was some priapic local sodden with drink. And I'm a suspect myself, it seems.

It's true that the police have called, a rumpled little fellow reminding me of the academics who disinterred the skeleton on the shore. His questions were plain and to the point. Where was I? Had I heard anything? Who was I with? No one, I said. I am alone.

'They can't,' I told her now. 'It was not me.' It was *him*, I wanted to say. It was the spectre marking its territory, letting me know that it's here.

Later, sated with each other, I showed her all the documents I have collated, the scale and scope of my researches. In the library I laid out seventeenth-century accounts, commonplace books from the 1750s, manor rolls, lawyers' drafts. I showed her secondary sources about the Norman aristocracy in Scotland, the French knights heading north to take up gifted lands – *Gaillon* and Gallondean. The Third Crusade, the fighting along the coast from Acre, the last march on Jerusalem in 1192. I showed her what I knew about the secrets of this house, and the death of Robert de Gaillon.

'It had no hands, you see,' I told her. 'The skeleton on the shore. And I found some reference to Robert's hands, "the severed hands themselves", as if… But if the skeleton is Robert and the hands are missing, then where did they go? It was a common practice back then to take body parts on Crusade, like relics. The Black Douglas took Robert the Bruce's heart with him, sealed in a silver casket, when he sailed to Grenada to fight the Moors. I have this image of William de Gaillon taking those hands, his father's hands. They had wrought evil, it was said. Perhaps he took them to the only place where that evil could be expunged? If the hands were tainted, then possibly he believed they should be hidden far away in the Holy Land, in the desert, where they could no longer trouble the world…'

'And what trouble did they do? What evil?'

'I don't know,' I admitted. 'The accounts don't say, not in any detail. Dark rumours, hints, allusions. Robert was a hated man, it seems.

A blasphemous man, although what that really meant in those days who can say.'

She passed her fingers over the parchment, the splayed-open volumes, and once again I wondered if I had spoken too much. Wrapped in my gown, her black hair loose, her eyes as bright as sunflowers in the lamplight, I had never seen a woman so ravishing. She looked as pure and beautiful to me then as Eve in the Garden. To draw my hands down those soft flanks, to feel her fingertips pressing on my ribs like piano keys, to close my eyes between her breasts – I can think of nothing else that would so reliably keep the night at bay. But I cannot ask her to stay here. I won't risk it. She is too much like Sarah. She would not survive. When I feel her body beneath me, I see my father's seething face, sculpted from smoke and oil, watching me from the corner of the room.

'It's like the Old Yellow Book, isn't it?' she said, looking through the papers. Seeing me raise my eyebrows, she explained, 'Robert Browning. There was an account he found in a book market in Florence, an old criminal case in Rome from the seventeenth century. All murder and thwarted passion. Very dark, very Gothic. He used it as his source for *The Ring and the Book*.'

'Then this can be your source, Esther,' I said, with sudden inspiration. 'For your poems. Gallondean can be a host of stories for you, all these tales hidden in the ages. All these fragments, these voices. Crusading knights, robber barons, lords and ladies. It goes deeper, I think, than anyone knows.'

I will gift all this to her. On a whim, and without breathing a word of it, I decided then to give Gallondean and everything in it to Esther Worrell when I die. The Lord of Gallondean is always condemned, but perhaps a lady would break that miserable fate? A healer, someone who has never killed, someone without the hard residue of spilled blood on her hands. There would be, perhaps, only one firm instruction: burn it down. Dismantle it. Tear the old house from its foundations and scatter the stones, and then sell the land for as much as you can get. Do not stay here as I have stayed, sharpening your weapons while you wait for the hound to howl.

Later: I write this quickly before I return – at last my patience has been rewarded. The chamber has been found.

There is a hatch in the kitchen floor that opens onto a narrow stairwell. The steps lead down into a basement storeroom on the northern side of the house. I've long been aware of it. There are shelves in there covered with old tins and jars, rotting preserves, coiled rope, crumbling wooden crates. A door on the far side, no more than five feet high, leads through a short brick-lined passage to another storeroom, which as far as I can tell extends under the terrace at the front of the house. If you stand silently in that store-room and listen, you can hear the waves pounding on the stone somewhere far above you.

I have explored the corners of that cramped space on more than one occasion, drawn back to it by the sense that something has been concealed there. The lineaments of the room feel wrong, the distance from the other storeroom and the kitchens, the length of the passage that leads to it. It is at an angle to the main house, pointing I believe towards the east. On the wall by the entrance is a niche for a lamp, and on the far wall there is an old iron sconce that would hold a wooden torch. The floor underfoot is unfinished stone, rough and irregular. With my lamp held high, I have scoured the walls and floor looking for evidence, but nothing has presented itself. An odd little chamber, buried deep. A holdover from the castle's ancient days, perhaps a cell for its dungeons or a forgotten armoury. It took me longer than I would have liked to notice that the walls are not medieval, but of a fine, grey-stock Georgian brick.

The old chamber has been sealed.

It was Rutherford who first realised it. On a cool, clear day, the spring sun shining, he paced out the length of the terrace from the back door to the balustrade and then repeated the process in the passage underground.

'Ten paces short, sir,' he hissed, his eyes wide.

'Meaning?'

'The sky does not mirror the land beneath…'

I felt on the very cusp of understanding. 'Fetch the mattock,' I commanded. 'Fetch the hammer.'

When he brought both, we descended.

It is easy to lose your bearings from the storeroom to the passage, from the passage to the secondary chamber beyond, but Rutherford was as keen as an old badger burrowing through a familiar sett. He tapped his mattock to the brick wall while I held up the lamp. The smell of him was ripe in my nose.

'Here,' he said. 'Past this, if we were above, is the last six or seven yards of the terrace. Beyond that's the sea.'

I nodded and directed him to swing. The mattock bit, loud as gunfire in that enclosed space. I cracked in with the hammer and together we tore the bricks down. A stale, musty smell came out to meet us. It was black beyond the hole we had made. I stayed Rutherford and stepped inside, the lamp held up before me. The light swam and flickered.

It was a space perhaps twenty feet by ten. The air was moist and cold. The ceiling was an arm's length above, the walls constructed of irregular slabs of sandstone. There was a thick layer of dust and rubble underfoot, such that it made me think the original chamber must have been at least a foot deeper. Distant, and yet strangely near, was the furious, beating voice of the waves.

At the far end was a long slab of black stone, five feet from end to end, waist-high. Basalt, I thought, or some other igneous rock spewed from the bowels of the earth. In the lamplight it was flecked with shards of mineral. I stepped cautiously towards it. Of everything in Gallondean, it seemed the least fit. Someone had brought it here, I thought, long, long ago. Someone had placed it deliberately in this hewn place.

Now, as I write, I'm sure it's only my imagination that conjures up the stains of ancient blood on its surface. It was the dancing of the lamp flame, nothing more, the writhing of a fantasy. What I know for a fact is that a rune had been carved on the surface of the stone; a flared and precise symbol, folding in on itself, a thing of lines and curves, oddly mobile in the lamplight. It is a glyph from no form of belief or religion that I have ever encountered before.

I have found the chamber then, of that I have no doubt. Here, in the depths of Gallondean, is where Robert de Gaillon wrought his evil. And though I don't have even a shred of proof or a scrap of evidence, I know – *I know* – that this is where William de Gaillon killed his father too. A soldier of God, he struck Robert down and then departed on the one journey that could cleanse a soul entirely of sin. To the Holy Land. To Jerusalem, taking his father's hands with him.

Monday 13th May 1918

Esther bought a quarter of mint humbugs from the shop beside the station, but hadn't thought how she was going to share them with Corporal Prevost. He didn't allow any of the nurses or VADs to help him at dinner now. She had often seen him sitting silently in a corner of the hall while one of the other soldiers cut up his meat for him, directing it a forkful at a time and with a strange tenderness into his mouth. The nurses were too solicitous perhaps, less direct; and after all they were women. The men *knew*.

The train shunted and a great blur of smoke passed by the window. Prevost sat opposite her, upright, his face taut with that strained enthusiasm he must have thought put others at their ease, but which just made Esther feel jumpy and tense. With the inside of her wrist, she felt the bag of sweets in her jacket pocket. It was warm on the train, the spring sun belting into the carriage. All the humbugs would have congealed by now. She couldn't imagine prising one loose and offering it to him, popping it into his open mouth. If she couldn't do that then she certainly couldn't eat one herself. A waste of a penny, she thought, and that the quarter had cost as much as a penny in the first place was something of a slowly released shock. She looked out of the window at the passing fields and let her thoughts drift. Prevost's hands. Hands taken to Jerusalem. Jacob Beresford. He was all ribs and spine, as slight as a girl in her arms. No one had touched her since her husband.

Her body, dormant, woken by a spell to a fresh flood of pleasure, and the sharp edge of guilt.

It was not me, Jacob had said, and for a moment she had caught herself suspecting a lie. But it couldn't have been him. He would not do that.

'Fine day for it,' Prevost said, intruding on her thoughts. 'And you'll be seeing Miss Stewart will you, when we get there?'

'Yes,' Esther said. 'I hope to, if they're letting her see visitors.'

'Dreadful business.' His face was grim. 'A real shocker that it should happen here. And Miss Stewart such a cheerful young thing as well.'

'Let's hope it hasn't affected her too badly. And that they catch the man responsible.'

'The war, Mrs Worrell,' Prevost said. He shook his head and the strain deepened on his face. 'Gets everywhere. Into everything. The war, miss.'

After a moment the disarming grin broke out once more, so frequently deployed. Esther nodded and tried not to meet his eye.

'Might be I won't be seeing these environs much longer,' Prevost sighed as he glanced out of the window. 'Kelso, the Major says. Depends on the doctors at the Infirmary I suppose, but Edenhall down in the Borders is my best bet.'

'A very pretty part of the world from what I've heard,' Esther said, trying to encourage him.

'Might be the hospital's outgrown Kelso though. The Major reckons there's too many men now with...' He jerked up his empty cuffs. 'There's plans to move it up to Musselburgh, so maybe I won't be too far from what I've come to know.'

'You've enjoyed...' Esther started. There was no option but to continue. 'Roddinglaw has been a pleasant place to stay?'

Prevost barked out a laugh. 'You could call it so, Mrs Worrell. All that green. I've seen worse, believe you me!'

And he laughed again, almost a shriek. Esther blinked. She looked out of the window, raw fields replaced now by the brown backs of tenements, a film of smoke. She saw Prevost sitting in the corner of the dining hall, chewing his food; ferocious, wild, without mercy.

The knife in Alice's back had pierced any sense of safety the other women felt – nurses, volunteers, skivvies and kitchen staff. Everyone now had some disturbing tale to share, though they grew, Esther was sure, in the telling. One of the cooks in the canteen, a local girl, had come screaming back from the village in hysterics, her wicker basket bare of everything she had been sent to buy from the grocer. A man, she said, his face hidden, had been crouching in the flower beds on the long lawns that rolled down to the main road. He had showed her a blade, a lustful hatred in his eyes. The girl's mottled face, red with fright, was a portrait of terror. But when the orderlies had mobbed up to investigate they found only the elderly gardener, Mr Ferguson, lost in his weeding, and no more capable of lustful hatred than he was of getting to his feet unaided.

Esther felt there was something irrational, nearly medieval, about all this infectious fright. No matter that it had rational roots, in her darker moments she almost felt there was something willed about it; that the front was growing so much worse it needed a corresponding horror at home. The war, the devastation, the grief – it was all reaching out for them now. They were being smothered by it.

She bought flowers from a barrow outside the hospital, and while Corporal Prevost went off for his appointment, she searched the wards looking for Alice Stewart. There was a flutter of nerves in her stomach that she couldn't explain. It wasn't the thought of the wound, but who or what had inflicted it that frightened her. The spring grasses in the garden, the towering ferns, the breath of the sea as the evening began to fall, and the young man standing there before his ruined tower with that sullen pride in his face.

It was not me…

Perhaps that was why she was so nervous to see Alice now. It was the same reason she had found herself avoiding Ida Lambert as much as possible over the last two weeks. Jacob was written in her eyes. Even to say his name would be to reveal how close she had become to him.

Was she ashamed? She didn't think so, and yet just a few months earlier sleeping with anyone apart from her husband would have been utterly inconceivable. There was tenderness with Jacob though, sympathy, a sense of carefully judged recklessness. He had given her that at least. She wasn't sure what she had given him in her turn, but why torment herself over what she had done with another man? As Corporal Prevost said, the war got into everything now. She saw no reason why it shouldn't have got into the relations between men and women as much as anything else.

She held the flowers to her nose, breathing in their scent while she walked the corridors. The wards were full of wounded soldiers, but deeper into the tangled complex of the hospital she found rooms still reserved for civilian patients. She thought them strangely incongruous, as if no one during a war should suffer from anything other than gunshot wounds and shrapnel, but here there were old women and young women ranked up bed by bed, all of them looking at her as she passed with the wide and artless eyes of the sick. She paused to ask directions of a nurse and was pointed on her way, and after a few more turns found Alice in a long room on the eastern edge of the Infirmary. Esther passed quietly between the other patients, many of them dozing, others lost in the dull reveries of their ordinary illness.

Alice was lying near the half-open window, asleep. Esther could hear voices rising from the Meadows outside, the clip and rattle of horse carts on the street to the north. She put the flowers on the table by the bedside and cleared her throat, but then she imagined what Alice would see when she woke up. She would read the truth in Esther's eyes. She would see that something had changed, and then Alice would tell Esther what had happened. The dusky path from South Queensferry, the afternoon drawing in, a rough-palmed hand over her face and a knife in her back before twisting, twisting to see the face of the man who was trying to kill her.

It wasn't him. It couldn't have been. There was no part of Jacob that could have done that. She just couldn't stand to hear Alice say it either way.

The younger woman lay there, troubled in her sleep. Her skin was bloodless, her lips almost blue. Esther sat down in the chair by the side of the bed and watched her. It was too much to lay on someone this young, a girl who had expected nothing from her life but a broad and undistinguished happiness. First Georgie, now this.

Esther tried to imagine what the rest of her life would be like, whether there was enough in Alice to shrug off these weeks and let them drift out of sight behind her, or if every one of her days from now on was going to be marked by what had happened. And then expand that question to everyone in this building, everyone through-out the city, the country, the continent beyond. What was going to become of them in all the days and years to follow?

She sat there, silently, thinking. It was quiet and warm in the ward, the only sound the gentle hushing of the other women's voices, and before long Esther found her eyes beginning to close. She roused herself.

'Alice?' she whispered. She looked over her shoulder but no one had heard. 'Alice, I'm sorry this happened to you. I'm sorry.' She leaned over and kissed her forehead. 'I don't know what I'm doing. Truly I don't. And I must be ashamed of him or I would have told you sooner.'

She sat back in the chair. After a moment she leaned forward again and took Alice's hand, lying there cold against the counterpane. The girl didn't wake, although a tremor passed across her face.

'Love will pierce the doubt...' she murmured. 'I don't love him though. Or I don't think I do. He was like a memory to me, for a while. I feel... pity, I think. Pity for myself, which is the worst kind. And pity for him as well. You've never seen a more haunted man, Alice. He's wounded too, in his way. I don't think he'll ever recover. It's such a dark place, where he lives. I hate it. Gallondean. No one could possibly get well between those walls.'

Her words faded. The hour passed. Corporal Prevost would soon be finished and ready to go back to Roddinglaw, the assessment complete. Kelso or Roehampton, or Musselburgh if the hospital for limbless servicemen moved north. Esther thought wearily of the short train journey back to the village, the hot carriage, the week stretching ahead of her. Then she thought of Jacob and was pierced again with that pity, that strange thrill. She let go of Alice's hand and left the quarter of mint humbugs by the bedside.

They walked back through the streets, Prevost as ever slightly hunched and trailing at her side like an attendant or an officer's batman.

'But it went well though?' she said, turning her head. 'The fittings, the assessment?'

'As well as can be expected, Mrs Worrell.' He grinned. 'Which isn't exactly saying much now, is it!'

Despite his habitual cheer, Prevost seemed more subdued than usual since they had left the Infirmary. He was trying a new innovation of thrusting his wrists down into the outer pockets of his blue jacket to hide the missing hands, and he walked with his elbows stuck out, slightly flared, so that he kept jabbing people as they passed. A string of complaints followed them both down the street.

'And did they give you any idea if you'll be transferred soon or...?'

'No idea, Mrs Worrell. None at all. But let me tell you, that's not unusual in the army, to say the least of it. Pardon my language, but I've always said: if you want something properly cocked up, you have to get the army to do it!'

He winked, and Esther showed him her easy and encouraging smile. Prevost shoved his wrists deeper into his pockets. There must be people writing poems about this, she thought. About dead men, men with their limbs blown off, men blinded and maimed. Whoever's writing them though, I know it can't be me. I wouldn't know where to begin. She thought of Daniel McQuarrie, slight as a spectre, floating through the halls of Roddinglaw. The deserts and the hills of Palestine were still in his eyes, but not everyone lends themselves so well to poetry. Perhaps it's the poetry that needs to change then? Find new forms to reflect this overwhelming pity. She ran her mind over her clotted notes, the density of all that Victorian allusion. It was wrong.

Love will pierce the veil... Love, an impulse towards an object, a person. Flashes of an image, a feeling. There is no narrative to it at all. You cannot compass in words what you do not love.

On the train Prevost sat opposite her and stared out of the window, quieter than she had ever known him. There was no one else in their compartment and he had folded his empty cuffs in his lap. Esther had wanted to suggest a cup of tea at the station – she had brought a straw with her to help him drink – but knew without asking that Prevost would have refused. He would have done it with a joke and a smile, but she had no idea what such things were costing him. She tried not to think of the sculpture she had seen him making in the art room. What would he have felt seeing the clay in front of him, resolute and refusing to conform? The sculpture had almost looked like an angel, a tall figure with outspread wings, mangled by his truncated hands. At the very beginning of the war, when the army fell back from Mons, they said an angel had appeared and unsheathed its flaming sword above the soldiers. Saved by its grace, saved to fight again.

The tenements slid away. The greasy verges stained with soot unrolled after a few minutes to the brown fields, the flat green of the distant farms. The smell of the sea was in the air already. She had missed it. She would never be entirely free of the sea now.

'Your husband, Mrs Worrell?' Prevost said. Esther was startled out of her daydreams.

'Yes?'

'In the service? Or…?'

'He died,' she said. 'At the very start. The navy.'

'That early, eh?' Prevost nodded, as though confirming a suspicion. 'I'd heard, some of the lads, they'd said you were a widow. And a Jew, is that it?'

Her eyes wide and her heart skipping, Esther said, 'What? No.'

By now though she wanted to say yes. Throw it back in Peter's face, let them all be confirmed in their narrow prejudice. Sister in the wards, even Alice. *You people.* What people? But prejudice yearns for the satisfaction of affront, and she would not give it.

'No,' she said again. 'Where does that come from?'

Prevost nodded sagely. 'Miss Lambert suggested as much. Always talking, that one. And I thought you might have been, just on account of the colouring. Very dark, you are. Dark hair, olive skin. And the eyes. Like a cat's eyes, Mrs Worrell. My old dad, he was down on the Jews. Always banging on about it. A load of rubbish, I always thought. It's not the Jews that keep us down, it's the bloody toffs, I said to him!' He winked again. 'Pardoning the language.'

'That's quite alright.'

'Strange, isn't it?' Prevost mused. 'I've met all sorts since becoming a soldier. And there wasn't one of them was what I expected. Even the toffs. I reckon that's a good thing,' he said. 'Perhaps that's the only good thing that's come out of all this, don't you think?'

He wanted a reply, a confirmation of this one lesson the war had taught him. She found that she agreed. 'Perhaps it is.'

'I'm sorry to hear about your husband. But you're young,' he said, very seriously. 'You'll find it again, I'm sure. Love.'

'Are you married yourself, Corporal?'

'I am. And with a little girl. They were going to come up and visit, but it's difficult. It's very difficult...'

He drifted away then, chewing idly at a scrap of dead skin on his bottom lip. The train shunted and staggered, and Esther knew they were near the village now.

'I was a compositor,' he said quietly. 'Typeface on the printing press. Words. Skilled job, that. And you need two hands for it, to say the least.'

'Corporal...'

'Kelso, I think,' he said sharply. 'The countryside. Always did like it. I reckon I'll stay. When this is over, Mrs Worrell, you mark my words, we'll all of us be shut away out of sight. Missing arms, missing legs, missing half a face. Shut away where no one can see us and be reminded of what it all cost. When you know what it cost, you see, then there's only one question worth asking. Was it worth it?'

'I don't know,' Esther said. 'Truly. I don't.'

Prevost only smiled.

They alighted in a gout of smoke. The village was huddled beyond the verge, a collection of slate roofs on the other side of the tracks. They crossed the bridge onto the far platform. Coming towards them, hissing as it picked up speed, was the express from Queensferry heading on to Edinburgh, drawing a long trail of carriages packed with sailors from the naval yards. The whistle blew, sharp and shrill.

Passengers stepped back from the edge. A porter waved a red flag. The brute engine bore down, blunt-nosed, black.

Corporal Prevost nudged her with his elbow. His wrists were back in his jacket pockets. He winked at her – and then Esther watched him step lightly off the platform and fall onto the tracks as the engine barrelled onwards, wreathed in steam.

From Jacob Beresford's journals, May 1918

Another visit from the policeman who came before; querying, disputing, slyly testing my alibis. He is younger than he seems. He has the dribble of a thin moustache on his lip, a worn collar, a pasty, putty-pale face. I wonder if he feels the immense relief of being in a reserved occupation, and therefore free from the army's grasp. Plodding Edinburgh streets must be infinitely preferable to plodding through Flanders mud.

'How you must chafe to get at the Hun,' I said. He gave me an askance look in which I read all sorts of suspicions.

'You say you live here alone, Mr Beresford. No servants? No family?'

'No,' I told him. I am no aristocrat, but I hoped the peremptory manner of one who owned such a strange and antique property would intimidate him. 'My factor, Mr Rutherford, is often around, but there are no servants. The war,' I said, as if that explained it all.

'And are you often to be seen in the grounds?' he said. 'Or do you keep more to yourself, would you say?'

Questions, questions, all saying in so many words: *Why are you not in uniform?*

'I take the air frequently, it's true. My lungs,' I said. 'The sea air eases them.'

The detective nodded. The grey disc of his dissembling face revealed nothing. Down went the nub of his pencil to the page of his notebook.

Miss Stewart has recovered enough to talk, it seems, but only reticently. She speaks of some dark and undistinguishable figure rising from the undergrowth, half-seen. The wildfire rumour of a stranded German sailor has alarmed everyone, from Grangemouth to Leith. Again, the policeman asks, what was I doing that evening, when poor Miss Stewart was attacked? I was here, at home in Gallondean. And was anyone with me, anyone who could confirm this? Alas, no. I was all alone.

Once more the pencil seeks the page. The facts stack up, the conditions are noted. He looks with mild professional interest at the odd foundations of Gallondean, the dark corridors, the smell of decay. It is getting worse, every bit of it. Wrenching sounds in the night, things falling apart, stones clattering from buttress and tower. And here I am, with no one to account for me, and no means of itemising my days.

Under normal circumstances I would rely on Rutherford to provide an alibi, but since we uncovered the chamber beneath the terrace he is nowhere to be found. I haven't seen him for days. I rely on the boy from the village to send my letters now, and to bring what few supplies I need. I made what explanations I could to the detective and mollified, for the moment, he drifted away. Back to Edinburgh, back to his office and his files, his deep suspicions. If they cared to look, they would find out about my father's accident, my seemingly precipitate flight into the web of the TB sanatoria. The mind of the policeman starts from a position of assumed guilt, surely, and only draws in the facts to establish innocence. We are in a police age, in these days of war.

But I *am* innocent, I want to say. Of this at least. And I am doing what penance I can.

Some evenings I spend in the uncovered chamber, kneeling before the slab of dark stone, running my fingers over the symbol in its side. It is freezing in there. The sea clamours far above me, hollow and dim. My fingertips slide over the carved lines, the curves and edges, an ideogram I can't read, a glyph I can't decipher. And yet, it doesn't feel evil as the rest of that chamber feels evil. Are those the desperate marks of fingernails I see, clawing at the stone? Is that rusty stain the remains of a stanchion that once kept iron manacles in place? Were there meat hooks hanging from the ceiling, and were skinning knives and eviscerating blades tossed bloodily to the ground when the butcher's work was done? The mind boggles. What happened here? What would survive of it after so many centuries? No mortal traces, surely, but there is a worn-out, ragged scum of misery still lingering in this place. I'm certain that this symbol on the stone was put there to keep this misery at bay. I'm sure of it. It feels like a warding mark, a warning, a way of stamping something out.

I thought of telling Lawson about all this, but I think I've tried his patience enough these last few weeks. The man seems to be at the end of his tether. His work consumes him. One recovering soldier threw himself before an oncoming train the other day, from what I've heard. The village boy was more than pleased to give me the details. I can't think of a greater blow for someone dedicated to healing those men than for one of them to decide the work wasn't worth the candle.

Everywhere there is this sense of people marshalling their exhausted reserves now. There is a feeling not just that the war is dragging on, but that it clearly will never end. Hundreds of thousands of young men turn eighteen every year. The age cap for conscription creeps higher – they'll be pressing men in their sixties into this before long. Industries will be utterly depleted. Shells and bullets will no longer be made, and instead soldiers at the front will cut each other down with sword and axe and spear, as our forefathers did so long ago. They will beat each other to death with bloody rocks. Why not? Why not just keep going until there are none of us left?

'Yours is an illness that can encourage delusions,' Lawson told me. 'Excitability, feverishness, and so on. It's very common. Have you, perhaps, experienced any delusions?'

I could only laugh. What is all this that surrounds me but an endless delusion? This life, this death.

What an awful spring it has been. What a terrible time.

You'll hear it before the end. The howling. But you shouldn't be afraid.

'Why do you make them, Dan?' Francis Goodspeed asks him, nodding at the jar in his hands. 'What are they for?'

They're sitting in the common room, staring through the bay window onto the grounds. Rain fades in and out. Clouds stream back and forth, dragging bands of shadow across the land. There's a smell in the air of stale cigarette smoke and pipe tobacco.

'It's hard to say,' Daniel tells him. He runs his fingers over the roughened clay. This one is better than the rest, more precise, sculpted with more confidence. He's had enough practice now to get it right. There are six altogether, most of them no taller than eight inches. This last one is wider-bellied, near a foot in height. Six is all he needs. 'Sometimes the hands make what the mind doesn't really comprehend,' he says. 'But still the hands have to make it.'

Goodspeed understands. If anyone does it's this gangling young man with the stiff arm and the bony face always tight with pain. He only opens up when he's with Daniel. Tentative and hesitant with everyone else, unable to meet the eye, but with Daniel he's almost loquacious.

Somewhere back there, in the past, Daniel has seen the jars. He knows this, but he doesn't tell Goodspeed. He's filled them now with earth from the ancient grave on the foreshore by Gallondean. *It's the same earth, every bit.* He has the nagging suspicion that this is of immense importance.

Francis Goodspeed cradles a lump of clay as long as his forearm in his lap, a hooked cylinder that almost looks like a ship's anchor. A flange or buttress projects from the body on either side. The top looks bitten, as though gnawed by someone's teeth.

'Did you hear about Prevost?' he says. He holds up the clay and Daniel realises that it's Corporal Prevost's angel; an abortion, deformed, a parody of grace pummelled by his weeping wrists. 'That narrow platform in the village. An accident, they're saying. That's the official verdict anyway. Did you know him?'

'Only by sight. I don't think I'd ever spoken to him.'

'I haven't much myself. Hadn't. There was *Peter Pan*, but I think he was only in that at Moore's insistence. I must say, I thought it was rather cruel, on his elbows and knees and all that. He seemed to enjoy it though. Prevost. It was like he was saying, "Well, here it is then." Do you know what I mean? It was right there in front of you, the injury, and there was nothing else to say. I suppose that's what acting is, in the end. Licence not to be yourself when you step onto the stage. Just pretend that it's not happening and then in some odd way I suppose it isn't. That's command in a nutshell.'

'It must have been difficult for him.'

'It must have been hell,' the other man agrees. 'Day to day. That was the biggest fear with my men.' He sounds almost shy as he admits this. 'Not death, being killed, but being maimed.' He grips his hands together and the words when they come almost stifle him. 'When I was wounded, I thought, I thought, when I lay there, I… There was an arm, a man's arm, blown off and lying there in the mud in front of me. It was mine, do you see? My arm, lying there. It wasn't, clearly, but just for that moment, that bare minute, it was. And the awfulness of that.'

'I'm sorry.'

Goodspeed stills his hands between his knees. Daniel looks at them, the way they shake.

'Even now, months later, I often wonder whose it was. Sounds silly, but sometimes I think it really *was* my arm, and what I have here is just something I've imagined to take its place. I've dreamed a new one, and here it is. What becomes of them, I wonder? Those pieces of ourselves that we lose.'

'I don't know,' Daniel says. He draws his own hand down the side of the jar. 'But the pieces aren't lost. They are taken.'

'It was the wrong wristwatch though, do you see?' Francis Goodspeed tells him, urgently, not heeding. 'I didn't recognise the wristwatch. That's how I knew it wasn't mine.'

Prevost's death was suicide, Daniel knows. The platform at the village isn't that narrow. Prevost would have thought of the burden he would place on others, and when the mind turns in that direction there are few other solutions to be found. It's a kind of love, for those left behind. He did it for love. But no one is a burden on those who love him. Love pierces the doubt.

Daniel had seen Esther Worrell the day after the accident, distraught as she went through the motions of her work in Roddinglaw. Her face was as drawn as if she'd spent a week under bombardment. The other nurse being stabbed in the forest, and now this. He holds the jar in his lap and wonders if she has enough material for her poem now. Palestine, the Holy Land. A knight at war, a warrior on Crusade. Is that how she sees him? He cannot think of himself as a warrior. Not anymore.

Goodspeed, with a pained sigh, levers himself up from the chair.

'Medical board soon,' he says. 'Did I tell you?'

'Do you think they'll send you back?'

'They will.' With an almost forgiving smile, he says, 'Back to Belgium. Back to France. We need everyone we can get.' He touches Daniel's arm briefly. 'I don't mind.'

Daniel nods at Goodspeed's shoulder. 'But it still hurts?'

'Oh, yes,' he says cheerfully. 'Like absolute hell. Don't worry though – I won't do what Prevost did.'

'The accident?'

'There's still duty, on top of everything else. That's all that's left really, in the end. Just pretend it doesn't hurt and then – well, there you go.'

He places the angel on the mantelpiece above the empty grate. In the daylight swimming through the window it looks utterly grotesque.

'They try to soothe our minds as much as mend our bodies here, don't they?' Goodspeed says, with a confidential glance. It's as though he's deciphered a puzzle that's occupied him for months. 'All this culture – amateur dramatics, cinema shows, painting and sculpture. I'd heard that Captain Magallenes wanted to start a literary magazine, poetry and the like. Culture as opposed to war. No one seems willing to admit that war is just another type of culture. Humans do it, give it meaning, organise it, conduct it with every sinew of their strength. All the best minds are geared towards its improvement. Animals don't wage war, do they? No point blaming God or the devil. It's just us. And we're very good at it by now.'

He pats the angel's lumpen head, the crescents of tooth marks clearly visible.

'I had thought I would take it with me when I go. The Angel of Mons and all that. But now I think I'll leave it here instead. Let it spread its wings over everyone who remains. I think that's what Prevost would have wanted.'

FROM JACOB BERESFORD'S JOURNALS, MAY 1918

My efforts have been rewarded and the stream of letters I dispatched from Gallondean have finally borne fruit. I have received a reply. I include it here in full:

Mrs Emeline Fernsby
23 Castlebar Road, Ealing
Middlesex
13th May 1918

Dear Mr Beresford,

Thank you for your letter. I must confess, it took me longer than I would have liked to reply to you. Your enquiry came as a surprise; I have tried not to think about Gallondean for many years. It has been thirty years, in fact, since my father moved us there. The memories are very painful, and in replying to you I was worried that I would dredge up moments that should be long forgotten. But even the most painful memories ought to be safely confronted, I feel, lest they grow in our minds and in the darkness come to shut out all the good.

You ask if I have any information about Gallondean, any documents or accounts, and I must disappoint you on that score. All I have is what I was told and what I saw. You also ask if there is anything I remember about the house that could 'help you understand it better', and although you leave this request vague, I feel I know exactly what you mean in the asking of it. I too would have liked to have understood Gallondean more when I lived there. I am not sure if my memories can serve you in this way, but for what it's worth I present them all the same.

I moved there with my father when I was fifteen years old. He was a prosperous man who had made his fortune in the railways, and like many self-made men of that period he felt his wealth deserved a grander setting. He had always been taken by the Scottish Baronial style of architecture, and I believe if the owner of Roddinglaw had been willing to sell his seat then my father would have bought it from him. Instead, half a mile further along the coast, he found Gallondean. It was vastly older, and in many ways a grander place than Roddinglaw. Antiquity has a value all its own, after all.

I always hated it. As I'm sure you know, and despite my father's attempts to renovate and repair it, Gallondean is a dank and dreary house. The cold gets into the bones there, and the only view is the grey salt sea and the brown slopes of Fife on the other side of the firth. It was more than just the discomfort of a primitive place that turned me against it though. Some places retain memories, I'm quite sure. I don't believe for a moment in ghosts or spirits, but where terrible things have occurred, the stones seem to suck the misery into them and breathe it out over the long years that follow. Terrible things happened in Gallondean, so the legends say. Or so said the legends I was told. I remember never being at my ease there. Sleep was difficult. The house seemed to tamp down the appetite, and all the natural joy and exuberance of a grow-ing child was crushed by the weight of that ancient stone. I became more morose and withdrawn the longer we lived there. It wasn't simple unhappiness, but a sense of being smothered – by the darkness in the corridors, by the long and awful history of that place.

If it was bad for me, it was worse for my father. I think this is why I have replied to you, when my first instinct was to throw your letter away unanswered. You describe your own father as becoming inter-ested in the history of the house, an interest you have taken up yourself, but I can read between the lines quite clearly. My father also became interested in Gallondean's history, but it was an interest that devel-oped all too quickly into obsession. He dug and rummaged amongst the records of the dead, trying to piece together its earliest days. He became convinced that Roddinglaw was keeping information from him, that it was some obscure revenge for my father's successful purchase of the house. There were ugly scenes, made worse when Roddinglaw commissioned the statue of the Crusader knight on his lawns, which you must have noticed. That was seen by my father as a provocation too far, a taunt, although I'm sure it was nothing of the kind. All I know is that my father accused him of straight theft, of ransacking Gallondean before we could take possession of it and stealing away important documents. I have no doubt that this was nonsense. Lord Roddinglaw was an honest man, but he knew what Gallondean was. He knew the history of what had been done there, what blood was mixed with its foundation stones. I don't have the full details myself – indeed, I doubt anyone does, after all these centuries – but Robert de Gaillon, who inherited Gallondean from his father, was a monster of a man, so the legends claim. A Gilles de Rais figure, a beast who preyed on the folk whose liege lord he was. Women would go missing from the surrounding lands. Children would disappear, never to be seen again. There were fearsome rumours, dark tales of unchristian acts. Talk of blood-pacts and devil worship; that he had a demon bound to his service. I leave you to decide on the veracity of the claims – they were made after all in a more credulous age – but I am certain that Robert de Gaillon was a cruel and unjust master. These were men, remember, not too far removed from their Viking past; Norman lords who a handful of generations earlier would have hanged men as sacrifices to their pagan gods. When such cruelty becomes habitual and the very source of a line's power, then why shouldn't the echoes of that terror remain in the places they build around them?

I said it was worse for my father. I was never sure exactly what he expected from Gallondean, but looking back on it now, I think he wanted nothing more than respect. As the owner of a great house, he perhaps thought he should be treated as a great lord in turn, but such status always eluded him. He was a man who had made his fortune through business after all. The enmity with Roddinglaw had left him an isolated figure locally, and he had few friends willing to make the journey north to visit. He became as grim and lonely as I was myself, although it was strange that in our loneliness we never took solace in each other's company, as father and daughter should. The house got into his mind, I think. Robert de Gaillon got into his mind.

He became more and more withdrawn. He wouldn't eat, and all he drank was the wine he had imported at great expense for his cellars, wine that he had always assumed would grace the table at the grand entertainments he would throw in Gallondean. There were no such entertainments though, no guests. He stayed in his library or in his room. He became a haggard, unshaven figure haunting the corridors, muttering to himself, a miser who refused to spend any more money on the upkeep of his grim castle. He frightened me, I admit. He began to say that he had made all his money out of murder, that the men who had died building his railways had died because of him. He was enriched by the blood of those men, he said, as much as if he had cut them down himself.

This went on for months, for years. I didn't know what to do, or how to escape, and you must understand that above all I loved my father. But his manias wouldn't leave him alone, his maddened obsession both with the history of Gallondean and with the blood that he felt was on his hands. Sometimes I would wake in the night and find him sitting at the end of my bed in the darkness, sobbing quietly, an empty bottle on the floor at his feet. He would show me those hands and ask if I could see the blood dripping from his fingers, but of course I never could. He was a good man.

It came to a head one night, deep in the summer. You will know by now of the legend of Hound Point, I'm sure. My father certainly knew of it. And I'm also sure that it was no more than the wind that night, the high summer breeze blowing through the gaps in the stones, but when I heard it, I knew exactly what my father would think it was: the haunting sound that seemed to drift along the coast, a fell cry like some great beast mournfully howling its grief. My father called out from somewhere deep in the house. Taking up a lamp, I scurried through the corridors looking for him, fearing the worst. All that summer he had been drowning in his delusions, and now it was as though they had all come true.

After long minutes of searching, I found him in the wine cellar. He was kneeling on the roughened stone, his back to the stairs I descended. When he turned to me I saw, for the first time in many months, something like peace in his eyes. He smiled and showed me what he had done. He had cut off one of his hands with a knife he had taken from the kitchens, and was only sorry that he was unable to cut off the other, having no remaining way to grip the blade. 'Would you do it?' he said to me. 'They are covered in blood, you see. And they have done evil.'

There is little more to record. After he died, I inherited Gallondean. I would have sold it to Lord Roddinglaw, who I suspect wanted to pull it down, but he had also passed away by then and his widow was not interested. For many years I couldn't bear even to think of it. My father is buried in London, but Gallondean remains his grave, as far as I am concerned. I moved away, trying to push the events of that summer from my mind. Eventually I sold the property to a trust that had some vague intention of renovating it once more, and I presume they sold it to your father when the costs became too much for them. I console myself that it cannot possibly last much longer, although it is true that they built things to last back then. These were the men who planted castles in every corner of these isles, and built the abbeys at Caen, and Rouen Cathedral, and Mont Saint-Michel.

I have written far more than I thought I would and told you something I have never told anyone else. That's what happens when you open the floodgates to old memories, especially the ones best left forgotten. All the detail rushes in to fill the gap. I will not reply if you write back. I have said what I needed to say. I felt that I owed it to you though, as the new heir. All I would say now is that you should leave that place, Mr Beresford. Leave Gallondean as soon as you can, and, if you can bear to, then pull it down. It is not that the stones are too strong for anyone to master, but that they are too weak. It is too old a place, and old things long past their time grow malicious. They seed malice in us, as they seeded a strange malice in my father.

Yours sincerely,

Emeline Fernsby

Friday 17th May 1918

Night, the scent of dust and paper in the air, the smell of libraries, old stone and altars. Esther sat nodding in a cone of light behind the desk of the nurses' station. The wings of Roddinglaw felt like the flanks of some great ship breasting an ocean, the grand staircase curling above her like the interior of a smokestack. She nestled in the prow as it cut through the water. The breeze was mottling a calm sea out there, but if she strained she could hear the sighing of the waves beyond the lawns, the crackle of the surf against the shore. Even now, in quiet moments like this, she thought of Peter. When night descended and there was nothing else to snag her attention, her mind often drifted away over the deep. She wondered if he had thought of her in those last moments – flailing, screaming, half-burned, afraid, however he had died. Did his mind reach back to her, or had it all been blacked out by the approaching void? There is, after all, no greater shadow on the mind or shackle on the senses than fear.

She stood up from the desk and wiped her eyes, surprised as ever to find that the tears came so easily. But then she did not hate him. She never really had.

The door to the common room was ajar and she crossed the hall to close it. Pausing a moment, shielded by the bulge of the staircase as it curved up towards the first floor, she heard an oiled click. A sliver of cool air, the flit of a white spectral shape threading through the shadows on the other side of the hall. Esther snatched a breath and clutched herself in alarm. Then, her eyes wide, staring, she realised that this was one of the patients emerging from the long gallery in the eastern wing. He was barefoot, hunched, a filled pillowcase slung like a sack over his shoulder, his face a white circle smudged against the dark.

She almost called out, but when she saw that it was Daniel McQuarrie she said nothing.

He crept past the nurses' station, feet silent on the tiles. Hidden in the shadows, she watched him reach the door beneath the spine of the staircase that led into the servants' corridors and the bowels of Roddinglaw; the passageways and storerooms, all the cupboards and pantries and linen presses.

There was a place in the house, he had said. One place in Roddinglaw where he felt safe, and where he could close his eyes.

She waited for the lock to click and then followed him, being as careful as she could not to make any noise. The cone of light fell away behind her, the stately silence of the entrance hall and its grand stair-case, the faint breathing of the men in the ward. She slipped through the door that Daniel had taken, passing into a long and moonlit corridor. The windows on the right, rectangles of black and silver, were high and narrow and looked out onto the bare, neglected scrub of the kitchen garden. The air was sharp and cold through here, the ceiling close above her, only an arm's length away. It was like tunnel-ling into the sheer slope of a hillside.

Her feet scuffed on bare stone and she looked up to see if Daniel had heard, but the ghost had passed on. There was a swell of disturbed air. Esther paused and held her breath. After a moment she continued, coming through into what she realised was the short hall outside the linen press. The long wooden table where she had folded the sheets with Alice was empty.

Setting her mind against the weight of the house and all its hidden spaces, Esther listened to the sounds of Roddinglaw asleep. She could hear the temper of the joists relax, the accommodating shift of beams and boards, the disturbance of someone coughing far above her in the upper rooms. A breeze frisked against the window glass, and again from far away she could hear a soft sigh; either the waves gasping at the shoreline or the low mutter of the wind passing through the line of firs.

She didn't know why she was following him, to what end. When Alice had discovered his empty bed that night, not long after he had arrived, Esther had been content to let Daniel keep his secrets. There was no harm in his absence, she had told herself, no danger to any of the other patients and little sign of any danger to himself. But then all his talk when they were sitting in the shade of the bronze horseman had made her wary of his state of mind.

Christ, and truth, and a place of safety…

This was a dark place, he had said. And it wasn't just Daniel who felt that. Even with a hundred other patients, Roddinglaw seemed such a lonely house lately. It was the war, the endless rolling tide of it inexorably pushing at their minds, a great black wave spilling across the sea from France. It was Alice attacked in the woods; Corporal Prevost stepping so calmly from the platform into that gout of steam, the brakes screaming; or Jacob Beresford girding himself for the fight, utterly consumed by whatever it was he feared on this stretch of coast. There was another darkness besides the war, dredged up from the deep foundations of Gallondean, or disinterred from his illness as it slowly consumed him.

There was no one she could talk to about any of this. Not Ida Lambert, affectionately hostile, seemingly so free with her opinions. Certainly not Major Lawson. Now Alice was gone too. There was only Daniel; a priest in his confessional, a saint assuming the burden of other people's sins. Talking to Daniel McQuarrie was like writing in her notebook, or communing with that second voice from which the poems sometimes came; the voice of art, or faith, or just moral endurance.

Esther picked savagely at the dry skin on the back of her hand. These were night thoughts, the perceptions only a large and empty house could awaken. Daniel was no priest. He was a sick man waiting to get better – wounded, and shocked by what had wounded him. There was no other source of darkness. It was just the war.

She was turning to head back to the entrance hall when she heard a noise above her. A scuffing sound, the soft thud of something shifting position. She brushed her fingertips against the plaster of the low ceiling. A light appeared under the line of the linen press door, flickering like a candle.

'Daniel?' she said, and then the flame pinched out.

She opened the door to the linen press and stepped into the dark. When her eyes adjusted she could see the built-in shelves of folded sheets and pillowcases on her right, the curve of the wall to her left reaching round into the depths of the press. There was no light. She listened. She could hear him breathing, somewhere above her.

'Daniel, are you there?'

After a moment he said, 'I'm here.'

There was an alcove above the door where he had hidden himself, and beyond it was a narrow passage that stretched back above the ceiling of the corridor outside. She could smell the burned wick of his candle. Turning, looking up, she could just see in the swarm of shadows the suggestion of his face staring back down at her.

'Is this where you go?' she asked. She found she was whispering. 'Where you feel safe?'

'Yes.'

'And how's your chest? You might have strained yourself climbing up there.'

'I'm fine,' he said, and his voice was flatly reassuring. 'Everything is fine.'

Esther closed the door and sat down. She had no need now for the brisk, sing-song tones she found herself using with the other patients, that bright and benign insincerity. There was something about Daniel McQuarrie that always invited the truth, she thought. Truth, and a confiding air. You could say anything to him, confess anything, and he would listen without judgement.

'Like the monastery you mentioned,' she said. 'It's like a cave, up there. I can understand. Burying yourself away, hiding. I'd like to do that myself sometimes.'

'What would you be hiding from?'

'Oh, I don't know. My fears. Regrets. The war. Do you ever feel that you're only waiting for something to happen, but the worst thing is

214

that you know it can only happen when you make it happen yourself? There is no one else. It's only you.'

'That can often be the hardest thing of all.'

'And doing so means letting go of so much, even of what has hurt you…' She tried to laugh and lighten her tone, but it came out as a sob. 'I'm sorry.'

'What is it that holds you, Mrs Worrell?'

'I'm unhappy. I'm so very unhappy, it feels like the most awful grief, but I don't know what I'm grieving for.' She covered her face and breathed deeply, stilling the tears that she would not let fall. 'I remember, when my husband died – rather, it was when I was *told* that he had died. It was such a beautiful day, still summer really, so early in the war, and… God forgive me, I was *glad*. Isn't that appalling? That I was free from him, that the burden had been taken away. I was so relieved that I almost laughed. I don't think I've ever forgiven myself for that.'

'Did you love him?'

'No,' she said. 'Not truly. And I don't think he loved me. The idea of me perhaps, but not who I really was. Whoever that is.'

'Then there's nothing to forgive.'

She looked up at him. 'Isn't there? Are you sure?'

'You do grieve for him, despite what you think. You work to help others. I was taught that faith alone could bring the sinner grace, but now I'm not so sure. I think it is what you strive towards as well. God looks with kindness on those who strive to be forgiven, and who do penance.'

'That's just it,' Esther said. 'What penance have I truly done? There are worse places in the world than this, aren't there? Better places for me to be.'

'I suppose penance is a harder journey than any of us allow. It's a long road. We might not like what we find at the end of it.'

'Like the knight,' she said.

'The knight?'

She looked up again to where the shadows hid him.

'William de Gaillon, the statue on the lawn. The son. Despite everything he did, taking himself to the East, fighting for what he thought was right, he was still killed in the end. The hound howled for him when he died. The hound will always howl for the heirs of Gallondean when they're about to die, so Mr Beresford says. He knows all there is to know about that legend, I'm sure.'

'His penance. His Crusade. He killed his father after all.'

'And cut off his father's hands as well,' Esther said. She gripped her own hands, thinking of Corporal Prevost. 'Mr Beresford thinks William de Gaillon took those hands to the Holy Land and buried them. The opposite of a relic, whatever that would be. Such a horrible tale when you think of it.' A blade of air cut in under the door and made her shudder. She hugged her knees again and felt the chill from the cold floor creep into her bones. 'To have the hands taken away like that, no matter what. You would be like a ghost, touching nothing… They were such brutes in those days.'

There was silence from the alcove above the door. Esther could hear his breathing, slow and steady. The quietness lingered, thickening. There was the scrape of a match and the sharp flare of an ignited wick. Shadows leaped and tumbled over the walls.

'Captain McQuarrie? Shall I get you back to the ward?'

His voice was strained when he spoke.

'No,' he said. 'Please. Here will suit me, until the morning. It's getting closer, you see. It's… I'll hear it. I'll hear it before the end.'

'Then get some rest,' she said softly. 'Take care. Please.'

His breath came more easily then. She listened to it for a while, the soft rising and falling, until she was sure that he had fallen asleep.

Getting carefully to her feet, Esther slipped out of the door and back into the corridor. The candle flame still flickered in the cave behind her. For a moment she stood there by the long table with her hand upraised, her fingertips skimming the ceiling beneath the place where he lay.

FROM JACOB BERESFORD'S JOURNALS, MAY 1918

Again, past midnight, I felt it in the room. I woke to see the shadows watching me, the lamplight no more than a brittle ember dying in the bulb. Darkness, thick as oil, bled across the floorboards. Eyes like distant starlight stared at me – my father's eyes, the eyes of Robert de Gaillon in that chamber underground. Evil is like a maggot in the heart and in the hands. I laugh at that evil, knowing that its days are numbered. But when I reach for Vishnu I find that the statue is cold, colder than death. The stone is chipped. The porphyry is beginning to crumble.

Sarah, I'm losing you. I should never have left. She is not you, I know. No one is.

It's like a cloud hanging over the coast, getting lower and lower; a sense of doom and dread. It makes my heart beat faster, freshens the blood, puts steel in my veins and sinews. A great black mantle is waiting to smother me and I yearn to tear it to shreds.

Sometimes, in my more lucid moments, I seem to recognise all this for what it is – nothing more than the shadow in my lungs, growing darker. I wake with my head on a pillow pink with bloody froth. A flight of stairs has me gasping for breath, with black spots dancing before my eyes. My hands shake, my limbs tremble. I am struck with strange zeal and crushed by the weight of abject misery. I have projected it all outwards, vomited it forth, until it has swept across the land from east to west. That's all it is. I am wracked in the sweat-drenched sheets, burning, burning, drowning in the dark.

I have called for her. I have sent a message to Roddinglaw, asking for us to meet. One last time, I think. I will let her know what she means to me, and what she can take from me when I am dead. For I am under no illusions that when I destroy this thing, I will destroy myself too. William de Gaillon fought the shadow and won, but death still reached him in the end. Death is the wages of sin after all.

Sometimes I think of him with kindness, my father. He did what he thought was best for me, and he was a man of an earlier age. He was under no illusions about the world and how it worked. Bobby, Sarah, they would have seemed to him beyond frivolous. He had nothing but contempt for them, and for me, but his reasons were just. It was not his fault.

What haunts the borders of my sight is both him and not him. The shadow only took his face – but then surely there must have been a face to give to it in the first place?

Tomorrow, I think, or the day after. Soon. None of them are safe now. Some nights I lie there and I pray for the dawn, for the coming day. And then at last for the night when it will all be over.

Sunday 19th May 1918

The cottage was bare and filthy. A stone sink in the corner brimmed with broken dishes and there was half an inch of grease on the iron range. No fire burned. Outside Esther could see the grass swimming in the sea wind, the bruised sky, the fading day. Inside there was a stale smell of sweat and spilled whisky, the long neglect of an unloved place.

'Going out, are you?' Ida had said as she left Roddinglaw. 'A stroll around the grounds, at this hour?'

There on the turn of the stairs, leaning on the banister, her long arms elegant in their starched white sleeves, she had looked down at Esther with her cinema eyes, her plump lips pursed. A wry resentment, envy, an evident hunger. But for what? Gossip, news, rumour, all of it the dark backing to make her own days visible to her? Everyone else was just the supporting cast to Ida, as Esther had eventually realised. She had thought they were friends, but now she saw that Ida could only ever commune with herself. She did not like other people so much as the rumours she could wrap around them, the suspicions of them that she could frivolously indulge. Esther had given the younger woman a bare nod and Ida had withdrawn.

'Well, be careful,' she said, falsely prim. 'After what happened to Alice. Eyes are always watching, aren't they? Hands waiting to grab. Don't do anything I wouldn't do...'

'I must apologise for the locale,' Jacob said now from the other side of the room. His voice was hoarse. 'Not the most salubrious, is it? But Gallondean is impossible, absolutely impossible... I'm sorry, but I won't have you in there now, it's... You will have to trust me. It's not possible, that place. Not Gallondean. Not anymore.'

He sat at the wooden table and picked at the grain. There was a cup of cold tea in front of him, untouched. Despite the chill he was perspiring, his face red, his coat fastened right up to the collar.

'Lawson asked me the other day if I suffered from delusions – the illness, you know – and I laughed. Now I'm not so certain.'

Esther, standing, turned back to the window. The glass was stained with salt. The front garden, if it could be called that, sloped down to the beach and was filled with drifts of sand. The gate hung askew.

'Whose is it?' she asked. 'The cottage, I mean.'

'Rutherford's. It's a bloody disgrace, isn't it? He's my factor, as was.'

'Meaning he is no more?'

Jacob gave a snort of contempt. 'God knows. I haven't seen the old bastard for days. By the strict letter of the law, it belongs to me in any case. He's my tenant, that's all.'

'So many assets,' Esther said. 'You're quite a wealthy young man, aren't you?'

'Through no effort on my part. I have my father to thank for that. He started with very little and made himself rich, quite an achievement.' He stabbed viciously at the surface of the table with his thumbnail. 'Not that being wealthy buys you respect if it's the wrong sort of money. You should see the way that policeman talks to me... No, it's a uniform that buys you respect these days.'

'I'll tell the police, Jacob,' Esther said. She stood by him and rested her hand on his shoulder. 'That you were with me that night, that it couldn't have been you who hurt Alice.'

'Don't. I need no alibis. It doesn't matter now.'

'But if you're under suspicion, then I can help. Please?'

He lurched from the table and started rummaging in the corner of the room. He dragged out a crate and the exertion had him coughing into his fist.

'When I first became aware of him, I thought Rutherford was just an old derelict, a hermit waiting to die. I didn't realise he'd been my father's servant. He'd recently been dragged from the sea by the coast guard, he told me, after he'd stolen a boat at Port Edgar. He was trying to row out to the islands.'

He took a stack of papers from the crate, and a large black ledger. The spine had crumbled away, leaving only the vague threads of its binding. He wiped dust from the cover with the heel of his hand.

'There's an old monastery out there,' he said. 'Inchcolm, I think. A ruin now, of course, but I always rather thought it had something to do with that. But who can tell with those who grieve? It makes you do strange things. His son was killed in the war. Along with all the other sons.' He looked around at the filth and degradation. 'He's at the bottom of the spiral now, I imagine. After his son died, after my father, the legend – perhaps he didn't see the point in going on. What are cleanliness and order and sanity itself but our revolt against fate? And fate has long had its hooks into Mr Rutherford, as it also has in me.'

He brought the book and the papers to the table. There was something gleeful about him now, an eager impatience. Every other moment he would clear his throat, coughing, shifting the weight in his lungs, the corrosion. He pulled out her chair and it screeched on the flagstones. The eyes, those hard grey eyes, were blurred with tears.

'I found these earlier. I've been here for hours, reading them. Esther, please – come and sit with me. Look. Rutherford had collected them all, do you see?'

She sat down as Jacob threw back the cover of the book. Pages of spidery copperplate, rusty ink, the paper yellow and dusty. She couldn't read a word of it.

'I don't know what I'm meant to be looking at.'

'It's about Robert de Gaillon,' he said. He drew his fingers across the lines. 'These are old church accounts, parish records and so on, for the lands surrounding Queensferry.'

Esther looked on them with new eyes. 'From the twelfth century?'

'God, no, nothing like as old. These can only go back a century or so, but ministers can get bored with their charges and find themselves delving into folklore and legend more than anyone else, I suspect. Always suspicious that the Christian graft will not take. Rutherford kept all this for himself. God knows where he found them, but he never showed them to me. I think the details excited him. Or perhaps he just didn't want me to know? Only someone armed with the truth can protect themself from evil after all, and I've never been quite certain that our Mr Rutherford had my best interests at heart. I think he feels that Gallondean must always devour its victims... There's so much here, noted down, hinted at, occasionally stated with the most appalling directness. Shall I tell you about it?' he said. 'Would you like to know what that place truly is?'

'No,' Esther said, firmly. Jacob, ignoring her, opened the book. He turned over a page and quietly began to read out the words.

'"The original stone keep was a dreadful place, grim and forbidding. Robert de Gaillon had reached the age when disease and illness begins to take its toll, and, aware that God's judgement was nearly upon him after a lifetime of the most indiscriminate and bloodthirsty violence, he secluded himself deep inside his ancestral tower, hoping thereby to keep the natural consequences of his actions at bay. Prey to strange delusions, fearful of the coming trial in which his soul would certainly be found wanting, Robert de Gaillon fell into that most dreadful temptation known to the Christian man. He began to consort with dark powers, with witchcraft and necromancy, hoping to cure himself of his ills by strange magics and spells. It was said that the windows of the house flashed with eldritch lights, and that deep in its hidden chambers the Lord of Gallondean summoned demons that could only be roused by the blood of sacrifice."'

Jacob glanced up. His eyes were like a shrouded midday sky.

'Wonderful stuff, isn't it?' he said. 'Very colourful.'

'Stop it,' Esther snapped. 'I have no interest in any of this.'

But Jacob ignored her. He went on.

'"It is claimed that Robert de Gaillon murdered over a hundred children in the chambers of his keep. He ravished and killed local women, riding out at dusk on a great black horse and snatching them from the fields. Women and children were tortured and skinned, their tormented flesh fed to those demons in the hope of buying from them long life free from illness. For it was not power that Robert de Gaillon sought, power which he already had as lord of this coast, but long life, and life everlasting.'"

Jacob was grinning now. Esther stood. 'I don't want to hear another word of this. Close that book or I will leave, I promise.'

'Awful things, *awful*... Imagine it, Esther. Cutting away children's genitals and eating them. Slitting the throats of little boys and girls and plucking out their eyes... dragging the guts from their stomachs with hooks... it's—'

'Jacob!'

She snatched the book from his hands and flung it across the room.

He laughed. 'That was all he wanted, do you see? He was afraid to die because he knew what would be waiting for him, on the other side of death. It's pathetic. He was a coward and a monster, rummaging about in corpses looking for the key that would unlock his prison. Imagine being his son. Imagine being William, standing there clothed in righteousness, sword drawn in that bloody place, waiting to cut his father down... It's almost over though,' he said. 'You understand, don't you? I've found Robert's chamber. It's the source of everything.' He slapped the table with the flat of his hand. 'And now that the wall is broken, it will come. The chamber has been revealed. The shadow is on its way, and I cannot risk you being there when I destroy it.'

Esther stood by the window with her arms folded. She wanted to leave. She felt sick. Beads of sweat were rolling down Jacob's face. She could almost smell the fever in him. The last time they had lain together, spent, he had wept against her shoulder and mumbled a name that she couldn't quite hear, but that she knew wasn't hers. She had held him against her, his skin as hot as a furnace, and in some agony of guilt and anger had tried to will Peter's body to take Jacob's place.

'I don't care about Gallondean,' she said. 'I don't know why you let this disgusting tale obsess you. It has no hold on you other than if you let it.' She started forward, reaching for him. Under her hand his shoulder felt like iron. 'Jacob, you must know, I'm leaving here. I've asked to transfer to the front. I've asked for my name to be put forward with the VAD. A man was killed, one of the patients, he took his own life, and I *cannot* stay here any longer. I can't. The field hospitals need as much help as they can get. I could even train as a full nurse, I can—'

He took her hand and laid his cheek against it, hot as fire. 'The front?' he said. 'But it'll be different soon. Everything will be changed. You won't need to go to France, Esther. It was the house, you see? That's what happened to my father. The malice was seeded in him, by whatever de Gaillon unleashed in there. I think it was seeded in me too, but I've kept it at bay for so long. And now I've found the source of it all, in the foundations. The chamber... Such horror there, Esther, you can feel it. It's bled into the stone, but if I can hold on just a little longer then I can confront it when it comes for me. I can stop it, at last. When the hound howls from the Point, when I'm ready to die.'

'Jacob—'

'It makes sense to me now. It was never a death sentence. It's when *you* are ready to let go that the cry is heard. Not before. My father knew that, I think. He wanted to come home and die here, but I took that away from him. I didn't mean to, but... He was dying, as I am dying. It's a release, and for me it will be a victory. I am the one against whom no victory by the dark is possible...'

He covered his face and coughed into his hands, shaking, retching. Esther rubbed his back. She couldn't understand what he was saying. Muttered, weeping confessions, something about America and money and the burial of the dead, his father. The brainfever bird calling from the tree, calling, calling; Sarah and Bobby and the shadow lengthening across the grass, as the sun blazed down and burned the world.

'Sarah!' he wept. 'Forgive me, please... I'm sorry.'

Esther held his head to her breast.

'I'm not her,' she soothed him. 'Whoever she is, whatever she meant to you and however much the memory of her keeps you going, I am not her. I must be myself. Don't you see? I can't be her for you. I can't be anyone but myself.'

He wrenched himself from the fit, gasping for air. His face was dripping with sweat.

'I'm trying to set you free, aren't I? Smothering you with what I think is freedom.' He clutched her hands and tried to smile. 'I'm going to leave it to you.'

'What?'

'Gallondean. When I'm gone it'll be yours, but you must promise, *please*, you must promise to destroy it. That's all I need you to do. Tear it down as soon as you can and pull it up by the roots. Let the waves wash over it, and what money you can get from the land will be yours.'

No neat phrase came to her tongue in response. There was no disgust or horror, no sense of being trapped by another's expectations. He genuinely thought he was offering her a gift.

'I don't want it,' she said, as calmly and as clearly as she could. 'I do not want it.'

She held him close as another fit burst through him. He spat blood onto the table. His body was a reed, buckling in the storm. He cried out and tried to stand, and she couldn't stop him falling. Sprawled on the ground, vomiting onto the flagstones, his eyes flickered white in his skull.

'Esther,' he slurred. '*Sarah…*'

It was no different from lifting any other patient into bed. Esther bent his knees and hooked his arm around her shoulders. There seemed no weight to him at all. She half-dragged, half-carried him through the grimy kitchen to the bedroom, where she laid him on the sagging mattress.

The coverlet stank and the pillow was stained with sweat. In a cupboard she found cleaner sheets and pillowcases, a musty smell about them. She changed what she could as Jacob lay there, shivering with cold. The sea bled against the sand outside. Dusk was falling.

She lay next to him on the bed and held him as he stumbled into sleep, his head against her shoulder. 'Sarah,' he moaned again, and she said, 'Yes. Yes, I'm here, Jacob. Don't worry, I'm here with you.'

What did it matter now? she thought. Let him take comfort where it could be found. After all, he was dying.

He thinks about William de Gaillon, and the hound, and the skeleton dug up along the coast. Robert de Gaillon, killed by his son, whose hands were buried in holy ground.

He thinks about the heir of Gallondean, his dark hair and sallow face, and where he has seen that face before. There was a cave far to the east, where the campfire burned and the earth gave up its secrets.

There's one memory above all others: his brother Simon sitting in the garden when Daniel told him his plans in those fraught days after their father died. The confession Daniel made, his hope, his commitment to serve the Church. He remembers Simon's easy, infinitely compassionate smile, so understanding. It was the smile of someone indulging a child's fantasy. Daniel only sees it now.

You don't have the strength for it, that smile seemed to say, without cruelty or malice. *Your faith is just smoke on the water, drifting away.*

How quickly that faith had fallen from him. How easily it was heaved into the dust. It was the truth once, and then it was only doubt. Perhaps it was always doubt. He had never really believed in the damned and the elect. Surely everyone would be saved by the love of God, no matter what? The father loves the child despite all his transgressions.

Deep in the alcove above the linen press, hiding through another night, Daniel sits and lights his candle and lines up his jars. In front of him is Esther Worrell's book, the volume of Robert Browning. The words of an extract from *The Ring and the Book* leap out at him. *'Tis a figure, a symbol, say;/A thing's sign: now for the thing signified...'*

Leafing through the pages, he finds 'A Death in the Desert' and carefully tears the poem from the binding. With the stub of a pencil he marks each page with the cross of Jesus.

He rips the pages into fragments and pushes each piece into the jars, one by one, burying them in the grave dirt, the earth of Gallondean.

There is an emptiness in him, but it is not a loss. Everything has been pared away. Not an emptiness, but an openness waiting to be filled by the breath of God. Dependence, a sense of peace.

Man is not God but hath God's end to serve...

226

A moment from his childhood intrudes. He remembers sitting in the parlour on a Sunday evening, his father's strong and resonant voice as he read from *Isaiah*.

Also I heard the voice of the Lord, saying, Whom shall I send, and who will go for us? Then said I, Here am I; send me.

No damned and no elect, only those who serve and those who refuse. Send me.

He packs the jars into his bag and drops from the alcove to the floor of the linen press. He passes on, into the corridor, across the hall, to where the front door opens to his touch. It is black night and no one sees him.

The air is fresh and cool. The stone of the doorstep is cold under his bare feet. The trees are swaying in the darkness. The grass is a carpet of green.

Taking the jars from the bag, Daniel lines them up on the edge of the path. When he looks to the trees he sees the shadow waiting for him, watching. It wears his face, and the German's face, and the face of Jacob Beresford. It is Robert de Gaillon, the Lord of Gallondean.

You must not be afraid.

He smiles. He looks to the bronze horseman and brings his fist down onto the jars, one by one, smashing the clay. Dirt spills to the grass, smelling of the grave. Scraps of paper flutter in the breeze. He plucks one from the air and crams it into his mouth, slowly chewing, swallowing it down. He takes the cross into his stomach and into his blood.

Wind and rain batters the desert, in the dry lands beyond the cave.

And then the hound begins to howl.

Jerusalem

December 1917

In the moonlight the wadi was bare and pale. There were round white stones gathered in the bed. He could smell the dry scent of the weeds and John Allynson's sweat as he crouched over his pack. Ruhi stood there like a patch of midnight in his khaki robes, holding the reins of the sorrel mare. The horse grunted once and hoofed the dirt. A breeze poured through the gorge, soft and fragrant. Above and behind them, on the near side of the riverbed, the hill bulged north and joined the crest of the ridge that shadowed the Hebron road.

Daniel heard the mare's light and nervous whicker. The breath rose from his mouth, pale as smoke. He was glad of the heavier drill. You didn't think of it being cold here, but the desert threw back the heat it gained by day. The pendulum always swings. There is no real twilight but a sudden and abiding darkness.

He trained the glasses at the slope on the other side of the wadi. The track disappeared into shadow. The clouds drew away and further up he could see the red flank of the hill, picked out in moonlit silver.

Ruhi picked his way through the strewn red rock, slipping past the stands of thorn and the wild amaranth and arum. He flowed like ink over the white stones of the riverbed. Daniel laid his finger outside the trigger guard of his revolver, the hammer back. Allynson drew the bolt of his rifle. Another man would have spoken now, unnerved by the silence and by the rolling, barren strangeness of the hills, but John had been a soldier almost longer than Daniel had been alive and he said nothing.

The horse lowered her head and browsed the weeds. She was small and hardy, a white diamond on her muzzle. She took every ounce of her work without complaint. Only sometimes did the night and the smell of the goats in the hills unnerve her. He remembered again with great pleasure the Anzac cavalry on the beach before Gaza, two hours before the dawn, the long jostling line of the riders gripping their saddles with their knees and the sea cold and mirror-smooth, a sweet smell in the air of cut grass and hay as the horses moved up. Then the dust billowing as the infantry crossed over, everything muted by it, making ghosts of your comrades. No distance anywhere, just the grains of dust settling over them and the thick coastal fog spreading out as the division moved up to the attack, everything with no more force or purpose to it than a dream. The battle itself he could barely remember, but he would always remember the fog and the dust and the horses and the way the mist made everything seem unreal.

The night grew colder. The breeze shook the thorns. Rain was on the way. He looked across the wadi with the glasses and where there had been only shadow he now saw Ruhi crouched there, serious, beckoning. The lean bearded face, the slow, laggardly gesture.

Daniel holstered the gun. For a moment it was more than distance that separated them. A gulf of time and meaning lay across the wadi. As he drew the mare down the last few feet of track onto the white stones he almost felt that he had stepped into the pages of scripture; a young warrior in the hills of Judea, in the shadow of Jerusalem.

There was fighting in the south when he woke the next morning. He could hear the crackle of rifle fire, the shout of trench mortars. The overlapping hills made it sound safe and perfectly contained, like a distant live-fire drill.

Ruhi went off to scout the trail. Daniel rose from his blanket and looked back to the land they'd passed through. Below them in the deeper hollows lay pools of unburned mist, grey and cloudy and hanging against the stone. The sound of gunfire rattled across the dawn.

'Bethlehem?'

'Could be,' John Allynson said.

The sergeant was strapping up his bedroll. Daniel looked south but the Hebron road was hidden from them. He could see the white line of the wadi they had crossed. He flattened his palm above his eyes.

'Those are British guns,' he said. 'The range sounds short though. The Fifty-third must be pushing up. Doesn't sound like much of a fight.'

'Never does from a distance.'

It never did. You could watch five thousand men advancing over a bare plain, hiking fast, pausing to crouch and fire, their bayonets catching at the steel light, and in moments the land would swallow them. They would disappear into the scale of the country. The land always had the greater force.

They saddled the horse and moved up, Allynson with his rifle over his shoulder, his head covered by the Ottoman *bashlyk* he'd taken in the Dardanelles. The horse whinnied, a mild sound in the freshness of the dawn. The cool air flowed like water.

When they reached the summit Daniel looked back to the rolling mass of the hills behind them. The crumbled stone reminded him of the pyramids in Egypt, stripped of their cladding. Up close the land seemed barren and scoured of life, but looking back you could see the long patches of green from the winter grasses in the rising light and the olive trees gripping the rock, all the land oddly contoured and creased like seamed, elderly skin. There were greens and yellows, streaks of red, everything fresh and rejuvenated. By the afternoon it would be parched brown again and would seem once more a Bible wilderness, but for now there was something harsh and beautiful and strange about it. A hardness in his soul responded to the hardness of the land. There were no words for it. For a moment he just allowed himself to feel it. That he should be here now, that these hills and mountains would always be here, always, contested and precious for what they kept revealing to the world.

They paced on over the brow. The track passed into a shallow depression a hundred yards across. The path was lined with rocks and carmine-coloured stones. Wrinkles of mist dragged a trail of rain across the hills and the rain soon stiffened. The wind cast it into their faces. Before long Daniel couldn't see more than ten yards ahead.

'This is it,' Allynson said. The sergeant's face was turned up towards the sky. Rain jewelled the blond scrub of his three-day beard. His hard blue eyes were narrow. 'Winter rains.'

'Just in time.'

'Like bloody clockwork.'

'On the plains I dreamed of rain,' Daniel said.

'You haven't known it, lad. This is the real symphony here, the main event. Everything else has been just the bloody overture.'

Rain rattled on the stones, louder than gunfire. From all the channels and gullies that cut through the hills and from the sunken wadis hidden in the mist could be heard the running water. It surged through the rocks. They were three thousand feet above sea level. The belly of the clouds felt an arm's length away. Beyond, like shapes dimly seen in the contours of a darkened room, the flat heads of the distant hills loomed north and east.

There was a terrace of stone at the summit of the hill, slabs of marble cut with dark striations. Here and there the boundaries of old buildings were marked by lines of weathered brick. The rain made the smooth flat stone slippery underfoot. Daniel pulled his weight against the reins of the horse. He could see Ruhi crouched amongst the thorns on the other side, where the ground dipped towards a shelf of rock. Water streamed over the edge onto the goat track beyond. Ruhi had unfurled his *bashlyk* and the ears hung down below his chin, the dark grey-brown wool stained black with rain. The British soldiers came over, not talking, the soft clatter of their equipment lost against the steady downpour. Ruhi raised a thin finger to his lips.

'Turks are near,' he said in a hoarse whisper. 'Ten of them over the next rise, flooded out of the wadi.' He flicked his fingers through his beard, shedding sparks of rain.

Daniel unclipped the holster and slid the revolver's lanyard around his wrist. The rain pooled in the crown of his cap and ran down either side of the brim.

'Where do they go?'

'North,' Ruhi said.

'A patrol?'

'Yes, my captain. I believe so.'

'Are they digging in?' Allynson asked.

'No, sergeant. But they take shelter now in the stones of an old farmhouse. They can cover us from the north. When the rain stops, they'll be for Jerusalem I would guess.'

Allynson scratched his chin. He wiped the rain from his eyes.

'Machine gun?'

'A Hotchkiss,' Ruhi said gravely.

Allynson looked to Daniel. The clouds filtered the light. It shone very pale around them.

'Sound like more than a patrol with the Hotchkiss.'

'Could be they got lost pulling back towards Jerusalem?' Daniel said. 'Or away.'

Ruhi agreed. 'True. And they were slovenly to my eyes, like men who run.'

Daniel thought this over. At all costs they must avoid the exchange of fire. They must not be seen or pursued. If they made any sharper contact they would be as well heading back to Brigade right now with nothing to show for it but the spent cartridges. He would not do that if it could be helped. They must see what travelled on the road to Jericho.

'Where does this track take us?' he asked.

Ruhi made a gesture. 'All the way down to the plains by the Dead Sea and the mouth of Jordan, by many twists and turns. But there are ways back north if we go east a mile, I believe.'

'You believe?'

'I know, my captain.'

He does hate the Turks after all, Daniel reminded himself. A sister raped, a brother pressed into their armies – whatever it was, this hatred had proved a boon to the 53rd for many weeks now.

'All right,' Daniel decided. 'Lead on.'

The goat track twisted down the slope. There were clumps of thorn on either side, flattened by the rain. For an hour's slow march Daniel led the mare, following Ruhi's slumped back. He pressed his heels into the muddy earth as they descended. He could smell the wet hide of the horse. It was sweet and homely.

Below them, growing louder as they approached, cool and still shaded by the flank of the hill, a stream of water frothed through a wadi's bed. On the banks were olive trees seeming crisp and revived by the winter rain, their bark black and their drab green leaves shivering. The stream flowed quickly. The water was milk-white and ankle deep. Gingerly the mare stepped through, Daniel holding onto its bridle. He hauled himself out on the other side, his boots streaming. He could see the goat track curling up the slope ahead. Higher up he could see it creep back on itself as it mounted the terraces, disappearing into the settled misty air of the summit.

The slope levelled out towards the north, then dipped into a wide bowl of volcanic stone. The rain slackened. For a moment the clouds unravelled and showed the pale blue sky of morning, still pink in places, pastel-smooth. On the western side, bathed in sunlight, the rock was very pale, but it grew darker and redder, almost a madder-rose as it steepled into the ridgeline stretching north. Below them the gorge fell away into darkness.

It's a fine country, Daniel thought. Severe, but nothing bleak about it, nothing. It strikes a very firm chord inside. Seeing it all, the lessons of childhood are more firmly painted in; the smell of dust from the hymn books as the sermon is read, the light gaining shape and colour as it passes through the stained glass. The land puts flesh on the bones of words like *wilderness*. Here is where Christ walked and steeled himself against the devil. Titus's legions marched these roads to crush the rebellion. Raymond and Godfrey and Bohemond, and all their Christian knights, the massacre of the Jews when Jerusalem fell.

He wondered what Allynson made of it all. Did the poetry of faith spark in that old soldier's soul? Or was it all one to him with South Africa and the North-West Frontier, and France and Belgium and the Dardanelles and Egypt? He went where the army sent him. There was no more to it than that.

They passed through the bowl and cut across the rim of a gorge that yawned beneath them. To the west, half a mile off, the hills fell in a series of stepped terraces. Daniel could see the black mouths of caves there. What looked like tracks led up to them across the terraces. He could see the steps that had been carved into the stone, worn smooth. He laid his hand on Ruhi's narrow shoulder and pointed.

'They are riddled through these hills,' the guide explained. 'Shepherds use them now, but they were places for holy men in times past. Prophets and hermits, hiding in the wild.'

Daniel looked down the length of the gorge and tried to imagine the perspective from the other side, from the cool shadowed openings in the rock.

'Why don't the Turks fortify them? Two machine guns and a trench mortar and you could hold off an army here.'

'They are foolish people,' Ruhi scorned. 'Who can explain why they do what they do?'

'I thought they had Germans with them. Germans would not have left all this alone.'

'Jerry advises, he doesn't command,' Allynson said behind him. He'd slung his rifle barrel-down on his shoulder. 'And the Jerries are pulling out.'

Later in the morning the rain withdrew and the clouds drifted west towards the sea. The sun burned off the dew. A veil of fog slithered greasily across the higher slopes.

They stopped to rest beneath an overhang of stone, on the shoulder of the trail. They lit no fire. Allynson prised open a can of bully beef with his bayonet and cut out a slice for Daniel. The meat was warm and soft in his mouth, oily with the residue from the tin. Daniel hobbled the mare and took from his store of Huntley biscuits, snapping the hard squares in two and sharing them out. Ruhi demurred, with much politeness. The food of the British soldiers, Daniel was quite sure, was unadulterated filth to him.

Daniel sucked the shard of biscuit like a lozenge, letting it dissolve in his mouth. Nobody spoke. Allynson filled the bowl of his pipe and smoked thoughtfully. Water dripped from the rock. Beneath them, twenty or thirty feet down, a line of olive trees and thorns coiled into the gorge. He could hear the soft, cheerful gurgle of a stream, the careful speech of the leaves scraping together. The rain had released their fragrance into the air, smoky and dark and almost stronger than Allynson's tobacco.

He couldn't say how many miles they'd covered now. As the crow flew, not much more than five. With each rise and fall, hacking in and out of gorge and ravine, it could have been three times that. They had moved now far to the north-east from the Hebron road. Daniel looked to the drifting sky. If I've mapped this right then Jerusalem should be nearly due west. If I've mapped this right, and if Ruhi has taken us the right way.

'Lieutenant Wake has that Austrian sniper rifle,' Daniel said. Allynson looked up, taken out of his daydream. 'I wish I'd borrowed it. For the Jericho road, I mean. We could have picked off the enemy officers if they withdrew. It would have been some use.'

'The only use we've to be is to watch,' Allynson said. 'Watch and note and report, whatever moves.' He bit his pipe stem. 'Besides, Lieutenant Wake was sold a pup. That rifle's nothing but a Mannlicher with a cheap Italian sight. I've seen it.'

'Don't tell Wake that.'

'He knows.' Allynson showed his teeth. 'That's why he makes such a fuss of it, because he knows what it's worth. Which is fuck all. No,' he sighed, 'don't be in too much of a hurry to shoot Turkish officers when there's no call for it.'

'I just want to—' Daniel said.

'What?'

'Be of more use. To help. The war.'

Allynson shook his head. 'You don't have to kill people to help. Any case,' he said mildly, 'with your shooting we'd have to get far closer than is strictly sensible.'

'What's wrong with my shooting?'

The sergeant gave an idle shrug. 'Nothing. For an officer, it's not bad.'

'And I suppose you were potting rabbits at three hundred yards with your father's shotgun before you could walk?'

'Not in Ardwick,' Allynson said. He laughed. 'Few rabbits there. And my father was what you might call an unknown quantity.' He laughed again.

'I'd never fired a weapon before the OTC,' Daniel told him. 'I fished with my brother now and then when we were boys, drawing lines for mackerel if the fishermen let us. But I'd never killed anything more than fish before.'

Allynson directed a gob of spit over the edge of the terrace. 'Fish don't count. And worry not, Captain McQuarrie, I still doubt you've killed anything more than fish. You've a spotless soul.'

Daniel smiled. He'd fired his revolver at Gaza, aiming at the dark, man-sized shadows that had fled before him in the dust and the fog, but it had been as much for the comfort of the noise as for the effect of the bullets. He doubted he had hit anyone. He was glad, if he admitted it. That would be a thing to colour your soul indeed.

'What about you, Ruhi?' He turned to the guide, who lay sprawled beneath the overhang. 'How many Turks have you killed in your time?'

'Oh, none, sir,' Ruhi said, abashed. 'I've killed nothing bigger than a goat, and then only for necessity. It is an event, to kill a man. It draws something dark into you.'

Daniel wondered how many of those events John Allynson had experienced in his time. He'd been twenty years in the army, at least. More. He should be an expert by now. And here they were at the gates of Jerusalem, and if the Ottoman front collapsed then the division would find itself back in France or Belgium. The front would never collapse there. It would never end. A hundred years from now and their great-grandchildren would still be fighting in Ypres and Flanders and on the Somme. It was where Simon had died. Daniel tried to think of his brother then. Tall and lean, the heavy jaw, the auburn hair catching at the changeable coastal light. He had taught Daniel how to tie a fishing knot, how to light a fire, where to find owl pellets and fox dens. I will join you in French soil, Simon. We will be together again, sailing on the broad waters, trawling in the deep.

He looked at Allynson, the ramparts of his high and almost Slavic cheekbones, the tanned skin like old leather, the creases that nearly buried the blue eyes. He looked at Ruhi, the graceful Assyrian cast of his face, ascetic, the black beard, the brown skin seeming paler in the shadows where he lay. Nothing else would have brought three such men together. We are joined only by war, and without war the paths we follow would never have crossed. This is the only good that truly comes from war, that three such men should meet and be brothers.

The rain came back when they had left the gorge, harder this time. The sky at noon was as flat as evening. Daniel drew up his collar. Ahead of him, taking his turn leading the mare, Allynson snatched off his *bashlyk* and let the water fall into his face, tipping his head to it, squinting, mouth open. Judean rain. Ruhi was further ahead, twenty yards up the trail as it petered into a narrow table of rock. A plateau of raised ground lay between the ridgeline further north and the complex of ravines they had left behind them. Fifty yards across, strewn with boulders, the tableland shimmered beneath the unrelenting rain.

The Mauser cracked from the northern ridge. Daniel flinched. He saw Allynson stagger and drop the reins. The mare clattered its hooves and bolted, white-eyed. Allynson clutched his neck and fell to his knees and there was red between his fingers. Across the terrace, screeching, the mare stumbled from the edge of the land and fell, dragged by the weight of the saddle bags. Nothing but silence followed, and then Allynson coughed and dug his fingers into his knees and blood burst from his mouth. The next shot broke his head open.

Daniel ran. The gunshot roared. Rugged slopes ahead, black in the sheltered sun. John, he thought. Jesus fucking Christ, John.

A bullet slapped the rock by his feet, skipped up across his temple. There was no pain, only a searing clarity. Blood in his eyes, the horse still screaming where it had fallen. He couldn't see Ruhi.

Running, the Webley in his hand now, lungs heaving. He fired just to hear the shots, like Gaza, the rounds thumping in the flat and rain-dead air. Rain smashed the blood from his face. He scrambled, dropped, hit the edge of the terraced stone. Runnels of red mud dripped around him. The screaming of the horse, and then he was throwing himself down the slope, sliding on his heels where the scree had been loosened in the rain.

The bed of the gorge was smothered in scrub. It curved around him and slipped away into darkness. He saw olive trees like twists of wire strung out along the slope, boulders of stacked red stone. He could see the mare writhing in the shadows, kicking, braying. One leg was broken, bent back at the hock, a ring of white around her eyes. There was a foam of blood around the bit, and then a hollow smack as another bullet found her flank. The gunshot tore at the wind. The teeth of the gorge gnashed above him. The mare shuddered, the scream so loud Daniel crammed his fingers in his ears as he crawled past.

He slewed up, fell, fired blind as he ran, aiming to the line of the gorge above, snapping shots into the black flank of the valley side. A bullet hissed through the olive trees. Daniel slapped the rough trunks as he wove between them. He tripped on roots, raised an arm to shield his face from their branches. Cold water burst up from his feet as he rushed down the stream in the wadi bed. He pushed through the thorns and the back of his neck trembled with the fear of the bullet that would pierce him.

Scrambling through the scrub, his foot kicked out into emptiness. There was nothing in front of him but the open air, the cringing roots of the trees as they grasped the tier of stone. He threw his arm back, tried to twist and scramble for purchase, but then he was in the grip of nothing but the wind and the rain.

He felt the Webley dragging on its lanyard, the hollow weightless rush of the fall. He had time to think of John and of his brother but they were just flashes, just the image and the feeling that gave it colour. Then there was no time at all, and no flash and no colour and no feeling left behind but the cold and the rain, and the dark red Judean hills.

A fire burned. Slats from an artillery case, crisping in a ring of stones.

'John,' he said.

The flames danced, very low and very dark. He watched them for a while. His hands were bound, his legs too. He didn't try to speak. He took in the warmth from the fire and told himself to think of nothing. Don't think about John or Ruhi or the mare. Don't think about Battalion or Simon or Jerusalem. Don't think about Christ in the wilderness, or locusts and honey and the legions of Rome. Don't.

241

A pool of orange light swayed across the ceiling. He was in a cave. A few feet to his left there was an oval of darkness opening to the air, beyond it the rain, the brittle report of artillery in the hills. Low in the distance, louder than the rain, came the sound of the British eighteen-pounders. The 60th, attacking from the south.

Slowly he became aware of the figure on the other side of the fire. A man in German uniform sat there, a Hauptmann by the bars on his collar. He was sitting on the lid of a metal strongbox. His head was bare, his black hair wet and slicked back, his face twisted with pain. It was a long, thin face, shadowed and grey. He looked like a charcoal sketch, smudged and dirty with fingerprints. He had taken off his right boot and his sock. His foot flexed in the dirt of the cave floor, pale and bloated. The bridge and the ankle were badly swollen, almost black with bruising. The boot, scuffed and red with mud, lay discarded on its side.

The Hauptmann breathed heavily through his teeth. Tentatively he massaged his ankle. His face was flushed with pain. Daniel watched. The ankle had swollen to the size of those small, golden-leather melons they had bought in the Cairo markets, the yellow skin marbled with khaki fibre, the flesh as raw and red as peonies. The German was never getting that boot back on. The foot looked fit to burst. It must hurt like hell.

The Hauptmann muttered and hissed and passed a hand across his face. He called out in a bastard mix of German and Turkish, and in moments an Ottoman soldier came into the cave, dishevelled from the downpour outside. The Turk's face was impassioned with gloom. There was a prickle of beard on his jaw and his eyes were downcast. He smoothed the rain from his hair. He had the two saddle bags from the sorrel mare over his shoulder and he dumped them heavily at the mouth of the cave.

He was a *nefer*, a private in the Ottoman army. At the Hauptmann's curt command he crouched by the bags and found the medical kit Allynson had packed at Brigade. The *nefer* took out a field bandage in its paper sleeve and wrapped it quickly and tightly around the German's ankle. The officer gasped and bared his teeth, pressing down on either side of the strongbox with his clenched fists, drawing back as if he could lift himself away from the pain.

Daniel saw his Webley tucked into the Hauptmann's belt. A naked feeling passed through him then. He was aware of a sickening throb building up in his temple, the crust of blood on his face, the silence that swelled and drifted around him. The cave swam away, caught in the tide.

He closed his eyes. There was no reason not to.

It was still raining when he woke. He could hear it hiss against the hills. The wind pushed against the terrace of stone outside, as soft and mournful as a foghorn. His hands in their bindings felt dead. There was nothing below his wrists.

The fire was low and the strongbox still squatted there in the dirt. The German seemed to be gone. The Turkish *nefer* sat at the mouth of the cave, a blanket around his shoulders and the Mauser on his knees. He looked disconsolately at the rain, dark stubble like paint dabbed haphazardly on his chin.

There was a grinding, crunching sound in the back of the cave. Daniel craned his neck. The German was crouched there. He was hacking into the dirt with an entrenching tool. His tunic was pooled on the ground beside him and he had rolled up his shirt sleeves. Again and again he punched into the earth with the tool, scraping the dirt aside. Cutting in, raking back. Daniel saw that his foot was still bare, the ankle encased in the white bandage.

There was a sharp click of metal on stone. The German paused. He leaned in and ran his fingers through the dirt and then called out to the *nefer*. The Turkish soldier cast off the blanket and laid the Mauser against the wall. Daniel peered through half-closed eyes. The *nefer* was wearing Ruhi's cap, he saw, and then he knew that Ruhi was dead too.

The hollow, naked feeling came back. It was only now that he realised how much of his hope had been borne on Ruhi's shoulders. He could have made his way back to the Hebron road, to Bethlehem, to Brigade. He could have taken a patrol back to the site of the ambush, and then they would have seen the flickering light of the campfire spilling from the mouth of the cave. But that wouldn't happen now, because Ruhi was dead. John Allynson was dead, and Daniel couldn't even say how long ago it was that they were both killed. The vast and barren silence of the hills had buried them. They had fallen into the gulf, alongside David's armies and the Prophet's men, the Frankish knights and Roman legionaries and British infantry. It was all over.

Get hold of yourself, he thought. You are here now, in this place. That is all you know and all you can manage.

The *nefer* joined the German at the far end of the cave. They both crouched and ran their fingers through the dirt. They pushed it aside with the flats of their hands. The Turk drew the bayonet from his belt and dug into the earth. Their voices were very low. Daniel tried to lift himself up.

'Water,' he said into the silence. His voice sounded strange to him. 'I need water. *Wasser, bitte.* And you have to untie my hands, I can't feel them. *Wasser, bitte.*'

What the hell was it in Turkish? He had never learned. The *nefer*, as if stunned by Daniel's words, lurched over and stood with the bayonet poised over him. He had the drooping, weary face of a man put too long under pressure. The Hauptmann stood up, resting all his weight on his good leg. His bare arms were streaked with dirt.

The German snapped his fingers and pointed at the strongbox. The *nefer* tucked the bayonet into his belt and started dragging the box to the other end of the cave. They had dug a hole there. They had dug several holes, although only one seemed deep enough for the strongbox.

The Turk grunted with the effort. There was the chink of metal, the unmistakable sound of coins clinking together. The German helped him lever the box in and held out his hand. The Turk passed him the bayonet, handle first. The German turned back to the hole, groaning as he crouched, and covered the strongbox with earth. He looked at Daniel. In English he said, 'We can spare a little water, Captain, I'm sure.'

The *nefer* took a flask from the baggage and held it to Daniel's mouth. The water was warm and silty. When he had swallowed, Daniel said, 'You need to untie my hands. I can't feel them.'

'I need do nothing, Captain,' the Hauptmann said.

The Turk capped the flask and stood with the hang-dog air of every private soldier unsure of his orders. He waited glumly for instruction.

'The circulation's cut off,' Daniel said. 'I can't feel my hands. Do you know that word? Circulation. The blood.'

The Hauptmann smirked. He probed gently in the soil with the point of the bayonet. His right leg was splayed out to the side, the foot bare and swollen and the bandages already dirty. He said something over his shoulder and the Turk took a thin clasp knife with an ivory handle from his pocket, and then knelt over Daniel and began to cut the ropes around his wrists. Daniel could smell the murky scent of sweat from him.

A flood of fire and ice came down into his hands, so hot it almost made him scream. For a moment he couldn't move his arms. The *nefer* massaged his biceps, said something low and encouraging and calm, and helped him to sit up. Daniel let his hands flop into his lap. They were dark and swollen, a corpse's hands. He tried to move his fingers. The blood began to flow. He rubbed them together and tried to ignore the pains that raced up into his shoulders.

'Good?' the *nefer* said.

Daniel nodded. 'Good.' He looked at the rifle where it leaned against the wall.

From the back of the cave the Hauptmann said, 'We will leave your legs for now, I think.' He laid the bayonet aside and dug into the earth with his fingers. 'It wouldn't do to have you running away from us, now that we've caught you.'

'You'll take me back to Jerusalem?' Daniel said. He had never been a prisoner before. It was a strange feeling. He was afraid, but he felt ashamed too. A sense of failure and humiliation. He found it difficult to look his captors in the eye.

The Hauptmann laughed. 'Jerusalem is under the British flag now, I fear. Yet another piece of incompetence to lay at the Caliphate's door. It is an empire out of time, I think.'

He prised and scraped at the earth, grunting. He was trying to loosen something buried in the soil. Daniel was too far away to see what it was.

'Then where? If not Jerusalem, where's left?'

'I suspect the road north is closed to us now as well,' said the Hauptmann. 'So the River Jordan, if we can manage it. A British officer may prove useful. After that, who can say.' He gasped as he shifted his weight. 'But not these hills, not anymore.'

'What happened to your foot?'

'I fell off a horse,' the Hauptmann said, cheerfully. 'And then the horse fell on me. I seem to be cursed with ill luck, and this damnable country is not an easy one to traverse at the best of times. During a winter thunderstorm, it is positively suicidal.'

'Your English is excellent,' Daniel told him, although he suspected the Hauptmann already knew this. He wanted to keep him talking. It was important to make the connection between them, to make the German see the British officer as a man and not just a soldier.

'I studied in your country. Mathematics,' the German said with a smile. 'At Cambridge. A far harder language to master than English.'

He laughed, again with that forced lightness. Daniel wondered how much pain he was really in.

'I have no German, I'm afraid.'

'This comes as no surprise,' the Hauptmann told him.

The *nefer* had settled himself back by the cave mouth. Warily he followed their speech. Daniel watched the German's back as he laboured in the earth, digging with the bayonet, scooping out the spoil with his hands.

'What did you bury there?'

'You're very bold with your questions, Captain,' the Hauptmann chuckled. 'Certainly for one in your position. If you must know, it is the soldiers' pay for much of the Ottoman Twenty-fourth Division.'

'You stole it?'

'Let us say instead that I have prevented it from falling into British hands by allowing it to fall into mine.'

He turned and grinned over his shoulder. His face was very grey now. The eyes were wild and unfocused, the smile oddly lopsided.

'I had hoped for an easier escape to Jericho. But matters as they often do in war have gone distinctly awry. We must make the best of our present circumstances, Captain. Not all is lost while your hands are full of gold.'

He pulled at the soil, gasped, grunted, reeled back and gave a shout of satisfaction. He scrabbled in the broken ground again, pulled something free, blew the soil away and dusted it with his fingertips. Daniel tried to see what he had removed. They looked like clay jars, he thought. Like Roman amphorae. They were no more than eight inches tall.

The German gathered his breath. He ran his hands over the jars. He was very still. He sat there contemplating them. Occasionally he reached out to touch them. He had forgotten about Daniel, it seemed, and the Ottoman gold, and Jericho.

After a few minutes he covered up the jars with his tunic and then lay down beside them. His teeth worked against his bottom lip. He tucked his hands into his armpits. The storm was up outside. The rain was fierce and the wind blew.

Daniel settled into his own thoughts again. He let his mind drift. He was tired and found it hard to keep his eyes open. He watched the firelight ripple across the ceiling of the cave and it drew to mind the scales of light on the surface of the water when his brother had taken him fishing. The boat rocking under them, the bite of the line in his palm, the sense of the sea speaking. He thought of the house where they had grown up and what might have happened to it, who lived there now. They had sold it after their father had died. He would give anything to see that house again. To go back, to return, to become yourself again.

With half an eye he watched the *nefer* at the cave mouth and the German lying silently further back, the ancient jars nestled under his tunic.

And when ye shall see Jerusalem compassed with armies, then know that the destruction thereof is nigh. Let them which are in Judaea flee to the mountains.

Luke 21. He had found that passage in his Bible when the division first moved into Palestine.

He saw Simon stilling his arm as the line jerked down into the water. *Give him some slack*, he said. *Now – strike!*

Daniel felt his hands. When they were almost back to normal the *nefer* came and bound them again. He banked the fire and all three of them tried to sleep.

In the dream the sea was black and Simon was sitting with him in the boat. There was something else in the boat with them, something dark and malevolent, but in the dream it was obscure. Neither of them could speak of it.

Simon was dead, Daniel realised. The jars were gathered around his feet. The sea they sailed over was as black and smooth as slate. Deep in its furthest reaches there were fragile points of light, like stars. Everything was very still. There was no sound.

Simon looked at him but Daniel couldn't see his face. His brother raised his arms and the hands were gone.

It's alright, Daniel told him. It's just that you're dead now, Simon. That's all. We're both dead. That's all there is to it.

Simon tried to speak but no words came. The black light of the sea flashed and shook.

The dark thing in the boat began to howl. There was nothing but the sea and the darkness where no wind blew. There was nothing.

He woke and saw the *nefer* curled up beside the fire, asleep. He was whimpering to himself, the rifle clutched to his side. It was still dark outside, still raining.

The dream swam away from him. The details faded. He moved his hands inside the bindings, relieved to find that they were still there.

The Hauptmann was digging at the back of the cave again. He was bare-chested, his shirt flung aside. Earth was scattered around him. There were more jars now, lined up beside the ones he'd already disinterred. One of them was larger than the others, at least a foot tall. The clay was rusty and dark with soil. The German's swollen foot lay there in the shadows. It didn't look like it belonged to him at all. For a moment Daniel thought he had hacked it off with the entrenching tool. It looked dead.

He was muttering to himself, cutting down again and again with the bayonet, scraping the soil away. Every movement seemed to cause him pain. Tenderly, as if afraid the least attention would shatter them, he drew his fingers across the sides of the clay jars. Daniel was sure that the Hauptmann had been doing this all night. He hadn't given himself a moment's sleep.

'Hauptmann?' the Turkish *nefer* said.

He sat up and warmed his hands by the fire. The German didn't answer. He didn't even look round. The *nefer* said something in Turkish and a look of abject resignation passed across his face. He lowered his eyes.

The German, struggling into his shirt, limped to the fire and muttered an oath. He saw that Daniel was awake and signalled for the *nefer* to cut his bonds. The Turk approached with the clasp knife, and again Daniel sat up and massaged his hands. He glanced at the officer's foot. It was twice its normal size. In the light of the fire it had a sallow, green cadaverous look. He could smell it, even above the scent of the burning wood.

'He wants to go,' the German said, in his flat and accentless English. He nodded at the Turk. '*Nefer* Berat. He wants to take the money while we can and make our way to the Jordan. But what happens then? I want to ask him. What happens when the Ottoman army asks what we're doing with all their gold? They will take it back, surely. I think he's afraid that I'm planning to kill him.'

'Are you?'

The Hauptmann laughed. Daniel saw it then. Something had gone wrong in his eyes. The *nefer* had seen it first and now Daniel had seen it too. The dead foot was poisoning him.

'Don't worry,' the Hauptmann said to Daniel. 'He can't understand English. I won't kill him, not yet anyway. I need someone to carry the box.'

He roared with laughter and struck his chest with the flat of his palm. *Nefer* Berat cringed by the fire and clutched his rifle. Daniel kept rubbing his hands, trying to make it seem as if they hurt more than they did. He looked at the Turk and his rifle, at the saddle bags with Allynson's supplies.

The Hauptmann limped back and forth and buttoned his shirt. He stared with naked longing at the clay jars. Whenever he hobbled towards the mouth of the cave he would always cast a look over his shoulder at them, reluctant to get too far away. He took a box of ration biscuits from the saddle bags and tossed one to Daniel, one to the Turkish soldier. The *nefer* mumbled something and began to eat, his eyes staring away into nothing. Daniel didn't know what the penalty was for desertion in the Ottoman army. In the British, it was death.

Daniel broke off a corner of the biscuit and let it soften in his mouth. The German stood there with all the weight on his good leg, lupine, ravenous, his eyes flicking between the Ottoman soldier and the clay jars. Always his gaze came to rest on them.

'What are they?' Daniel asked.

The Hauptmann wiped his mouth with the back of his hand. He moved his weight, tentatively, onto his bad ankle. He closed his eyes and moved the weight back with a long, exhausted sigh.

'I'm not quite sure. They are very old though, I'm certain of that. Not Biblical, not quite that old, but even so.'

'How can you tell?'

'Nothing more than my intuition, and long afternoons spent in the Museum of General and Local Archaeology at Cambridge.' He smiled broadly. 'These are, I believe, centuries old, not millennia.'

'Centuries is still very old.'

'Indeed it is. This is an old land. It is fitting that it retains old things, in old and secret places.'

'They seem Greek,' Daniel said. 'Or Classical, at least.'

'The Hellenistic influence is a long and enduring one, Captain.'

'Perhaps from a burial? Grave goods of some kind?'

'Perhaps,' the German agreed. His face glistened with sweat. He moved his weight again, as though he enjoyed the pain it gave him.

'We had a guide,' Daniel said, wanting to keep him talking. Everything felt very close and uncertain in the cave. Something was approaching, he knew it. 'Ruhi. He told us that there were caves scattered throughout these hills. Prophets and holy men, hermits in the wilderness. Men seeking God.'

The Hauptmann nodded eagerly. He was still smiling. He wiped the sweat from his lean, hard face. Daniel had the oddest sense that he was in a seminar and the Hauptmann was guiding his thoughts, teasing the correct answers from him piece by piece.

'This land is the womb of faith,' he said. 'Heretics and radicals, prophets and priests. All have preached their gospels in these hills. Judeans, Jews, Samaritans. The cults of Moloch. Christians, Crusaders, the men of the Prophet, like our friend Berat here. Places for the faithful.'

The *nefer* made a sound in the back of his throat on hearing his name. He couldn't meet the German's eyes either.

'Have you any faith yourself?' Daniel said.

The Hauptmann laughed again, a brittle sound. He was very pale now.

'I was raised a staunch Bavarian Catholic,' he said. 'But war has erased whatever faith I might once have had. War and mathematics, and certain griefs, certain disappointments.'

'Before the war,' Daniel said, surprised at the confession, 'I wanted to be a minister in the church. At least, I thought I did.'

'And now?'

'I'm not sure. Not anymore. The war, and other things.'

'The war. *Der Krieg. La guerre. Savaş.*'

Berat looked up again. He frowned and leaned his forehead against the barrel of his rifle.

Daniel felt ashamed. It was as if he had bargained for his life with a secret. He had never told anyone that, apart from his brother. He remembered the moment, after their father had died. The garden dark around them in early summer, the smell of the clematis in the air. Daniel had told Simon how much he believed, how much he felt that light in him, and Simon had smiled and reached out and laid a hand on his shoulder. He had understood. Perhaps he didn't share the faith, but he knew what it meant to his brother. It was the sea and the woods around Cramond, and it was the stained glass in the church at Newhaven. It was the smell of the hymn books and the scent of the flowers in the night, and the black rags of the bats above them. It was his brother by his side. It was the mystery of the world, the love he felt for it. It was the light in the darkness.

251

'So, a true Christian,' the German said. He shuffled to the cave wall and rested his hand against it. 'Do you know your Bible well, Captain?'

'Well enough.'

'Then you'll know that we're very close to the scene of the parable… when the traveller came from Jerusalem to Jericho and fell amongst thieves? And here you are now, on the same road. Who will be your Samaritan? I wonder. Who will bind up your wounds and set you on his own beast? For make no mistake, Captain, I know perfectly well that I am a thief.'

He limped back down the throat of the cave, shifting the Webley on his belt. With an effort he took up the bayonet from the dirt. The clay jars were all lined up as if in an exhibit.

'You dreamed of these, didn't you?' the Hauptmann said. 'I dreamed of them. Berat here dreamed of them. I saw your faces, in the dream. I heard you both cry out in the night. They whispered to me in my dream, but I was already awake. Isn't that interesting?'

He leaned and lightly tapped the bayonet against the largest jar. The clay rang out like struck steel.

'Jesus cast out unclean spirits, do you remember? But where did they come from in the first place? A pity for the world that we still await Him, that we have no Jesus with us now.'

He turned his face towards Daniel. It looked wild, unrecognisable. The skin of his foot was threaded with black veins. The smell of putrefaction lingered in the air.

It was not madness, not exactly. It wasn't just the infection or the strain of battle. Shell shock could carve men down to mere shavings, but this was more than stress. It was something to do with the cave, and the hills, and the old, old land around them.

Daniel knew that the *nefer*, Berat, saw it very clearly. He was frightened, but his fear wrestled with his greed for the gold. There was the gold and a captive British officer and the wounded Herr Hauptmann who was losing his mind, poisoned by his broken foot and by the little clay jars that he couldn't leave alone. To Berat, he was trapped with a man as wild as any prophet in the wilderness.

Winter winds trembled in the hills. Rain drew a curtain of water across the mouth of the cave. The war felt very distant.

'What is your name, British captain?' the German said. He slumped heavily to the ground and cradled the largest jar in his lap. '*Wie heißen sie? Name, Rang und Service nummer!*'

'McQuarrie. Daniel McQuarrie.'

The German rocked backwards, clutching the jar. Laughter was torn from him.

'Daniel!' He brushed the sweat from his face. His whole expression was vague, smeared out. 'Of course it is. Of course. And I am Hauptmann Erich Löwe, my captain. At your service.'

The German stood and gave a parody of a clipped, Teutonic bow – and then, with a snarl, he threw the jar onto the ground.

The clay shattered with a dull flat crack. Berat jumped. Daniel shielded his face. A spray of dust, a gasp of air. The jar's belly split open and fell away. All three of them, Daniel, Löwe and Berat, stared at what lay there in the wreckage.

They were clothed in scraps of flesh, as brown and tough as leather. Beneath those scraps the bones were yellow.

It was a pair of human hands.

At dusk Berat fixed the bayonet to his rifle and went outside into the rain. What sky remained out there was a sodden grey.

Löwe sat at the back of the cave, barely moving. He brooded over the severed hands, staring at them, his own hands occasionally straying to his swollen ankle. The foot was beginning to turn black. The pain must have been excruciating, but he gave no sign of it.

When he wasn't massaging his foot or wiping his drawn and lucent face, Löwe kept stroking the butt of the Webley in his belt. It wouldn't be long, Daniel knew, before he used it on them. The road to Jericho would be a hard one, if it was still open. The Ottoman army could have abandoned the whole of Southern Palestine while they huddled in this cave. Löwe had two anchors on his escape; a captive British officer and a reluctant Turkish *nefer*. Two .455 cartridges would solve those problems neatly.

Berat returned after an hour. His uniform was dark and wet. When he spoke, the Hauptmann reacted angrily. Daniel couldn't understand them. He lay there by the red embers of the fire, hands bound again behind his back. Berat came and sat by the mouth of the cave and took the bayonet from the rifle. He looked close to tears. Mechanically, he began to clean the Mauser. He checked the cartridges and then sat there staring out at the rain, the butt of the gun pressed into the dirt and his cheek resting against the barrel.

Löwe knelt by the clay jars, hands steepled, his chin propped on his pressed fingertips. After a moment he arranged the severed hands in front of the line of remaining jars. He stared at them for a long while. Now and then he reached out and laid his hands against the bones, and it made Daniel feel that he was trying to draw some comfort or meaning from them, that he was trying to will a fellow feeling into the man who had once been joined to them. He couldn't imagine how old they were or how long they had rested in the earth.

Later in the afternoon Berat held the water bottle to Daniel's lips. Their eyes passed over each other. Daniel could see how nervous and unhappy the private was. He moved to untie the ropes but Löwe snapped at him and he withdrew. Löwe's voice was harsh and grating. Berat, apologetic, took up his rifle and settled himself to watch from the cave mouth again. The rain streamed down. It was dark and cold.

His hands were less of a problem, Daniel decided, than his legs. If his legs were free he could at least run. He tried to draw Berat's attention. He nodded at the bindings on them and then jerked his chin at the handle of the clasp knife in Berat's pocket. The *nefer* shook his head sadly. His eyes were very dark and moist. He glanced at Hauptmann Löwe, but the German was too absorbed in the withered hands to notice.

Löwe suddenly pivoted on his knees and crept over to the dying fire. He fed in the last few sticks of wood from the broken artillery case. Daniel could smell the rot from his foot. One firm strike would split it open. The German's eyes were raw, his face glassy with sweat. Through the rising flames it looked like a death mask.

He grinned and shuffled back into the shadows, where he picked up the clay jars and put them down, laid his hands on the bones, rocked back and forth, muttering, snarling. Spit sprayed from his lips. For the rest of the day, his foot stinking, Löwe did little else. He didn't sleep. He didn't eat. He hardly seemed to know the others were there, but sometimes he would call over his shoulder in German, and then more and more often in English.

'You are Daniel in the lion's den,' he cried. His voice seemed wrenched from the gut. His hand strayed to the gun in his belt.

Another time he said, 'Jerusalem is yours. Would Christ be pleased with your work, do you think? You have praised him with blood. Well done, Daniel. Well done. You are one of the Elect, one of the saved.' A string of spittle fell from his lips.

Later, he said, 'Can you see it? The writing on the wall. The writing is calling to me. Translate it for me, if you please. You have great insight into visions, into dreams.'

Also, relentlessly, 'But it was God who shut the lion's mouth and kept Daniel safe from harm. Is that not the case?' He looked to the roof of the cave, hidden in the shadows. 'Where is God, to shut my mouth?'

A night and a day and on into another dusk. Daniel and Berat ate the hard army tack and drank the water the *nefer* had gathered from the rain. Löwe shunned everything. He would not move from the back of the cave. He lurked there, his eyes savage spots of light staring out of the dark. He would not leave the bones alone. Every time Berat moved, Löwe screamed at him to be still.

'They cut the hands from sorcerers,' Löwe said. 'They cut the hands from thieves. Very simple, very effective. They cut the hands from those who consorted with demons and bound those hands with spells. I saw it happen, in my dream. He came from very far away, and it rained there too. A great transgression, for the son to kill the father.'

The night dropped into the valleys between the hills. The rain fell. He said, 'You should not scorn the followers of the Prophet, Crusader. They have given us the numerals without which no science is possible. Remember that, before you sheath your sword. The *Principia Mathematica* was all the rage at Cambridge, all the rage. I saw him once, you know. Russell. Extraordinary. Why I am a Hauptmann of infantry I shall never understand. And Palestine? I was going to be an engineer. In India once, I thought to build a bridge… But then there is no logic to govern a man's life, is there, Captain? Nothing is fated or planned. Accident, happy or otherwise, that's all. War is such ludicrous chaos.'

Much later, deeper into the darkness, Daniel woke. He heard the dull crunch of the broken clay and it made his heart beat faster. Löwe was smashing the jars.

The fire had fallen to a faint red glow. It was cold in the cave but Daniel felt the heat in his stomach rising and spreading into his limbs. He felt afraid.

The sky outside was troubled and dark. Streaks of light registered the dawn. The wind came threading through the gap of the cave mouth. Berat had woken now too and he pointed the muzzle of the gun at the vague shadows where Löwe picked through the broken shards.

'*Guter Gott*… God's very eyes…' Löwe mumbled.

'What is it?' Daniel's voice was too loud in that quiet. 'What's in them? What have you found?'

The German's breath came fast. He was shaking. Whatever they were, he was laying them out along the ground by the severed hands, arranging them piece by piece. Daniel tried to see past the hump of his back. It looked like scraps of parchment, squares and rectangles of paper, very brittle, some of them rolled into tubes that fell apart in his hands. Carefully Löwe picked them from the broken clay.

He made a clicking noise in the back of his throat and muttered words that Daniel couldn't hear. He was very still, very serious now.

'What have you found?' Daniel said again.

He couldn't stop his voice from shaking. He couldn't explain it. Being in this cave now was like being in deep water and seeing dark shapes pass silently beneath you. It was the body noting the scent of the beast before the mind was consciously aware.

'There is writing on them,' Löwe said. His voice drifted weakly to the mouth of the cave. 'I thought Hebrew, but now… I'm not so sure. Not Greek, no. No, I cannot say, truly I can't. I would almost think that they were numbers.'

He smoothed away the broken pieces of clay.

'The jars with this writing have been arranged around the hands,' he said, pointing. 'The hands were in the middle, and the other jars were circling them. Truly, they are like an equation... almost, almost.'

He stared down at the parchment and fell silent. For a long moment he stayed like that, rigid and bowed over the pieces, his back to the cave. Then he began to speak, softly, but it was in no language that Daniel had ever heard.

'What are you saying? What is that?'

Löwe didn't answer. Daniel looked to Berat. The *nefer* shook his head. He clutched the rifle like a shield, his mouth drawn.

'Berat,' Daniel whispered. 'Please. *Bitte.*'

The Turk shook his head. The shadows grew darker in the throat of the cave.

The fire was almost gone now. There was only a white dust in the ring of stones, the smouldering ash. Hauptmann Löwe said nothing. He didn't move. There was darkness in the sky, and soon the grey of the cave mouth and the grey of Löwe's back had blurred to the same drab, extinguished colour, and for a moment it was as though the German's hunkered form was the entrance to the world outside and the cave mouth was just the passage to a greater darkness.

Daniel watched him from the corner of his eye. Carefully he drew up his knees and rolled onto his back, his bound hands beneath him. He shuffled against the cave wall until he was sitting up and hissed at Berat, but the Turkish soldier still crouched there with the Mauser.

'Berat. *Bitte!*'

Daniel kicked his legs out. He turned to one side, displaying his hands. Berat's eyes flickered. Slowly, still focused on Löwe, he drew the knife from his tunic pocket.

The German hadn't moved but there was a sound in the cave now and it could only have come from him. It was a droning sound, like a prayer muttered in chorus. He knelt there before the severed hands, the scraps of parchment. Daniel saw that his foot had split open along the arch and was leaking a thin black gruel into the dirt, black as oil. It stank.

Berat, on hands and knees, dragging the rifle, skirted the dead campfire. He laid the Mauser down and unfolded the knife. Daniel felt the blade biting at the rope.

His hands shook as the bindings fell away. He fumbled with swollen fingers at the knot around his ankle while Berat folded the knife and groped for the gun.

Löwe moved. The droning was shut off suddenly, like music by a slammed door. Resolute, purposeful, he took up a piece of the parchment. His head shivered. There was the wet, unmistakable sound of him slowly cramming it into his mouth, his jaws chewing, slick with spit. He reached for another piece, folded it, choked, began to chew. The moist champing click of his jaws, the wet smack of his lips. He was picking shreds of flesh from the dead hands and eating them. He crunched the bone, he gnawed the sinew.

'Hauptmann?' Berat said. His face was dark and shone with sweat. Rifle in hand, he crawled to the square of earth where the strongbox had been buried. '*Ich nehme das.*' He set the rifle down and dug into the soil with his hands, grunting as he prised up the handle of the box. He watched Löwe, just a few feet away. Careful, very careful. '*Es ist auch meins. Ja? Meins.*'

The rope was tight around Daniel's feet. The *nefer* must have been a fisherman because it was tightly woven into what felt like a turtle knot and his fingers could get no purchase on it.

Löwe reached again, delicately. He tore another strip of parchment to pieces and stuffed it into his mouth. Then he ripped a string of dry leather from the bones. He sighed and chewed, luxuriating, a strangled whimper in the back of his throat. Berat had pulled the strongbox from the hole. Daniel could hear the soft, muted clink of the coins shifting inside. There was a drumbeat pounding in his head as he picked at the knot in the rope. He had not felt like this before, not even at Gaza. He was terrified.

'Hauptmann,' Berat said again. '*Ich gehe.*'

'Berat,' Daniel said sharply, his voice shaking. 'Nefer Berat, get back. Get back now.'

The air had changed. The fire was dead. The shadows in the throat of the cave were like ink. They flowed over the German and swallowed him down, and when the light briefly flared from a last splintering ember in the ring of stones, what crouched there in the cave was no longer Hauptmann Löwe. It looked like him, but it was not. It was something else.

Daniel wrenched at the rope. He seized his nerve. It was like being under fire, the bullets whipping past like skimmed stones.

The rifle was there on the ground. Dive across the cave and snatch it up, lever the first round into the chamber. One shot into Löwe's back. Smack the bolt and put the next into Berat. He could do it. His heart was racing. Fingers bit rope. Stagger through the hills, wade through the rushing wadis, find his comrades. Jerusalem by morning. Kneel where Christ was laid to rest, whence he rose once more into a glad morning full of mystery. Give thanks on the rim of Golgotha for this deliverance.

A red noise rose up around him. The cave roared with it.

The German was shrieking, as though scorched by fire. He tore at his hair with his hands, screaming, screaming, fingers wrenching at his face. Berat shouted, a cry of absolute horror – and then Löwe was surging towards him, clawing the Webley from his belt. Two rounds barked into the *nefer's* chest. The noise was loud as thunder.

The rope slithered from Daniel's feet.

The *nefer* crumpled, pink foam in his mouth, gagging, a copper stink in the air and blood spattered across the cave wall. The German tossed the gun aside. He lurched and settled, whipping around on all fours, face a mask of shadow. Slowly, hissing and gurgling, he crawled through the dead embers of the fire. The ocean was in his eyes now. The darkness was filled with points of light. There was a smell of hot metal and burned hair, a deep-trawled stink of rotting flesh.

Lunging, he grasped Daniel's legs and dragged him through the ring of stones and the white ash. Daniel clawed at the earth beneath him, twisted onto his front, felt the German's steel fingers probing and frisking him. The curtain of rain was dripping from the overhang only an arm's length away – the crisp air, sullen with cold; the dark sky and the scent of winter gorse, the bruised and smoky olive trees. Everything out there was fresh and clean and bright with purpose. Daniel shouted and reached for it, he would clutch all of it to him, snatch it all up in both his hands and breathe the surging life into his lungs.

The fingers were like iron in his flesh. Hands snaked round to choke him. He heard himself try to scream and then the German twisted him round and leered into his face, drooling, lustful. The eyes were marbled jasper. They fumed in the dark, burning. There was a shadow in him.

A howl on the wind, crying from the depths of the earth, a shriek across the sea. The German's face was awry, it was not human. The fingers were like shards of bone plunging into Daniel's mouth, as if he would tear the jaw away. Bloody drool slick on his chin, the gagging choking horror as the fingers pushed deeper, and then the stale rotten stink of parchment and dead flesh, the German thrusting the scraps into his mouth; ink, burned leather, all the ancient buried horror of it dissolving in his throat; the scroll as the angels showed it to Ezekiel, he thought madly, Ezekiel choking down the parchment, to take inside him the very Word of God...

He couldn't breathe. A shroud had been thrown over his eyes. Everything was black.

Daniel, heaving, kicked out and felt the weight withdraw from him. Scrabbling in the dirt, he flung himself forward, choking. He could taste the dust, taste the ashes. The world was a smear of light and shadow.

A roar shook the darkness behind him. He rolled to the lip of the cave. When he turned he could see the dim shape of Berat up on his knees and coughing blood, the Mauser in his arms. Half the German's head was hanging down onto his shoulder, arms flailing as he tried to push it all back together, fingers slipping in the blood and meat. One eye blown away, the other burning like fire. The long raw disjunction of the mouth was screaming, spitting teeth.

Berat snapped the bolt and shot again. Löwe's skull erupted. Berat fell and was still.

Daniel rolled to the edge of the terrace, streaked with rain. Down the tiers of ancient stone, end over end, and even as he fell he choked the flesh and parchment down and felt it seed its madness in him. He felt his throat tear, tasted blood. All the letters on the parchment, those curling symbols, were sketched in fire behind his eyes, their dark mystery.

He lunged for thorn roots and grasped for stone, skinning his palms. A rib cracked. He retched air into a struck lung. When he fell onto the wet white stones of the riverbed a flame licked down into his heart. It sang in his bones.

He looked up and the evening sky was stained with purple and silver. There were great spools of light weaving together as the darkness flowed through him. He clawed the earth. The rain shook. There was thunder, oceans breaking in the wrack. He looked at his spread hands beneath him. For a moment they were wizened claws groping on a ledger of black stone. Something from beyond this world of light and life was growing inside him.

Pieces of memory ran into the stream as it passed through his fingers. He tried to snatch them up before they were gone, jewels that he brought out into the dusk. He saw Simon turning to him as the line struck, dipping his hands into the salt water. He was in the garden at the end of summer, with the yellow smell of the clematis thick in the air. They were walking down Broughton Street to see *Peter Pan*, and then he was sitting in the quiet of the church, his father beside him, the light moving cleanly through the glass behind the pulpit. Red and green and gold.

The darkness swam through him, vein and sinew, blood and bone. The severed hands and the scrolls of parchment, infecting him, pouring through him and scouring him away. He was Captain Daniel McQuarrie, floundering in the wadi as the water streamed through, and he was a thing of the dark in a chamber underground, where pain and torment was his meat and drink. Shrieks and laughter, the cruel grip of the void. Soon there would be nothing of him left.

Some dim part of his mind reached out for scripture.

Let God arise, let His enemies be scattered...

His brother, the scratch of khaki as they embraced before he left for the front. The smuts and ashes of the idling train, waiting for the journey south. The fishing line descending into the dark waters, all the life that flitted around the bait, quick and silver and secret. Fresh rain and the green earth, and life.

'Christ,' he cried out. He felt the shadow flicker and surge inside him. 'For God's sake, help me.'

...as wax melteth before the fire, so let the wicked perish at the presence of God.

Pain ripped through him, white fire. His eyes were black. He called in prayer, pleading.

'Take this from me, please, cast this out of me – for God's sake.'

He retched again. The wind screamed and he could smell the olive trees, the fragrant scrub. Fire was on the breeze, as cold as ice. He retched again, every muscle and tendon in his body wrung out like a ragged cloth.

'Jesus help me,' he whispered.

Buckling, bent double, lips kissing the torrent of water as oil and shadow spewed from his mouth, black and gauzy like rotten lace. A tide of pollution pooled onto the stones, and where it hit the water it hissed and smoked and drew away. Daniel heaved and gagged, a hook in his belly drawing his guts up into his throat. He wept, and all he could hear was the shaken air as the sky was broken and the rain clamoured in the earth.

The darkness fell away from him. He watched it through weeping eyes, and in the leaden, uncertain light the smoke and oil began to coalesce. The shadow swirled and quickened into form. From where the water swayed in the wadi bed a blanket of darkness was rising. The German had choked him with it, and God had drawn it out. There was a stone malice in its eyes.

He looked into the shadow's face. Free from the prison of the earth, the cell of the clay jars and their enveloping spells, his own face looked back at him. And then it was Löwe's face, and then he recognised nothing at all.

Daniel raised his arms. He reached out, surrendered, but the shadow drew back a smoking blade and struck.

A lance punched through his chest, harder than steel. A sword of ice water, flooding through him. He couldn't even scream. All the air was burned away. He was stretched out like a silver thread, hanging in the deep.

Voices came from the distance then, beyond the rain. They were flat English voices, calm and unexcited, and then shouting as a crack of bullets split the air, the hot whistle of passing rounds. He could hear the crunch of army boots, the clatter of rain striking steel helmets.

The water was as cold as winter around him. The shadow withdrew and flowed away across the desert, into the hills, biding its time. There was nothing in the sky and nothing in the rain. He felt his life passing away.

'It's gone,' a soldier said above him. Then, almost impressed: 'Christ. He's still alive.'

PART IV

Monday 20th May 1918

In the dream she was in Florence. The taste of wine in her mouth, sharp as salt. A cry, far away in the distant streets, lonely, desperately lonely, and then there were hands gripping her, binding her, tearing, tearing…

Come on, come on, tell me what you are…

The room was dark as she surfaced. There was a dull pain at the back of her head. Someone had been screaming, a dream that seemed to pass into the waking world. The echo of it lingered, a heartfelt fading cry. A shiver ran through her. There was something out there, howling and discordant. Foxes, she thought. A hissing, viperish sound. It came again as she lay there, very faint now – dragged across the fringes of the night, frayed and lonely and full of the most desperate grief. Esther felt fear like frost across her skin. She clutched herself and clenched her teeth.

For a moment she thought she was in the dormitory at Roddinglaw. One of the patients had woken – Captain McQuarrie crying out, that same lonely panic, that same dread. But then her eyes adjusted and she saw the contours of the room around her, the bare floor, the old dresser in the corner and the rag of curtain draped across the dirty window.

'Jacob. Jacob, what in the name of God was that?'

She reached for him but he was gone. She felt cold and terribly alone. A chill had crept off the sea and slithered up the beach. The air in the old cottage was freezing. She called his name again but there was no answer.

She straightened her clothes and crept fearfully into the main room. A blade of moonlight cut across the flagstones. The empty cups were still on the table, the old ledger. There was a musty, animal smell in the air, a lingering scent of unwashed clothes and beef fat and tea leaves. Esther felt the taut, primed certainty that someone had been watching her.

'Jacob?' The cold was as hard as stone. She shivered again. 'Jacob, are you there?'

The last threads of her dream broke up and fell away, and the howl was just a memory that had dragged out of her sleep. That's all it was, though it lay across her shoulders like a sheet of lead. A howling.

He had been very clear about it. He was certain. The hound is supposed to howl when the lord is about to die...

The night was sullen out there and pressed against her. She left the cottage and cut along the path through the trees, her hands shaking. There was no need to run. Whatever was happening now would happen regardless. The howling had been clear in her dream. It had been a dream, she was certain, but the coastline was still poised with the memory of it, hunkered down, aghast. The branches were black spiderwebs above her. The cow parsley was tall and wavered in the darkness, spindle shadows. She stumbled on the rugged ground. The cold gripped at her and her breath was a trail of smoke.

She came by the path that turned off to the cliff-face of Gallondean. The stone was black, no torch or lamplight shining in its windows. The sight of it repelled her. She found herself flinching from it, as repulsed as if she was passing an open tomb. It was an awful place. She stood there before the rusting gate, gripping the bars, looking at the sunken, ramshackle garden, the black slab of the oaken door, the flat Norman walls and the blunt, iron crown of the tower. For the first time she saw the house for what it was. It had never been a home. It was only a place to project power and to dominate, to frighten and bully and corrupt. That's all it was. A boot on the face of the shore, pressing its heel down, the people inside trapped by the masks they had made for themselves, waiting with terror for the howling to release them. Horror had bled into the stone.

He would be in there now. Brooding in the midnight dark, all those documents feeding into his fever, sorting through his scraps and fragments and forcing them to cohere. He had heard the call from Hound Point and had risen from her side, taking himself to the castle in preparation. Death was coming. She knew he would meet it gladly. He was chained to the rock, waiting for the tide to rise, but she wouldn't go to him. She would not be drawn into that water. She refused. No one's expectations would ever grip her again. Let time deal with it. Let the waves of the years crash against the stone and gnaw it all away.

Esther shuddered and turned from Gallondean, and from wherever Jacob Beresford was waiting. She was no Catherine clawing at the window, no Mina locked to her vampire count.

I reject. I will not have. I do not want.

When she came to the lawns of Roddinglaw, feet slushing through the night-wet grass, she saw the door hanging open. The house was dark and silent. She felt cold and oddly frightened, crowded with that same sense that she was being watched. Eyes that had hungrily appraised her had only just drawn away.

Something crunched under her feet. Stooping, Esther saw shards of clay scattered on the path before the door, handfuls of black earth and broken jars. There were scraps of white paper tumbling in the breeze. She picked one up. Torn pages, she saw, two or three or four. Columns of disjointed words. *Yellow summer stone and sand.* 'A Death in the Desert'. Here and there a cross had been scrawled on the torn pages. She let the scrap fall from her hands and the breeze cast it far away. As she crouched on the ground she took up a handful of spilled earth and rubbed it between her fingers. It was dry and smelled of the bones it once held.

Something dark flitted between the trees, a silhouette, a black shadow with blazing eyes, free as smoke. She caught her breath. But then it was gone, and the only sound was the cool frisking of the leaves as the wind picked up and broke against the shore.

I write this with no peace in me and no need for confession. I have moments left. It comes. I am ready.

I have destroyed Sarah's statue. Vishnu's garlands are faded and dead. The porphyry has been cast to the ground and shattered. The circle of salt is broken. There is nothing that can protect me. The hound has howled and I have heard it.

God, how I have heard it now! It ripped the silence apart, piercing and shrill. Hoarse, as discordant as a cracked bell, the howl awoke all the echoes in the sea and fell against the stones and the trees and the black earth. It tore across the centuries. Snatched from sleep, half-drowned by my rotting lungs, I woke to it skirling in the night, a banshee scream that frayed my nerves and crushed my heart. I could not have designed a more discordant sound. It was a green sound, sickly, whining and yammering and rising higher and higher as I lay there paralysed by it, pressed into the sheets, a dreadful bludgeon that I could not escape. Esther stirred beside me, and it was as if I was suddenly in the very depths of summer, burned by the Indian sun. The hound was howling from the branches of the almond tree, rising, rising, and my father was dying beneath me in the grass; reaching in his death throes for this awful house, this tomb, this bloody chamber.

I staggered from Rutherford's room, stumbling in my haste and kicking something that skittered brightly across the warped floorboards. I snatched it up, a knife that I realised only as I plunged into the cool night air had belonged to the old factor. He had been there, watching us as we slept. He had stood in that foetid squalor and watched us breathing, waiting to gird his nerves for our murder. I have the knife beside me as I write. It was held at our throats, I know, but it was not for the old man to end my life.

I ran then for Gallondean, and the hound screamed exultant in a great curdling shriek that spread along the shore like the breath of hell. Battle was come down, at last. Death was with me.

Here, on the desk in the library, he has left a final missive; another document to add to my overwhelming profusion of texts.

His handwriting is as to be expected, but by the light of the oil lamp I parsed it well enough. I include it here, for the sake of completeness:

My lord – did I ever tell you of my son, young Leonard? More and more often these days I think of him as a boy, when he was fresh and innocent and full of promise, the feel of his soft hand as we walked the clifftops by the Solway, where the grinding rock is bitten by the waves beneath. He died in France as I have told you, snared on the hook of a whore's temptation. But the temptation would not have been there but for the war, I think, and the war would not have been there but for the darkness that swims in Gallondean. I am sure of this. It is an old thing, ever hungry. It must be fed and it must in the end be sated with the soul of its master. It has always been thus. I have done my best to keep its appetite sharp, my lord, until you were ready. I have killed, yes, but only the lives of animals. It was I who cut the whore in the woods, and when I have finished this I will hunt down the whore who services you so that you can feel the full measure of my anguish and know that there is nothing left for you but to hear the hound and die. It should have been your father, you see. If he had come back as was meant and not died in India, if he had died here in the halls of Gallondean as he intended, then the darkness would not have slipped its bounds and spread over all the world as it has done these last four years, feeding on the lives of innumerable young men as it fed on the life of my son. Instead, if it had swallowed old Mr Beresford, it would have stayed here in Gallondean, safe and contained by all the old memories of its terrible deeds. Darker deeds are needed now though, and then you will know. I too have read in the parchments how Robert de Gaillon was a monster who seized women and skinned children, spending his unnatural lusts on the innocent, his crimes as red as the devil's. All who command the stones of Gallondean in his wake will die. It is God's judgement. Even Robert's son, doing the Lord's work and taking those foul hands to the Holy Land, could not escape that judgement. But then William paid God's price without complaint, as you must too. Your heathen idol and your pagan salt will not avail you now. Only your blood.

And did I ever tell you, my lord, of the monasteries out there tumbled to the bare stone of ruin, where the monks of a greater austerity once removed themselves from a faithless evil world? That is where I shall be, when the hound awakes and his howl splits the night. I shall plunge into the freezing waters and swim there, and lie at last after that grand mortification with good Christian men whose eyes were clear. I will be free from grief, and darkness, and the deeds of Gallondean.

Let me only gain that light and be remade with the body of my son, and let your death when you welcome it close that darkness once more inside these awful stones. It must be so. The shadow must consume its master.

Yours in faith and sincerity,
Edward Rutherford.

What stayed his hand? I wonder. When he had us at his mercy, and all his instinct was telling him to kill the woman at my side, what stopped the blade from falling? It was the howling of the hound. What tore me from sleep must have struck him first, as he stood there trembling in the ruins of his life. A baying of grief and horror, and not an inch of the shoreline safe. The knife will have fallen from his hand, and in moments he was out there in the freezing sea, gulping down water and retching up salt, thrashing through the waves until they cuffed and fastened him in their unyielding steel.

There is blood on the page now, blood dripping from my mouth. Where it touches the paper it burns. If this is in any way a record of my time in this house, then let these journals be found beside me when I am dead.

There is of course only one place to confront the thing that has pursued me all these years. I will go now to the depths of Gallondean, to the chamber where the stone was laid, and where that darkness first came to light.

The hound's dead scream frets at the water and the trees. I hear it still. The last yawling note buffets at the stone of this dreadful house, never-ending. I will write no more. The fire in my lungs burns in every sinew of my body. My touch could ignite the very air.

I am *Sattva*, and Sarah is with me. I am a torch to set against the darkness. I am the last pool of light in the depths of the void, around which all the shadows swim. They will smother me, but in the smothering I shall burn them all away.

How freeing it is, as Bobby knew. How wonderful to meet death and know that only you can stop it.

The howling of the hound is the guns of war. Bullets scream and mortars bark their rounds into the hills. Fire burns in the dark. Men scream, their nerves shredded, rising, always rising, a horror that cannot be endured.

Daniel is deaf to it. He can hear the sorrel mare shrieking, her leg broken, and he crams his fingers into his ears as he passes. The German screams against the darkness as the darkness takes him, but he ignores it. The shadow buried in the cave and conjured in the depths of Gallondean is near. Over deserts and oceans it has followed him home.

He lopes across the grass, a wolf choking on the cross. The house rises from the night before him. It commands the shore. No lights glow across the water and all the engines of the ships are still. Darkness lies against the land but he blazes with God's holy fire. He is a scourge, a flame.

Rain peppers the trees. Beyond the shore the waves are hissing and whispering like dust in a desert sandstorm. The rain falls in a curtain beyond the cave. The flames dance against the walls. There is a smell of earth and smoke and unwashed men, and the dreadful scrape of a knife in the dirt. There are jars full of grave soil and severed hands.

He clutches at his heart. The wound in his chest is burning and there's blood beneath his fingers. He reaches out and sees the long beam of his shadow grope across the castle's garden.

To die... To die will be...

They would cut the hands from sorcerers. They would cut the hands from thieves.

A shadow was once summoned in this place, and then with the blow of a righteous sword it was banished. A knight took it to the Holy

Land and buried it, sealed it with scriptures and symbols, until the German dug it free. It has dogged his steps every foot of the way.

I came when you called. But you did not see.

The door yawns wide to welcome him. The shadow is waiting. He is a knight, a soldier on Crusade. He is a warrior of Christ, and the scriptures are his sword and shield.

Daniel steps forward and is swallowed by the cavern's throat.

Deeper in the house, far beneath its weight of stone, Jacob prepares himself. He lights a candle and listens for a moment to the muted boom of the waves above.

High tide. Strange though, it should be low at this hour. The sea should be pulling back and revealing the beach, the long fields of the mudflats glistening under the moon…

No. He understands. It's not the sea but the boom of artillery, the battering guns. It is the war, dragged in the shadow's wake, like a stream of phosphorescence by a surging ship.

He stands before the slab of dark stone with Rutherford's knife. He places a leatherbound notebook on the altar, his journals of Gallondean. Everything he knows about this place is in there, everything he understands. He draws his fingers across the rune carved in the stone's side, a thing of nested lines and curves. It's William de Gaillon's work, he's certain; a symbol to seal away evil and keep it safe. Where did the knight first see it? In his father's books, his scrolls of devilry and magic? A sign to bind a demon to your will? He turned evil against evil, and then he swept those blood-stained hands away with one blow of his sword. In the end, perhaps he did not trust the cross of the risen Christ.

It happened here. Jacob is convinced of it. He lays his hand against the stone. It's warm. Gripping the knife, he looks to the entranceway, the ragged hole into the cave beneath the castle.

There are shards of glass around him, streaked with red. The pressure of the steel Indian sun is crushing him, the light so fierce it almost blinds. From high in the branches calls the brainfever bird, its mindless trill; laughing, mocking, alive with madness. Howling from the Point.

It was in his father's eyes, like oil on water. He sees it now. It couldn't have happened any other way.

The bird stops calling. Jacob wields his blade and laughs.

The crack of the Mauser. John Allynson clutches his throat and falls. Ruhi runs. The rain hammers down, hard as iron. He vomits out the shadow and sees it pooling in the water.

...as wax melteth before the fire, so let the wicked perish at the presence of God.

Simon is sitting in the garden, waiting for him. He is holding his father's hand and the theatre fumes with light before them. The fishing line glints in the water and there are secrets in the deep, just waiting to be caught. The light flickers in the cave. He moves towards it. The sea beats the shore like the sound of distant guns. He is Peter Pan stalking his unstitched shadow amongst the sleeping children. He is a British soldier, a captain of infantry. He is a knight on horseback with his faithful hound at his heels.

He bears his weapons and there is a cross upon his chest.

A scuff of stone. Jacob rises as the shadow pours into the cave. The knife glints, burning with a secret fire. He bares his teeth, grinning, screaming, the lungs twisted in his chest as the air turns to ice. He throws himself forward, flicking the blade, feeling it bite against flesh.

Daniel looks on a pool of gathered darkness. Its eyes blaze like twin stars buried in the void. The fire quickens and the air around him boils with fury. The darkness slithers to grip his hands, to wrench the sword and shield away. But God is with him now, Christ is the sinew in his flesh. Blood pours from the wound in his chest, but he bends and twists and the shadow buckles. He breaks it on the dark altar and cuffs the blade from its hand.

Hauptmann Löwe looks back at him. Jacob sees his father. He is William de Gaillon cutting down his sire with a mortal blow, and then plunging the knife into his chest. He feels it pierce the bone and the shuddering heart, and he weeps – *God forgive me!* – his mailed fists pressing down, the hilt burying itself in his father's breast. Blood spews up around the blade. The old man cries out once and shudders, retching, screaming as the dark light dies in his eyes. Threads of shadow spool like black water across them. The air is colder than the bottom of the ocean. The darkness flickers, the torchlight fades, and all the fell symbols on scroll and codex blaze with fire.

The chamber is thick with smoke, stinking of sulphur and blood and burning flesh. William drags the dead arms across the altar and cuts the hands away, hacking the sword down and watching them spring from the bloody wrists. He takes them up and wraps them in a sheet of cloth, the blood staining the fabric, a stink in his nose of rot and decay. He will bury these foul things far from here, bind them with spells in the land where our Saviour brought his light to the unbelieving. Good Christian men go to make the sacrifice in the Holy Land, and if he can die after he has done this one good thing then he will have done God's will, and the darkness will have faded from this awful shore. There will be only light, he prays.

His heart buckles. He leans on his sword. The sky is discoloured with purple and silver. Out there, Jerusalem burns. Blood stains the altar, and it will never wash out. Blood pours from his chest. Daniel looks down at the body beneath him, the light fading from its eyes. The shadow melts away. A sword swings, and it is made of smoke.

Esther stands up from the grass and wipes her hands on her skirt. For a moment there, she thought she heard the howling. Hound Point mourning its master.

But then the wind changes and the clouds begin to shed their rain. The moon withdraws. She looks up at the face of Roddinglaw. The cry comes again, but it is only a soldier waking.

EPILOGUE

He saw her crossing the hall and called her name. He was standing by the entrance to the western ward, his arms hanging awkwardly at his sides, wondering if he should go in search of her and half-hoping that she had already gone. And then she briskly crossed the tiled floor ahead of him, and he had said the words before he realised what he was doing.

'Mrs Worrell?' Major Lawson said. She turned and smiled, and he tried to imagine that there was just a little germ of disappointment in her eyes. 'You've made your decision then?'

'Yes. I applied at the county branch, it's been arranged. I'm catching the London train from Waverley. I'm sorry to leave you short-handed, Major. Perhaps Miss Stewart will return when she's better? If I have time, I could go and see her for you?'

'No,' he said. 'I shouldn't think so. It would be cruel to ask her back. She needs her family around her now.' He gestured with his hand. 'Not this.'

'There we are then.'

'And then the front,' Lawson said, pressing on.

'If I can. If they'll take me.'

'Well, let us be optimistic and hope it's over before you arrive. We must have faith that it will all work out.'

'Indeed so, sir.'

Lawson smiled and nodded and rocked back on his heels. He was trying to be the commanding officer, he knew, a role with which he had never been very comfortable. He felt the mask begin to slip. At least it was not something he would have to endure for much longer. He glanced up into the wash of light coming through the window, and then he took her elbow and gently drew her aside. Esther left her bag by the door. They stood by the desk at the nurse's station, empty now this early in the day.

'Esther...' he began. He searched for the words. Not the expected ones, but the ones he wanted to say. But no, they were as elusive as ever. 'It's been a difficult time, I know,' he said. 'With Corporal Prevost, and now with Captain McQuarrie. I understand. We train ourselves for patients to die, but not often this far along in their convalescence, and not quite ... well, not quite in this manner. And then with Mr Beresford too, it's been a shocking experience. Truly shocking.'

He had guessed the relationship between them. Beresford had hinted at it, although he had had the tact not to say it directly. What did it matter now though? The man was dead, and that's all there was to it.

Esther Worrell steadied herself, and although she tried to look unperturbed he could see the strain in her eyes, her jaw.

'It has,' she said. 'And I'm sorry to hear that you'll be leaving Roddinglaw, sir. I thought—'

He demurred. 'It's to be expected. Indeed, it was unavoidable. The army makes a decision and that's all there is to it. There are other hospitals, other institutions where I can serve. But a strange business all round,' he said carefully. 'I thought Captain McQuarrie's wound was healing, but it went deeper than we realised, perhaps. He was frailer than we knew. Was there any connection between them, do you know? The captain and Mr Beresford? Any source of friction or enmity they may have had?'

'No,' Esther said. She gestured with her open hands, seemingly as lost as Major Lawson was himself to find any meaning in it. 'I doubt they ever exchanged a single word.'

'Then who can tell why he did it. In the end,' he said, 'it's the shadows of the mind that are the hardest to cure. The body is one thing, but the soul another. I always felt that Captain McQuarrie had left a good portion of himself behind in Palestine. You see it now and then. Some wounds pare away an essential part, and it's never truly recovered. A wounded man is rarely whole again.'

'We do the best we can,' she told him. She touched his sleeve. 'You couldn't possibly have done more.'

Lawson forced himself to brighten. He escorted her to the door, taking up her bag and carrying it out onto the drive. It was a warm day. The grass in early summer looked fresh and green upon the lawns. There was a clean salt smell in the air. The knight on his plinth looked new-polished, aglow.

'I was wondering, before you go,' he said, 'whether I might ask a favour of you?'

'Of course.'

'Robert Browning, that book of poems. I saw Captain McQuarrie with it once, and he mentioned it was yours. I was wondering, and it's a bold request I know, whether I could borrow it? Something...' He cleared his throat and looked away. 'Something to remember you by.'

'I didn't know you were a man for poetry, Major Lawson,' she said. Was that a pitying smile, one of shy commiseration? He would take it, if so. He would take anything she offered.

Lawson, with a self-deprecating bow, said, 'It's more the provenance of the volume than the contents. But then, one's never too old to learn.'

'I'm so sorry, sir, but I don't have it,' Esther told him. She looked sincere; her face had flushed a gentle pink. 'It would be yours, I promise, but I'm afraid I haven't the least idea where it is.'

'Ah.' Lawson smoothed his moustache. 'It'll turn up, I'm quite sure. If I find it before I leave, I'll do my best to send it back to you. Well then,' he said.

The words were right there, unspoken. The gesture was just waiting to be made. In moments she would be gone, and he would never see her again. The dark hair, that gentle smile, the charge she put into his heart. He felt the pulse throb in his temple. His hands were cold. I love you, Esther Worrell.

'Goodbye,' he said.

'Goodbye, Major,' she said.

They shook hands. Major Lawson stepped back inside the house. There it was then. That was the end of it.

She had said goodbye to Ida Lambert already. Standing in the dormitory, looking down on the grounds, they had kissed the air beside each other's cheeks, and as Ida squeezed her hand, grinning, her eyes oddly hard, she had said: 'What will I do without you, Esther? Alice likely never coming back, and now you heading away for adventure, and the whole coast in such dreadful upset over that poor chap at Gallondean...' With a sly glance she dared Esther to say more. 'I will *so* miss our little chats.'

'I'm not sure, Ida,' Esther had said. She drew her close, still clutching her hand. 'Who will you have to slander and gossip about now? Just think, perhaps you'll actually have to do your job for once.' She pressed her fingertips into Ida's arm, clutching the flesh. 'Enjoy going back into your cage, Miss Lambert, when the war is over.'

Ida gasped, and Esther did not look back as she left the room.

Now, after watching Major Lawson gain the sanctuary of Roddinglaw, she turned to go. There were still shards of brown clay beside the path, parts of the jars that had been broken there the night Captain McQuarrie died. The rest of the debris had been cleared away.

She was halfway across the lawn, heading for the Queensferry path, when Lieutenant Goodspeed caught up with her. He was in uniform and carried an overnight bag, and he looked happier than she had seen him in months. The creeping, hesitant Peter Pan had become a dashing Captain Hook.

'Would you mind awfully if I walked with you, Mrs Worrell?' he said. 'I've time to kill and I'd rather not get the train from the village just yet.'

'Of course.'

'And what a beautiful day it is,' he said. He tipped his face to the sky. 'It does the heart good to walk in sunshine, doesn't it?'

They passed beneath the trees, walking in dappled light as it was broken by the branches. Goodspeed breathed deeply, filling lungs too long constrained by an airless room.

'I say,' he announced, 'would you think me a little odd if I told you how eager I am to get back in service? I feel as I did when I first got my commission. Keen as mustard, and no doubt just as thick.'

'Aren't you frightened?' she said. It never did to remind the men too much of what they'd faced, but Esther set that aside for once. 'After all, you know what it's like.'

'I think that's just it,' Goodspeed said eagerly. He took off his cap and rubbed his forehead where the hatband had made a shallow red impression. 'I know exactly what to expect. *Exactly*, and so it doesn't trouble me as much. It's mystery that frightens, isn't it? That old fear of the dark.'

After a while they came to where the path branched off towards Gallondean. The great slab of the old house sat there at the end of its overgrown drive. In the fortnight since she had last passed this way it seemed if anything to have grown more decrepit. The windows were dark and the door looked permanently sealed. The procurator fiscal, as far as she knew, still had both the bodies. There had been no surviving family on either side to claim them.

Goodspeed, she saw, had taken a shard of clay out of his pocket. He must have picked it up from the grass when he left Roddinglaw. He rubbed the broken edge with the ball of his thumb.

'Why did he do it, do you think?' he said. 'Dan, I mean? Stabbed him through the heart, I heard. Poor sod.'

'I don't know. It's beyond me,' Esther said. 'It's awful, and I can only hope…' Her voice trailed away. 'God, I can only hope that he wasn't in any pain, at the end. Either of them.'

She turned away from the house. She never wanted to see it again.

'They're wondering now if he attacked Miss Stewart as well,' Goodspeed was saying. 'The same knife was used apparently. I can't see it. I don't know… There are always so many rumours floating around with this kind of thing, aren't there? Bits and pieces, different voices saying different things. Where did he get the knife from for a start? You never learn the full truth.'

'And the partial truth becomes a legend given enough time,' Esther said.

'Indeed it does, Mrs Worrell. Like the Angel of Mons, or the bowmen from Agincourt. You know, he always seemed half there to me, Dan. I liked him, but he was in pieces still. There was something missing there. Something taken away.'

'I liked him as well,' Esther said. 'Very much. I think he'd been more deeply hurt than anybody understood.'

They walked on. As they passed Hound Point, Gallondean now behind them and hidden by the trees, Esther realised that she had left her book in the dormitory: *Aurora Leigh*. She should have offered that to Major Lawson, and for a moment considered walking back to find it. But no, the moment had passed. The volume would instead become a fortuitous find to whoever took her place in the dormitory and on the wards. She hoped they appreciated it. Although she had taken more from that book than from anything else she had ever read, she had no need of it now. No need for knights and Crusaders either, or for grand narratives with an orchestrating voice. Only *this live, throbbing age/ That brawls, cheats, maddens, calculates, aspires…*

Was that Aurora's lesson? Look to the world as it is, now and forever? Don't look back, or, like Jacob, build an obsessive truth from accumulated scraps. She didn't know. Either way, she didn't have the words, not yet. She didn't have the voice – lean and capacious, varied and strict – but she was confident that it would come. London, Paris, the front; wherever she ended up, under her own steam she would find it in time.

Queensferry came into view as the woods fell away, the great red iron span of the rail bridge, the haze of smoke, the Hawes Inn.

'I always envied him a little,' Goodspeed admitted. He gave an embarrassed smile. 'Daniel, I mean. For fighting in the desert, for seeing Palestine. Jerusalem… Rather more romantic than Flanders mud, wouldn't you say?'

He took the shard of clay from his pocket again. After a moment he threw it far out towards the shore.

'And for being present at a victory,' he said.

'It's summer now, Lieutenant,' she told him. 'Spring is over. Have faith. The victories are all to come.'

ACKNOWLEDGEMENTS

TK

A NOTE ON THE AUTHOR

TK

A NOTE ON THE TYPE

The text of this book is set in Minion, a digital typeface designed by Robert Slimbach in 1990 for Adobe Systems. The name comes from the traditional naming system for type sizes, in which minion is between nonpareil and brevier. It is inspired by late Renaissance-era type.